MEMORY REBORN

Steven M Nedeau

This book is dedicated to
the memory and stories of
Philip K. Dick.

A special thank you goes out to
Mackenzie Littledale,
Criss Bubacz,
Mike Brown,
Brooks Hayward,
J. M. Grenier,
April Nedeau,
Joe Hiltz,
and Michael D. Nadeau.

Chapter One

Report Subject:	**Darien Mamon**
Origin Location:	**Oneida, NY**
Current Location:	**Tucson, AZ**
Subject Age:	**27**
Subject Status:	**Viable**

Haunted by the depth below, Darien clutched the writpad tight to his side and focused his eyes on the door across the span of glass. Muscles in his neck constricted, sending thin lines of pain into his back. Steeling his resolve, he stepped forward, shoes clicking across the surface as sweat collected under his white collar. Reaching the opposite side, he pressed the call button for the secured resident and waited for the response.

Stepping out onto the glass floor always unnerved Darien. Clear and flawless, the floors allowed light to travel down the old missile shaft to each level with little to no reflection. Looking down displayed the depth of the organization with figures traversing the central hub appearing smaller and smaller as the tiers descended into the earth. So clean as to be nearly invisible, every floor of the facility had them.

"Yeah?" an electronic voice responded through the speaker.

The writpad in Darien's hand buzzed a command and Darien pressed the back of it to the black acrylic door. Inside the secured residence, the information from the writpad displayed across the door vid-screen. Darien held the pad, watching his screen as the secured resident's messy signature appeared across it. Confirming the scrawl matched the signature on file, or was at least close enough, Darien made his way back across the span.

"Only five more," he reminded himself.

Passing through the door to the stairwell, Darien breathed a sigh of relief and rolled his neck away from his collar, feeling the sweat collected there as it cooled. His fingers wrapped around the handrail, squeezing. The metal didn't give. It was a reassuring feeling.

Keeping one hand on the handrail, Darien made his way down the stairs, ticking off one item from the list of his morning duties. Each appointment waited on a different floor. Darien frowned. Each appointment would require one more trip across his fears. He dreaded stepping onto the central hub floor, felt the swing of falling in the back of his skull as he placed his first foot down on it. Time and again he expected his foot to pass through the plane and tumble him into free fall.

He didn't mind the stairs, however the central hub and its depth illusion was another thing entirely. At least the stairs had a solid feel to them.

Everything in the rest of the facility felt like plastic, a smooth surface sticky with the feeling of impermanence, though none of it was.

This underground work silo had been in use for nearly thirty years since its refurbishment. Sometime in the twentieth century this location had housed a nuclear missile. Men worked here, ready to annihilate the planet on the order of one or two powerful politicians.

The facility didn't look that old. During refurbishment the silo itself had been widened and at each level additional rooms were added around the outside. Underground tunnels were then constructed, connecting this silo to others, some as far as several miles away.

It still felt sticky.

The metal stairwell Darien liked so much had been in place for over one hundred years. Painted every year, it held its age well, serving as the concrete and steel backbone for the newer materials that constituted the rest of the facility.

Darien scrolled through the list of secured residents. He had been one until recently. The secured residents were generally the new employees. MemorSingular imposed a three-week quarantine while the files and backgrounds of every new employee underwent a meticulous review.

Darien did not enjoy his time in quarantine. He answered questions about the people in his past, his education and study techniques, his hygiene routines, his sexual partners and orientation. Doctors visited often, poking and prodding him, taking blood and DNA samples. Test after test of his mental acuity were administered as his psychological state was scrutinized. All in all, with the attention given, he had not been as lonely as he expected to be during the three week isolation period.

Now he was a signature runner, his first assignment as a member of the MemorSingular staff. Door to door and resident after resident, he traveled the halls and central hub, learning his way around, recognizing some faces he passed in the hall. Most took no notice of him. A few stopped to read his red badge and date of employment. Darien wrote these people off as plain clothes security though their badges always said something different. *What good is being a secret security officer if it said security right on your badge*, he asked himself.

There were several different badges, black badges, blue badges; Darien had even seen a few green ones, but his was the only red badge he'd seen so far.

Looking up instead of down, Darien tried to forget the distance below him as he made his way across the glass floor of the central hub to the resident room on the opposite side of sub-level seven. He noted the steel beam supporting the glass floor at sub-level six, one level above. The only floor with a steel frame under it, sub-level six spoiled the illusion of a sheer drop underneath when you were at the higher levels.

Darien shook his head at the silo designers. If they had installed something similar at every floor, he would feel a lot more comfortable walking across them. He pressed the call button and waited for an answer. After a few moments he pressed the call button again, looking up at the steel beam as he waited.

Annoyed, Darien lowered the writpad and checked the resident sensor panel beside the acrylic door, rolling through the list of biological sensor data.

Blood pressure, *low.*

Heart rate—

"Oh, shit!" he said, slamming his hand into the alarm.

Waiting for the medical team he read through the list again, making sure the heart of the resident was still beating on the sensor. The readings looked grim and Darien could only watch anxiously as they got worse.

Hearing footsteps behind him, Darien turned to beckon the medical team on, but two black clothed security personnel tackled him to the floor, pushing his face into the glass. A knee pressed down on Darien's head while someone else had Darien's wrist and arm twisted painfully. The weight of the security officer on Darien's head felt like there were six people on top of him.

Through the commotion, Darien heard the medical team punching the open code followed by the hiss as the door slid up into the ceiling.

"Stay calm, sir!" one of the black clothed security personnel said sharply in a tone not likely to induce calm in anyone.

Darien's eyes squeezed shut in pain and, unable to reply, he only grunted in what he hoped was a compliant tone. He did not want his wrist twisted any further.

The guards struggled, needlessly, to press all their weight onto Darien as the hum of the electric gurney passed by. Then, all at once, the weight was gone and the guards were moving away.

Darien rested his forehead on the glass, trying to reorient himself, and experienced a strong sense of vertigo as he looked down several stories through the crystal clear floor. He fought the dizziness gripping him and focused his attention on the drool, his drool, on the glass in front of him. He tried to calm himself, keeping his eyes trained on the drool until he regained control of the spinning in his head.

Darien got to his feet, placing his hand on the wall, rolling his wrist with his other hand to drive out the pain. He was alone on the floor, both the security team and medical team having gone as quickly as they had come.

"What the hell was that all about?" he whispered out loud. Lifting his head, Darien glanced into the residence. There on the floor by the door was a large pool of blood smeared by the footsteps of the medical team. Papers and photographs were strewn about, littering the desk and bed.

Leaning forward to inspect the room, Darien was almost struck by the black acrylic door as it slid down rapidly from above, leaving the blood ringed footprints traveling to the elevator as the only sign anything had occurred.

The footprints.

The bloody footprints marred the illusion of walking on the nothingness of the central hub. Darien gathered his writpad and knelt down next to a crimson print, pressing his finger into the blood, smearing the print.

Man, I hope that guy, Darien checked the name on his writpad, *Martin, is going to be all right.*

He stood up, changing his focus to the smudge his face made where it had been pushed into the see-through floor, and saw her. Below Darien by one level, a blonde woman looked up at the bloody footprints, hands motionless on her writpad.

You know her, Darien thought, *from college. That's Shara's friend.*

The blonde lost interest in the blood overhead and turned her attention back to the calculation on her writpad.

It can't be her, Darien thought. *College was nine years ago in New Miami and on the other side of the continent.*

Still thinking about the girl from college, he watched the blonde tuck her writpad under her arm, turn her back, and walk away. After she passed out of sight, Darien's eyes rolled up to the ceiling, trying to remember her name.

Nancy, was that it?

Yes, he answered himself, *Nancy.*

Shara and Nancy had been inseparable in college, almost living together, always eating together, even visiting the amusement parks in central Florida. Darien had been jealous of the time Shara devoted to Nancy and, he had no doubt, she had felt the same about him. She had been there when Shara asked

Darien to lunch for their first date. She had also been there at the end of the relationship, watching as Darien's actions drove Shara away.

A pit formed in Darien's stomach, pulling at his sides. The shame of that day flooded him, igniting a rising burn in his face. All of his relationships ended badly.

He had four more doors to visit.

The writpad buzzed in his hand. "Darien Mamon, please report to HR, sub-floor 1, room 1D," shone in sharp red letters. The list of duties had turned gray, noting his immediate priority was to answer the summons from Human Resources.

They must be worried I'm going to sue, Darien thought. *Well, you can't go smacking people to the floor.*

Once through the door to the stairwell Darien grabbed the railing and looked forward to giving HR some hell about their security personnel.

"If you continue to perform outside of your required duties, we may be forced to redefine your role here or terminate your status as an employee."

"I'm sorry. I don't understand," Darien replied to the mousy, middle-aged woman sitting behind the desk. Her writpad was open and she was viewing a continuous loop of the event at the resident door of sub-level seven.

"Look here, at the thirty-second mark of the vid, after you were released by the security personnel. You looked directly into the residence."

"Are you kidding me?" Darien asked incredulously. "Did you see the way they slammed me to the floor? I'm lucky I got up at all."

"And here," the mousy woman continued.

Seeing her take no notice of his complaints, Darien's ears started to burn.

She continued, "The door almost hit you in the head. Are you aware of the complex mechanisms required to assure smooth operation of those doors?" She closed the video on her writpad. "I'm afraid you're going to have to be more careful in the future."

"What about my wrist?"

"Is it broken?"

"No."

"Is it sprained?"

Darien flexed his wrist, remembering the pain. "No, I don't think so."

"Then what's the issue?"

"They threw me to—"

She cut him off. "You'll find our security personnel are extremely efficient. They go through weekly training. When an alarm sounds, they assess the situation and try to eliminate any potential threat."

"If I was the threat I wouldn't have sounded the alarm," Darien shot back.

"You were at the scene of the disturbance."

"A disturbance I discovered and called for help about. What happened in that room?"

She made a note on her writpad and turned it off. "I'm afraid this incident is none of your concern."

Darien shut his mouth. He needed this position, as strange and secretive as it was. He wasn't sure why everything was so sensitive but it didn't matter.

Back at sub-level seven, Darien watched the maintenance men cleaning the blood from the glass floor. The team, dressed in off-white, armed with squeegees, made short work of the task, restoring the floor's frightening transparency. As the cleaning crew filed into the elevator, Darien opened the stairwell door. He shouldn't have come back to this level after the incident but he couldn't help himself.

The black acrylic residence door on the other side sat closed, nearly indiscernible from the walls. Reaching the door, Darien activated the lighted panel beside it. The man who had been in this room, Martin, was either deceased or no longer connected to the system. The biological data on the secured resident was zeroed out.

Check your writpad, idiot.

Darien's writpad had been scrubbed by the mousey woman in HR, who did her best to remove any solid information as to whom this secured resident was. There had to be something left, just for the sake of keeping accurate records.

Darien powered up the writpad. Martin's last name was classified, as was his age. Darien expected the man's work history might be restricted as well, but he was wrong. Martin was not a new employee as Darien had suspected. Three years ago, Martin had been hired by MemorSingular as a memory software consultant. A list of tasks scrolled under his name, several of each type: software update, system refresh, parameter mismatch correction, assistant to Randy Hollister.

The last one caused Darien to pause, *Randy Hollister?* Dr. Randy Hollister was a legend in memory retrieval. *He's working here?* Darien felt a happy chill run over him. Just the opportunity to work with such a genius was a dream Darien had never dared imagine. His reasons for accepting this job had been purely financial. So far, his duties at MemorSingular had been menial and mind numbing. Working alongside Dr. Randy Hollister could do more than pay down his debt. It could propel Darien Mamon's name into the textbook pages.

Look at you and your delusions of grandeur, he thought. *That guy, Martin, has been here for years. You've got a long way to go, my friend.*

He pushed the writpad page further into Martin's work history but saw no other mention of Dr. Hollister. *I wonder what kind of work they were doing?*

Still digging into Martin's work, Darien absently walked across the glass floor to the staircase door without giving the space below him a single thought.

Back in his own residence, Darien mulled over the events at the sub-level seven room. The HR mouse had been rather upset he looked into another secured residence. *Why?* Apart from the papers and the blood, it didn't look any different from his own. Martin must have been someone important. *Working with Hollister.* He had to be something special.

Darien walked to his door. The vid-screen was blank. Lockdown had occurred only ten minutes prior, and from his experience so far, Darien reasoned the lockdown periods always happened in four-hour blocks. At least he hadn't seen one shorter. At every lockdown thus far, Darien had received a warning on his writpad that he must return to his room, and he had done so without question. They must serve some purpose for the company, but he had yet to figure out what it could be. Perhaps, it was used as a way to perform a headcount of the employees presently in the facility. Maybe, it was a way to hold their personnel to a schedule. All he knew was, if you were outside of your area there could be serious consequences. It was even reasonable to assume someone outside of the facility would be locked out for the duration.

Stupid, he thought. He wanted to get out, to get into the city for something different to eat. *What good is having a job if you never get to leave to spend any of the money?* He winced at his answer, *debt.* This job was going to put a nice size dent in his debt balance.

Darien placed his palm on the vid-screen and it sprang to life.

"State your name," asked the pleasant feminine voice in a British accent.

"Darien L. Mamon."

"Access request?"

"Financial."

Spreadsheets flashed onto the screen, his assets on the left and his obligations on the right. The right side of the screen held the number considerably larger. He winced at the balance. The medical debt alone was mind boggling. They had garnered his wages. After taxes, eighty-five percent of every dollar he made went straight to MedCare.

Darien looked at the balance of his paycheck. On the outside, it wouldn't have covered a week in a body bag. The body bag was the street name for a three foot wide, three foot tall, by six foot long sleeping unit, officially called an EasyRest. He had spent too many nights in those. They weren't easy, but they were better than sleeping with the mosquitos.

Darien swiped the screen closed and sat down on the bed.

This company had been a lifesaver at the worst possible time in his life. His pay at one of his previous companies, Synapse, had barely kept him fed. Fifty-five hours a week sitting on a stool and coding technical documents online for syntax errors and missing colons meant he had to find somewhere else to be for the remaining one hundred and thirteen hours of the week. Thankfully, the weather in New Miami was such that he was rarely cold, though he was often wet. In the end, he had taken refuge in abandoned travel pods. The windows were missing and he had been assaulted by flying insects, but it had kept the rain off him.

In comparison, his room in the silo was a mansion. The desk was clear of any clutter, holding only the writpad, and matched the black acrylic of both the bed frame and the door. The bed was wider than he was accustomed to, though in his childhood, his bed had been quite large. Nothing in the room showed any personality or marring of the cold black sterile environment. Even the lights shone down without any appreciable warmth, cold blue beams reflecting dully, barely illuminating the space.

He tried not to touch anything. The feeling of plastic was always present.

Darien looked for something to occupy his time. He didn't have any books. The screens didn't accept broadcasts, local or nationwide. He didn't have any kind of phone or communicator, not that he had owned one prior to coming to his current location. A phone was just one of those expenses he couldn't afford. Picking up his writpad, Darien decided to lay on the bed and study.

His eyes went wide as he looked next to the bed. Shining out of the black acrylic wall was an illuminated music system. It hadn't been there this morning. Hell, it hadn't been there five minutes ago. Giddy with excitement, Darien moved his fingers around the dials and typed artist names into the lighted keypad.

He typed, Solar Fire Band.

"Not Found," was the response.

Thinking about the oldies from his time in college he typed, Mark Bental. He had listened to Bental's songs in college, reveling in the singer's unusual voice. A thought caught Darien's breath in his chest. He had been with Shara, listening, dancing, kissing as the music freed them of worries. Her skin had been so flawless, her smile, beautiful, the smell of lilacs on her neck. How they had listened to the music and held each other.

He typed, *Daydream on Mars*. And after listening for a moment, he entered, *Love Today*. Oh, they had danced until they were out of breath and laughing, their dance becoming a playful teasing until they had fallen down to the floor and made love on the carpet.

Darien closed his eyes to better concentrate on the music, embracing the memories of her touch, her voice, her laughter, and her breathing. It had been so many years ago, and it had ended so badly.

In the back of his mind he wondered if she still thought of him. *Does she still dance?* A wild thought struck him and he remembered Nancy. *Was that Nancy today?* If it was, *does she still have contact with Shara?* In his mind he fashioned a scenario where he would ask her about Shara, to find out Shara had been asking about him, that she missed him and thought about him all the time.

No.

Darien tried to reroute his thought train. He couldn't go down those tracks again, pining for a girl who he knew would never take him back. She was gone and he had to accept it.

So much had changed since his childhood. So many people in his life had come and gone. The emptiness in his chest weighed on him. Shara Musabayana was the only person he missed, the only person whose absence left a scar on his emotions.

The song ended, Mark Bental's voice trailing away with a barely imperceptible, "Never gonna fall for". The media player shuffled to *Hold Me* by Broken Keys, a crushing beat and synthetic dance number from just after the turn of the millennium. As the keyboards danced, the vid-screen on the inside of the door faded up from dark.

Pulsing across the screen, changing with the rhythm of the music, short videos and pictures displayed. He was in every one, hundreds of them. Some were obvious parts of his collection. Some were surveillance video from stores, nightclubs, traffic intersections, public transport, taxi pods, and even college hallways. In the images he appeared younger and younger as if the videos and images were being played chronologically in reverse order. There was an image of his home, of him walking with his parents, of soccer games held at his estate. There was one of him in Hawaii, surfing.

Darien stepped back. He had never been surfing. *How old am I in that photo, fifteen?* More images scrolled; his room, his basketball court, the soccer team again. There was one of him kissing a girl, another of a girl pushing him away. His mother was in one image, holding his grades, unhappy.

At the sight of his mother a flush of guilt crept into his ears. He could feel the embarrassing heat of the unconscious blood flow.

After the image of his mother came a video of Darien hiking a trail, high, high in the mountains. The camera appeared to be connected to Darien, catching mostly his face as he climbed along. He spoke into the camera.

Watching himself, Darien could not tell what he was saying. Reading lips had never been one of his skills and the music of Broken Keys drowned out any sound that might have been part of the video.

One thing was certain. Darien had never been mountain climbing, never been hiking. On one side of his video self was a sheer rock face, on the other side, a drop of hundreds of feet, shown clearly as the person in the video looked up, allowing the camera to glimpse the chasm behind him. In the video, Darien stepped easily holding the handrail chain driven into the cliff face. How old was he here, thirteen? The height was dizzying, even in a video.

Darien reeled and sat back on the bed. The song ended, and with it the video display went blank.

Staring at the door, Darien felt a chill roll up his back. That could not have been him. He had no memory of such a hair-raising experience. However, there he had been on the screen, nonchalantly walking next to a fall of certain death, without fear.

After several seconds, the screen sprang to life again, displaying a news article next to a portrait of his smiling ten year old face. Darien's eyes traveled from his image to the words on the screen, but he only read a few before they faded away.

"Paramedics could not save youth."

Chapter Two

<table>
<tr><td>**Report Subject:**</td><td>**Darien Mamon**</td></tr>
<tr><td>**Origin Location:**</td><td>**Oneida, New York**</td></tr>
<tr><td>**Current Location:**</td><td>**Tucson, AZ**</td></tr>
<tr><td>**Subject Age:**</td><td>**27**</td></tr>
<tr><td>**Subject Status:**</td><td>**Viable**</td></tr>
</table>

Darien woke early, the pictures and videos still haunting him. Duties for the day waited, rolling across the writpad screen on the desk. Sitting down, Darien flipped through a few coding requests from the programming resource department, stepped through the list of secured resident rooms he was supposed to visit, and blinked in surprise when he reached the end of the list to find he had a meeting scheduled with the MemorSingular programming section head, Dr. Randy Hollister.

He could not believe he was going to meet Dr. Hollister so soon after starting with the company. Only the day before had he learned of the affiliation between Dr. Hollister and MemorSingular. He remembered his studies at South Miami Technical University and how entire curriculum paths followed Dr. Hollister's discoveries. The man had pioneered the collection of human memory into already existing storage devices by reducing the size of the memory file, much the same way music files were reduced in size near the end of the previous century. Anything not seen or heard by conscious human senses had been removed. Darien had thought the concept far-fetched.

When he had been studying Randy Hollister's achievements in Synapse Technology 201, Darien had asked his professor, "How could anything not perceived by human senses be part of the original memory file to begin with?"

"Ahh," Professor Becker had remarked. "You'll notice I said *conscious* human senses. Your brain notices things that it filters out of your consciousness. If you lived near a major transportation center, your brain would eventually filter out the noise of vehicles. The algorithm of Dr. Hollister takes those unconscious filters into account when storing the memory."

Becker's grey beard betrayed his otherwise youthful appearance. His energy and enthusiasm for the material made the class something to look forward to. When Professor Becker had asked for volunteers for the virtual reality module, both Shara and Darien had put their hands up.

She had looked beautiful, Darien remembered. Her smile lit up a room, breaking everyone's heart and answering the questions you hadn't asked yet.

Professor Becker chose Darien for the experiment and the plastic circuit band sat tight around his head.

The technological advances were astounding. A century before, anodes and cathodes had to be taped to people's skulls in order to read their brainwave statuses. Only fifteen years prior to this experiment, a new system emerged where the nanometer wires were grown, like layers on a microchip, meshed together within the plastic headset. This new technology not only read the subject's brain waves, it altered them, changing the experience, molding the flesh to the program flickering through the digital gates.

Darien's first mem-sim was a birthday party, his birthday, but he wasn't him. Seven or eight years old, his pigtails shook as he sang along with the music coming from the media player embedded in the walls. He was a girl. Scanning the room, Darien saw a large woman approaching, carrying a double layer cake with seven lit candles flickering as she walked.

My mom is awesome!

Darien, engrossed in the memory of the little girl, felt his mouth curl into a smile and he blew out the flames, smelling the smoke and melted wax. Reaching for a candle, intending to lick the frosting from the bottom, the little girl burned her finger on the still smoking wick.

Taking off the headset at the end of the recorded experience, Darien looked at his finger. There was no redness, no mark.

The pain was still there, a dull memory of the persistent ache one often experienced after a burn. He shook his fingers as the instructor explained the lingering sensation.

"The memory makes the pain real." Professor Becker walked over and lifted Darien's hand, showing the class there was no mark on the skin. "Do you still feel it?" he asked. "This wasn't the beginning of memory capture. It was the first recorded occurrence of physical pain. I don't have to explain the ramifications of such a discovery."

Professor Becker walked to the window. "What color were the drapes?"

"I don't know," Darien said. "Were they blue?"

"There weren't any drapes," Professor Becker responded. "That information wasn't necessary and thus it was deleted from the end file."

The next assigned memory flashed across the screen in front of the class. Many smiled and groaned, their obvious disappointment clear to Darien. They had not volunteered for the experiment. *Oh, well,* thought Darien. *You snooze, you lose.*

"Are we all going to have a chance to use the set?" a young man in front asked. His elbows rested on his desk and he didn't lift them off the surface, even with his hand raised.

"No, I'm afraid there isn't time to share the simulation with everyone."

The young man put his hand down and looked longingly up at the screen. Darien followed his gaze to see the largest roller coaster he could have imagined. He had some experience on roller coasters with his day trips to the Florida theme parks. He and Shara had been on the Falcon three times in a row despite the two-hour wait. The largest roller coaster there, Kobayashi, had thrilled Darien with its wide and rolling loops, even if he did prefer the quick turn and drop.

Darien smiled, thinking, *This is going to be fun.*

The classroom faded into white light as the sun shone down from over the corners of the building facade. Around Darien, statues of ancient Norse gods held swords and a mix of other weapons. The crowd pressed into rows winding back and forth under the expansive canopy. This was the line for Thor, the newest roller coaster at the Seventeen Nations amusement park.

As Darien neared the front of the line he glanced behind him and saw holding his hand the most beautiful girl. She was thin and blonde, and she was smiling at Darien adoringly. Her fingers squeezed his, and the smirk on the corner of her lips held a secret. She winked. Darien's eyes darted to the ground and a grin flashed across his face to hide the blush. From her sandals, to her long, tanned legs, up to her cutoff jeans and avocado green tank top, she was a picture of loveliness.

Their fingers intertwined and she pushed Darien with her other hand, never letting go of their connection. The line had terminated, and the sexy blonde and Darien were boarding the roller coaster car. He allowed her to enter the car before him, though he was next in line, and watched her ass as she crossed in front. *Love those shorts,* he thought as he climbed in behind her.

Before the cars moved on the track, the blonde dropped her hand from her pull-down safety bar and squeezed Darien's leg, sending a thrill of sensations rolling through him before the cars slid away from the station on their way to the first hill.

Without the clack of an old steel roller coaster design, the magnetic levitated cars sped up the hill and directly into a loop. Exhilaration soared as the blue sky rolled away from view and back again. The turns elicited screams of joy, causing both Darien and his date to grab for the safety bars.

In one continuous turn, sensations of his amorous thoughts, experienced only moments before, dissolved with the arrival of an unexpected burp. Darien began to feel queasy.

Each turn and dip lasted forever as the sweat formed on his brow. *Sick on a roller coaster?* Disoriented, Darien fought against the memory simulation. *I don't get sick on roller coasters.*

A sheen of sweat covered Darien's brow and the sickening feeling increased until Darien was leaning his head to the side against the pads of the pull-down safety bar. Each new twist and turn had him swallowing, trying to maintain.

The last drop did it.

Uncontrollably, hands trying desperately to hold back the

flow, he threw up all over the beautiful girl and the front car. For the remainder of the ride Darien lay limp in the seat, the vomit coating his fingers as the beautiful girl in her avocado green shirt cried next to him.

The simulation ended, going dead at the worst possible moment, and not a second before.

To Darien's relief, he had not actually vomited in the classroom, but several classmates looked uncomfortable. Someone in the back moved to open a window, enveloping everyone in the humid warm air of the Miami springtime. The influx of heat didn't make Darien feel any better.

Darien sat spent at his desk, sweat running down his temples. Shara draped an arm across his back, holding his hand. Her eyes, those beautiful brown eyes, looked at him with concern. He gave her a weak smile and put his head on the desk.

"So," Professor Becker began, "what color was your shirt?"

"My shirt? I don't know. Her shirt was green," Darien said without lifting his head.

The professor turned his attention to the rest of the class. "Did anyone else notice the color of Mr. Mamon's shirt?" Silence answered his question. "As before," he continued, "the color of the shirt worn was not important enough to be included in the memory."

Professor Becker turned his attention back to Darien. "Are you ready for the next one?"

Darien groaned.

"I'll do it," Shara said, still looking at Darien. Relieved, Darien held out the plastic headset and she set it on her head, brushing the black hair out of the way first. Professor Becker helped her with the adjustment, and then, with a keystroke on his writpad, started the simulation.

Darien, still spent and queasy from his own experience, watched the screen with his chin on his arms. He swallowed hard and listened to the reactions of the class as they all witnessed Shara's memory simulation experience.

Boats floated in a circle. She swam in deep water, smiling, watching her friends. Several people were climbing and jumping from the boats, laughing, trying to outdo one another. With a shout, a young man leaped from one of the higher decks, somersaulting to hit the water feet first. He came up from the splash with a terrified shriek.

"Shark!"

Choking on the water from her gasp of fear, Shara swam toward a boat. All around her, friends splashed, each alone in their effort to escape an attack. Shara was far behind everyone else. One by one they pulled themselves out of the water, calling for those behind them to hurry, their arms outstretched from their position of safety. The first to see the shark, grabbed a coiled rope from the deck and threw the line to Shara.

She grabbed it and the man on the other end began to pull her toward the boat when the massive shark brushed against her leg, scraping off skin with its abrasive hide. Shara gasped again, choking. Every ounce of her strength poured into reaching the boat, pulling hand over hand on her end of the line. A jagged grip snatched her foot, dragging her under.

Sputtering and coughing Shara resurfaced, clawing her way through the water toward the boat and safety. The screams of her friends cut off as she was pulled under again.

The simulation ended.

Displayed on the board were Shara's biometrics, her heart rate accelerated to near dangerous levels. Tears streamed from her eyes and she wiped them away, embarrassed.

"I'm sorry," said Professor Becker. "I should have warned you."

"No, Professor, I'm sorry. I didn't understand how real it would seem." Shara removed the headset. "I was there, in the water. I could feel everything. My muscles ached with treading water. The rope burned my hands. My hair was in my eyes and I could taste the salt. I could feel," She took a deep breath, "the teeth."

"It's not unusual for people to lose themselves in a mem-sim, Ms. Musabayana." Professor Becker sat on the desk in front of her and looked around the room. "I need to tell the class that the woman in the water survived the attack. She donated this memory to the school just last year. We cut the memory at this point because the conclusion is a bit bloody. But, like I said, she survived. And prosthetic limbs are a dime a dozen these days." Professor Becker looked at Shara, concerned. "Do you wish to try another one? I can't promise it will be pleasant. In fact, the next mem-sim in order is rather disturbing."

"OK, then," Shara said. "I'm gonna sit this one out." She took the headset off and held it out.

"I'm ready," Darien said. "I can go again."

The professor took the headset from Shara and handed it back to Darien. "Are you sure?"

Darien placed the set back on his head. No one else in the class appeared interested any longer in being part of this experiment. Shara still breathed heavily, wiping the tears of her frightening experience from her cheeks.

In the next simulation, Darien walked between two other men, his hands in shackles and his clothes orange. A man in black walked in front. No sound came from the simulation, no footsteps. He should have been hearing the shuffling of the sand under his feet. There was nothing. Without the sound of the footfall to accompany them, every step felt like a sponge.

Wind played through his hair. Grass clippings strewn across the concrete gave a scent, sharp and clean, like a Saturday morning in the suburbs. An orange sun hung on the horizon. Unable to tell if the sun was setting or rising, Darien wondered at the memory he was reliving.

Is this an ending, or a beginning?

Looking up, he marveled at the cloud formations, colors vivid and magnificent. The display of orange and red rolled away into a purple, darkening to a cold deep blue.

They approached a chain link fence, shut securely with a lock. On top of the fence, barbed wire spun circles of razor. The man in black turned to allow one of the guards to unlock the gate.

A priest. His white collar finally showing, he looked with pity at Darien.

Through the gate they continued, walking now on an asphalt

path with a fence on either side. In front of them a staircase climbed up between two solid walls. A wide view of the valley awaited at the top of the stairs. Houses and churches sat sprinkled between trees painted in vivid fall colors.

Several men in black robes, like those of a long past court, waited at the top of the staircase, sitting off to one side behind a table, clad also in black. The guards let go of Darien as a portly man, hair grey from his years and wearing a blue suit, began speaking.

Darien struggled to wake from the simulation.

He could not hear the words of the man in blue, but the man's lips moved and Darien read the words, "Sentenced to death. Under the power vested in me by the state of Missouri, I grant immunity to the executioners in their duty to carry out the sentence." He met Darien's eyes. "May God have mercy on your soul."

Grabbed again by the two men, Darien resisted as he was dragged to the edge of the raised ledge. Looking down, the realization of the means of execution engulfed him and he collapsed in their grasp, dizziness crushing him as he recoiled from the drop in front. Strong hands hoisted Darien to his feet. Seconds later those strong hands moved him forward and let go, dropping him off the precipice. With a silent scream, the simulation ended.

He was in the classroom again. The other students held their breath, waiting for Darien to say something.

"Can you read lips?" Professor Becker asked.

Darien tried to swallow his anger and failed.

"What? That's all you have to say?"

"I'm sorry, Darien. Are you all right?"

"Well, yes," Darien said.

"Do you need a nurse?"

"No." Darien dropped the plastic headset on the desk. He wasn't doing another one of those experiments.

"Can you read lips?" Professor Becker repeated.

"No."

"You could in that simulation. The subject," Becker checked

his writpad, "a mister Wilson, was deaf and he could read lips as his way to communicate. You, Mr. Mamon, don't have that ability, but the skill was temporarily yours for the duration of the simulation."

Professor Becker paced the room, explaining the reason behind this simulation. "One other point to note; in Ms. Musabayana's simulation, the subject survived the attack, allowing her memory to be recorded years after the event. In your last simulation, the subject died and the memory was recorded post mortem using electrical stimulation." Professor Becker took the plastic headset and placed it back in its case. "Another point of record, did you notice that this memory-sim was incredibly detailed? Every little thing, every smell, visual display, every sensation, the wind in your hair, the smell of grass and the way it connected to childhood memories, everything was important. Our subject, on his way to an execution took a look around him and felt everything was important, everything was burned into his memory, written in exquisite detail. Everything was so important to him that this last memory was the only thing that could be recovered. Time and again, when attempts have been made to recover memories of those that experienced death, the only one remaining consisted of the moments leading up to it."

Professor Becker had been the head of Memory Engineering and Technology for more than a decade at that time. Darien had since heard he took a job at some company in New York. They had to be paying more. That was the problem with careers in academics, no money.

Professor Becker opened the minds of his students into new worldly experiences. Some might have thought it odd Darien had such affection for someone who had been the ignition of so many unpleasant experiences. Friendships begin in many ways. Sometimes they start with a fight.

"You have memories of my memories," Dr. Hollister said as he looked over Darien's credentials. "The roller coaster where you got sick, the girl in the green shirt, that was mine."

"So what color was your shirt?" Darien asked.

"To be honest, I don't recall. It was a detail that wasn't needed and so not saved."

"So how mad did she get?"

"After I threw up on her? Pretty mad. Thankfully, there was a relatively large washroom nearby and we were able to clean her up, not that I was much help, as sick as I was. Is it pointless to say it was our last date?"

Darien laughed, remembering the look on her face.

Dr. Hollister put his feet up on the desk and leaned back into his chair, still scanning the writpad with Darien's college record. "So what did you do after college?"

"I answered that in the forms required for my application. Isn't it there?" Darien asked, embarrassed to have to talk about his past.

"That was an application for employment with MemorSingular, Incorporated. Right now, I need to decide if I can work with you, if you fit the needs of the program in question."

Darien leaned forward in his chair. "I guess I am a little star-struck. I studied your work for a year."

"Look, I'm only a man, like you. I just had a few good ideas that took off."

Dr. Hollister was not a young man, looking younger than Darien expected, but still distinguished. His hair was gray and trimmed short in a military fashion. Even at his age he wasn't frail. At over six feet he didn't fit the bill of a lifelong programmer and engineer scientist. Darien could easily see Randy Hollister lifting weights in a gym, giving advice to those around him. 'No, don't lift it like that! Straighten your back and look at your reflection in the mirror. It'll help you keep your form correct.'

Darien snapped out of his assessment of Dr. Hollister and gave an answer to the doctor's original question. "Well, I didn't have much chance for direct opportunities after college because of—"

"Because of the alleged cheating," Dr. Hollister finished for him.

"Uh, yeah," Darien said, embarrassed again. "My first job was with Femto Bloodsystems. For them I was a code correction officer."

"It says here that you were assigned to work on syntax and math verification."

"Yeah, that's right."

"And that led to a job at Integrated Blood Incorporated. Why did you leave them?"

"I got a better job offer at BioMedTricks."

"And why did you leave BioMedTricks."

"I got sick. Cancer."

"It says here that you were dismissed for frequent and extended absence."

"Well, they get to write the record, don't they?"

"Including the time you spent in the hospital, how long were you out of work?"

"A year."

"Did you code at all throughout that year?"

"Only a little."

"And what did that entail?"

"I wrote a game program with a kid that was sick in the room next to mine."

"And your debt to NationalMedCare, what is the percentage garnered from your income?"

"Eighty-five percent."

Dr. Hollister whistled. "Well, that's steep."

"Yes."

"Your next job was with," Dr. Hollister checked his writpad, "Synapse."

"Yeah, I was there for two years. BioMedTricks wouldn't take me back. They said that with my debt I was an unnecessary security risk."

"And where did you live during your time with Synapse?" Dr. Hollister was flipping through the history on his writpad.

"Look, all of this information is right in front of you," Darien said. "I'm sorry to be a bit of a dick but why didn't you review this before I arrived?"

"Embarrassed?"

"Yeah, a bit." Darien shrugged his shoulders, feeling lost, unable to guide the conversation at all. "I was homeless a lot of the time, living hand to mouth. Every penny was accounted for and I was barely keeping myself fed. Have you ever been there? Have you ever been hungry, ever given your last bit of food away to someone less fortunate than yourself while at the same time not knowing when you'll eat again?"

"Was it a new feeling for you?"

Darien lost control of his temper and his voice blurted out his thoughts before he could revise them. "Are you a psychiatrist, now? Look, if you're looking for a reason not to add me to your group, I'm sure there are plenty."

Dr. Hollister didn't answer. He rose from his seat, walked to the door and opened it.

Darien watched him and sighed heavily. After a moment of self-loathing he took his writpad from the desk in front of him and walked to the door.

"I'm sorry, Dr. Hollister."

He received a nod in reply and the door shut quietly behind him.

"Well, that sucked," he said out loud. Darien's stomach turned and the tightness in his shoulders emanated all the way down to his fingers. "Another opportunity, down the drain."

Shoulders drooping, he checked the time on his writpad and discovered it was still within the allotted breakfast service. He didn't feel like eating. Darien walked toward the staircase, the metal staircase he liked so much. His fingers wrapped around the cool handrail, feeling the dried paint pooled on the underside from the last painting. He stopped to lean against the wall at the landing below. Mind reeling, he could not believe how he had lost his temper again, this time missing out on the chance to work with a legend.

One group of people sat at the far end of the near empty cafeteria, eating and laughing. Their raucous behavior came to an abrupt stop at the sight of Darien entering. Nancy, or the girl Darien had thought was Nancy, was with them, her blonde hair pulled back into a ponytail. Stealing a glance, Darien tried to determine if it was indeed her.

The buffet table had the look of a scavenged carcass, bones appearing through the torn meat. He shoveled the last bits of scrambled eggs from the tray to his plate and collected some half slices and slivers of cold bacon. At least the coffee was hot. One thing he could not stand was stale coffee.

He was jolted out of his self-pity by the humming of the writpad notification signifying an incoming message.

HR again, Darien thought drearily as he lifted the pad. To his surprise the screen read, "3 PM. Dr. Hollister."

Chapter Three

Report Subject:	**Darien Mamon**
Origin Location:	**Oneida, New York**
Current Location:	**South Miami Tech**
Subject Age:	**18-19**
Subject Status:	**Non-Viable**

"Why do you date him? He's an absolute ass. Do you think he cares about you or your feelings?" Nancy shoved a whole slice of bacon into her mouth.

The lunchroom at South Miami Technical was bustling with students carrying trays, backpacks, and projects to their tables. Writpads were propped against coffee mugs and ketchup bottles as hungover teenagers tried desperately to learn the lessons they were about to be quizzed on. The bright painted colors of the walls and pillars were supposed to help the students start their day off on a vibrant, positive note. To a teenager with a hangover, they were like a needle in the eye.

"I know Darien's not perfect. Who is?"

"Perfect? Perfect?" Nancy said around the slice of bacon. "Did you know he was flirting with Sue Wesson last week?" Nancy threw her hands into the air with the last question.

Shara was about to take another bite when a young man set his tray down a couple of spaces from them. He was thin. His clothes were wrinkled and his hair stuck out at odd angles from his head. As they watched him, he lifted one foot after another over the bench seat and sat down with a sigh of exhaustion. Eyes closed, he popped the top on his caffeine energy drink and drank half of it before he looked from around the side of the can to see Nancy glaring at him. The young man swallowed and slid with his tray to the other end of the table.

"And I flirt all the time, too," Shara said, poking a breakfast sausage on her plate and dipping it into the maple syrup.

Nancy did not look convinced.

"He has a lot of good qualities. He's eighth in the class so far, right behind you and me, actually. His temper is nowhere near as bad as people say. I don't know how he didn't deck Frank yesterday. And," Shara continued, lifting her eyebrows, "he always brings me coffee in the morning."

"Well, you wouldn't survive without your coffee," Nancy teased. "And Frank would have killed him." Nancy shoved another slice of bacon into her mouth, folding it in, and continued talking with her mouth full. "Did you read his paper on social mobility? It was absolutely barbaric, going on about worker ants and social classes. It made me wonder how he really feels on the subject." She swallowed the bacon in a lump and catching her breath, said, "Heartless prick."

Shara chewed the slice of sausage and thought about Darien. He wasn't staggeringly handsome. He wasn't ugly, either. He wasn't tall. He also wasn't short. His appearance was common, unremarkable. Nevertheless, he did have a way about him. He wasn't a good singer, but he sang anyway. He wasn't a good dancer, but he never minded when someone laughed. *Smart, he's smart*, she reasoned. That wasn't what had drawn her to him.

South Miami Technical, built over in the new state extension area on pillars of concrete and plastic, allowed for students to live in the most southern state without the pests of the swamps. The pod door opened to salty air, a warm breeze, and a painful sun.

He looked like a lost puppy, Shara said to herself. Classes had already started. This puppy was coming in late.

"Five hours in a pod and my head is still dazed," Darien grumbled. "This is unacceptable." His clothes were too warm for the South Miami climate, a sweater, long denim jeans and boots. Staring around, he tried to orient himself on the map. He looked like a child, glancing left and right, peering down at the jumble of colors and lines on the vid-card in his hand as the sweat poured off his head, dripping off his nose when he bent down.

Taking pity on him, Shara approached the boy and touched

his shoulder. "Hey there, nubess," she said. "Are you OK?"

He looked at her hand on his shoulder and brushed it off. "Yeah, I'm fine," he said, squinting and holding the vid-card up close to his face.

"Well, you don't look fine. You're holding that upside-down. And look at this," Shara snatched the vid-card from his hand and pointed it at the ground. A hologram of the campus appeared at their feet. Buildings were named, as well as streets, campus sections, and there, off to the left, raised up from the plastphalt street, was the hologram representation of his assigned dormitory.

Shara pressed a corner of the vid-card and next to the 'you are here' blinking star appeared the name of the street they were standing on, Childress Ave.

"Uh, thanks," Darien said, blushing a little.

"Yeah," Shara said nodding. "Looks like you're here." She pointed down and poked the dormitory building hologram. At her touch the hologram disappeared. She handed him back the card, which now displayed directions to the dormitory.

"How did you know where I was going?" he asked.

"Most people don't bring a suitcase to class. And no one heading to class around here would be wearing a thick sweater and jeans. Maybe you're one of those weird people that do, maybe not. I took a guess." She smiled as she walked away. "Welcome to smami tech."

"He's still a prick," Nancy said, waking Shara from her reverie.

Shara blushed for a moment as the memory hit her with a needle of shame. She and her friends had been trying to create a nickname for South Miami Technical since they had started a year earlier. It wasn't catching on. It wasn't catching on in a big way and she had become a victim of ridicule over it. Some students even made stickers with her photo on them alongside the moniker "Smami ditz".

Shara took a large gulp of coffee to hide her embarrassment, making it worse as a splash of coffee escaped her mouth, spilling around the sides of the cup to stain her new shirt.

Nancy burst out laughing, "You're a mess today."

Shara joined Nancy in the laugh, letting go of the embarrassment and grabbed some napkins to wipe up the coffee.

"All brains and no coordination. I swear, I don't know how you made it this far," Nancy said, helping with the napkins. "You better put some water on that. It's going to stain."

It was the second time Shara ran into Darien he expressed any interest at all. The girls had been sitting in a group at the middle table of the library, poring over digi-books and flipping calc-sims for answers. Nancy saw him first.

"Hey! Don't look now but we got a gargoyle on the second floor checking you out."

"Where?" Shara asked, smiling.

Nancy typed at her writpad and swiped a calculation away. "In the glass room, group study A." Shara looked up and received a poke from Nancy. "I told you not to look."

Shara looked up again anyway. "I know that guy."

"You do? What's his name?"

"Oh, I don't know him. I've met him."

"Not the same thing."

"Is he still looking?"

"No, he's gone back to the board."

Moments later, Shara was at the door to Group Study Room A. Inside, the 'gargoyle' described by Nancy was walking through his calculation on the magnetic Gaussian board attached to the wall. Shara's tap at the clear glass door made him jump. Seeing her, he put down his magnetic pen and opened the door.

"Hey Nubess," Shara said, smiling.

He smiled back.

"What are you studying?"

"Calculus, parametric surfaces."

Small talk, he wasn't good at it.

"Are you understanding it?" She walked past him into the room to stand in front of the magnetic board. "I had trouble with it in my first year.”

Darien joined her to stare at the equations. “I’m getting along all right with it. I just looked and spotted an obvious error on the elliptic paraboloid. Trying to get my brain to accept the math isn’t the easiest thing.”

“Are you almost done?” Shara asked as she looked through the calculation. “I thought we might get some Thai food.”

The grin on Darien’s face showed his answer. “Yes,” he exhaled and laughed, “Sorry, I was holding my breath for some reason, there. Thought you were going to point out another mistake.”

She held out her hand. “I’m Shara.”

“You only have a first name? Like all those singers from last century?”

“Shara Musabayana.”

He took her hand. “Darien. Darien Mamon”

They sat across from each other in the small Thai restaurant as the waitress brought their drinks, a hot tea for Darien and a beer for Shara.

“I’m not in the mood for tea,” Shara said, pouring the beer into a glass. She filled the glass to the rim and finished off the bottle, annoyed the glass hadn’t been large enough. Sighing, she pushed the empty bottle toward the table edge for the waitress to collect when she returned, and looked up to see Darien smiling at her.

“What?” she asked.

“Nothing.”

“Oh, it’s going to be one of those dates?” she said, rolling her eyes before meeting his and demanding mockingly, “What?”

“I hate it when the glass is too small, too. All glasses should hold at least a full beer.”

“Right?”

“But then people would be drinking whiskey out of beer glasses, so I guess it’s a no win situation.”

“No whiskey for me. Beer,” she said. “Hard to beat a good beer.”

"Which one is that?" Darien asked, scanning the menu.

"Hiragana."

"Do you mind if I have a taste?" he asked.

"Sure." Shara pushed the glass across the table and, to her surprise, Darien stood up, leaned across the table, and kissed her. It was long and sensual. His lips were soft and wet, and her tongue played against his upper lip. Shara did not pull back. She leaned in, shocked at her actions but enjoying every moment. She began to feel a warm tingle in her stomach.

When the kiss was finished, Darien sat down and smiled. Picking up his tea, he met her eyes. "Yeah, I like it."

Shara blushed and answered, licking her lips.

"You know, I lied to you the day I met you."

"You did, huh?" Darien said, sipping his tea. "Lying to me on my first day? Kinda cruel, isn't it?"

"I asked if you were all right. You said you were fine. Then, I said you didn't look fine." Shara picked up her glass of beer. "That was the lie." Shara lowered her voice to a whisper. "I thought you looked very fine."

Nancy wiped at the coffee stain. Shara watched her in the mirror of the girl's bathroom. Nancy's blonde hair always looked intentional. If it was ever messy it was because she wanted it to be messy. The same went for her clothes. Even the most frumpy of outfits looked like a billion dollars on her. Shara compared herself to Nancy all the time. Her best friend was everything Shara wanted to be, beautiful, unafraid, classy, easy-going, and smart. *Well,* thought Shara, *I'm smart, too.*

"There, that should do it," Nancy said backing away. "That shouldn't take all day to dry, even with the humidity today."

The front of Shara's shirt was now two colors, the color she left home with, a breathtaking sky blue, and now a darker version of the same color.

"I should just go back to the dorm and change," Shara said, brushing at the wet spots in the mirror.

"Don't be silly. You'd never make it back to Control Systems in time. We have a quiz today, remember?"

Nancy was right. She was always right.

The quiz in Control Systems took the whole class period. Shara looked through her work, scanning for mistakes, knowing she was going to miss some of them. This was her worst class. There was always one formula needed for these quizzes she hadn't memorized and she spent a good deal of time working out the solution without it. The clock at the front of the room ticked away toward ten minutes to eleven. Setting the paper toward the front of the desk, she gathered her things and prepared to leave.

"Time," Mr. Warner said from his desk below the clock.

"I don't understand why we can't just do this at the dorm." Shara leaned on the railing and looked out at the ocean. The water, sixty feet below them, lapped quietly at the pillars of concrete and plastic. "Still, it's nice out here."

"Because, I told you, I never know when someone is watching me."

"Why would anyone want to watch you?" She stopped herself with a thought. She liked watching him. Still, this was different. "You're talking about surveillance. Give me a moment to consider that the man I've been dating for a year might be a little off his rocker, two sandwiches short of a picnic."

"I'm telling you I saw them. And," he dug into his pocket, "I found this." He held up a battery and handed it to her.

It was about two inches long and a half inch in diameter. Shara looked it over. "It's a battery," she said, shrugging her shoulders.

"Shake it."

Shara shook the battery and looked at it again. "There's something in there," she said. "You can feel it spinning around the axis."

"See?" Darien said quickly.

"That doesn't prove anything. It could be defective."

Darien took the battery back and threw it over the railing into the water. "I'm not taking any chances."

"What the hell? You can't just throw your garbage in the ocean." Shara watched it plunk into the small waves.

"Anyway, that's why we're out here."

"OK, paranoid, I told you to lay off those THC infused lollipops. You can't just go buying them anywhere."

"Where will you be going this summer?" Darien ran his hands up and down the sleeves of his own shirt.

"What do you mean?" Shara asked.

"Are you going to be taking an internship somewhere?" Darien looked over his shoulder.

"Well, I had a couple of offers but I haven't decided which one to take."

"I have an internship," Darien said flatly.

Shara scoffed, shaking her head. "You're a sophomore. How could you have an internship somewhere? Sophomores never get an internship."

"Well, I've got one. Only one company expressed interest and I don't think I have a choice but to go. The money is running out."

"How? You haven't had the classes."

"I've had the classes," Darien said.

"I've seen your work."

"Not all of it. I came here on an accelerated plan. In fact, I'm going to be graduating with you."

A jolt of excitement shot through Shara and she jumped a little. "That's great! Why didn't you say anything?"

"I couldn't. Dr. Becker's been helping me out. I've been simulating classes. I'm not really supposed to talk about it." Darien was running his hands over his clothes as if he were looking for something, checking and rechecking his pockets.

"That's good news! What are you so uptight about?"

"Someone followed Becker the other night and beat the crap out of him. Said he's broken all the rules and wanted to know who he was helping."

"And that's why we're out here?"

"Yes." Darien sat down with his back to the railing and pulled her down next to him. "When I arrived here I had some of the classes already under my belt. I tested out of a few. Becker helped me push through to my senior year and I tested out of the rest last month."

"How could you get all that done, even in four semesters?" Shara asked, incredulous. Darien was acting odd. He was so serious.

"Do you remember that class we had together, the one about memory storage and recovery?"

Shara nodded.

"Well, the first classes I tested out of had the same feeling as some of those memories I relived with Professor Becker."

"What do you mean?"

"Did you try the headset?"

"You know I did."

"Well, when you look back to that memory from the headset you know it wasn't yours, but it's still there as if you lived it. A lot of the answers for the first classes I tested out of came just like that" he snapped his fingers, "like, the memories were mine, but not mine." Darien hadn't stopped searching his clothes. His fingers ran slowly along his collar, along the belt-line of his pants, and around each button of his shirt.

"So, you think you might have had classes taught with mem-sim before even coming here?"

"Yeah, and I think I was chosen for that assignment by Professor Becker on purpose, or for a purpose." He took off his shoes, feeling around inside them. Shara watched him in silence.

Then, with a moment of realization, he lay on his back and fished a pocket knife out of his front pocket. Opening the knife, Darien cut the shoelace for each shoe at their lowest eyelet. One of the laces didn't cut easily. As Shara watched, Darien drew a thin wire from out of the shoelace, unraveling the lace from the shoe in the process, until he held in his hands five centimeters of wire. At the end of the wire was an oblong metal piece Darien inspected closely, holding his breath.

"Well," he said, "there's no apparent microphone." He dropped the wire and the cut laces over the railing, watching them fall away to the water. "That one's just a tracker. Lucky."

"So how long do you think they've been following you?" Shara pushed the paper bowl of French fries across the table to Darien.

"That's the thing. I really don't know that any more than I know who." Darien picked up four fries and ate them in one bite.

"What other kind of devices have you found?"

"Other devices, like the battery?" Darien swallowed the fries.

"Yeah, like the battery."

"Well, I don't really know for certain the battery was a device. I might have been paranoid. I haven't found any other types of devices." He shoveled in four more fries, talking with his mouth full. "Do you think I should be looking for other types? Like what? Everything else I've found, that I'm for sure about, has been woven into my clothing in one form or another."

"I suppose there's all kinds of tracking devices out there. I don't suppose you've done any research, maybe saved one of them and looked up a serial number or something?"

Darien stopped mid-reach for more fries and laughed. "Do you ever have one of those moments where you suddenly discover how dumb you are? I just had one of those." He laughed some more, a deep and silent chest constricting laugh, one of those laughs where it's impossible to take a breath, his eyes closed tight, hunched forward over the table placemat in front of him. When he could finally breathe, tears were streaming from his eyes and he looked up to see Shara laughing along with him. "No. No." He took a deep breath, sucking in the air, filling his lungs with just enough for another few words. "I destroyed them all." He took another breath. "Dropped them all in the water."

Shara snorted in her laughter, causing her to laugh even harder, the French fry in her hand forgotten.

When Darien finally composed himself he took the french fry from Shara's hand and ate it, smiling at her playful indignation at losing a single fry.

"How many did you find?" Shara asked.

"Like," Darien scrunched his eyes, "eight."

"You found eight and didn't think once, 'I should find a microscope and see if there's any identifying information on this.' You're right to feel stupid." Still smiling, Shara pulled the paper bowl of french fries close to herself again. "You're going to have to wait until it happens again, now. Or," she raised her eyebrows, "you could learn how to dive and go find the one you threw away an hour ago."

"Yeah, I think I'm good with that."

"So, eight, in how long?"

"Six months."

"You're finding more than one a month?"

"I found the first three at the same time."

"They had three on you at the same time? Seems like a bit of overkill." Shara reached for the ketchup.

"That's what I thought too. I mean if this is the lawyers from my parent's estate then it's a terrible way to keep track of me. And for what purpose? To get back the tuition money?"

Shara started and looked up at the clock on the wall behind Darien. "Oh, crap. I gotta go. I'm supposed to meet Nancy for a study session in her room." Shara stood, shoved a few fries in her mouth, and kissed Darien on the cheek between chews. "Keep the next one you find and we'll look at it together."

The walk to Nancy's dorm room allowed Shara to get her emotions in order. Spending time with Darien turned her heart to jelly. He wasn't like anyone she had ever known before and she couldn't stop herself thinking about him.

You need to tell him.

Guilt swam around her thoughts. His life was going to stray far from his goals. Everything he reached for would be pulled away and she didn't know if she could bear to witness it. Being in love with him didn't make it any easier.

Punching in her student key, she opened the door and pressed the button for the elevator. Darien never took the elevator. Unlike her, he hated them. She enjoyed the silence, watching the lights blinking the floor numbers as they went by.

Opening the door, Nancy didn't look happy.

"Do you remember what time we were supposed to meet?"

"Of course I do. I was talking to Darien and lost track of the time." Shara brushed past Nancy and dropped onto one of her soft couches. "Are we still going to make the call?"

"No, I already did that." Nancy shut the door, opened a packet of tea flavoring, tipped it into a mug, and filled it with water from the jug at her feet.

"So, what did they say?" Shara asked.

"They said," Nancy stirred her drink, "that we need to keep on doing what we're doing. They also said I need to bring my grades up. Apparently, no-one anywhere is going to hire me if I don't have the four point zero GPA."

"Grades are one thing. Drive is another."

"That's what I said." Nancy held up another tea flavoring packet and nodded to Shara questioningly.

"Yes, I'd love some." Shara watched Nancy make another drink, her mind going back to Darien, again. *Eight, he found eight tracking devices.*

"They also said there's another subject you need to take, something about management of personnel." Nancy handed Shara her drink. "You're always better with people than me."

"That's a strange subject for a memory engineer. Are they asking for a double major?"

"They didn't say." Nancy sat on the couch and rested her head on Shara's shoulder. "I'm so stressed. We've been working so hard and there's always something more. I'm starting to wonder if any of this is worth it, if we shouldn't just say, 'To hell with all of it.'"

Shara brushed Nancy's hair with her fingers, draping the long blond locks away from her eyes. "I'm tired too. But, we've come so far. What's the alternative at this point?"

Nancy lifted her head and sipped from her mug before placing her cheek back on Shara's shoulder. "Maybe we could skip some classes and hit the amusement parks, again." She chuckled. "Maybe I could find a date this time."

"It's a good idea. Can I bring Darien?"

"Find me a date first."

Shara sipped her tea. "It'll get his mind off things. He found another wire on him."

"Another?"

"Yeah, he was pretty upset."

"You need to hide those better." Nancy lifted her head and took another drink.

"Do you ever think maybe we're on the wrong side?" Shara said, leaning back into the couch.

"No, I never think about it. But, like I said, what's the alternative?" She turned her head to look up at Shara. "You like watching him?"

Shara shrugged her shoulders. "Of course I do. He's young and handsome."

"To you, maybe. Just remember why we're here."

Chapter Four

Report Subject: **Darien Mamon**
Origin Location: **Oneida, New York**
Current Location: **Tucson, AZ**
Subject Age: **27**
Subject Status: **Viable**

Several levels below, workers were cleaning, increasing the transparency of the glass. Looking down at them twisted Darien's stomach into knots. He focused instead on the sub-level six steel support beam helping to mar the depth illusion of the glass floors. He took a deep breath, letting it out slowly, and walked across the terrifying span to the acrylic door on the opposite side.

He would have to get used to this facility or it was going to be a long year. Perhaps he could request a transfer to another location next year. He had heard the Sierra Vista facility just outside of Fort Huachuca was like a vacation resort in comparison to Tucson. *At least at that location all the buildings are above ground,* he thought.

Pressing the button alerted the secured resident and Darien placed the writpad against the door.

"Hey," said an electronic voice from inside. "Who is that? Hollister?" The electronic voice cut off abruptly with the last word.

"Sign, please," Darien said. This was the first inhabitant who had tried to communicate outside of a simple 'hello' or 'yeah.' After noting the writpad had been signed, Darien asked, "You work with Dr. Hollister?"

He waited for the voice to answer and, guessing the electronic system had cut off intentionally, he turned to leave.

"Can you hear me?" The electronic voice representation was gone. This was a human voice. Looking around, Darien tried to see who was talking when the voice spoke again through the speaker on the door, absent of any hint of electronic voice manipulation. "Are you still out there? Can you hear me?"

"Yes," Darien wasn't sure he should be speaking to anyone. Only a day prior he had received a reprimand for just looking into a room unauthorized. "Hello?"

"I'm Sam Matheson. Remember the name. Sam Mathes—" The voice clicked away.

Darien looked at the door, searching for the break in the surface that would have allowed the inhabitant to speak to him without using the standard electronic system, understanding Sam Matheson had managed not only to turn off the voice manipulation algorithm, he had even managed to override the initial system shutdown. Darien's mind sped off into the code that might accomplish these feats until he became jumbled in a loop of functions and objects so complex he forgot he was standing on a sheet of glass.

The writpad buzzed. He read the message out loud, "Darien Mamon, report to Human Resources, immediately."

Darien dropped his head. *Not again*, he thought to himself. *How? How do I always wind up in these messes?*

Attached to the command to report to HR was a signature, Emily Stone.

Who the hell is Emily Stone?

He needed to get better at learning names. Only the day before he had been in HR talking to that small mouse-like woman. Darien corrected himself; he was being reprimanded. He must have been standing at her desk for ten minutes. Her name was written in recessed letters on a shiny silver plaque. He could see the desk. He could hear her voice. *What was her name? Was it Emily?* He couldn't remember and admonished himself over it. *Asshole.*

The metal staircase railing rang with a gong as he rapped his knuckles against the painted surface. The vibration of his blow stopped as he placed his hand on it. He hit the railing again as he climbed, enjoying the sound. HR had called him to the office again, twice in only two days. There was a firing coming for sure.

The only thing he could think of that he might have done wrong was to talk with the secured resident Sam.

It wasn't even a conversation, he argued inside of his head, running through the possible talking points in the coming encounter. *No, I didn't initiate communication. Look here, all I did was get the signature. He talked to me, said his name was Sam.*

Reaching the landing on sub-level one, Darien stood outside the door to HR and took a few moments to regain his breath. Sub-level five to sub-level one meant climbing four double flights of thirteen steps each. *Not liking the elevator might pay off for my waistline,* Darien thought.

With a final deep breath, Darien grasped the doorknob and twisted, expecting it to open the door, and slammed his chest into the, still closed, wooden barrier. It gave off a resounding thud. The door was locked. Darien turned the doorknob again. *Yup, definitely locked.*

The writpad buzzed again.

"Please, report to HR immediately."

"I'm trying," Darien said in exasperation as he tried the knob again.

From one of the other doors on the HR level, six men wearing the black uniforms of security came toward Darien.

"Hi, guys," Darien said. He found himself on the floor again, writpad flung away to clatter against the glass, wrist painfully twisted so the slightest pressure sent distress levels of pain through his nervous system. Mouth pressed against the floor he managed to say, "Seriously?"

"State your business," the man pressing the back of his head demanded as he pressed harder.

"I wa carred to ayarrr," Darien said.

The pressure on his head released a little and the man in black asked, "What?"

"I was called to HR!" Darien repeated.

One of the security personnel picked up and examined the writpad. "According to his schedule, he is to report to HR. It says, 'immediately.'"

"Can you see who initiated the command?"

"Yes, sir. There is a signature attached to the command."

"A signature? Whose?" The man on Darien's back increased the pressure on Darien's head. The question wasn't for him.

"It says Emily Stone, IDA," the security team member holding the writpad offered.

The painful pressure on Darien's head released and he was dragged to a standing position, his arm still twisted uncomfortably behind his back. Darien winced as the man wrenching his arm adjusted his grip to remove a plastic restraint from his belt.

"Ziiip," the restraint tightened on Darien's wrist. He didn't struggle as his other arm was aligned with the first and the other end of the restraint was tightened.

Finally able to speak, Darien asked, "Hey what's the big issue here? I was only answering the call I received." The only reply he got was to be roughly shoved into one of the doorways the security personnel had come out of.

The hallway stretched away from the central hub, painted in the same dark green paint of the metal stairwell. Darien looked down at the sides of the hallway and was confused to see an elaborate spring system holding the floor suspended from the ceiling. The coils, an inch thick as they spun around seemed a fair amount of overkill to hold the weight of the men traveling down the hallway. Then Darien remembered the original reason for the creation of most of this facility. This was a nuclear silo. Much of the electronics would have been held in this wing of the underground bunker, set on springs to protect the men and equipment enough so they could retaliate, even after a nuclear blast had occurred outside.

All these thoughts transpired in a moment, for that was all the time it took to walk down the hallway to the room at the end. Darien was set down into a chair with his arms still restrained behind him. He looked around the room. The electronics and vacuum tubes that would have been the heart of this room during the Cold War standoff were gone, replaced by tables with glossy black tops, chairs, and padded walls. The room had four doors, one on each wall through which most of the men who had dragged him in here disappeared, and a large glass mirrored window.

For the first time Darien got a look at the man in black that had pressed so firmly on the back of his head. He was just over fifty, Darien estimated. His dark brown hair had long been overrun by the gray of middle age. The man was physically powerful. Darien had already learned this outside of HR, but he looked it as well. His nose was crooked or just off center giving him a rugged appearance. As Darien inspected the man in black further a spot of recognition flooded through him, and Darien said, "Mark Engles?"

"No," the man in black replied.

"You're not Mark Engles?" Darien asked. The man in black ignored him, sitting down at the opposite side of the table and opening Darien's writpad. "You worked at BioMedTricks out near Bucktooth Sally's in Miami, right?"

"Nope."

"You've put on a bit of muscle," Darien looked closely at the man in black, leaning forward in his chair. "But, if you're not him, you're related."

Rising from his chair, the man in black leaned forward over the table to show Darien the ID card attached to the retractable cord at his belt. The ID had a photo of the rugged looking man and a name below the photo in bold black letters, *Lawrence Enderby*. Lawrence let the card slip from his hand as he sat back down and it flew back to its position at his waist.

"Well, nice to meet you, Larry."

"Lawrence."

"Not Larry?"

"As far as you are concerned, you may call me Mr. Enderby."

"All right," Darien said. "Mr. Enderby, can you please explain to me why you guys keep smacking me to the floor? Why did you drag me into this—" Darien looked around him, "interrogation room?"

"It is for your own protection."

"My protection?" Darien almost yelled. "And let me guess. I'm still restrained in case I might want to cut my own throat with my fingernails?"

"Something like that. People do crazy things." Lawrence scanned through the writpad. "You have a meeting today with Dr. Hollister?"

"Yeah, three o'clock."

"You're not going to make that appointment. Give me a moment. I'm rescheduling your meeting." Lawrence's fingers moved with precision, quickly sending a notice to Dr. Hollister. "How about ten AM tomorrow?"

"I can't afford to miss my appointment."

"Sucks to be you." Lawrence flipped the panels on the writpad closed and set it on the table. "Better be there at ten, tomorrow, then."

"Are you going to tell me what's going on? Why you guys keep harassing me?"

"I'm not at liberty to say just yet."

"Liberty?" Darien sat up in his seat. "I demand to know what the hell is going on."

"You do. Do you?" Lawrence asked, smiling. "Well, I'm afraid I can't say anything, not until I can get some confirmation you aren't the leak."

"Leak? What leak? What is there to leak?" Darien asked. His hands were beginning to go numb.

"Suffice it to say, for the moment, we found an information leak. Until we learn some more about you, you'll have to just sit tight." Lawrence pulled a data cord out from under the table and plugged it into Darien's writpad. The screen became a picture of white noise, rippling through several patterns of video recognition before it relaxed to show the order to report to Human Resources. Lawrence's fingers typed a flurry of keystrokes into the writpad. "There, that should do it."

"Do what?"

"I opened your writpad to remove the encryption." He reviewed his work. "Damn. I forgot a piece." Lawrence frowned and pulled a plastic card out of his shirt pocket, visibly annoyed at himself. He pulled Darien's writpad back to himself and turned the power off and then on again. When the system refreshed, Lawrence held the card up to the screen and it rebooted again. "That's what I get for showing off. It's so much easier with the card."

"Do you want me to look at it?" Darien asked, mockingly. "I'm pretty good at this stuff."

Still working on the writpad, Lawrence said, "Hey, pencil-neck, I don't need your sass."

"If you just tell me what you're trying to do with it—"

"Ah! My last statement wasn't clear enough." Lawrence raised his eyebrows and said, "Shut up."

Darien watched the large fingers hitting the keys until Lawrence finally sat back with an air of success.

They sat there for the next twenty minutes in silence, Lawrence Enderby stared across at Darien, as relaxed as if they were only having a conversation about an extended warranty on a travel pod. He was even smiling a little.

A short man in a black uniform entered through the door behind Lawrence. "What the hell?" he asked, shutting the door behind him. Picking up Darien's writpad he asked Lawrence, "What the hell did you do to this thing?"

This man, unlike Lawrence, had a slight appearance and was obviously not a fan of physical exertion. In his eyes, however, one could see he was not a man to be trifled with. Clean shaven and close cropped, he had the stern look of a military general.

He sat down next to Lawrence and fiddled with the writpad, pulling the cord. "Where's that card?"

Lawrence fished in his shirt pocket again and drew it forth.

"Well, that explains a lot." The short man in black took the card from Lawrence and snapped it in half. "Old card. I still have your new one." He searched his pockets and pulled out two plastic cards. One of these he handed to Lawrence and pressed the other against the screen of Darien's writpad.

A myriad of data scrolled across the writpad with such speed it could not be read or recognized until finally the screen displayed the message, 'record not found.'

Are we good?" Lawrence asked the short man in black.

"Yes, Larry, all set," the short man said as he sat down at the table.

"It's Lawrence."

"All set, Lawrence." The short man in black rolled his eyes.

"This is Agent James Curtis," Lawrence said, gesturing to the short man. "He's just cleared you based on your data streams. We've been monitoring you since the day you arrived, common procedure. Every new employee gets the same scrutiny. You might be an idiot, but you're not the leak."

"Well, thanks," Darien replied.

Agent Curtis said, "Someone, however, believes you to be approachable as an asset. That's why you received the invitation to HR this morning." He picked up the writpad and flipped it off again. "Who is Emily Stone?"

"How should I know? I figured that was the name of Mrs. Mouse in HR."

"Mrs. Mouse?"

"I didn't get her name, little mousey looking woman, sits behind a desk."

"Ah, Helen. OK." Agent Curtis said these words without inflection, as if he were only speaking to himself. This peculiarity faded as he asked his next question, "So, you have no idea who this Stone person is?"

"No, I figured I was in trouble again, getting called to HR."

"Oh, you are in trouble, just not with HR," Agent Curtis responded. "I think we can remove those restraints. Larry? Do you mind?"

"Lawrence."

"What?"

"My name is Lawrence."

"Yes, Lawrence, would you mind removing the restraints?"

Getting up from his chair, Lawrence walked around behind Darien and, pushing Darien's upper body forward in his seat, snipped the plastic bands with a tool from his belt. Darien rubbed at his wrists looking at his writpad in Agent Curtis's hands.

"Sorry for the rough treatment, Mr. Mamon," Agent Curtis said. "Or should I just call you Darien?"

"Darien will be fine."

Lawrence took his seat again next to Agent Curtis and Agent Curtis continued. "Mr. Mamon, do you know what the acronym IDA stands for? It's used after Emily Stone's name in the message requiring you to report to HR."

"To be honest, I didn't really look at the name. The call to report to HR had a pretty good hold on my thoughts. Last visit to HR didn't go as expected, you know?"

"We know. So," Agent Curtis prodded, "what do you think the acronym IDA stands for?"

"I assume it means integrated development assistant. At least, everywhere I've seen it, that's what it meant." The color was starting to return to Darien's hands with a tingling sensation but there were still indented red marks from the plastic bands. Darien flexed his fingers to help the blood circulate.

"In our field that is normally the case, but not in this instance. You see, there is no Emily Stone working at this facility. It is a fabricated name."

"And," Darien said slowly, "I should have known that?"

"Only if you were, in fact, the leak would you have known that information." Agent Curtis closed the writpad.

"Well, I'm glad we cleared this up."

"This is no laughing matter, Mr. Mamon."

"Darien."

"This is no laughing matter, Darien. Do you wish to know how we knew about the name being a fabrication?"

"Not particularly." Darien leaned forward in his seat. "I can't say I'm very fond of you fellas. I think I'd like to go."

Lawrence winked at Darien, smiling. In his hands he played with the broken restraints on the table.

Agent Curtis shook his head and continued. "I'm sorry, Mr. Mamon, but according to the contract you signed at your employment agreement meeting you are required to help us. Failure to comply will result in your immediate incarceration pending the conclusion of this investigation. We have no way of knowing how long said investigation could take." Agent Curtis handed the writpad back to Darien. "So, I think, from my experience in these matters that you will want to hear what I have to say."

Darien sighed. He would have to start reading everything placed in front of him. Still, he reasoned, given his financial situation, he probably would have signed the agreement even had he seen the assistance clause.

"It's an address," Agent Curtis said.

"What's an address?"

Agent Curtis pressed the palm of his hand to the table and the internal screen sprang to life. He typed while speaking. "The name, Emily Stone, IDA stands for M. L. E. Street, Oneida, O, N, E, I, D, A, in the state of New York." A map displayed on the table screen and Agent Curtis spread his fingers out against the surface of the table. The displayed map zoomed to the address, showing a long, isolated street. Agent Curtis swiped his hand across the map and it became a satellite image of a sprawling corporate office.

"Our organization has many branches that seem independent but are connected in ways that will become apparent in the near future. Here in this facility our doctors and engineers were working on gene splicing." Agent Curtis sat back in his chair. "You've heard about the eradication of some of the more dangerous diseases. This is the type of facility that makes those advances in medicine possible."

Agent Curtis swiped his hand across the map again and he said, "This is the same address as of this morning."

The new satellite image showed a smoking hole. Trees once covering other areas of the map had become brown litter laid to waste by a massive explosion. Buildings once housing the daily activities of people devoting their lives to the pursuit of knowledge were reduced to piles of rubble and flat black footprints.

The flat aerial photo became a video of the carnage. Bricks, broken and reduced to dust, littered the road where the cameraman was standing. A roaring fire spat black smoke into the air. The video zoomed in on the parking lot of transportation vehicles, windows shattered from the blast, plastic melted by the heat. The cameraman reduced the zoom and began walking, panning the camera left and right to show the extent of the damage. A voice, the cameraman likely, began speaking. "And here we have the organization in charge of human traffi—" Agent Curtis swiped the video away.

"We're still trying to determine the identity of the cameraman. You were our first clue."

"Not much of a clue," Darien said. "This is in New York? I don't know anything about this."

"As has been proven by your data stream." Agent Curtis said leaning forward again. "Mr. Mamon—"

"Darien."

"We are concerned a terrorist organization may have infiltrated our facility. We would like you to become our eyes, our ears, until we can get to the bottom of this tragedy, until we can find this bomber. We're fairly sure the origin of this particular bomber is the terrorist organization named Hiraeth. It's based here in this country but Hiraeth's arms stretch to Europe, Asia, and Africa." Agent Curtis ticked off the continents on his fingers. "This isn't their first attack on PEPM, and their attacks are not limited to us. Last year Hiraeth killed six hundred people globally at these locations." He spread his hands on the table again to display a flat global map. Several cities had black stars to mark the targeted locations: Savannah, Houston, London, Marseilles, Saigon, Shanghai, Minsk, and Rabat.

"I don't know. I'm a programmer. I write code. I'm not a spy or an agent or some kind of detective."

"We're not asking you to be James Bond," Lawrence said, shrugging his shoulders and splaying his hands. "Just keep your eyes open and report to us."

"Us?" Darien asked. "Just the two of you?"

"There's a lot more than just the two of us, but yes," Lawrence answered. "We would be your contact for both the security personnel and anything having to do with this investigation."

"I'm not sure. Am I in danger?"

"Did you see the size of the blast radius in that video?" Agent Curtis asked. "Do you have any idea the tonnage of explosive material large enough to make a dent like that? We're dealing with something bigger than just a nut who thought the local company was poisoning his well."

"I'm pretty sure it is safe to say that we're all in danger," Lawrence said. "If some person or organization has the type of access to plant explosives of this magnitude inside one of our facilities, who knows what else they have access to?" He was still playing with the plastic restraints, scratching his fingers with the sharp edges left by his snippers.

Agent Curtis pressed another button on the table display. The global map became the video of the destroyed buildings in New York and was soon replaced with an image of body bags lined up along the side of the road. The haze of smoke still filled the air. Emergency vehicles, lights blaring, lined the explosion site. In the new video, men were shouting, wearing fire protective suits and yelling about how it wasn't safe to get any closer to recover the remaining bodies.

A list of names replaced the images, scrolling past like the credits of a movie, hundreds of them. Darien's eyes recognized one, Becker, Professor Becker.

"As you've said, 'you're not very fond of us at the moment.' But these," Agent Curtis said, "are the names of the employees lost at this facility today. If Larry has been a little harsh with you in our interactions thus far, I believe he can be forgiven."

"It's Lawrence."

Chapter Five

Report Subject:	**Darien Mamon**
Origin Location:	**Oneida, New York**
Current Location:	**Tucson, AZ**
Subject Age:	**27**
Subject Status:	**Viable**

Dr. Hollister pushed the indicator light on the front of the old metal receiver, frowning at the result.

"I think the LED is bad. This is supposed to be on. What channel is it set to?"

"I don't know, sir. I've never seen one of these." Darien peered at the connections and their appropriate labels on the back.

"Well, this system accepts old radio waves at relatively low frequencies. You adjust the frequency with the variable resistor attached to the knob on the front."

"I know what a radio is. I just haven't seen one before. What are you trying to do with it?"

Dr. Hollister stopped poking at the old receiver and walked over to the wall display in his lab. "Well, most of the higher frequencies are taken by the newer methods of communication. I'm trying to use the AM range to receive messages from long distance."

"Seems like a fairly unreliable system," Darien said, still inspecting the old metal receiver.

"Not so. You're looking at the first radio frequency setup there, my friend. Some AM signals could travel further than the FM signals adopted by the radio industry. Put on a heavy cloud cover to bounce off and the AM signals could travel even further at night. I studied it a bit during my earlier years."

"Sounds stupid."

"Does it? This," he said, pointing at the old radio, "is the birth of everything wireless." Dr. Hollister pulled out a chair and positioned it in the middle of the room. He took special care to maneuver the legs over taped X's marked onto the floor. "Sit here."

Darien sat in the chair and immediately felt a rushing sensation. Colors danced past his peripheral vision, always out of focus, always blurred into each other. A great windstorm buffeted his ears, spinning from left to right as if he were rotating around the sound. Then, he found himself standing in a foggy town square, one of over a hundred other people.

Looking down, he examined his clothes to see they had changed to rough fabrics and simple fasteners. In the center of the square a wooden A-frame had been constructed. Hanging from the center of the frame was a rope tied into a noose.

Darien looked around. *There must be someone coming, leading the damned man to his sentence.* He searched the crowd around him, inspecting each, wondering what wrong they had all suffered to be so eager to watch a hanging.

People of all ages stood waiting, smiling in the mist. Men held toddlers on their shoulders. Women, young and beautiful, held hands with their betrothed or lovers. All seemed ready for a good show, a well-deserved execution.

Behind Darien, a hush took the crowd and they parted for the condemned. It wasn't a man. It was a child.

A boy of ten, shirtless and dirty, struggled against the tall, heavyset man holding his arm. The boy's hands were tied in front of him and he did not have the strength to pull away from his much larger jailor. The child's eyes were wide with fright, flitting left and right, searching for help from anyone in the crowd. Tears streamed down his face in brown lines through the buildup of dirt. Around Darien the crowd jeered and yelled toward the boy. The faces of the young and beautiful women stretched into those of wiry old hags, lines and wrinkles indenting their features as they screamed in fury.

"Yeah! Now, you're about to get what you deserve!"

"String him up!"

"Filthy thief!"

Stunned at their callousness, Darien wondered again what the boy had taken from them more precious than the life of a child. *What was his crime?*

Darien walked, pushing through the crowd, towards the A-frame as the jailor tightened the noose around the boy's neck. Winding his way through the people toward the child, Darien lost his breath as the jailor pulled on the other end of the rope to lift the struggling boy off his feet.

With a jerk, Darien snapped to his feet from the chair.

"Ah, I was wondering how long that would take," Dr. Hollister said. "Are you all right?"

"What the hell was that?" Darien asked, feeling like he was going to puke. "It felt like a mem-sim but I wasn't in anyone else's memory." Darien shuddered. "I was me."

Dr. Hollister beamed. "We call that experience 'situational memory replay.'" He walked to the wall control display and checked on the feedback information while he continued. "How was the entry?"

"What?"

"The entry into the situational memory, how did it feel? How long did it take?"

"Um," Darien said, moving away from the chair. "It took a couple of seconds."

"Any sensations?"

"It was loud."

"Loud?" Dr. Hollister made a note on his writpad.

"And colorful." Darien stepped further away from the center of the room and the wooden chair with the marked X's on the floor. "What was it? It wasn't a memory-sim."

"You're right. It wasn't someone else's memory. We took a situation and placed you into it, inside of your mind." He looked over his shoulder at Darien. "We hijacked your consciousness for a moment and made you a new memory."

Darien reached up to touch his own neck. The boy had shown genuine fear. The smell of the crowd hung in Darien's memory. Standing away from the chair, Darien asked, "Is this why we started this conversation with the old AM radio? Are these technologies connected?"

"Quick," Dr. Hollister nodded in approval. "Back in school you needed to wear the plastic headset. It read your brainwaves and synched its output to match, giving you the situations, sensations, even emotions embedded in the mem-sim."

"This wasn't a mem-sim," Darien said. "This is totally different."

"Yes, let me finish." Dr. Hollister pressed 'save' on the experiment displayed on his wall. "I read your brainwave patterns from a distance with this new system. It calibrated itself and broadcast the simulation. Calibration is still a bit off. That's why it was so noisy."

"But it wasn't a memory simulation. That wasn't anyone's memory. You created a new memory in my mind based on what? Parameters you programmed into the system?"

"Yes."

"That's scary as hell. Who's to say what happened or what's real?"

"You do. Did the simulation feel so real you would be confused with reality?"

"It was eerily real." Darien shivered. "You did this with AM radio?"

"No. Though the theory is the same. AM radio isn't nearly as powerful as the simulation requires, and AM is intended for longer distances. Eventually, situational memory replay will be possible at a greater distance. Right now, this only works inside this room," Dr. Hollister spread his hands out, palms up, "So far, it only works on a subject sitting in that chair, placed at that exact spot. See the marks on the floor?"

Darien leaned on the desk far away from the chair. He had a creepy sensation when he thought back to the hanging of the child, like he should have stopped it.

"Your simulations, how flexible are they? Could I have intervened? Could I have saved the kid?"

"If the simulation had been written out extensively like those old books, what were they called? Choose your own adventure. If we had written the code to that extent, then, yes, you could have intervened."

"Who was the kid?"

Dr. Hollister sat in the chair, first pulling it away from the marks on the floor, and began typing on his writpad.

"Would you mind," he asked, "filling out a brief survey about the experience?"

"Uh, yeah," Darien said, taking the writpad offered to him. "Because it's fresh in my mind, right?"

"Yes," Dr. Hollister said. "I can't do the experiment on myself so I don't know what's missing. I don't know the lingering effects or how long the memory will last."

"I don't know if I should be happy to be your guinea pig. This stuff isn't proven? How did you get the authorization?" Darien ticked off the answers to the survey as he spoke.

"I didn't." The chair didn't have any armrests and Dr. Hollister crossed his arms. "To be honest, I don't think the company will be too pleased. It's expensive, and right now we're funding the whole thing ourselves. I've been considering reaching out to investors." He pursed his lips and raised his eyebrows. "I imagine the porn industry will be the driving force behind this eventually," Dr. Hollister said. "Why not? They've been the driving force behind most of the technological advances for the past one hundred and fifty years."

"Porn?"

"All that aside, maybe it's best that we keep this test between us for now."

"Who am I gonna tell? I don't know many people here, except for the goons who keep dropping me to the glass."

"Who?"

"Guy's name was Larry."

"Oh, Lawrence." Dr. Hollister took the writpad back from Darien and scanned the answers. "Yeah, I know him, security, strong as an ox. I'll have a word with him, ask him to settle down a bit."

Outside the door, Darien leaned against the wall. Worse than any mem-sim, Darien wondered if every session with Dr.

Hollister was going to be as painful. His vision had a funny edge to it, like everything in the hall was out of focus. For all he knew he could be in another situational memory. His writpad buzzed, reminding him of his duties. There were more signatures to collect, more secured residents to not meet.

The thought of the secured residents sparked a latent outrage in him again at his encounter with HR. *What the hell is that about? What's the harm of meeting some of the new employees?* He still couldn't understand the unnecessary secrecy at play in this company.

He let his eyes stare at Hollister's door. *Situational memories.* He shook his head. Situational memories were the classical Pandora's box story. Misuse of such a thing was inevitable.

Well, he thought, *if I am still in a situational memory, I'm going to do what they don't expect.* Darien turned off his writpad and walked up the stairs toward the surface entrance.

"So, what's next?" he asked himself aloud in the echo of the empty staircase. "Feel like sitting for another memory?"

"Oh, I think that's enough for today," he answered. "I think I'll go for a walk outside." He'd been in this hole in the ground for what, three or four weeks? *You should take a pod to the city and see some of the sights.*

"Ha!" Darien laughed at the thought. Slightly out of breath from climbing, he answered himself again, "You can't afford to go to the city, scrub! Keep digging! That med-debt will ruin you."

Chapter Six

Report Subject: | Darien Mamon
Origin Location: | Oneida, New York
Current Location: | Tucson, AZ
Subject Age: | 27
Subject Status: | Viable

The solar panels at the ground level angled automatically toward the sun, leaning like plants and trees towards the light, soaking in the greatest number of BTUs in a continuous pattern. They lined the land in all directions, meticulously cleaned and adjusted by a handful of workers in wide brimmed hats and white shirts.

Darien walked between the panels, shading his eyes from the reflections. He remembered his awe when he arrived here the first time. That day, his questions concerning the solar array were quickly forgotten as he had entered the underground system to begin his interview. Now, they were back.

Why doesn't the place just connect to the power grid? Maybe they're not using much electricity and the whole operation is solar powered, or maybe they're using so much power their usage could be seen as suspicious.

Another thought occurred to him, *Is this an illegal operation?*

Out of the corner of his eye, Darien saw someone from the cafeteria. Her white hat was pulled low over her eyes and he thought he knew her when she glanced his way. Darien hadn't found the courage to speak with her in the cafeteria but there was no time like the present.

"Uh, hi," Darien said, stopping and turning to her. "I'm Darien," he extended his hand and she shook it with a firm grip. "I'm pretty new here and I don't know many people but I've seen your face before in the cafeteria."

"I'm sorry," she said. "I never eat in the cafeteria. We're not allowed below. We just maintain the power system." Her eyes were so dark Darien could almost see his own reflection in them. Her brown skin contrasted nicely against her white shirt.

"But you've been to the cafeteria. I saw you just the other day sitting with a blonde woman."

"No, you're mistaken. That wasn't me."

"I'm very sorry," Darien said, embarrased. "She looked very much like you. My name is Darien."

"You said that." She returned to the control panel she had been adjusting. "So, haven't been here long?"

"No."

"And what did you say your name was?"

"Darien, Darien Mamon."

"Nice to meet you Darien, Darien Mamon. I'm Leslie." She smiled, still working on the solar panel in front of her. Darien looked down at her badge and noted that it was tan. He hadn't seen a tan badge yet. "Don't get outside much, do you?" she asked.

"No, I don't," Darien said. "No reason to leave if you can't afford to go anywhere. I'm paying off my debt." Darien winced at his oversharing. *Stupid, stupid. Stop talking, Darien.*

Leslie turned away to punch the keypad on the post holding up the solar panel and said, "Well, that sucks. Why are you in so much debt?" She bent down to pick up her tools from the ground and Darien found himself looking at her ass. He took a deep breath as quietly as he could and answered her question.

"I had cancer. The payments are going to be taking eighty-five percent of my income until it's paid off."

"Oh, the price of life," she said standing up. "You're lucky, I guess. Not many survive that strain of cancer at all."

Confused, Darien said, "But I didn't tell you the strain."

"You're working here, love," Leslie said, "only one strain it could have been."

Darien was taken aback, his voice weak. "Excuse me? What are you talking about?"

Leslie turned to look him over. "Do you have a badge? Why aren't you wearing a badge?"

"Yeah, I have a badge, but I'm not inside so I stuck it in a pocket. The pin keeps poking my chest." He pulled his red badge out of his pocket.

Her eyes went wide.

Leslie shut the control panel door. "I'm sorry. I have to go." She shoved her tools under her arm and walked away toward the end of the solar panel row.

Darien walked after her. "What were you saying?"

"Look, don't follow me. You're going to get me in trouble," she said over her shoulder.

"But—"

"You're not even supposed to be out here mingling with us. Go back inside before you get someone killed."

Darien stopped. "Killed? Why would anyone be killed?"

Leslie kept walking, her small frame taking long steps. Darien watched her walk for a few seconds, enjoying the way her hips swayed, before turning back towards the underground facility. This was the most confusing place he had ever worked. He turned his head to look at her again and made for the staircase.

In the cafeteria Darien looked at the four hard-boiled eggs on his tray. The apple next to them was a deep red. *Leslie*, he thought to himself. He could have sworn that he had seen her down here eating with Nancy, at least the girl he thought was Nancy. Instead of his usual seating area, Darien walked to the table where he had seen the women eating just the other day and put down his tray.

The cafeteria was a bustle of activity again. People sat at every table engaged in conversation. Some of them spoke in low quiet tones but several of the tables were raucous and laughing.

He sat down and picked up one of the eggs. "Not much of a lunch," he said to himself.

"No, it isn't," said a woman's voice from behind him. "Can I sit down?"

Darien coughed on the egg, catching a little in his throat and he managed to say with a wheeze, "Sure, no problem."

"Good, this is my usual seat."

She sat next to him. Darien looked at the girl and was surprised to see Leslie. She wasn't wearing the wide white hat and shirt any longer but a pair of tight jeans and a thin red sweater.

"I thought you said you weren't allowed to come in here."

Her brown eyes looked back at him and a smile broke her face. Her teeth were remarkably white in contrast to the dark brown of her skin. "Been topside recently, I see. You met Leslie?"

"You're not Leslie?" Darien looked her over. Same hair, same eyes, same face, same body, same ass, this had to be Leslie. Her name tag wasn't tan, though. It was red, like his.

"No, I'm Cindy. I work in memory config for Genetibotics. Leslie is a solar engineer. People confuse us all the time. I've never met her, but people say we look a lot alike."

Darien looked at Cindy's name-tag. It did say, *'Cindy Barnett.'*

This was his second case of mistaken identity in as many days. He had already confused Lawrence Enderby with another person he knew from South Miami. "Well, I suppose I should introduce myself. I'm Darien." The hard-boiled egg still in his right hand he reached across with his left to shake hers.

"Do you have a last name, Darien?"

"Mamon."

"Darien Mamon? Nancy was right."

"It is her? I was just going to ask you if you knew a Nancy Williams. You were sitting together." Darien smiled. Knowing at least one person here made him feel a little less lonely, even if it was Nancy.

"Well, this is my spot. I always sit here." Cindy took a sip from her milk. "Nancy says you're an asshole. She didn't ask me to send a message or anything, but that's what she said."

Darien laughed. "I could see Nancy doing that. 'Oh, and if you see Darien, tell him he's an asshole.'"

"Well?"

"Well, what?" Darien asked, taking another bite of his egg.

"Is she right? Are you an asshole?"

"Everyone's an asshole sometimes. I've been trying to make

certain corrections in my public persona these last few years. I'm really hoping I've outgrown that aspect of my personality," Darien said, still struggling to swallow the dry yolk of the hard-boiled egg. He sipped at his water, washing it down. "It does appear my reputation will take longer to recover from my years of indiscretion and villainy."

Cindy laughed and wiped egg yolk from his sleeve. "You made a fairly large impression on her. When she saw your name on her writpad I think her exact words were, 'No effing way.'" Taking a knife from her tray, she cut her sandwich into quarters.

"She said effing?"

"Well, her word was more explicit." She put down the knife. "Are you still cheating on your exams?"

"Whoa! How much did she tell you? That was a long, long time ago."

"You used to date a friend of hers," Cindy said, looking over at him.

"I did," Darien explained. "I have a history."

"Don't we all?" Cindy took a bite from one of the sandwich quarters on her plate. "You make it sound like there's a lot more to hear about."

"Oh," Darien frowned playfully, "I've said too much."

They sat together in silence a moment as Cindy chewed another small bite of her sandwich. After she swallowed the small bite, her attempt at being dainty failed and she shoved the rest in all at once. A quick swig of milk washed it down and she inhaled deeply.

"Are you all right?" Darien asked.

"Yeah." Cindy shrugged. "I only eat once a day and sometimes I get a little overzealous. I'm trying to lose weight."

Darien snorted. "Really? Why?" He had been checking out her frame as they spoke, the same frame as top-side Leslie, he mused.

"I'm working on a new genetic trial and they're comparing the metabolic variances based on mealtimes and frequency. My manager suggested it has something to do with lifelong nutritional advantages gained through childhood regiments."

"I thought MemorSingular was strictly an analog-to-digital-memory-recovery company," Darien said. He picked up the apple, took a large bite, and chewed.

"No, not only. You forget, you work for PEPM, Phoenix Electronics and Pharmaceutical MicroSystems. They have their fingers in all sorts of things. To be honest, my pay statement says I work for Genetibotics. My boss works for MemorSingular, though." Cindy finished her sandwich and milk. "Hey! Don't worry about me. I have it easy. There are some people working here at Genetibotics—" she waved her head side to side and corrected herself— "PEPM, that are taking part in this experiment and they don't even know. Imagine taking your tray up to the line and being turned away when they swipe your ID tag."

Darien asked, "So, how many people work here? Are there a lot of different companies?" He had so far only worked in the main hub of the silo. It was true the silo had been expanded in diameter following the removal of the missile, but from the look at the crowd in the cafeteria it was apparent they couldn't all work in the same area.

"I think there's three or four." She looked around and pointed. "Those doors over there lead to another silo about a half a mile from here, north. And those doors over there lead to another silo a half mile south from here. This is the center. That's why the cafe is here. Bit of a pain in the ass really."

And such a nice ass, thought Darien.

"How long have you been here?" Cindy asked, eyeing one of Darien's eggs.

"Not too long. Not long enough to get bored and too long to get lost. I've never seen anything outside of this silo."

"You're not curious about seeing the other sections?" she asked.

"I didn't know there was anything there worth looking at, until now." He lifted an eyebrow.

"Nancy didn't say you were such a smooth talker," she said laughing.

Darien blushed. "I'm sorry. Was that too forward?"

"No, no, I barely noticed," she lied. Taking on a motherly tone, she said, "Been a little lonely in your room, have you?"

"Well, haven't you?" Darien asked. "I've not really been able to talk to anyone. I was even reprimanded for seeing too much."

Cindy furrowed her brow. "Seeing too much? That sounds like a conspiracy."

"Well, they didn't actually say that," Darien corrected himself. "They said it was because the door almost hit me in the head."

"You only got eggs and an apple?" Cindy was eyeing his plate again. "What door?" Cindy took one of Darien's eggs.

"You know what? It doesn't really matter." Darien reached for his egg and missed as Cindy took a bite, laughing again.

Darien put another hard-boiled egg on her tray and she covered it with her other hand so he couldn't take it back. "I'm going to eat that," she said, nodding with her mouth full.

"Would your boss consider taking the food off my plate cheating on your diet?" Darien took a bite out of his apple after removing the stem. Cindy shrugged her answer, her mouth still full. Darien asked another question. "So, what silo are you in?"

Still chewing, Cindy waved her hand in the direction of the doors to the northern silo.

Suddenly noticing the time, Cindy picked up her tray and, swallowing the last remnants of Darien's egg, said, "It was nice to talk to you," she shrugged mid-sentence, "meet you. I'll tell Nancy it really was you." She smiled. "And thanks again for the compliment. I haven't been noticed in so long I was beginning to forget what it felt like." She bit into the second egg and chewed it as she walked away.

Darien watched her turn and set her tray on the washing stand. She winked at him, still eating the egg, walked to the doors for the northern silo, swiped her badge and went through.

Yup. Same ass.

Chapter Seven

Report Subject: **Darien Mamon**
Origin Location: **Oneida, New York**
Current Location: **Tucson, AZ**
Subject Age: **27**
Subject Status: **Viable**

"But what about the person on the receiving end of these memories?" Darien asked.

Dr. Hollister was recalculating the frequency of the transmitted signal. His hands, covered in magnetic gloves, traveled the Gaussian board on the wall, correcting numbers in the equation. "Imagine," he said, "if we could boost the signal, pushing it even further than this facility. We could broadcast a new memory simulation nationally, even globally. During the mid-twentieth century they used to play sitcoms on everyone's living room television. *I Love Lucy* was the talk of the town, back then." He stopped working on the Gaussian board and put his hands on his hips. "Advertisers eventually ruined television. They went from five minutes of commercials for a thirty minute show to a two minute commercial for a one minute clip."

"Yeah, I know the history. This feels more..." Darien searched for the right words as he copied the calculations from Dr. Hollister's Gaussian board to his own writpad. "It's invasive, dangerous."

Dr. Hollister waved him off. "Every major advancement in science and technology has faced the same argument. How could this be misused? And most of the time the hysteria died away as the people eventually accepted it as the norm."

Darien shook his head and leaned forward toward Dr. Hollister. "You're not talking about adding two minutes to an episode of *Laugh In*. This could change the world, make a selective group of people insanely rich with direct product placement, change the opinion of a politician, maybe even start a war."

"Or end one," Dr. Hollister said, pointing at Darien.

Darien stopped copying his calculations. "What is there to stop this technology from being even more real than it already is? It's going to follow the porn curve."

Dr. Hollister laughed and spilled his coffee on the floor. "You were listening. Gave that one some thought, I see. You even created a name for the phenomenon, 'porn curve.' I like it." Dr. Hollister wiped the coffee with a towel. "OK. Let's hear it."

"You said yourself that pornography is often the leading financial interest in upcoming technology."

"I did say that. Continue."

"Well," Darien said, "throughout time humans have always have made some form of porn. It existed in painted caves, carvings, sculptures, paintings," Darien ticked off on his fingers, listing as many as he could think of, "analog photography, digital photography, film, magazines, digital media, holograms..." Darien trailed off. "Every decade a new form comes out, each one more real than the last. This," Darien said, waving his hands at the Gaussian board, "is going to be the new one, and it will become so real some people will lose grip on what real is."

"You're worried some people will be trapped within their fantasies?"

"Yeah, why should I ask Susan out when I can have Ms. July or fifteen other porn legends tonight, instead?"

Dr. Hollister spilled his coffee again, this time adding the additional mess of it streaking down his white lab coat. "For one thing, it will never be as real as the real world."

"And why is that?"

"Because of the Municci Effect." Dr. Hollister waited for some hint of recognition from Darien pertaining to the term.

Darien shook his head and shrugged his shoulders, raising his eyebrows at Dr. Hollister.

"Didn't cover that, huh? The Municci Effect states that mem-sims and memory can only be deemed as reality in the unlikely event both subjects have identical DNA, like identical twins or clones."

"Cloning was outlawed fifty years ago." Darien walked to the sink and retrieved another towel.

"And marijuana was illegal in most of the world at one time, too. Did that stop its use?" Dr. Hollister said, taking the towel from Darien and wiping up the new mess. "There are always things in this world that shouldn't be happening, but are. Even slavery hasn't been completely eradicated."

"So, with identical DNA, what can be expected?"

"Even then, nothing is guaranteed. No two minds are alike, but with identical DNA, as in identical twins or clones, the brain can be trained to accept the same patterns and molded to react the same as the brain of origin when exposed to memory stimuli."

Dr. Hollister crumpled up the towel and attempted a basket shot for the bin, missing horribly. "Initially the memory simulation would seem just like that, a simulation. As time goes on, the simulations begin to feel more real until they are unrecognizable from a subject's organic memory." Dr. Hollister's attention was pulled away as he glanced at his Gaussian board. He cocked his head, leaned in, and made a correction. Stepping back, he admired the result and continued, "At least that's what we've learned so far."

Now, there was a question hitting Darien in the face.

"How?"

"How, what?"

"How have you learned it? Clones are supposed to be illegal." Then Darien remembered his conversations with Cindy. She worked for another arm of the corporate structure, Genetibotics. *Does her section of the company delve into cloning? Just how large is PEPM?*

Dr. Hollister peered at the Gaussian board, made another correction in his calculations and said, "Want to try a few more mem-sims? I have two new ones. I'm trying to figure this section of the calculation and some feedback on the overall wavelength response could close up some of my loose ends."

"It's not going to be that strange radio based system, is it?"

"No, that one is still being tested. I had a bad experience with it yesterday with another subject. The power system isn't refined enough to supply adequate levels. Something is wrong with the phase locked loop. It never settles."

"Just two sims? I'm not going to be falling out of a window, am I?"

Dr. Hollister checked his notes. "No, actually. It should be pretty fun. I think you're going dancing."

The beat pressed into Darien's chest, rhythm thumping like a new heartbeat. He grinned. He loved this song. The nod of his head became a flexing at his knees and he grooved out onto the dance floor holding his drink as steady as he was able while he let himself disappear into the music.

My mic is a magnetic prosthetic
  Integrated circuits embedded
  with no anesthetic
  so don't even sweat it
  It only hurts if you let it
  Simple surgery, splurging
  But not simply cosmetic
  Swerving, nerve system shredded
  Now my spine is synthetic
  Electro-kinetic is it, if you can get it
  Genetically programmed for each man
  You just set it
  Do you understand where I'm from?
  No? Forget it.

Mid-verse, Darien stopped singing long enough to finish his drink and continued dancing, holding the empty glass. His dance partner smiled down at him, pearly white teeth looking purple in the nightclub black light. The smile was infectious and

Darien gazed with love at the man keeping time to the beat along with him.

They danced, holding hands, caressing each other lightly, playfully, in the crowded room.

Look out people
  Because I'm becoming technological
  Why? I don't even know
  and didn't even think it possible
  Or Plausible
  Don't understand how I became robotic
  Record company keeping me working
  To try and make a profit

Darien watched his partner. The tall man gazed back at him, squinting his eyes, smiling ever so slightly. Darien's hands explored him, gripping his belt to pull him closer. Sweat dripped from the taller man's forehead and soaked the shirt around his collar. Placing his hands on his partner's hips Darien matched his tempo.

The stubble on Kenny's cheeks as he smiled gave Darien a small thrill that took his breath away.

Kenny, the tall man is Kenny. Darien's waking mind had surfaced during the mem-sim.

The ecstasy of the dance was abruptly stopped by an elbow to Darien's back. A couple dancing behind him had become overly enthusiastic.

"Oh, wow!" a voice said over his shoulder, barely understandable over the din of the music. "I'm so sorry. Are you all right?"

Darien winced and his partner frowned at the offender.

"Dancing out here is gonna leave us with more bruises than a rugby match," Kenny said, taking Darien's hand.

"Kenny, it's all right," Darien said pulling at the tall man.

"No, let's get another drink." Kenny looked back at the offender, a short, chiseled man in his mid-twenties. "C'mon Sam."

I'm Sam.

"I said I was sorry." The young man grabbed his own partner and moved to take their spot on the dance floor.

The name registered in Darien's mind. In this mem-sim, he was Sam.

"Let's get that drink," he said.

They walked through the crowd of gyrating bodies to the crowded bar. Getting the bartender's attention was a little more difficult.

Kenny ordered. "Can I get a gin and tonic and," He looked at Sam, "a slippery nipple?"

Sam nodded.

The bartender looked at Sam. "Can I see your ID please?"

Grinning, Sam pulled his ID out of his wallet and handed it over.

"Sam Matheson, twenty-five?" The bartender frowned, pulling out a book of state ID definitions. He looked up New Hampshire and compared it to the card Sam had given him. Everything checked out and he passed the card back to Sam. "You look young for twenty-five."

"Yeah, I get that all the time."

They lay on the couch. Kenny had rented the attic apartment, four flights up, just this past summer.

Winter roared outside, bending the trees, wiping the snow from one surface to pile it high somewhere else. Snowflakes fluttered against the plastic siding, rolling across the surface from one side of the attic to the other, accompanied by the banshee's wail of the wind.

The power was out, a result of the storm, and the candle flickered from the breeze in the drafty space. A gas fireplace and fan ran on a back-up battery supply, a necessity in Northern Vermont.

Sam ran his hands up Kenny's arm to his shoulder, tickling his neck before planting another kiss on the man. Breaking, he looked into his lover's eyes, those beautiful brown eyes, and said, "So, are we going to be here all day? I thought we were supposed to go skiing."

"You have something else you'd rather be doing? You weren't complaining an hour ago."

"Well, that was an hour ago." Sam looked out the window. "I don't suppose it's safe to drive."

"I haven't heard a plow go by, yet."

Sam shot up from the couch. "I'm hungry. Is there any of those ribs left from last night?" He headed to the kitchen draped in a long tan blanket and nothing else.

"Sam?" Kenny called from the couch as Sam rummaged the refrigerator. "Do you think they're still watching you? We haven't had a peep from them."

"I haven't been able to lose them, yet. They've found me every time. I can only imagine."

"But the sensor scan came up empty."

"The scanner, where did you get that thing?" Sam said through bites of an apple he found in one of the drawers.

Kenny laughed, looking at Sam, and said, "Where did you get that thing? I haven't bought any apples in months. Is that any good?"

Sam smiled and swallowed. "It's fine."

"I got the scanner from a friend of mine and he told me not to ask where it came from. I'm guessing he picked it up when he was working in New York." Kenny got up from the couch and walked naked to the gas fireplace. Standing with his back to it, he reveled at the warmth and let out a long contented sigh.

The open window brought the sounds of traffic wafting in along with the smell of the hot dog cart on the corner below. The air wasn't fresh. Those weren't electric pods below. They were the old combustion vehicles pouring smog into the air and leaving galvanized rubber particles along the road's edge. A mixture of oil and water filled the potholes in the street, covering the surface with a rainbow haze.

Sam took the wallet from his back pocket, opening it, and dropped all of the identification cards and credit chips onto the counter. Sifting through them, deciding which to discard, Sam came across a number written in blue ink on the back of a paper business card, 704. The number kept appearing in his dreams. Sometimes it was a room number. Other times it was a street address. Once it was a winning lottery number. And yet another time it was the balance in his bank account. It kept coming back, over and over again. He turned the card over and read the name of the business so eager to get their name out they'd spent a fortune on these expensive pieces of garbage, Little Jimmy's Roofing Supply House in Waterbury, Maine.

Sam turned on the gas stove and held the paper card over the flame, letting it burn, enjoying the smell before dropping it into the sink. He wouldn't need the card to remember the number. It was burned into his brain. If he came upon it there was no way it would slip past without him noticing. Maybe then, he would understand why the number had so many times frequented his dreams.

Maybe Hollister put it there to mess with you.

Sam pushed the tap up to let the water extinguish the smoldering paper and he filled a glass taken from next to the sink. The water in the glass had an iron taste to it. Swishing the water around the bottom of the cup Darien looked at it. The micro-particles floating around in it spun lazily. Shaking his head, Sam rinsed out the glass and refilled from the tap, swallowing it down with a gulp.

He walked to the closet and pulled out several shirts before choosing one, a black t-shirt emblazoned with a yin and yang symbol of dragons. Pulling the shirt over his head he adjusted it to fall over his shoulders correctly and checked himself in the mirror. He stood there looking over his clothes, appreciating the fit. Then, he gazed up to appraise his hair and saw his face.

Darien snapped out of the mem-sim. That was his face. In that brief instant he wondered if he were watching a memory creation sim instead of a prerecorded memory, and then, the fantasy world enveloped him again.

The mirror image was hazy. Sam couldn't see himself. Grabbing a rag from the sink, Sam scrubbed at it, rubbing in circles. No matter how much he cleaned it, it did not give off a reflection of any quality. He took the mirror down from the nail holding it in place and put it on the table next to the rag. *It was clear a moment ago. What's going on?*

A kaleidoscope of colors swirled around him, as disorientating as a house of mirrors. Pain rolled across the back of his skull. He was seeing double. Knives exploded in his stomach, buckling him over onto the floor. His tried to focus on the wood grain and his fingernails scratched across it, sinking into the grooves. Shattered in the cruel sensations, Sam's consciousness reduced to nothingness and he groaned an inhuman sound of feral despair. The double vision went away as the pain drenched into his limbs, spiking nerve endings within his joints, igniting fire in his veins.

Sam rolled onto his back and looked up at the ceiling as his vision started to fade away again. The colors drained out of the frame as a white light entered his eyes, driving straight to the back of his head.

"So, is this him, Sam Matheson?" a man's voice said. It was crisp and deep like the edge of a knife.

"Yeah," said a woman. Her voice didn't sound natural, having a digital quality to it, like it had been synthesized badly. "He ran again. Lucky for him the drug put him out or I'd smack him around a bit. I hate New York."

Sam's heart pounded through his chest, echoing in his ears, slamming into the pressure crushing his brain. Looking behind him, knowing he was being followed, he ran through the maze of solar panels. They had to be following him. It had been so easy to get out of his room. Heat beat down on his head and he gazed upward away from the rising sun. Were the satellites active today? Were they tracking his heat signature?

I'm Sam again, Darien thought during the simulation.

The sun was rising. Sam watched the details of the mountains getting brighter. He had to hurry. Agent Curtis was sure to be in pursuit.

He pushed through the desert, winding his way through the scrub and thorny trees strong enough to thrive in the low moisture environment. He hadn't brought any water and he had no idea how far it was to the city proper. Was it better to walk and get there late or run and get there early? He didn't know the answer to that either. Maybe he could hide in the shade of a tree during the noon sun.

His wrist held a plastic band with his name on it. *Yup, Sam Matheson again*, Darien thought through the sensations of the mem-sim.

He was wearing a red flannel shirt and jeans and he carried nothing but a handkerchief. He should have brought water. Even in the silo underground you dehydrated quickly. He never needed to drink so much back home in New Hampshire.

You're not from New Hampshire. Darien's thoughts rippled away, half inside and half outside the mem-sim. *I shouldn't be able to identify my own thoughts through the sim*, Darien thought before the code pulled him back fully into the mind of Sam.

The last three times he had escaped it had been at night. Heat had not been the issue.

After walking for two hours Sam came across a road and turned north. His face and neck itched with sunburn. If he didn't find some shade soon he was going to be in some serious pain later. His last time on this road a young woman had picked him up, saving him from the heat, and he scanned far into the distance looking for the dust cloud of a car, any car. Sure enough, a cloud was approaching. By the side of the road, Sam waited until he caught a glimpse of the driver.

Agent Curtis wore his black uniform and he didn't look happy. In fact, he looked downright pissed.

Sam bolted off the road into the brush, running as fast as he could. Thrusting the vehicle into park, Agent Curtis was hot on his trail. Parched already, Sam ran himself out and fell to his knees after the second mile. He dry heaved, trying desperately to cough the dust out of his throat. Behind him, Agent Curtis was the picture of efficiency, running with measured breathing and a steady pace. As he reached Sam he didn't waste time in discussion.

The electric wires hit Sam in the back, dropping him like a stone to the orange gravel and scruff of the desert. He screamed in pain as the current pulsed through him.

The gloss black and white of the room looked familiar to Darien. Sam's room was just like his own. Everything matched, from the desk, to the bed, to the frame around the door and the walls.

On the plastic black desk sat a silver knife. The blade had been easy enough to sneak out of the cafeteria, tucking it into his sleeve as he left his tray at the wash station.

Picking it up off the desk, he looked at the blade, its edge serrated in tiny lines for cutting meat. The handle was dull black plastic, uniform to countless kitchens around the planet.

He pictured the factory somewhere making these knives. Endless production lines heating the steel and cutting out the desired shape from the metal blanks. The clank of blade after blade falling to the production trays rang with a continuous drone, one after another landing and sliding off the pile.

His life, was his life any different? Moments from his childhood rang like the dropping of the blades through his head, falling into his mind and flitting away with the flood of other memories. A history of events he was not present for came back like the scenes of an old movie watched too many times. His memories were not his own. He had experienced the past of countless other men, of other women.

Is anyone living my memories?

His fingers traced the line on his forearm before the blade, scratching the surface where he intended to cut. A thought went through his mind, *This isn't my arm.*

The blade didn't care.

Darien took off the plastic headset and placed it on his lap. His fingers tingled and his arm ached with the after effect of the memory-sim blade. The blood didn't drip from his arm, but it ran through his mind.

The last three memories had been frightfully disturbing. Was he supposed to have seen them? Did Dr. Hollister know they had come through? Two, Dr. Hollister had said. He was supposed to witness two memories, not five. The last three, how had they entered the system? There had been a grain to them, Darien thought, as if the code had been embedded in the two intended sims. Thinking back over them he was sure he had seen the ghost of the last three mem-sims within the initial two before they played in full. He was certain they had played simultaneously with the other sims, like a double exposed analog image. Someone had hidden those mem-sims in there.

For me?

In front of Darien, Dr. Hollister was standing, coffee stains running down the front of his lab coat, snapping his fingers, and calling Darien's name.

"Darien! Darien, can you hear me?" Hands clapped in front of Darien's face and he reacted with a start. Had he been outside of the memory-sims and yet not back in his own consciousness? Darien raised his eyes and looked through Dr. Hollister.

"Hey, welcome back, Darien. You didn't snap out of the sim right away." Dr. Hollister hurried to the sink and wet a fresh towel under the cold water. "Maybe we should take a break on these for a while."

"What?" Darien asked.

"Thirty-seconds, at least, you just sat there and didn't respond, even after you removed the headset. Your eyes were open but they weren't focused on anything. I didn't think those two memories were as intense as all that." He came back with the towel after wringing out some of the water. "Are you all right?"

Darien had questions, even if he was afraid to ask them. He took the towel from Dr. Hollister and wiped his face, letting the questions wash away, almost all of them.

Is Sam Matheson dead?

Chapter Eight

Report Subject: **Darien Mamon**
Origin Location: **Oneida, New York**
Current Location: **Oneida, New York**
Subject Age: **15**
Subject Status: **Viable**

"She used to visit me when I had vid-tests with the tutor. She was there at Christmas, at birthdays. One time she even ate with me." Darien pulled at the grass under his shoes.

"Not much of a mother," said the girl, a new gardener's assistant. "My mother hardly lets me leave her sight, except for work and school and when I'm over one of my friend's houses." The girl chuckled. Darien took this to mean that she heard the words as they came out and maybe realized how much freedom she actually had.

Darien leaned in front of her, trying to get a glimpse of her eyes, her intoxicating blue eyes. He was only half listening to her, examining her. Her job had shaped her body as well as any gym membership. The shapeliness of her shoulders accentuated her slender neck. He liked her freckles, particularly around her nose, and her bottom lip kept drawing his eye.

"My father was around more often," Darien said, looking away from those enticing lips. "He watched me play soccer with my team. They always came to my house." Darien lay back on the lawn, hoping she would lay back with him, and threw aside the grass he had been yanking out of the turf. "Practices, games, events, tournaments, all took place on my private field."

"A private field sounds amazing," she said. "There aren't many free fields around where I live. There are fields, sure, but I get paid to cut them, not play on them. Did you like playing? I always wanted to."

"Yeah, I guess. It was never a really big deal for me. My

parents set it up, thought I was going to be some kind of athlete or something. My father would sit up on the balcony next to his bedroom to watch and cheer me on. Sometimes he would clap, but only if he wasn't on the phone."

"So, the private field," she asked looking around, "where was it?"

"On the south side of the house, where the pool complex is now. Speaking of which, we should go swimming."

She pushed his leg. "I don't have time for swimming. I'm only on break."

"You work for me. We'll extend your break."

"No, your dad hired my dad's company. I work for my dad's company." She lay down on the grass, propped up on one elbow, looking at him. "Besides, I think the only reason you want to go swimming is to see me out of these jeans," she said laughing.

"You're not wrong."

She sat up on the grass again and took off her gloves. Her hair fell over her shoulders as she removed her hat, red curls shining in the afternoon sun. Her smile was genuine, something Darien had come to notice when it appeared. The life of wealth meant many would flash a fake smile for a bit of favor.

Darien sat back up and kissed her, pressing into her bottom lip. She leaned in to him.

Darien was accustomed to getting what he wanted. The estate was well over a hundred acres. If he wanted something, his father just had it built. There had been private concerts, visiting celebrities, and other major events at his home throughout the years.

Scores of people filtered through the house. The tutors came and went. So did the nannies, nutritionists, trainers, and friends.

Some things Darien excelled at: numbers, spreadsheets, programming; but writing, grammar, and words always troubled him. When Darien was twelve, his tutor came to discuss his paper on the economics of the Congal Republic. The numbers were correct, but she said his writing style was anything but technical.

Aside for a few servants who had looked after him, Darien didn't say hello. He didn't reward good work. He didn't punish bad work. His real issue was that he didn't see them. They just worked there.

He never pushed a lawnmower, never washed a dish, never scrubbed a toilet. One day, Darien learned he could get his way by saying two simple words.

"You're fired," Darien told his tutor, Sandy.

She had been his soccer coach two years prior. Still young and beautiful, her synthetic leg whirred as she tapped her foot. Stretching from her hip to her toes, the synthetic leg, black and acrylic casing reflecting the lights of the learning hall, had been the first thing Darien noticed about her when he was ten. Her skills on the soccer field were a thing of beauty. The leg was perfectly tuned to her movements and her shots on net spun the ball in a graceful arc, further decreasing the chance a goalie could make the save.

Synthetic limbs in professional sports were banned after a player from Brazil amputated his own legs in favor of a synthetic advantage in the World Cup a decade prior. Perhaps that explained why Sandy was only a coach and not a national player. Even with the stigma of a false limb, and the shame of being only a coach, she rarely covered the leg. Darien could picture a closet full of one-legged pants.

Reading over her notes on his paper, Darien rolled his eyes. The words in red ink stung. He threw the paper to the floor.

"You can pack your bag and the guards at the door will show you out."

"You're firing me over the grading of your assignment?"

"Yes, I am. My last tutor was never so critical."

"You can't rely on feedback that isn't critical of your work, especially if your writing ability is so lacking. You have a long way to go."

"Whatever." Darien rolled his eyes. "Good luck with your attempt at teaching in the future."

She cracked her neck, visibly annoyed, and told the twelve

year old brat exactly what she thought of him. "You're an asshole."

She stormed off past the gate guards in their black uniforms, her acrylic leg matching the other perfectly in stride. She hadn't even taken the time to pack a bag. The heavy iron doors closed with a bang only moments after she walked through them and the gate guards took up their positions on the inside of the gate wall after radioing the tower of their now secure positions.

It never occurred to Darien as a child that the guards were on the inside of the gate.

He never left the estate. Anything he needed was given to him. When he was hungry, they hired a chef. When he was lonely, they brought him a friend. They paid those friends, and it was just as well, because Darien didn't know how to be a friend. He bossed the friends-for-hire around until they left, all of them except for one, Tim. Quick witted, smart, and handsome, Tim was always just a little bit better at every game they played. Darien despised Tim. He reminded Darien of everything he himself was not.

Every game played against Tim was a challenge. He never gave up easily and he never let Darien win if he could help it. The one time Darien had beaten Tim at a board-game, Darien danced around gloating about how he had won, thrusting his fists in the air and trash-talking.

"I told you I'd beat you!" he shouted triumphantly in Tim's face. Tim only smiled and reset the pieces into their starting places.

"I like this game. Good win, Darien. Do you want to play again?" he asked.

"What? You enjoy getting your ass beat? I suppose if you like being a loser I can help you with that."

Darien won the second game, too. His victory dance increased in intensity. His arms pumped the air and spread out wide to accept the cheering of the audience inside his head.

"Twice! You really suck at this game. Want to play again?"

"Sure," Tim said arranging the pieces again.

"If you think I'm going to go easy on you, you've got another thing coming."

"No, don't do that."

"Do what?" Darien asked.

"Go easy. Don't. How will I ever learn if you don't give me your best?"

After the third win, Darien was practically singing with the elation of his success. He marched around the room, finally having something he was better at than Tim.

Ooka Chaka, ooka Chaka, woo-woo!" he shouted. "Do you hear that? Do ya? That's the steam train rolling over you, loser!"

Tim won the fourth game and Darien slapped the board off the table.

When Darien and Tim were eight they climbed a tree far from the house to find out how far they could see. Tim ascended gracefully and confidently through the branches passing Darien near the bottom. Climbing the tree had been Darien's idea. Here was something, he thought, he would be better at than Tim, having already climbed this tree before, though he had not made it all the way to the top.

He watched Tim go higher and higher, past the point he had been previously. He watched, indignant this boy would show him up once again.

I need to go higher. Stretching out his arm he grabbed the next branch, swinging his leg up and over as he braced himself against one of its extensions. The pitch stuck to his hands, aiding his grip on the bark. *Another branch,* he thought. Moving back toward the trunk he leaned up against it and reached up. Grabbing on to the next clump of branches, Darien wrapped his knees around the tree and shimmied up.

Kneeling on the branch, Darien peered up to see Tim even higher than he had been only a moment ago. The top of the tree swayed with his weight.

"Show off," Darien muttered and, bracing against the trunk, he reached for the next branch and missed.

His chin slammed into the branch below him and he tumbled like a rag doll, hitting three more branches before landing on the forest floor with a thump.

In the pine needles and leaves, bloody, crying, and screaming in pain after the wind returned to his lungs, Darien yelled for his mother. He wrapped his hands and arms, sticky from the pitch, around himself in pain.

Tim was has his side moments later, having climbed down the tree nearly as fast as Darien had fallen. Tim, fingers gently touching his friend, said, "Hey, man, I'll be back. I'll get your mom." Tim pulled away, sprinted to the house and that was the last time Darien ever saw him.

Lying in bed with two broken ribs and a broken left arm he cursed himself. Calling for his mother had been a stupid thing to do. She never came. There were servants for that.

Tim had looked genuinely concerned and scared before he ran to get help. After the tree, Darien knew Tim would never be allowed to return. As he lay in bed wishing away the pain, Darien decided he would never climb another tree, and wondering if he would ever find another friend, he cried himself to sleep.

Chapter Nine

Report Subject:	Darien Mamon
Origin Location:	Oneida, New York
Current Location:	Oneida, New York
Subject Age:	18
Subject Status:	Non-Viable

Sunlight streamed through the windows in the otherwise dark room. Set up on castors over a red carpet, the pair of coffins cast a dark shadow into Darien's mind. He looked at them, two identical temporary receptacles imported specially for the funeral of his parents. They were closed, the results of the pod accident being too horrible to view. After the ceremony the bodies would be taken from the coffins and burned in a simple wooden box.

Just burn the coffins, Darien thought. He didn't really know the procedure, having never had to deal with death before.

After the teams of undertakers wheeled the coffins away Darien stood in silence next to the photos of his parents. The framed images showed them separate, as always. At this moment he couldn't recall how often he had seen them together.

He stared into their photos and they stared back at him. Darien didn't know which of his parents he looked like. Some people told him he had his father's eyes, not the color, just the shape. He couldn't see it. Others told him he had his mother's nose. *That's just crazy,* Darien thought. *She has this line down the middle of her nose and mine doesn't do that at all.*

Darien reached out to touch the black plastic easels and wondered if he could break it by only clenching his fist. He bent one, applying the slightest pressure.

Taking each of the photos from the thin easels Darien walked to his room and placed them on the tall fireplace mantle.

It wasn't until he walked to his father's study, pulled out a glass from the cabinet, and defiantly opened a bottle of rye whiskey from his father's collection that he cried.

The relationship between him and his parents had never been strong. It was something he had come to terms with at a very early age. The distance between them cushioned the impact of losing them together, but he had never felt so alone.

The alcohol did little to ease his mood, no matter how much he drank. He walked the halls of his home, carrying both the glass and the bottle. He walked to each of their rooms and opened the doors without knocking, for once. He sat on their beds and looked out the windows. Darien's night ended on the balcony off from his father's room, sitting in a chair and watching a soccer game from memory he himself had played in a decade earlier.

The pod accident taking both their lives as they left a party at a friend's house had been the headline of the day. News channels throughout the house displayed the gruesome story as staff members searched for information regarding their futures.

Lawyers invaded the house, having no respect for boundaries. With their briefcases, suits, and calculators, they came in like an advancing army, occupying the conference rooms, rescheduling the duties of the servants, changing mealtimes, and getting on Darien's last nerve.

"They interrupted my movie," Darien complained to his butler. "They keep calling all the time." Darien threw his phone across the room. "I ignored them."

Darien's butler, Andy, had been someone Darien could speak to when his parents were absent, which had been often. Andy was of average height and build. His hair was gray but Darien had no idea of his age. Hell, Darien was surprised he remembered the man's name. He often didn't.

Maybe, he mused, *I'm better off. Maybe I'm finally growing up, taking charge of the estate.*

He rolled through the changes assailing him this week. One would think the loss of his parents would have been the most painful of all, but Darien had lost them years ago, lost them at five years old when he understood he was not important to them. His grieving for them had begun thirteen years before their eventual demise. Even the tears Darien had shed after their passing had been for himself and not them, a moment of self-pity.

Many years ago he had learned which servants he could reach out to when he skinned his knee or fried his computers. In reality, the servants had become his parents, guiding his education, his schedule, and well-being. He looked at Andy with an affection he had never before realized.

"Ignored them? Are you sure that was wise, sir?" Andy asked. "I imagine whatever they have to speak with you about is important, possibly in regard to your parent's estate."

When the lawyers finally had enough of being ignored, two men came to Darien's theater room to force him to attend a meeting. The two dragged Darien through the estate, him complaining the whole way, before dropping the young man unceremoniously into a chair in front of a thin wiry man of about fifty. The thin man sat behind the desk of Darien's father and he didn't look up when he addressed the arrogant teenager.

"Mr. Darien Mamon," He said, still not looking at the boy. The mag-pen in his right hand scribbled across an electronic spreadsheet in front of him. "We had the reading of your parent's will last night. You missed it."

"I don't follow your schedule," Darien spat back. "You work for me. Maybe you can read it again."

Darien looked behind him to the two men that brought him to his father's office. They were, most certainly, augmented. One of them had the scars of nerve enhancement, visible at his wrists and forearms. The other had shoulders that couldn't be strong enough to pick up Darien by the collar. He still did. The man had lifted him like a rag-doll.

Darien turned back to face front. "You two will be working in Ecuador, tomorrow. I'll buy a quiet little ranch tonight, something with lots of cattle."

"No, Mr. Mamon," said the thin man, looking up finally from his electronic spreadsheet. "These men don't work for you. They work for me and we all work for the estate of your parents, Mr. and Mrs. Joe Mamon. I am the executor of said estate." He returned his attention to the Gaussian spreadsheet in front of him and the mag-pen continued scribbling. "And I don't believe you'll be buying anything tonight," he said.

The thin man sat scanning his spreadsheet in silence.

Darien stood up. The men behind him sat him back down.

"You know who I am?" Darien struggled against the men holding him in his seat. "I could fire you and move your whole family to the backwoods of Kentucky." Darien was furious and struggled under their grip.

The executor met Darien's eyes. "Mr. Mamon, this is no longer your house." He looked around appreciatively. "Your parents in their compassion have written a clause in their will that the estate will pay for the first two years of your college education. I suggest you work hard in those years. I am to understand you have already had a number of college courses?"

The executor waited for Darien to answer but the boy was being stubborn. "Take as many extra classes as you can. After a period of two years, you will no longer be receiving funds from the estate. To have any chances of making something of yourself, your college degree will be a necessity. Your aptitude is in science and math. We have enrolled you in the South Miami school of Technology."

The executor waved him away, "Goodbye, Mr. Mamon."

The transport pod doors locked and the whine of the electric engines sent him away. The two men threatened with Ecuador had picked Darien up and dragged him from the room, screaming the whole way to the front door. Darien had been unable to get a grip on either of them as they deposited him into a transport pod.

He should have been in South Miami in a couple of hours. Three hours into the trip, using a portable communication device, Darien connected to the travel pod software and found where exactly he was going. It wasn't hard to find. However, when he tried to trace the route back to his home, in an effort to reprogram the pod to take him there, Darien found an encrypted system blocking his path.

The executors and lawyers had deliberately routed the pod so the starting address would not be easy to trace back. Out of ideas, he watched the system requests sending the pod in an unnecessary direction on more than one occasion. He looked again at the multiple changes the pod made. His journey from home to school wasn't only being kept from him. The pod had been programmed to avoid detection from any outside entities as well.

If the windows weren't blacked out this might have been a good sightseeing tour.

Darien lay on the floor, having abandoned the plush seat in despair. Cool air circulated around the pod interior, hitting the back of his neck.

Eventually the windows of the pod lost their blackness and Darien rose to watch the world pass by. The pod skimmed over the swamps and low-lying neighborhoods of central Florida, staying high enough to miss anything reaching up from the surface but low enough not to be recognized as a commuter in the general pod traffic. Looking down out of the windows in the floor Darien noticed he was flying over the railway lines, typically known for being in the poorer, more industrialized sections of a state.

When the pod door opened, a wet heat engulfed Darien. He felt like he had stepped into a steam room. Darien grabbed his communicator and the bag someone at his house had packed for him and disembarked.

The school, South Miami School of Technology, was constructed over in the new state extension area. White pillars stretched high, their windows reflecting the sunshine and blue sky. Walkways reached out above the water, connecting the buildings and gliding up gracefully to reach the higher levels of the towering white structures without ascending too aggressively.

In Darien's bag was a writpad and a plastic map card. He fished them out and looked over the pad. Bland and cheap, the pad was one of the lower scale models, not at all like the Tosa model he had at home.

Classes start today, Darien thought after powering up the pad and seeing a schedule.

He flipped through the schedule noting all of the classes he could already drop. This wouldn't do at all.

He checked the time on the pad to find he had already missed one of the classes. *Dammit. How am I supposed to figure this all out?*

After hours in a pod Darien's head was still dazed. The salty air, a humid breeze, and painful sun did not help. Only that morning he had been a wealthy man. He looked down at the bag containing his only clothes. "This is unacceptable." Shouldering the bag, Darien tried to follow the plastic map card to the dormitory.

Half a mile from the pod Darien poked at the map. *That's not correct,* he thought, looking up at the sign posts. Putting down the bag, Darien turned around trying to get his bearings. He must have looked lost, glancing left and right, looking down at the jumble of colors and lines on the vid-card in his hand because a young woman approached him, touched his shoulder, and said, "Hey there, nubess. Are you ok?"

Chapter Ten

Report Subject: **Darien Mamon**
Origin Location: **Oneida, New York**
Current Location: **Tucson, AZ**
Subject Age: **27**
Subject Status: **Viable**

The door system did not respond when Darien pressed the call button. Darien pressed it again. He backed up to check his writpad, ensuring he was at the proper location. *Sub-level five, room H. Seems right*, he thought. He stepped forward and pressed the call button again. There was no response.

The writpad buzzed in his hand.

Checking the screen Darien watched as both the list of rooms and occupant statuses updated, flashing to one of four options, Viable, Non-Viable, Expelled, and Terminated.

Terminated. That's a scary status, Darien thought.

'Terminated' seemed so final. Were those employees just removed from the facility or was there something more permanent in their status? Darien looked through the list again.

'Expelled,' that means removed.

He counted six entries with the subject status listed as 'Terminated.'

The subject status option displayed for this room, Sub-level five, room H, changed from 'Viable,' to 'Non-Viable,' to 'Expelled.'

"You think they would update the status list before I started my rounds, but, no!" Darien complained under his breath.

He scrolled through the list to find out where he was supposed to go next, forgetting for a moment the clear floor beneath him until a glance past the writpad in his hand spun the sensation of vertigo around the back of his head. He stepped forward onto the black plastic edge near the door.

Regaining his composure Darien searched the pad screen for this room. It wasn't on the list.

As he scrolled, the writpad updated again. Rooms listed only moments ago as either 'Expelled' or 'Terminated' now said, 'Open' and the subject name previously listed had been removed from the status. Scrolling the writpad screen, he counted the number of rooms with an 'Open' designation, fifteen. He searched again for this room and found, according to his writpad, this room was now empty.

Shaking his head, Darien turned to leave as a voice buzzed over the communicator.

"Hello? Is someone out there?"

Darien stopped and looked back at the door. Sub-level five, Room H. He checked the writpad status, 'Open.'

And one more thing, the voice was definitely a woman. It was digitized and altered but it was definitely a woman. There hadn't been any women in these rooms so far, at least in any of the ones he visited. Had the new round of employees started?

Darien walked back to the door and answered, "Hello, yes? I'm Darien Mamon. Can I help you?"

"Can you open the door?"

Darien looked at the outside of the door, scanning the black acrylic where the illuminated open symbol should be. It wasn't there.

"I'm sorry," Darien said. "The plastic is dark out here. I don't know where the open control is without it highlighted."

"Hmm."

"What's your name?" Darien asked. "I have on my pad this room should be empty."

"I'm Elizab—" The speaker cut short.

"Hello?" Darien said. He scanned the acrylic again, looking for the open symbol, guessed roughly where it should be and poked the wall. With a musical jingle the door slid up into the ceiling. A small woman in her early twenties, blonde hair tangled and unkempt, eyes puffy and red, peeked out, and seeing Darien hugged him, pulling him into the doorway.

"Stay in the doorway." She backed into the room and when

Darien moved to follow her she pushed his chest with both of her hands. "Stay put. Stop. Stand still, right here." With her arms outstretched she continued to back away, keeping her eyes on him.

"Ok?" Darien said questioningly.

The small woman grabbed a brush from the desk and walked back to Darien, brushing her hair. "Can you answer a few questions?"

"What?" Darien asked, confused. "Why am I standing in the doorway?"

"I want the door to stay open in case I need something that's still inside, but I'm afraid the door might close again and trap us both. And I can't go walking around with my hair a mess. That would be too suspicious." She looked him up and down. "I don't know you." She shrugged. "That's a good thing. Where am I?"

Darien was confused. "Huh? You're at MemorSingular, in Tucson."

"Arizona?" She looked out to the central hub. "What day is it?"

"Friday."

"The date?"

Darien was taken aback. "Uh, March tenth. What did you mean by suspicious?"

"They kept me under for a week? No wonder my arms and legs hurt. Where are the stairs?"

Darien pointed across the hub. "What are you talking about? Under for a week? You haven't been here a week. I come to this door every day and yesterday Louis Waterlen was in this room."

"Then, they kept me somewhere else." She looked around outside of her room. "Where are the cameras?"

"I don't know about any cameras."

She slapped him hard and snatched his red badge from his chest. "You're coming with me."

"What was that for?" Darien asked rubbing his face.

"Checking to see if you're awake. Of course, there are cameras. Where do you think you are?"

"MemorSingular, Tucson, Arizona. And, yes, there are cameras, I just don't know where they are."

"Idiot." She threw the brush back into the room. "C'mon." She took Darien's hand and dragged him across the hub to the stairs. As they left the doorway to her room, the door slid shut behind them. When they reached the stairs, Darien expected Elizabeth would head up towards the surface, but she didn't. She led him down the stairs, toward the cafeteria at the bottom.

"Where are we going?" Darien asked.

"You said we were at MemorSingular."

"Yeah."

"You can't get out from here, too many guards. We need to get to one of the other silos." She relaxed her walk as they reached the cafeteria and, still holding his hand, walked him to the doors leading to one of the other silos. Reaching the door, she kissed him and said, "All right, honey, are we still on for dinner?" She squeezed his hand hard, pushing the bones in his palm together painfully.

"Uh, yeah," Darien said, struck dumb by her actions. She kissed him again, swiped his ID card and disappeared with it through the door.

He stood there and contemplated his next action. His ID card was gone. He was going to have to report it missing and get a new one. Turning, he looked around the full cafeteria. At several of the tables were faces he recognized from his rounds through the silo. They paid him no attention.

Seeing an empty spot at one of the tables, he headed for the food line before realizing he couldn't get a tray without his ID badge.

His mind was spinning.

Who was this girl? He wanted to know more about Elizabeth. She had been here against her will, that much was obvious. But, why?

His lips still held the taste of hers. The kisses she planted on him weren't a wet display of affection, neither soft nor sensual. She had pressed her tight lips against his with a pecking sound. Her smell filled his nostrils. His heart swam and he chastised himself at his moment of childish fancy.

She used you.

She had taken his card. His hand went to his chest where it was supposed to be pinned. If he reported the ID card missing before she had an opportunity to get out of the facility or to wherever she was heading, she might be caught.

Why do you care? He asked. The answer came to him. *Because you've seen someone trying to get out or at least trying to communicate here already, Sam Matheson. And, you still don't know what happened to that guy, Martin. Was that just an accident, or a suicide attempt?*

What do you really know about this company?

Holding the handrail, Darien headed for the security office. As he climbed the stairs he couldn't stop thinking about Elizabeth, the smell of her skin as she pressed her lips to his, how her hair, neatened by the hairbrush, still had that 'just got up' look to it. She hadn't been there yesterday. Why had she been there today?

His writpad screen went black, its security functions making it inaccessible without his ID card in the vicinity. It couldn't be helped. He would have to go to security and deal with Larry or Agent Curtis to get another, and he wasn't looking forward to that. If there was any luck at all, neither of them would be there and he could just deal with someone else.

Though he had agreed to report anything unusual to Larry and Agent Curtis he wasn't sure they were on the right side. Something was happening here. The first time Larry had thrown Darien to the floor was because Darien had interrupted, what? An attempted suicide? And now Darien had been coerced to help in an escape attempt. He expected, with good reason he assumed, to be called to HR any time now. There was no way his aid to Elizabeth would not have been captured on the camera system.

Darien swiveled his head around as he climbed. *Where are the cameras?* He hadn't thought much about it before. He hadn't seen a single obvious camera sticking out from any of the walls or down from the ceilings. *They have to be in the walls.* It was the obvious spot for them. If the plastic on the walls had a transparency to them to allow for screens, they could probably have the same level of transparency for a camera system.

He pulled himself out of his distraction and back to the matter at hand, the missing ID card. Perhaps it was better to own up to the situation sooner rather than later. As he climbed the stairs to the security office at sub-level one, he passed a team of black uniformed men heading down. Stopping and pressing himself against the outside wall of the staircase, he gripped the metal handrail, expecting at any moment to be thrown to the floor.

Barely touching him, the guards rushed past and continued down the stairs.

Sitting on the top step at sub-level two were Agent Curtis and Larry Enderby, waiting for him.

"Darien," Agent Curtis said.

Out of breath, Darien said, "Hi, Agent Curtis. Hi, Larry."

"Lawrence."

"I lost my ID card." Darien continued climbing until he was eye to eye with the two sitting men.

"No, you didn't," Agent Curtis said. "We were watching the cafeteria monitor when she took it from you."

Darien blushed and felt a rush of sweat at having been caught in a lie. A fog filled the space between his ears and his mouth hung open slightly. He tried to clear away the haze and come up with a reasonable explanation. Having none, he leaned against the railing and waited to be arrested. He felt sick.

"Don't worry," Agent Curtis said, his voice echoing in the stairwell. "You did just what we wanted you to do. We've been monitoring Elizabeth. We were keeping her in another location and we moved her to this one to try and get her to escape. We transferred her to room H, sub-level five?" He said the last bit as half question and half statement getting a nod from Larry in response. "We expect she is part of the Hiraeth terrorist group we've been tracking. We wanted her to get away. She has a tail."

"Excuse me?"

"We have someone following her," Larry said.

"Hiraeth? You mentioned them before. What's a Hiraeth?

What are you talking about?"

Agent Curtis looked miffed. "You really have been sheltered, haven't you? It's the terrorist group. Remember that explosion site I showed you? Hiraeth is Welsh for 'homesickness' or something like that."

"Oh." Darien wasn't sure if he should say anything more, so he just asked, "Can I get a new card?"

"Yeah," Larry got up and motioned Darien to go in front of him. They walked up the stairs leaving Agent Curtis behind.

"Larry?"

"Lawrence."

"Why was Elizabeth here? She seemed fairly keen on getting out."

"Not everyone here is an employee," Larry explained as he climbed. "Some violated the contract and are only here until they can be moved into incarceration."

"You seem to keep pretty on top of things around here."

"So?"

"So, I wanted to ask you about the first time you threw me to the glass."

Larry chuckled.

"That guy, Martin, did he die?"

"No."

"Do you know why he did that to himself?"

"We work underground. Some people can't take it."

"It's more than that and you know it."

"I do, huh?" Larry brushed past Darien, opened the door to the security center, and motioned Darien inside. "Look, we put a lot of money into every employee. The training alone is expensive as hell. You signed a contract when you started, just like everyone. Is it our fault if some people don't read it?"

"Is that why Elizabeth wanted out?"

Larry nodded and led the way to a desk and shelf system in the back.

"And there was another in room—" Darien checked his writpad. It was still black. "Well, I don't have the room number but his name was Sam, Sam Matheson. He tried to talk to me but someone was controlling his system."

"You remember when you started?" Larry asked. "It's a lot like that. You gonna get a little isolation until quarantine is over."

Larry selected an ID card from a shelf on the wall and ran it through a scanner on his desk. Darien's photo and information appeared on the face of it. At the initialization of the new ID card, Darien's writpad power came back on.

"What about all the new people? Where did they come from? And where did all the others go that were in those rooms?"

"You sure have a lot of questions today. Gettin' a little suspicious, are you?" Larry sat behind the desk. "It's a business. People come and go. Some went to work in the other sections and some were let go. It ain't going to work out for everybody."

"It's just—"

"You been cooped up in here too long. You haven't been to town since you got here." Larry leaned back in his chair. "I think maybe we should take you with us tonight."

"Well, that all depends on where we're going." Darien could not afford to spend anything.

"Oh, we're headed out to the desert. There's a little training exercise. We'll call for you later." The lights on Darien's writpad flashed a notification. "That would be Dr. Hollister."

Darien shrugged, looking at the writpad. "How did you know that?"

"We're security, man. It's my job." Larry smiled. "Get to your appointment with Hollister. See you tonight."

The writpad in Dr. Hollister's hand buzzed and a voice informed, "Simulation complete."

With a gasp, Darien slumped forward out of the chair to sit quivering, gripping the desk for reassurance. Chills ran across the back of his head. His chest hurt and his breathing came out sharp and erratic. Falling back to rest on his heels, pushing away the chair in the process, Darien tried to compose himself. His pulse throbbed in his neck and his heartbeat sounded like the fingers of a talented typist striking the keyboard.

"Darien, can you hear me?" Dr. Hollister asked.

"Yes," Darien said without moving.

"Do you think you can resume your seat?"

"I'm not putting on the headset again."

"I understand how painful facing your fears can be. You don't need to sit through another memory-sim again for a couple of days at least."

Darien pushed away from the desk, rolling from his haunches to sit on the floor. He placed his left hand on the seat of the chair and stood, feeling a bit wobbly still. Gaining control of his balance, he pulled the chair to the desk and sat in it.

Dr. Hollister sat across from Darien, moving the chair from the center of the room. "It can't really hurt you if it's only in your mind."

"That is a reassuring thought until you realize it's your mind deciding what's real and what isn't," Darien said, rubbing his temples. "It's harder, building memories instead of reliving someone else's. In someone else's memories you can use their skills, gain their strengths—"

"Feel their fear," Dr. Hollister interjected. "And that's why we need to keep trying these memory creations. We picked one issue with you, your fear of heights."

"Other people are afraid of heights."

"And that is also true. But your fear is fairly deep. Were you always afraid of heights?"

"No. Yes. I don't know. I used to go to high places, climb trees, partly because it scared me. After I fell, I stopped doing that."

"You fell?" Dr. Hollister asked.

"Yeah." Darien cringed at the memory.

"Can we download it?"

"You want to download the memory of the fall?"

"If we can use it to reduce or eliminate your fear of heights through the creation of new memories, wouldn't you want that?"

"I suppose I would," Darien answered.

In response, Dr. Hollister's fingers were flying over his

writpad.

Watching a change in Hollister, Darian said, "Well, that perked you up. There's a catch isn't there?"

"It's minor, but because of the way we want to use the memory, you're going to have to relive it. We can't just extract it."

Darien felt the sweat build up in his hairline. This was something he definitely didn't want to do. "So how does this work?"

"We'll blend it into a few other memories so it shouldn't have the same impact. It'll pop up like a flashback in a movie." Dr. Hollister walked about the room as he brainstormed and explained the steps needed to extract the memory. "This way you won't have to relive the whole thing all at once. Then, we'll piece it back together into a whole instance, the whole experience."

Darien still didn't like the idea.

"You're going to be experiencing some memories of another subject, Sam Matheson. Every once in a while, you'll fall out of the simulation and experience a flashback of your own memory for just an instant. Then, you'll immerse back into the simulation of Sam's memory again."

"Are we using the headset or the wireless system?"

"No, you can sit right there. We're going to need the more direct connection through the headset. Put it on again."

"Today?" Darien asked exasperated. "Can't this wait?"

"Yes, it can wait." Dr. Hollister looked deflated. "But I'll make you a deal." He spun through his files, displaying them on the screen. "Record this now and maybe I can let you have a few extra memories, things that don't involve heights. Want the best seat at a concert? Who's your favorite? It doesn't even need to be a current band. They could be anyone from the last hundred years."

"You have live concerts stored and we've been doing all of this creepy stuff? What, you don't get any satisfaction out of a happy memory?"

"You want a few happy memories? We can do some of those.

But it's not satisfaction we're after, it's data. Building new memories is a hard item. They need to be believable, and to make them so we have to stretch into some of the harshest environments, otherwise the easy ones will look fake."

"Music," Darien mused. "I know this is a stretch. If you have a Mystic Piglets concert in there, you have a deal."

Darien watched Dr. Hollister's eyebrows rise and at once knew he would be sitting through another harrowing simulation. Closing his eyes, he winced at his mistake. Virtual front row seats to a Mystic Piglets concert was a low price when compared to the anguish he knew was in store.

Sam's fingers raced across the keypad at the door. He could swipe his ID card but that would be a sure give away. Reading the numbers written on his hand, he punched '36547*.' The door opened with a beep. Checking to make sure the cafeteria was still empty, he slipped through the doorway.

Twenty feet wide, the tunnel stretched into the distance, a shaded and round fluorescent light hanging every ten feet. The circles of light illuminated the long straight tunnel further than he could see.

Darien swung onto the lowest branch of the tree. "C'mon!" he called to Tim below him. "Scared?"

Tire marks scarred the floor of the tunnel. Along both sides, electrical wiring and pipes stretched, bringing power, water, or trash from one facility to the next.

Sam checked to see how much room there was behind the pipes. On foot he couldn't outrun an electric tunnel car but he might be able to hide from the drivers if he could squeeze in behind the pipes.

Darien stayed close to the trunk of the tree. He knew the branches well, having climbed this tree several times before. It didn't stop Tim from passing him on the climb.

***

Some of the lights were out. Sam watched the dark spots as he walked along and noticed they fell at regular intervals. Perhaps they were used to measure distance.

Darien gripped the branch and tried to calm himself down.

At the tenth dark spot in the tunnel, Sam took a left into another corridor branching off. A sign above it read, "Genetibotics."

Darien reached for another branch. He hadn't been this high before.

The warm sunlight near the window fell on Sam's back. His elbows on the table in front of him, his hands supporting his face, he listened to Jenna.

"I don't know why we don't just go to the party. There's going to be lots of people there, music, dancing probably."

I'm not in the tunnel anymore.

"I don't need a party right now. I need to finish the report. My GPA is going to take a massive hit if I get anything below a C on this."

"Suit yourself," Jenna said. "You're the one who keeps saying you need to get out more." Jenna got up, and slinging her backpack over one arm, left the campus coffee shop.

After watching her leave, he stared at the blank page of his writpad. He typed a few sentences and erased them. He looked around the shop for anyone who he might recognize from class. Seeing no one, he got up and walked to the counter.

"Hazelnut, small," he said to the girl behind the register.

Darien's fingers closed around the tree branch. He could see Tim climbing above him.

* * *

Sam waited for his coffee, thinking about the report. With a start, he remembered he had left his writpad on the table of the crowded coffee shop and turning to make sure it was still there, saw a tall man standing over the table looking the writpad over. He was beautiful.

Self-doubt crushed Darien as he tried to reach the next branch. Certain of winning this game, he was ashamed Tim had passed him. Balancing, he stretched against the trunk of the tree, hands reaching up for the next branch, and missed.

"Hey," Sam called. The tall man picked up the writpad. "Hey," Sam called again, hurrying over to the table.

"Oh, hello," The tall man said. "I was just reading the title. What class is this?" He handed the writpad to Sam.

"Materials of the Technical Revolution."

"I thought it sounded familiar." He smiled and held out his hand. "I'm Kenny. I had that class last semester." He sat down. "Do you need some help?"

"Seriously?" Sam asked.

"My price is one coffee. Chop, chop," Kenny said, winking.

His head hit the first branch, crashing a white light through his vision. The second branch scraped along his arm as he flailed for purchase.

Sam looked back at the table. Damn, Kenny was handsome.

The next branch hit the small of his back.

I wonder how he takes his coffee. Sam thought.

The impact with the ground stole all of Darien's breath away.

"Hello, again," Sam said to the girl behind the counter. "Can you make that two Hazelnuts?"

Pain.

Chapter Eleven

Report Subject:	**Darien Mamon**
Origin Location:	**Oneida, New York**
Current Location:	**South Miami**
Subject Age:	**18-20**
Subject Status:	**Non-Viable**

His advanced knowledge made Darien the target of his classmates. A series of groans cascaded around the room whenever his hand went up to answer or ask a question.

"Are you kidding me?" a voice sounded from behind him.

Darien turned around and looked at Lance. "What? You don't know this one?"

Lance whispered his response, "I think you better watch that tone, rich boy."

Darien smiled back, but his guts turned at the thought of a potential confrontation. He didn't want to fight. Everyone else seemed to want to. Lance was larger than most, and he was a scuffleball player. Even his desk had trouble holding him. His knees pressed against the front bar of the chrome leg supports.

One large hand reached out and pressed on Darien's shoulder, turning him around again to face front. "Eyes forward, rich boy."

At least he's smiling, Darien thought. *If I can make him laugh, he might not kill me.*

The professor continued on with the lecture, ignoring the two.

An hour later as they were packing up their materials, Darien glanced at Lance and said, "See you tomorrow."

"What? You don't want to play ball today? We've got a scuffleball game starting in another hour."

"I've never played scuffleball." Darien laughed. "I don't even know the rules."

"There aren't many rules to worry about." Lance smiled. "It's all part of the fun."

"How do you play?"

"You've seen soccer?"

"Yeah."

"It's nothing like that." Lance led the way down the stair risers to the front of the lecture hall. "Injured players stay on the field. If they're still conscious, they can grab your legs as you try to run by. It creates a unique obstacle course on the field every time you play a round."

"Every time I've seen it, all I could think of was that it looked like a fight."

"Sometimes it is. You're allowed to punch other players but you have to have possession of the ball."

"I don't know why you don't just call it fightingball."

"We did." Lance opened the door to the hall and let Darien walk out first. "We got a cease-and-desist letter from a bunch of guys in wheelchairs that play rugby. Those guys are hardcore."

"Wheelchairs? Can't they fix those injuries now? Hell, I've seen a few artificial legs." Darien thought of the tutor and soccer coach he had fired as a kid. Her artificial leg was as good as any organic.

"Some of them get a spinal switch to turn off the legs so they can still compete."

"Yeah, no thank you to that."

"All right," Lance said, "your loss. We'll see you tomorrow." He punched Darien's shoulder, sending lines of pain down to Darien's fingers.

"I must admit, I avoided leaving the dorm room for a couple of days. I had to share it with some idiot from Massachusetts, or as I began to call it, Dumbassachusetts," Darien joked to the kid in the seat next to him. "This guy expected me to pick up my clothes, make my bed, and even do my own laundry."

Moments later the seat was empty and Darien laughed to himself. They didn't like him. Everyone except Randy avoided him like he carried communicable diseases. He knew this. He didn't care. He was better than any of them.

Soon after his arrival at South Miami Technical, an advisor had called Darien on his vid-card to set up a series of entrance tests. Every student that had not used the public education system was required to take the collection of tediously boring standardized tests. Filling in circle after circle, Darien fell asleep twice. The results of those tests pushed Darien into second year classes. Already ahead of the game, Darien slacked off, drinking more than he should have, sleeping less than was wise. He didn't attend a single class in the first week.

He reasoned to himself this was all just review. What was the point? He skipped lessons. Even with the stupid roommate, Darien was enjoying himself. He had never experienced this level of freedom. Being in a different place was invigorating and Darien wished he had paid more attention to the Florida scenery as the pod approached the school.

When he did decide to go to class, he sat confidently down in the back of the room and let his mind drift away. Twenty minutes in, as his mind became bored with the view from the window, he started to listen to the lecture.

A student presented her work to the class, using terms unfamiliar to Darien. He skimmed the information on the magnetic board, eyes bugging out in surprise. Foreign symbols danced inside obscure formulas. Nothing looked familiar, nothing at all.

What is that symbol? he thought, panicking. *I don't know that symbol.*

I'm in trouble. It's going to take me forever to catch up!

He was behind, by a long way. Darien Mamon was going to have to work. Late night calculations in the school library, algorithms, difficult and hard to follow, and if one did something wrong they wouldn't find out until they simulated the problem at the end: that was his life for the next month as he tried to understand the sections he missed. Looking back, it was clear to Darien: He wasn't only an asshole, he was a fool too.

He dove into extra study sessions, imposing himself into already existing groups. Feeling at first like a burden on the other members, he worked hard to prove himself a reliable study partner, finding unique solutions to problems, often arriving at the same answer as the teacher but without following the same format.

Maybe they still hate me, Darien told himself. *But they know intelligence and ingenuity when they see it.*

By the end of the first term Darien had climbed to the top of the class behind Shara and Nancy.

Shara was in her last year at South Miami, smami as she called it, just getting off an internship at Electromed in Sierra Vista Arizona.

Darien and Shara only had one class together. In that class, she was always the one with her hand up, her questions revealing a keen mind, bridging gaps, and further expanding the topic of discussion.

Darien dreaded his other classes. Engineering, even medical engineering classes, were filled almost exclusively with men. Having many other classes together, these men were a tight group. His solo education, guided by some of the best private tutors, resulted in Darien looking awkwardly on, unsure if he should participate as the others joked and spoke among themselves. Only one bright spot presented itself in those classes. As Darien struggled his way through the hardest chapters, watching his own grades dip, the others seemed to be having it worse.

That's to be expected from the public education system, Darien thought, looking down his nose at them.

Before passing in a take-home test, as they neared the end of semester, Sven, an older student, approached Darien.

"What did you get for number seven?" he asked, scanning his own paper.

"I'm not going to help you cheat," Darien replied.

Sven held up his paper, showing his calculations, typed and complete. "I'm not trying to cheat," he said. "I just want to see if I did it right."

"Well, I'm not showing you my paper," Darien stated flatly.

Sven moved off to confer with the other members of the

class and Darien heard him say softly, "Prick." The other members of the class roared.

Darien struggled to fit in socially outside of his study groups, but apart from Randy, who no longer seemed to want to kick his ass, he had not made any friends. Months of interaction with the other members of the student body had not changed that.

Shara and Lance kept him grounded. Shara's smiles held him up and Lance's ideas always got him into trouble. Whenever Darien was feeling down, Shara was there. Whenever Darien was feeling goofy, Lance did his best to push it to the next step.

The big man had a zest for life Darien had never felt. Always eager to try the next thing, he often pushed Darien outside of his comfort zone. The only things Darien ever backed down from involved heights, things like base-jumping. Jumping from a tall building using only a parachute was high on the list of, 'yeah, not for me' adventures.

If he wasn't with Lance, he was with Shara. His initial annoyance at her, *She's smarter than you*, had been melted by her persistence, humor, and amazing smile. Shara and Darien laughed and sometimes made love in an empty travel pod if they could ditch Shara's best friend, Nancy. The two girls used the travel pods to get around campus and sometimes they would take one up north to the amusement parks in Central Florida. Shara had worked there in her first year at South Miami and knew all of the secret places within the parks. The first time they allowed Darien to accompany them, the trio visited backstage at the Animal Extinction Exhibit where the staff let Darien touch a tiger pelt, a rare opportunity.

Often left behind by the two, Darien was giddy at any chance to accompany them, and though he didn't enjoy Nancy's company, he endured it to spend time with Shara.

"If you could stop glaring at me, that would be nice."

"Well, stop acting like an asshole and I'll try."

Shara knew so many people. They all loved her. A flurry of hugs hit her whenever she entered a room. Many times, this left Darien standing awkwardly off to the side as she caught up with her old friends. She always introduced him but he just couldn't speak to any of them. "I'm sorry," he would say, but the real problem was that he felt they were beneath him. Most of them weren't even studying engineering.

The relief of signing up for his final semester of classes didn't last. Both Shara and Darien needed the same class, a third year category on memory storage called Calculations and System Design.

The class explored the impulses and memory requirements of the human brain versus various computer systems. It studied the transfer of emotions, the storage of traumatic experiences, and the history of mental retention and distribution.

Homework filled their nights. The assigned problems fell together like pieces of a puzzle, building as a whole to display a full picture of how the formulas worked together.

Darien followed along, placing each equation in the correct order. However, when the tests came, his mind went blank. Frustrated, Darien studied harder than he ever had, but it didn't change the outcome. During the tests his thoughts always came out jumbled.

Homework sessions doubled in length. He avoided social functions, much to the chagrin of Shara. He drilled himself on the formulas and their functions. It didn't help. By the time the third exam came around Darien was in serious trouble. The first test hadn't been too bad, a 75. The second test was worse, a 66. The third test hit hard, 38.

Darien looked at Shara's test score. She was flying through all three tests in the high eighties.

"Look, you're doing it all wrong," Shara said looking over Darien's shoulder during one of their homework sessions.

"No," Darien said. "It works better this way." Darien compiled the program and pressed the run button on the writpad. The pad hung with a static screen for over a minute before it cleared as the pad rebooted itself.

"I just can't follow the class system in this design," Darien complained, shaking his head. "That should have worked."

Shara grabbed the writpad after the reboot. "If you follow the algorithm listed on the student page put together by Dr. Becker it comes out fine."

"But, it's so slow," Darien complained.

During the final exam, Darien sat next to Shara. He had to pass this. She was used to him sitting so close to her and, in desperation, Darien began to look at her calc-pad.

Ah, that's what I was missing, he thought to himself as he copied her solution. Again and again, problem after problem, he found himself looking over at her work. Her calculations and methods followed the order shown in the homework, something Darien had experienced trouble replicating during the exams so far. He didn't need to copy her calculations, just her method. The numbers didn't matter if the method was correct.

When Darien handed in his paper, he watched the professor place his calc-pad, along with Shara's, in a pile separate from that of the rest of the students. His heart sunk, weighing down his chest as if it were filled with lead. Walking back to his seat next to Shara, Darien could not meet her eyes.

At the end of the exam the two were summoned to the professor's office. The results were predictable. Darien Mamon was expelled for cheating. Shara Musabayana was stripped of her honors. They did not accuse her of cheating, but of knowingly allowing someone else to cheat. Why did she let Darien sit so close to her if she had not been complicit? She still graduated, but her thesis on the human mind as a read/write system, a year of research, was denied publication.

Darien's indiscretion ended their relationship. She was furious.

"You never gave any thought to what might happen to me on this. How much of my work did you copy? How long have you been cheating off of me?"

"Just this exam," Darien answered. "I was just trying to pass the class." A cloud filled his mind, raining hate and self-loathing.

He watched the tears rolling down her cheeks. He saw the

flush in her face and all he could do was hang his head in shame.

She turned away from him, wiping the tears from her eyes with her knuckles and her last word stung at Darien's heart with its simplicity, its tone of finality. "Go."

Walking to the public pods on the North side of campus, his ears burning, his eyes puffy, he cursed his weakness. In one decision he had lost both his education path and his best friend. Her smiles, her touch, her laughter were not for him any longer. He was alone again, single again.

He pressed his palm to the dorm keypad and the light turned red. "Access denied." The door to the dorm had already been locked out.

Darien punched the light, screaming at the top of his lungs.

All of his clothes, everything, was in there. They were not going to let him retrieve any of it. The veins in his neck pulsed with fury. The sweat on his head dripped onto his shirt, his only shirt. He screamed again, tears streaming down his face. Students avoided him, walking past him to use another door. Maybe they'd witnessed this before. From their expressions, Darien knew they were not going to help. He had been cast out.

Lance met him at the door.

"I can't let you in, man."

"I just need to get my things," Darien pleaded.

"Your things," Lance said, "were flushed out by a team of janitors over an hour ago."

"An hour ago? That was during the exam. How did they know so fast?"

"I don't know, man. All I know is you're not allowed to come back into the building." Lance looked sympathetic. He reached into his pocket and gave Darien a plastic vendor card for a local coffee shop.

"Hey, there's enough on here for a couple cups of java." He leaned against the doorframe. "You're gonna have trouble finding work, now."

"Why?"

"You don't have a degree."

Darien put the java card in his pocket.

"Companies and corporations, looking to save a few bucks, hang out near the college, looking for dropouts. You could try the pod station on the mainland."

"So I can get exploited for pennies on the dollar?"

"What choice do you have, man? It'll start that way, sure. But you're not one of those who couldn't hack it. You just fell down at the finish line. You're going to have to punch a few people to finish the game."

"Scuffleball reference?"

Lance smiled. "You don't know me by now? I'm sorry I can't do more for you." He gave Darien a bear hug, nodded a goodbye, and shut the door.

Sitting on the step, Darien made a note of his assets. The education fund set up by the lawyers of his parent's estate had dried up by then, of course, but his private finance account had some money in it, containing what he earned from small part-time work at the school. Wiping his tears and wearing or carrying in his pockets everything he owned, Darien walked to the pods.

Dirty and stained from the students, either from partying to the point of regurgitation or from promiscuous sex, the pods would take him to the mainland. He chose the cleanest one and pressed the destination, flinching at the price. The mainland was almost foreign. He had only traveled there with Shara on rare occasions.

Some of those stains might have been ours, he thought, laughing at first but, then, wiping a tear from his cheek.

Chapter Twelve

<pre>
Report Subject: Darien Mamon
Origin Location: Oneida, New York
Current Location: South Miami
Subject Age: 21-23
Subject Status: Non-Viable
</pre>

The company representative on the mainland introduced himself as Evan.

"Hi, I'm Evan. Do you have a moment to hear about Femto Blood Systems?"

"Yup."

Evan ushered Darien into the broken down storefront painted in turquoise and orange. The wages he offered were substandard, barely enough to get an apartment and keep food on the table. Luxuries like entertainment, health products, and cleaning supplies would be hard to afford.

The offered post was one correcting code. However, during his employment at Femto Blood Systems, Darien saw several opportunities to rework functions and improve efficiency. The response was always the same.

"That's not your job."

It soon became apparent Femto Blood Systems was a fly by night scam company. It didn't matter. He didn't have a choice. As the weeks turned into months, and months became over a year, Darien paid close attention to his funds. He didn't travel. He didn't date. He didn't eat properly.

He began to look differently at the people around him. Were they as miserable as he? They didn't appear to be. Day in and day out they came to their desks, shutting out the natural light for the dull fluorescent glow of the screen. Faces changed so often Darien stopped trying to learn names. Loyalty for Femto Blood Systems was a non-issue. When someone quit, the company just went back to the university pod station.

After thirteen months of toil, Darien walked into his supervisor's office, displayed several hand gestures, and quit. After a walk to the university pod station, he signed on for a job with Integrated Blood Incorporated. They were a smaller company, but they were beginning to advertise on the electronic flyers around town. It didn't matter. Eight months later he was looking for work during every hour he wasn't chained to his desk.

BioMedTricks pulled him out of Integrated Blood Incorporated. Their deal with customers sounded so good it just had to be a scam, but Darien wasn't concerned about that. With the salary offered he could take a shower every day. He could eat what he wanted when he wanted, not having to wait for payday. He could get a better apartment. Maybe he could even take a vacation.

For so much of his life he had looked down on those who had to work every day. Here he was now, one of them. Perhaps he had been wrong about them. Perhaps there was more to learn, and he was learning the hard way. The BioMedTricks offer in his hand, Darien called a realtor to improve his surroundings.

During his time at both Femto Blood Systems and Integrated Blood Incorporated he came to realize that no one paid attention to a broken man, and that's what he'd been. He had done it to himself. He knew this. The contract with BioMedTricks would give him a chance to claw his way out of obscurity. Over the next few months, entertainment entered the menu, dating became an option, and Darien started to stand taller.

On his own time, Darien began writing code on the company writpad. Programs to increase his productivity at work filled up folders and were integrated into his daily routine. Before long, his employer began to notice.

"Mr. Mamon," his supervisor, Eddie Likmand, called out as Darien was walking past his office. Darien's hands were filled with his writpad bag, a hurried attempt to put together a lunch, and a change of clothes.

Darien backed up and looked into Mr. Likmand's office. "Yes, sir." The word still sounded odd to him. He never called anyone 'sir' during his formative years. A bit of respect was required in the working world as he had quickly learned.

"You were tardy yesterday. You left early last night and you are tardy again this morning." Mr. Likmand displayed his writpad screen on the wall behind him so Darien could see the proof. "I'm writing you up and you will lose two days' pay in your deposit."

"Has my work been slipping?" Darien asked.

Mr. Likmand scanned his writpad. "No, actually. Your output has increased twenty-three percent." Mr. Likmand scanned the writpad again, confused. "How has it increased so much?"

"I automated the code at my station so it operates continuously whether I'm there or not."

"Did you have authorization to modify the code?"

"No, sir." There was that word again.

Mr. Likmand furrowed his bushy eyebrows and said, "Bring me the modifications you implemented before you log in this morning."

Darien nodded and walked to his cubicle desk.

After Mr. Likmand looked through Darien's code he called a closed door meeting with all of the other supervisors. Through the windows Darien watched each of them read through the code, watched each of them smile and point out changes to their peers. Following the meeting Darien was called into Mr. Likmand's office again.

"Darien, after careful consideration and review of your changes we have decided you will not be permitted to continue using them. It is our conclusion that the modifications put the system at risk." Mr. Likmand took a sip of his water. "In addition to your two days docking of pay from your next deposit, we have decided to decrease your overall income by ten percent. You will also be suspended for one week without pay, effective immediately."

Dejected, Darien returned home. When he returned to work

the following week he found his code had been integrated into the entire BioMedTricks mainframe, Mr. Eddie Likmand's office had been moved up one floor of the building, and Eddie's old office now held a new supervisor in charge of Darien and his activities.

Furious, Darien stormed away from his desk and headed for the bathroom. In the stained sink he ran the cold water and splashed it over his face, wetting his sweatshirt around the collar. He let the water run.

Mr. Likmand and the other supervisors had stolen his code and used it to further their own positions while punishing the very person who wrote it. The twenty-three percent rise in productivity for the entire group was immediately recognized as a boon for BioMedTricks and Mr. Likmand had received a promotion to System Head.

The surge of anger pushed through his veins. Sweat soaked his forehead. His shirt felt sticky with it. He'd been sweating a lot recently and he splashed a little more water around his neck, not caring if it soaked his sweatshirt.

The reflection in the mirror faded to black. His grip on the stained sink slipped and he fell forward into it, ripping it from the wall as he fell. Water cascaded from the broken pipe hitting the underside of the mirror and pouring down the wall.

In the growing puddle, Darien's head lolled and his limbs gained weight as he attempted to move. His hands were heavy. Lying on his stomach, he turned his head enough so he could breathe above the pooling water.

Hands were pulling him, rolling him onto his back. "Hey! Are you all right, man?" The water soaked into the back of his sweatshirt. Darien rested his head on the floor and focused his hearing on the voice. It was moving away, calling for a medical transport.

The grit of the floor pressed against his fingernails as he scraped them into the grout. The water had now soaked his pants, spreading like the weakness through his body the instant before his collapse.

Running feet, Darien could hear the sound of running feet

and then the voices.

"What happened?"

"I don't know. I opened the door and there he was on the floor."

"Is he breathing?"

"Yeah, I think so."

"Is someone calling the med transport?"

"Mark is calling them."

"LaLiberte?"

"No, Engles."

After a brief pause someone said, "Look at the sink. Mr. Likmand is going to lose his shit."

The bathroom remained out of focus and the darkness became a bright light, causing Darien to clench his eyes, warding away the intensity. However, the light came from inside. His eyelids could not shut it out.

Chapter Thirteen

Report Subject:	**Darien Mamon**
Origin Location:	**Oneida, New York**
Current Location:	**Tucson, AZ**
Subject Age:	**27**
Subject Status:	**Viable**

"So, you're a tough guy?"

"Keeping the panties wet and the powder dry." Larry pushed another bullet into the magazine. "Someone's gotta be that guy. Might as well be me."

Darien smiled. "Well, it couldn't be me." He felt good. One thing missing from Darien's childhood had been camaraderie. Growing up alone and protected, he had never been the one invited to sleepovers and he imagined that's what this moment must have felt like.

When Darien arrived at the security door, Larry opened it and invited him in as if they were old friends. They walked down the spring suspension hallway to the interrogation room at the end where Martin waited for them at the table. Martin looked in good spirits, much better than he had when Darien last saw him. This thought made Darien laugh a little. *How much can you see with your face pressed to the floor?* Coincidentally, that had also been the first time he met Larry, and now the three were sitting at a table joking and loading magazines with copper jacketed bullets.

Larry handed Darien a magazine and pushed a box of bullets in his direction. "Never be you? Why not? Don't like girls?"

"Of course I like girls."

"So it's not a problem with the panties but a problem with the powder?"

"I don't have any experience with guns," Darien said, shrugging his shoulders.

"Not even the new electric rail guns?"

Darien shook his head.

"Caseless ammunition?"

Darien shook his head again.

"Pulse rifles?"

"Nothing."

"Well, you're gonna like this." Larry hefted the pistol Martin had been inspecting when Darien arrived. "Semi-automatic. It's an antique but we've added some wireless functions to it. The sites have been improved to align themselves to the trigger motion of the user."

"Trigger motion?"

"If you don't have a lot of practice you can turn the gun slightly as you press on the trigger. It takes a lot of practice to shoot straight. The electronic sight learns your issues as you use it. It reads the circular motion during the trigger pull and aligns itself to offset."

"Well, it sounds like this gun was made for me."

"A lot of the newer handguns have this already, especially the rail guns." Larry handed the gun to Darien. "It's as easy as landing a punch."

"Well," Darien said, "I haven't done a lot of that either."

"Never been in a fight?"

"No. In all honesty, I wanted that experience for a long time. I studied Aikido when I was younger but the only person I ever used it on didn't know he was in a fight. I've never had someone come after me. There was one guy in college I was pretty sure was going to turn me into a puddle, Lance. He and I actually became pretty good friends. I'm happy it never happened. Even with the training, I think I would have panicked."

"Martin, have you ever been in a fight?" Larry asked.

"I've only been in a few fights, but I've been in several beatings."

Larry guffawed, snorting and doubling over.

"Well," Martin said, "is it really a fight if you never get a chance to hit back?"

"No," Larry replied, wiping a tear from his eye. "I suppose it isn't. What are you, some kind of pussy?"

Martin didn't reply and took a long pull from the beer bottle in front of him.

"Don't worry," Larry continued. "I like you. You're funny. Not like Darien here, he's got a stick up his ass."

"Back off, man. I didn't put it there." Darien had never loaded a magazine before. He pushed a bullet in and felt the tension of the spring.

"Well, you got to learn to relax, man. That's why you're here, both of you. We could have tried drugs, but they're way too expensive." He opened his eyes wide. "And you never know what kind of side effects they might have. A little fun-time is a much better cure."

"Fun-time?" Martin asked. "Any ladies coming with us?"

"Not that kind of fun-time, fool." Larry thought for a moment. "It's a good idea, though. I wish I had thought of it. I definitely think I could have hooked something up."

Martin put down his magazine. "Well, allow me to place my vote."

"Next time," Larry said. "I'll see what I can do."

"You got yourself a stable of women out back?" Martin asked. "I've been here for months and I keep striking out, every time. I'm lucky to get a damn name."

"As a security agent I have a little access to the personnel files. I'd be lying if I said I didn't use that information to my advantage."

"Files, huh?" Martin picked up his magazine again and pulled the box of bullets closer. "What kind of information is in one of those?"

"Smut, some of it. Most of it is a dating history: preferences, likes, dislikes. You answered the questions when you started working here. They did too."

"Well, let me know if you come across any of them that have a fetish for a scrawny guy with a little dick."

Larry and Darien both burst out laughing.

"Yep, I like you, Martin," Larry said as he sucked in a breath.

Darien looked at Martin. He was just a little taller and much thinner. His black hair hung limp on his shoulders. A stubble showed on his face and it was apparent this man could not grow either a mustache or beard in less than a month. Darien guessed Martin's age to be around twenty-five.

The stitches ran along both of Martin's arms. Only a little over a week prior he had tried to take his own life. Since then, he had resided in a medical ward where he could be closely watched. Larry had visited every day.

"So, what are the plans?" Martin asked. "You have a few guns here. We loaded a lot of clips. How many clips are there?" He counted quickly, "Ten? Why so many? Don't you think you could hit us with fewer bullets?"

"Funny." Larry puffed out his lower lip in obvious appreciation of the dig. "Don't worry. There's a shooting range outside. I figure a little target practice would be a good remedy for the funk you've both been in."

Martin displayed his arms. The stitches ran in tight rows surrounded by yellow bruising. "A funk?" He grinned and grabbed Darien's forearm. "Where are your stitches? This guy ain't in a funk."

"Give me time," Darien said. "I'm working my way there."

"See?" Larry said to Darien. "Sarcasm, very important to humor. You could be funny. You're not, but you could be."

Larry had an odd sense of humor. He was brash. Darien really didn't see the humor in joking about attempted suicide, even if Larry and Martin both seemed to be fine with it.

Darien finished loading his magazine and opened the beer in front of him. The first gulps were like an elixir of happiness. He hadn't had a beer in weeks. It was cold and bitter by just the right amount.

As he finished his second beer, Martin pushed the last of the loaded magazines to Larry, who was collecting them in a black nylon bag and, after placing the last one in, he zipped it shut and emptied his own beer in three long swallows.

Larry belched loudly and walked away toward his desk at the back of the room, returning with three pairs of shooting glasses. He handed one each to Martin and Darien. Then, he opened a fridge under the table and handed another six pack of beer to Martin.

Drinking and shooting, thought Darien. *Great way to get yourself killed.* He hoped that wasn't the intended outcome.

"I think that's everything." Larry patted his pockets, "Keys. OK, let's do this."

Living inside the climate controlled facility, Darien never got used to the blast of heat enveloping him when he stepped outside. It took his breath away. The light wind felt like a hairdryer. He walked slow, conserving his energy, squinting in the bright sun, and drained his first bottle of water before they were one hundred yards from the facility.

Larry trudged along, talking about the plants growing near the path. Mesquite trees sat low and stretched out wide. There were bushes and trees filled with evil looking thorns, tall spindling cacti and low dry grass. The dirt had an orange tint as if high in some metal, perhaps copper, but according to Larry, who remarked on his knowledge of Arizona, copper was more likely to be found around Bisbee.

"There's a deep rift in the earth near Bisbee called the Lavender Mine. I can't remember when that operation closed down. I've always wanted to visit Bisbee," he said. "Seen a few pictures and it looks quaint and cozy. I've heard good things about it. Maybe, one day."

The range was a wide span dug down into the desert to a depth of about ten feet. The sides were left rough and sloped to, according to Larry, keep any fragments of bullets from ricocheting back towards a shooter or spectator. Within the expanse of the sub desert depression were single level buildings, standees and target lanes.

Larry dragged a folding table from inside one of the buildings and set out the contents of the bag, a semi-automatic pistol, ten clips, a small stack of assorted targets, and a bottle of ninety proof rye whiskey.

"Well, there's an accident waiting to happen. Isn't the beer enough?" Martin said picking up the whiskey.

"Don't be such a pansy. I forgot the tampons," Larry chided and opened the bottle, the cork emitting a squeak followed by a low frequency pop. He put the bottle to his nose before pulling a glass out of his pocket. He poured a half inch of the whiskey and took a small sip of the amber liquid. His eyes closed as he savored the taste. "I never understood why anyone would want to drink this out of a shot glass. God Damn, it's delicious. You waste all that flavor in an attempt to get drunk quickly."

"Some people like being drunk," Darien answered inspecting the pistol.

"Then, drink something that tastes like old bandages, tequila, maybe."

"Whoa!" Martin said. "Watch yourself around here. Tequila is sacred."

"Tequila, tequila…" Larry reached into his back pocket and brought forward a metal flask that read on its face, 'Drink like you're already dead.' "Want some?" he asked.

Martin took the flask and tilted it back, sipping the contents. "All right." He coughed. "This one's not bad."

"Do you think we can save the drinking until we're done with the loaded gun play?"

"Darien, what? Are you on your period?" Larry asked, but he also put away the booze.

Larry handed noise canceling signal generators to each Martin and Darien. "Put these behind your ears where that bone pushes out from your skull."

"You mean my skull? Is that the bone you're talking about?" Darien asked.

Larry stared at him. "You know what I mean. Put these on your skull behind your ears, like this." Larry turned his head left and right so they could see where he had placed his hearing protectors. "It won't cancel all of the sound but it should reduce the decibels enough that it shouldn't damage your ears."

"Yes, sir," Martin replied.

"Who's up first?" Larry picked up the black semi-automatic pistol and handed it to Martin. In response to Martin's surprised look he said, "Nothing makes you feel more like a badass."

"I didn't think I'd get to go first."

"Someone has to." Larry lined up the magazines on the table absently as Martin checked his initial reaction and hefted the weight of the pistol in his hand.

"Two hands." Larry took the pistol back and demonstrated a two-handed firing stance. "Just point and pull the trigger. Don't ever point it at anyone you're not interested in seeing dead." He handed the pistol back to Martin. "Wait here and we'll let you know when to start."

"What do you mean start?"

"There's going to be a maze of assailants, holographic. Just follow the lights."

Larry pulled Darien into one of the buildings and locked the door. Once inside, Larry walked over to the control panels and turned on the microphone. "Can you hear me out there?"

The control panel screen showed Martin nodding his head.

"Straight ahead and you can start whenever you want."

Martin followed the lights into the maze of targets.

Inside the control booth, screens lined the walls showing multiple angles of Martin as he fired at moving targets jumping out of the ground or from behind walls in sequence.

In awe, Darien asked, "How many cameras do you have out there?"

Larry nodded his head, looking sideways at Darien. "It looks impressive, doesn't it. It really isn't that many. The cameras are on drones. They just follow him around the maze, and because they're linked to the gun they manage to keep out of the line of fire."

They watched Martin.

"Hey, Larry," Darien said.

"Lawrence."

"Did you guys ever get any more information about that explosion in New York?"

His eyes still watching the screens, Larry answered, "Agent Curtis went out there. He's been following the electronic trail. You know, credit hits, image discoveries, stuff like that."

"Sounds tedious."

"Yeah, but the systems are getting better all the time. You can do most of it from one room. For instance, we took an image from the site of the explosion and cross referenced it to find it led to images of people we know, some of those people are even here at the facility."

"I don't understand 'cross reference of images.' What does that do?"

"Have you ever heard the old term seven degrees of separation? It's like, you know one person and they know one person, and so on, and so on, until you can connect them to someone famous. This system is like that. It takes a photo of you and scans every face in the photo, then it takes a photo of the target and scans every face in their photos. Then it follows the same pattern through the web for the faces in those people's photos until the two inquiries collide."

"Hey, there's a memory equation there."

"We use it to find out how many connections it takes to get from one person to the other. Remember that girl Elizabeth? Between her and the terrorist bomber it only took three photos. It's a lot better than it used to be." Larry pressed a few buttons to replay some of Martin's shots. "That was a good one," he remarked, pointing.

"It used to be that everyone kept their photos, an old term, images," he corrected, "separate and relatively private. That was before free storage in the cloud systems. We can browse through that like butter on a hot plate."

Larry turned his full attention back to the screens and Martin's exercise. After the last target fell, Martin stood looking at the pistol in his hands. It should have been empty, the slide in a locked open position. It still appeared to be loaded.

On the screen, Martin looked down at his forearms where he had tried to open his veins only days before.

Larry's eyes went wide. "Dammit!" he shouted and rushed to unlock the door. He fumbled with the lock, dropping his keys as he swung the door wide and ran out.

Darien watched Larry leave and turned his attention back to the screens to see Martin looking at the loaded gun thoughtfully, smiling all the while. Larry tackled him with a smack and Martin's reflexes squeezed the trigger, causing the empty cartridge to eject as the weapon fired into the ground. The cartridge hit the sloped side of the shooting range and rolled down to the two men struggling in the dirt.

Larry reached for the gun in Martin's hand.

"Get the hell off me!" Martin yelled when his breath returned. "What, did you think I was going to try and off myself again?"

Larry grimaced a response, "Look, man, I shouldn't have taken the chance."

"But you did. And I'm all right. At least, I was until you came flying through the air like a damn freight train."

Martin got up, rubbing his ribs, pushing Larry away, and walked to the control building. Larry wiped dust from the pistol.

The drones following Martin returned to their positions on the side of the control building.

"He doesn't have to keep such a close watch on me. I'm not a damn baby." Martin watched the screens replaying his run through the maze.

"Martin, you already tried once," Darien said.

"Shove it," Martin said, not taking his eyes from the screen. "Look at that one." He pressed rewind and replayed the footage of himself and his reaction time coming around a corner. "Like a machine. I stopped thinking by this time. Just point and shoot. Look here." Martin rewound all the way to the beginning. "Look at the hesitation. I was afraid," he said in disgust.

Darien sat down in one of the chairs next to Martin. "Everyone's afraid of something."

"Oh, yeah? What are you afraid of?" His eyes followed the video, overly critical of his movements.

"Heights, can't stand them. I get all jiggly inside, dizzy, like I'm going to fall over."

"Heights? That's stupid. If you're somewhere high being afraid just makes the chances of you doing something stupid and dying all that much worse. You might as well be afraid of the dark."

"Who says I'm not," Darien said laughing.

"You're a trip, Darien. I like you. I don't care what they say about you."

"I've been working on my fear of heights since I got here. Walking around the Central Hub is like an exercise in 'How much can Darien sweat'? Dr. Hollister has even been using it in his study. It seems half the vids and memories I have with him are of me climbing a radio tower, or skydiving, or jumping off bridges. I even had one where I was hiking a trail on the edge of a cliff." *Like in the photo*, Darien thought suddenly.

Martin turned away from the video. "You're working with Hollister? Me, too."

Darien was surprised to have forgotten this bit of information about Martin and the look on his face showed it. "That's right," he said. "I saw that on your files when—" Darien silenced himself.

"When you found me," Martin said, sitting down and putting his feet on another chair. "Don't sweat it. I'm trying to put that day behind me."

"What kind of work have you been doing with Hollister?"

"I've been running vids and memory sims for about ten weeks but I've not done anything with heights."

"What kind of stuff do you concentrate on?"

"Violence."

"You really screwed this up," Larry complained from outside. "I can't believe the crud in here. What? Did you shove it into the dirt on purpose?"

"Asshole," Martin said under his breath, then yelled his reply, "You're the one who made me, Larry."

"Lawrence," came the muted reply from outside.

Darien couldn't leave his conversation with Martin alone after his last response. "What kind of violence?"

"What kind of heights?" Martin asked, scrunching up his face and shaking his head before smirking and saying, "Fights, shootouts, executions, war, genocide. Violence is a lot harder to do up close. Pulling a trigger is cake compared to strangling the life out of someone."

"What the hell?" Darien gasped.

"No violence for you, huh?"

Darien shook his head.

"It started small, fistfights in grade school, watching my father beat the crap out of my mother."

"Is that how you grew up?" Darien asked.

"Not even close. But the mem-sims and memory creation are really messing me up."

Darien looked at Martin's stitches. "Is that why you cut yourself?"

"Who knows? I been pretty dark lately. I lash out. Sometimes I just punch everything. You should see the walls in my room. I haven't managed to break them but there are fist prints everywhere." He showed his bruised knuckles.

"All right," Larry called. "I got it clean again. I'm going next." He poked his head in. "Close the door and lock it. When you lock it from inside, it turns on the flying screen bugs." He pulled the door shut and Darien locked it with the keys Larry had dropped.

They sat down and watched.

Larry knew the course. Larry knew the gun. The pistol in his hands fired with precision and speed, his fingers well trained to squeeze the triggers without disturbing his sight alignment. The maze had reset the targets after Martin's run. Each target snapped up from the floor to catch a bullet dead center. Larry's considerable size flowed with grace and certainty, traveling through the exercise with practiced perfection.

Martin watched in awe, tracing the course in his head, fingers flexing as the targets came into view, smiling at the best moves, and laughing when Larry made a shot that should have not been possible. "Look at him go!" Martin exclaimed. "How many times has he run this course. He knows what's going to happen before he gets there."

At the end of the course, Larry dropped the empty magazine out and put it in his pocket. He waved the gun in his hand so the drones following shook along with it. "Unlock the door. We don't need the drones anymore."

Taking the keys from Darien and unlocking the door Martin walked out to meet Larry, putting the keys in his pocket as he walked. "What the hell, Larry? That was amazing!"

"Lawrence."

"You didn't miss a single target."

"I never do." Larry walked to the table and put the gun down. "Let's see the replay." Darien and Martin followed Larry into the building and sat again in awe watching a master at work.

"I could watch that over and over," Martin said.

"Well, we have to get back soon. Darien, are you ready to give this a shot?" He motioned the two back outside to the table.

"Remember," Larry said, "the holograms will jump out at you, but they can't hurt you. It's just a 3D image. If you get too nervous to continue, just put the safety on and the system will shut down."

Darien picked up the gun and Larry handed him a full magazine from the bag. Darien pressed the magazine into the gun and dropped the slide, chambering the first round.

Larry laughed. "You pick it up pretty quick. Now, the safety is still on but be careful where you point that." Larry ushered Martin back into the control building and the drones flew into position behind Darien.

In the heat and blinding sun Darien walked through the firing maze, carefully aiming and taking his shot on target after target. One after another fell in a holographic death scene. The ear protection behind Darien's ears held the sound to muffled cracks, but he could still feel the pressure change as the lead left the barrel. It was loud even with the noise canceling signals.

His finger squeezed the trigger as he engaged each target, and before he knew it, the maze was over. The gun slide had snapped to the open position with the last shot.

Moments later Larry and Martin were walking his way. Larry was smiling. Martin wasn't.

"Jesus, Darien, nice work! A solid shot on every target, all dead. I'm gonna start calling you Deadshot. Your time could use some work but what do you expect for a first run?" Larry took the gun from Darien. "You did a sight better than Martin here. True, it's his first time on this range but he's had other training. You haven't!" He turned to Martin. "What do you think?"

Martin punched Darien in the mouth.

Chapter Fourteen

Report Subject:	Darien Mamon
Origin Location:	Oneida, New York
Current Location:	Tucson, AZ
Subject Age:	27
Subject Status:	Viable

The handhold crumbled away leaving the left hand supporting all of his weight. Unprepared for the stress, his fingers strained at the sudden change and lost, causing him to let go. Time slowed perceptibly as awareness increased, a result of the sudden rush of adrenaline. His heart, beating ferociously, drowned out all other sounds, thumping in his ears like the echo of a bass drum. He fell.

The first impact against the rocks shattered his arm, destroying any chance to grab a handhold. Pain stretched up through his shoulder and across his back, cascading down his spine to his hips. The second hit was a glancing blow, sliding against the rock, pressing the gravel into his flesh like a rash. He thrashed through the pain, seeking purchase on the stone ledge, anything to stop his descent, losing more skin from his fingers and palms. It did not help and he was thrown into free fall again. The tree limbs broke his ribs, flexing just enough to fling him away after the impact.

He came to rest in a heap of pine needles, dirt, and broken rock.

"That didn't wake him?" Dr. Hollister's hands flashed across his writpad. "I thought for sure he'd have woken up at the initial fall."

Octavio Medina perked up. "Do you think that means your sessions are working? He stayed in the dream-sim all the way to the bottom. Is his fear of heights lessening? We're way behind schedule on this one, Randy."

"I know, I know," Dr. Hollister said. He searched through simulation files on his screen. "I'm going to try to add some new elements. Maybe if we induce some other fears, at low intensity, of course, it will lessen the effects of the greater phobias." Dr. Hollister selected another nightmare, loading it into memory, and pressed the 'commit' key.

"You're playing Dr. Jekyll, Hollister," Octavio Medina said. "If this doesn't work, it'll be years before we can even come close to a proper replacement."

"There are other methods we could be using," Hollister said. "We could try actual situations, not simulated. A few of those might lessen the intensity."

"Something outside." Octavio Medina rubbed his hands together.

"Well, the floors in the central hub scare the bejesus out of him but I think the effect isn't as pronounced as it once was. I think we're on the right path, but we need to up the ante if we're going to meet our deadline."

"That's a good idea, Randy." Octavio Medina headed for the door. "Call Helen and have her schedule it."

The images flashed through Darien's head, rolling into his thoughts, rolling over his history. Which ideas were his? What fear owned him? The air left his lungs and he lay face down on his hospital bed gasping and grasping the steel bars on the sides.

Legs garbed in white pants and comfortable shoes hurried to the bed to disconnect tubes and wires from Darien's arms and chest. He couldn't see their faces. Their voices blurred like vision underwater, meshing together into a drone of similar audio frequencies.

The owners of the legs and feet unlocked the wheels and guided the bed out of position before fading away, allowing the bed to move down the corridor, propelled by the unknown. Darien pressed against the mattress, trying unsuccessfully to lift himself, his face falling back to the sheet.

Is this a hospital?

The infected environment spoke silent words. It was dirty, not visibly but you knew it was, there on the floor, at that spot on the corner, on the handle of that door or the button of the elevator.

The bed stopped at the end of a hall. A transparency dissolved across the sheets and Darien found himself able to see through the mattress like the glass of the central hub. He could feel the impermanence of plastic and through it he saw, stacked along the floor, stainless steel bins like those used in cheap 'all you can eat' buffets. Row upon row stretched wall to wall in the now expanding hallway. The hospital bed faded away to nothing, leaving Darien floating mid-air like a ghost trapped between planes and dimensions.

Present in the stainless steel bins, fading in as the bed had faded out, were bodies, small bodies. Children lay within each bin, lifeless and orange.

Small, they're so small.

Some of them babies, some of them toddlers, others as old as ten, lay in the bins, their skin as orange as a sprayed-on tan. Darien's eyes scanned left, his weightless body following his vision until the bins rested directly beneath him. The children were each deformed in some way, broken like the discarded toys of an overindulged brat. The leg of one of the boys stretched out of the bin, stiff with rigor-mortis, appearing more mature than the body of the child should have allowed.

Looking back to his right, he slid through the air like a fog to witness the mutation of girls similar to that of the boy, broken, malformed, no longer holding the beauty and innocence of children but the cracking of time as they crumbled to dust.

Movement off to his right brought his attention back to the bin of a little girl. He reached for her, his heart breaking. She was moving, trying to stand.

Darien's breath came back in a gasp as he snapped upright in his bed. Panicked, he scanned around him. This wasn't a hospital. The floor was the same black acrylic it had been last night.

A dream. It was only a dream.

Darien pulled his knees tight to his chest, hugging them as tears flooded his eyes. The sheets held no warmth, their folds cold and wet. He was six years old again, imagining the monsters that cause a house to swell and creak, trying to make sense of the sounds in the night, imagination running wild until the innocent heating elements, dishwashers, or wind revealed themselves to be the source.

On the desk the writpad buzzed and Darien let go of his knees to wipe his eyes and answer the message. His schedule for the day awaited him. Would he be Dr. Hollister's guinea pig today or would he be visiting the shooting range again?

His upper lip puffed out, making any attempt to speak or lick his lips awkward. Martin had socked him a good one. He had been jealous of Darien's success in the firing maze. He shouldn't have been. Darien didn't care for guns. Martin's violent mem-sims appeared to be wearing off on the young man.

Grabbing up the writpad, Darien read the instructions.

Rest and relaxation, no guns.

That left Larry out of the day's events, Martin too, probably.

After a quick shower, Darien dressed and walked down to the cafeteria. He made a small selection of items from the vending line, picked a plate of eggs, and made his way to an empty table where he seated himself before looking around. The other people in the cafeteria paid him no attention. Over his eggs, Darien wondered what he was going to do with the day. Then, as he dropped a bit of egg onto the sleeve of his shirt, his mind went to Cindy. *Where had she said she worked, Genetibotics?*

On the far side of the cafeteria he found the door Cindy had left through after they had shared a meal. At the table near that door was Nancy, sitting alone, her blond hair cascading across her shoulders. She had always been attractive and Darien noted she had become even more so with maturity.

She hates you, man, Darien's inner voice said to him. His blood started pumping at the possibility of a confrontation. A pit in his stomach grew at the dread of her imminent rebuke. Many times in college she had hit him with a remark so damaging as to drive his self-esteem off a cliff. Her gaze always held the sting of contempt.

You know her, he reasoned. *Maybe she's chilled out a bit now that she's left college.* Darien grimaced at the next thought. *Maybe she'll just slap you and walk away.* He pushed that image away, shoved it down deep. *Maybe she knows how to get in touch with Shara.*

Getting control of his heartbeat, Darien rose from his seat, picked up his tray, and walked toward her. She wore a more professional outfit than most of the other employees in the facility. The grey suit stood out against the mono-color uniforms of almost everyone else present and she ate while jotting notes on her writpad.

"Keep walking, mimic," she said as Darien neared, not even looking up.

"I'm sorry to bother you," Darien said. "Is your name Nancy?"

"Yeah, so?"

"It's Darien, Darien Mamon from South Miami Technical." It wasn't a question but it came out like one, his voice rising at the end in hopes of recognition. He wasn't disappointed. She looked up. She even smiled.

"Really?" She looked him over. "I'm sorry. I didn't recognize you." Nancy dropped the fork and walked around the table to hug him.

Darien accepted the hug gladly, still holding his tray in one hand, and though she had never hugged him before, Darien felt like he had come home. He was sure she had never liked him.

Nancy pushed him away to look at him. "I'm so sorry I didn't recognize you before."

"That's all right," Darien said, putting down his tray. "It's a weird environment."

"What happened to your lip?" She lifted her chin and pointed.

Darien's hand went to his face. *I must look awful.* "Oh, I got into a disagreement with a friend."

She smiled. "Yeah, that sounds like you."

"You should have seen it last night. I looked like a completely different person. Most of the swelling has gone down."

"Does it hurt?"

"A little." Darien rolled his lips over his teeth.

"What have you been doing since college? I haven't seen you since—" she shut the statement down at Darien's grimace.

Darien took a deep breath and answered her question. "I've been working at a few different companies, coding mostly. Have you been here this whole time?"

"No." She reached down to flip her writpad facedown and continued. "I went on to get my doctorate, Shara too." She smiled. "Holy crap! She's going to flip when I tell her this."

"You're still in touch with her?" Darien's face flushed.

"We weren't just acquaintances, dumbass." There it was, her old nickname for him. She winced at the familiarity and said, "Sorry, old nicknames die hard. I won't use it anymore." She looked him up and down and asked, raising her eyebrows, "You're not still an asshole, are you?"

"I am, but I am no longer in denial about it. Means that I can make necessary adjustments to reduce the intensity."

"Smart-ass," she was still smiling. "Yeah, Shara finished her doctorate and started working here before me. She's my boss." Darien took in a sharp breath and she squeezed his arm. "Calm down, Romeo. She's married."

Darien's heart sank. "Married? That's great!" he faked excitement. "Is he a good guy?"

"Better than you," she said winking. Her writpad buzzed and she flipped it over and read it before shutting it off.

"Damn, I need to go." Nancy hugged him and picked up her things. "I'm sorry I have to run. I really am. Are you free for supper tonight? We could go over old times."

"I'm actually free all day," Darien said.

"I'm not." She hugged him again and said, "Seven o'clock, right here." Darien watched her hustle away before picking up her tray and stacking it with his.

That was unexpected. A cursory nod, a two minute hello, a dismissive wave, those would have made more sense. She had appeared genuinely happy to see him even if she didn't immediately recognize him. You never think your appearance has changed all that much. Then again, you see it every day.

Darien ate his breakfast and dropped off the tray in the kitchen before making his way back to the door to Cindy's silo. Pulling out his new red ID card, Darien gave it a swipe over the sensor and frowned when the sensor light turned red and beeped at him. It needed a code.

Darien drummed his fingers on the door. *I haven't been given code-level authorization to travel the corridors between silos.* It didn't matter. He knew a code. He had seen it work in someone else's memory. Sam had written the numbers on his hand. Reaching back into his memory of Sam's mem-sim, Darien turned his hand, just as Sam had done, and visualized the sequence.

Lifting his eyebrows with a 'here goes' expression, Darien punched the digits from Sam's memory, '36547*.' The door opened with a beep. Putting his ID card away, Darien grinned and walked into the tunnel as if he belonged there.

Chapter Fifteen

<table>
<tr><td>**Report Subject:**</td><td>**Darien Mamon**</td></tr>
<tr><td>**Origin Location:**</td><td>**Oneida, New York**</td></tr>
<tr><td>**Current Location:**</td><td>**Tucson, AZ**</td></tr>
<tr><td>**Subject Age:**</td><td>**27**</td></tr>
<tr><td>**Subject Status:**</td><td>**Viable**</td></tr>
</table>

Hanging every ten feet, shaded and round fluorescent lights lit the tunnel as it stretched into the distance. The tire marks scarring the floor of the tunnel seemed a waking dream. It wasn't his memory he was accessing to find his way and it faded along the edges like a remembered nightmare at the rising of the sun.

Darien checked the pipes and electrical conduits running along the tunnel sides. He couldn't imagine trying to hide behind them and wondered what Sam must have been thinking to consider squeezing himself in there. It looked tight, and Darien reasoned it was probably better to just be caught in an area considered out of bounds than scrape himself to shreds trying to hide.

As in Sam's memory, some lights along the corridor were out, leaving alternating light and dark areas. At the tenth missing bulb, Darien saw an opening to the left and turned in that direction, walking under the dusty sign for Genetibotics.

These silos once housed nuclear missiles and warheads. The tunnels between the silos came much later, after the silos had been repurposed, some of them in preparation for the eventual collapse of civilization, some of them for storage of who knows what, others as dwellings for communities and religious cults. When they eventually became too expensive to upkeep, many were abandoned. It was at this time a wealthy conglomerate bought the silos, all of them. The tunnels were one of the first things completed after the critical gutting and reframing.

Hell of a walk, Darien thought. He hoped he would reach Genetibotics soon. He had to use the bathroom. The tunnels didn't have that function and though Darien was sure at least one of the pipes along the walls was connected to that particular utility, he knew he couldn't just crack it open to take a leak.

The writpad had proved useless. Darien pulled it out shortly after entering the corridors to use as a map but found he was not authorized to view the inter-connective tunnel system. The hanging lights came on and on. The pressure in Darien's bladder grew and only when Darien considered peeing behind the pipes did the door appear in his vision fifteen lights away.

Hurrying to get through the door, Darien used his ID card, *it worked,* and once through, he beelined it to the nearest bathroom.

After his emergency, Darien sat in this silo's small cafeteria scanning his writpad. He searched for Cindy Barnett in the directory and was pleased to discover his writpad automatically connected to the silo system without any trouble. After learning the directory code pattern he found Cindy Barnett registered to sub-level 6, Karsis, row G, number 17. So many more people were in this silo than his own. *How are the silos designated?* he wondered. *What's the name of my silo?*

Ten fifteen AM, read the time on the writpad. That explained why the cafe was so empty. He gazed down the vending line. *No hot food? With so many people housed in this silo?*

Darien climbed the metal painted staircase, happy to feel the strength of the railing as he swung himself around the corner at every landing. At sub-level 6 Darien was breathing heavily, sweat beading on his forehead and around his collar from the climb. He found several branches traveling out from the central hub, each one with a name; Bilbo, Potter, Tyrion, Thargus, Falkor, Karsis, Conan. *Fantasy characters?* He thought, *The place is run by a bunch of nerds. They could have named them after cities, or rivers, or historical warlords like Genghis Khan.*

Cindy answered her door on the third press of the

illuminated button. Her face, still pretty, was gaunt and drawn, her eyes lacking the shine they had in the cafeteria not so long ago. She looked at Darien with a dazed expression only recognizing him after a matter of seconds.

"Are you ok?" Darien asked.

Her bathrobe hung open, showing off the tight tank top and panties. Even though he hadn't seen a naked woman in over a month Darien couldn't get over her face.

"How much weight have you lost?"

She didn't answer, saying instead, "Hi, Darien. Took you long enough to visit." She looked him up and down. "What happened to your lip?"

Darien reflexively raised his hand to his face. "A friend of mine punched me."

"In the mouth? Sounds like a good friend."

"I don't have many friends," Darien said. "I figure I can't go picking any favorites, right now."

She smiled. "Well, I figured after our lunch that you'd be knocking on my door sooner than this." She backed away from the doorway and closed her robe. "You want to come in?"

Darien felt a rush of blood hit his cheeks when she covered up again. Was she embarrassed? Should he be? He walked past her into the room. Inside, Cindy's room was much like Darien's. There was a desk, a bed, and a bathroom. Darien heard the hum of the running bath exhaust fan. He sat down on the edge of the bed.

"I thought you might be from Central Office," Cindy said. "I have an appointment. S'why I'm not dressed yet. They're going to take out the tracker wire."

"The what?" Darien asked as he watched Cindy walk to the bathroom and turn off the fan.

"The tracker wire," Cindy explained. "I think I've had mine for about," she stopped to think, frowning. "As long as I can remember. I don't need it anymore. To be honest, I've only known about it for about six months."

"Did they put a wire on you to track your movements when you started at Genetibotics?" Darien asked.

"I don't think so. It came up on a full body scan last week. Maybe my parents put it in. They were dicks, always making me prove where I'd been. Anyway, I'm getting it out today."

"Where is it?"

"The scan says it's in my leg." She sat on the bed next to Darien and, opening her robe, pointed out a spot on her inner thigh, lifting her foot off the floor. "It's funny. I never felt it until the scan pointed it out." She grabbed Darien's hand and pushed his fingers into the spot she had indicated.

Darien felt around with his fingers, looking for the wire. His focus expanded and he was feeling her thigh, squeezing.

Surprised at his loss of control, he flushed and looked up into her eyes. She was biting her lip.

Darien stopped squeezing, leaving his hand on her thigh and stammered the beginning of an apology before her hands grabbed his collar and pulled him into a violent kiss.

"Ow! Ow!" Darien said, pulling back a little, his lip pulsing with the sudden pressure.

Gently this time, Cindy's lips explored his as her hands left his collar and reached around his back. His hand on her thigh slid around to the outside, pulling her closer. They wrestled like that, overcome with passion, trying to become one with the other, their breathing and heartbeats increasing with every second.

"We shouldn't start this now," Cindy said between breaths, but she wasn't stopping. She pushed Darien onto his back and fumbled with the fasteners on his collar before diving to bite his neck.

Darien's hands pulled the robe off her shoulders and he said, "Why?"

"The Central Office," she said stripping off the robe. "They could be here any minute."

Darien laughed, "Well, then we have plenty of time."

Her hands explored him, gliding over the front of his pants. "It's not too late is it?"

"No. No," Darien said. "It was just a joke."

Darien slid his hands up the back of her tank top and pulled her down to him, kissing her lips, biting ever so gently. She fell onto him, resting her weight on his chest. The heat of her body against his excited Darien. He moved his hands to Cindy's hips, slowly pulling and thrusting his body against hers. Her tongue explored his.

The ring of the door alert snapped them apart. Cindy sat up, grabbed her robe, and threw it around herself. Their shared body heat dissipated as she climbed off.

She smiled and her face flushed as she tied the robe. "Looks like we're going to have to finish this another time," she said.

Darien, still lying on the bed, laughed at the timing. Months and months he had been celibate, with all the time in the world to himself, and the first chance he was given an opportunity to have sex, there was no time.

Cindy checked the vid-screen on the door. Two men in white uniforms waited outside with a wheelchair. "Yeah, that's my ride."

Cindy pulled Darien from the bed until they were standing in a tight embrace. Her eyes looked into his. *Those beautiful brown eyes*, Darien thought. Standing on her tiptoes, she planted a soft wet kiss on Darien's lips. His hands fell to her ass and Darien pulled her against him. She gave Darien one last squeeze and opened the door to let him out and the two uniformed men in.

"Cindy Barnett?" asked the man pushing the wheelchair.

"Yes, that's me."

"Good, if you would just sign here." He extended his writpad as Darien squeezed past them. Cindy reached out and swatted his ass, winking when he turned to look back at her.

Darien walked away towards the metal staircase, back toward his own silo. He could hear her joking with the two men as the wheelchair carried her in the opposite direction. Her laughter was beautiful.

This day had turned out to be a great day. The taste of Cindy's lips lingered. The intensity of her passion made goosebumps roll down his arms and across his back, like a happy spider running a race. As he descended the stairs he looked at the markings designating his location and memorized them. He would be coming back here.

His thoughts of Cindy brought back his topside encounter at the solar devices. *What was her name, the girl? Leslie*, he answered. She looked so much like Cindy, same brown eyes, same smile, same ass. He pictured them together, pictured them kissing, and kissing him. The swelling in the front of his pants brought him back to his senses.

You haven't had sex in months and you want two at a time? You'll never be that lucky, he scolded himself.

I don't know, he argued. *You have a dinner date with Nancy tonight.* The very thought made him laugh out loud. Nancy's romantic interests were miles away from him. He was exactly 'not her type.'

Chapter Sixteen

Report Subject:	**Darien Mamon**
Origin Location:	**Oneida, New York**
Current Location:	**South Miami**
Subject Age:	**24**
Subject Status:	**Non-Viable**

The rows of fluorescent lights shone down, blinding and irritating. Darien awoke in a white bed, plastic and impermanent, disposable for a more sterile environment. His gaze traveled from the lighted ceiling to the walls around him and finally to himself. Clear plastic tubes with clear liquid were taped to his arms. There was another in his foot, and one more in his…

"What?" Darien tried to shout, recognizing where he was. "I can't afford this!" His eyes, wide in their sockets, flashed around the room, taking it all in. Chest heaving, sucking in air, his body preparing for fight or flight, he tried to understand how he had arrived here.

"Not to worry," said the finance professional, his clothing the same white as the surroundings. His hair was black and he had a greasy look to him, like a hitman in those old gangster movies. He was here to represent the hospital. The man grinned. "With your non-verbal consent we were able to garner your future wages until the debt is paid off."

"Why am I here?"

"Well, the A.M.T.—"

"A.M.T.?"

The grinning finance professional cleared his throat. "The automated medical tech," he nodded, "suggested at first that the diagnosis was operational exhaustion, but your blood-work has confirmed that it's a rare form of cancer, Pheochromocytoma." His eyes rolled upward, as if to check his pronunciation, and apparently satisfied, he nodded his head.

Darien was overwhelmed. Even with the gene therapy and advances over the last hundred years, people still died from cancer, and it was expensive. If he survived he was going to be in debt for the rest of his life.

Goodbye, apartment. Goodbye, adequate food. Goodbye, showers.

"Well, we figure sixty percent of your wages until the debt is paid off is sufficient for our forecast."

Grinning that greasy grin, the finance officer left and a nurse unit entered the room, electric gyros whirring softly inside the insulated housing.

"And how are you feeling today?" it asked in a pleasant female voice.

"I'm feeling about as well as you can imagine." Darien's head was pounding. He wiped the sweat from his face and ran the back of his hand across his nose, expecting to see a long swath of blood across it.

The next week was a blurred dream, with time ticking away counted as a series of intravenous bags changing color as they hung suspended around him: Chemicals and saline and nanobots trying to repair his glands. He couldn't afford the femtobots made by the company where he was coding.

You can make and design them, but you can't have them, peasant! he thought wryly.

For two weeks following the initial treatment he spoke only to the nurse unit and the AMT. The finance officer visited once more, grinning all the while, that fake grin you get from real estate purveyors and fast food screen attendants. He was there to change the terms of the care-patient agreement to seventy-five percent.

Scores of nanobots pushed the chemicals, breaking cell walls to force the healing, all while Darien's body tried to fight them off. The results were constant nausea, bursting headaches, and fatigue.

His face pale from regurgitating his morning breakfast, miserable and longing for information, Darien hacked his door panel, forcing it to give him access to the hospital med-net where, after several misspelled searches, he found treatment notes regarding Pheochromocytoma. He shook his head at seeing the information, instantly regretting it as the motion caused his stomach to turn again. *This should have been an easy cure,* he thought, disgusted as he continued reading the small screen. *Minor surgery followed by minimal chemotherapy and hormone replacements.* Long nights, suffering the chemotherapy effects should have been unreasonable. The hospital wasn't following any of the normal treatments.

Finding his med-file, he clicked on it.

Access Denied.

The screen went dead.

Darien heard something in the next room. Someone else was throwing up, and they were having a tough time of it as well. The spasms and shouts of despair echoed. The door to his soundproof room was open a crack, allowing in the sounds of someone else's misery. The AMT usually kept it locked.

Darien peeked out into the hallway. Seeing no one, and no mechanical, he walked to the door of the adjacent room, put his ear to it, and pushed it open. This door wasn't locked either. The sounds of despair did not continue. Whoever had been losing their breakfast appeared to have finished.

He pushed the door further open to peer inside. Walking toward the bed, pale and tired looking was a teenage boy. His eyes brightened at the sight of someone new.

"Hi," he said. "I thought Mr. Sanding was the only person working here."

"Mr. Sanding?" Darien asked.

"The finance officer."

Darien hadn't even asked the grinning fool's name. The finance officer was the only human Darien had seen in three weeks and he never asked for his name.

The boy looked at Darien's hospital gown. "You don't work here? Cancer?"

Darien stared, smiling at the boy, happy to see another person, and realizing he was ignoring the boy's question, answered it.

"No, Capricorn." Darien waited for a laugh. Not getting one for the bad dad joke, he followed with, "Yeah, it is cancer. You?"

"Cancer, a really rare form. It starts with a P but I don't remember it." The boy waved his hand beckoning Darien into the room. "I haven't seen anyone else in," the boy counted in his head, "five weeks."

"You've been here five weeks? These walls really are soundproof. I've been here three weeks."

His name was Philip Tulley. The boy suffered from the same form of cancer as Darien, Pheochromocytoma. Having a common enemy, the two began to spend some of their healthy hours talking together, in one room or the other after that.

Philip was seventeen. Darien was taken aback by how alike they were. They could have been brothers. Philip reminded Darien so much of himself as a teen, except the boy wasn't an asshole. Philip's story was similar to Darien's. His home was a large estate north of the hospital. All of Philip's education came from private tutors and professors. His parents were affluent and he almost never left the estate. When he did, he usually had a contingent of bodyguards and closed vehicles. It appeared Philip's first night in the hospital had been his first time sleeping away from the estate.

Two months passed. Philip and Darien became as close as brothers. Seeing no one else, they comforted each other following the procedures that left them so ill.

Philip had a programming background and he was talented, despite his youth. He had been working on a game prior to Darien's stay at the hospital, and when Darien found out about the game the two dove into the class definitions, interrupts, and functions needed to bring it about.

They worked through their pain and discomfort. Philip's headaches would have him groaning at the screen as he tried to fumble through his coding assignments. Rushes of adrenaline followed every small success, leaving him sweating on his bed and out of breath. The setbacks were many. The successes were few. They found themselves duplicating work when they were apart but also making great progress when they were together.

"I wish I had a bigger screen," Philip said scrolling through his code to find the interrupt required for 'ground attack mode.'

"I think we're lucky to have even a couple of writpads to work on." Darien said as he dialed his writpad to connect with Philip's.

"Maybe we can break into the hospital system and use the ones in the visitor room after hours," Philip posed.

"If we're going to break into the hospital data system, I want a couple of beers. Let's start with the mechanicals. They should be easy enough to hack into."

"I could use a beer," Philip said. "I know, I'm too young, but if I'm gonna break the rules, I'm gonna break the rules."

"I don't know," Darien said. "Dealing with what you're dealing with, I think a beer or two won't hurt you too much. Stay away from those foreign brands, though. The alcohol content in those is a little high."

Every compile left more questions and pointed out more mistakes, instigating a flurry of work for the two. In a matter of six weeks of sickness and coding, they were beta testing game play, discovering new errors. A crash kept occurring when the hero would jump out of a helicopter to attack the game villain and the glitch seemed impossible to get around.

"All right," Philip said. "Jump."

Darien pressed the controller in his hand and watched the hero on the screen leap into the air. A moment of queasiness rolled across the back of his skull at the thought as the hero plummeted toward the ground. The hero's impact was interrupted by the glitch twisting the image of the hero into a warped outline of his shape, half inside out and half normal before the screen froze.

"Did you see that?" Darien hit the back button and jumped the character again. "Look," he pointed out, "during the fall, when the player point of view rolls around him, time slows down a hair. Is that taken into account for the gravity calculation? Pull up the function."

Philip pulled out his writpad and started punching keys on his screen. His fingers stretched the image, moving it around, letting him view the game hero from every angle. "That's it, I think. The calculation is right. But I called the wrong class there to account for the camera rotation effect." Philip scrolled to his mistake and noted the location for Darien. They had been searching for this glitch for two weeks, scanning over the code, rerunning the simulator.

Philip saved the change and restarted the game. Grabbing the controller he switched it to two player mode and handed another one to Darien. "Wanna play?"

"You know I do."

Wearing only a hospital gown and a pair of shorts, Darien stood in the hall. He had gently opened his door, quietly and as slowly as possible, looking for signs of any person or mechanical orderly. Satisfied all was clear, Darien walked to Philip's room and pushed on the door. It didn't open. Placing his ear to the smooth wood he couldn't hear any sounds from inside.

Maybe the boy was having one of the treatments on floor six. Those were never pleasant. Darien made his way back to his room. There was no sense hanging outside of Philip's door. So far, the mechanicals had not shown any signal they were aware of the friendship between he and Philip, and there was no sense in giving those rolling buckets of bolts a reason to start locking them in their rooms again.

When Darien returned later the door was still locked. The vid-clock on the walls noted it was after regular hours for the human staff, not that they ever came to this area of the hospital, but he did see them often on floor six. He cringed at the thought.

I hope he's not still getting a treatment. He's going to be sick for hours.

Darien wanted to play the game again. They had finished it only the day prior and Darien owed an ass-whupping to his young friend. The boy had dominated every scenario they played, laughing at each of his successes.

"You know, Darien, you really suck." Philip hit the reset

button on the screen.

"Well, you keep camping me. Let me get out of the respawn room, you cheating twerp."

Darien left his room again to visit Philip hours later, after lights out, but the situation had not changed. No sounds came from the room. He tried to punch up the electronic chart on the door but it wouldn't accept any code he tried to enter. The last one he tried had been an expletive he typed in frustration.

Still frustrated, he looked around. The hallway was empty of mechanicals and he decided to try some of the other doors.

Locked.

Locked.

Locked.

Open.

He had never ventured this far from his room on his own. Thus far, in his health-regiment/imprisonment, every time he had traveled down this hall he had been on a rolling gurney ushered by a square mechanical orderly.

Darien pressed on the unlocked door and waved his hand just inside to turn on the automated lighting system. Racks of blue vials filled wall to wall white refrigeration units. They stretched from floor to ceiling and glowed with a soft white light inside. As Darien approached each unit the interior light brightened to illuminate the tubes, and though the tubes themselves were blue, the liquid contained in them was a deep red. *Blood.*

Each vial in this refrigerator rack had a name printed on it, Jackman, Vance. He checked the next, Wallace, Jennifer. Every rack held a different name. In his head Darien did the math. Twenty racks per fridge, sixteen fridges, three-hundred and twenty names. Next to each name on the vials was the word Pheochromocytoma. "You have a rare form of cancer, Pheochromocytoma," they had said to him. It didn't seem rare at all.

Darien looked at the dates of Jennifer Wallace and noted they were fairly recent, no more than a few months old. *Is Jennifer still a patient?* Checking the writing on the front of the rack again Darien read, 'Jennifer Wallace: Deceased.'

He scanned back to Jack Vance, "Deceased," he said aloud.

"Deceased," Darien said scanning the next rack. He read the racks from top to bottom in the refrigeration unit, all deceased. Taking a deep breath as he raised his eyebrows and rolled his eyes, Darien moved to the next unit.

"Dead, dead, dead, dead." He moved to the next unit to find the same results. Refrigeration unit after refrigeration unit, the outcome of the patients were all the same.

Noticing they were arranged alphabetically, Darien found his own name.

"Mamon, Darien: status pending." He cracked his neck and stretched a little, mumbling to himself, "Well, that's good news. I was worried I'd be deceased."

A thought occurred to him and searching the refrigeration racks he looked up another name, Tulley, Philip.

'Deceased.'

His shoulders drooped as the pit fell into his stomach. In a daze, Darien walked out of the refrigeration room. The pinpoint lighting cans, operating under limited lumen output this late at night, shone down in small circles. Darien felt he was looking into the past. The hallway stretched away from him, making the walk to his room, and to Philip's room, longer than it actually was.

They got the game working yesterday.

Only yesterday.

Philip's laughter echoed in Darien's ears. Now, the only things ringing in Darien's ears were silence and emptiness. They finally played the game. Victory after victory had washed over Philip in a few moments of joy. Had that been the moment Philip had been waiting for, playing the game? Would he have held on for another day if he had lost? Darien had read once about terminally ill people holding on to life until they reached the end of a book or video series, unable to let go until they knew the outcome. Had that game been Philip's reason?

Darien walked away from the rooms and down the hall to the elevator banks. He pressed one of the buttons. It did not light up. He pressed another to the same result. Grief took him. Tears landed at his feet as his head hung low. The spasms of his sobs buckled his knees and he fell to the floor in front of the silver of the elevator doors, gasping for breath, taking long gulps of air in between his bellows of sadness.

Spent of emotion, he lay exhausted in front of the elevators. This boy, this child had been his friend. He had been innocent, strong, funny, and he had always been happy to see Darien.

That's only because there wasn't anyone else. He brushed away the thought.

The coolness of the white tile floor against his face snapped him back to his senses. Sitting up, he looked around. Was this a hospital or a prison? He had joked about it before. Now, he looked at his surroundings with a new eye. How many racks were in that room? Was he free to go or would he be kept here until it said 'deceased' next to his name?

"If you're looking for Mr. Philip Tulley, please be informed he is no longer among the living." The mechanical's voice was soothing.

Darien left his room that morning not caring if anyone or anything saw him. He was going to leave.

As he passed Philip's door he stopped to run his fingers on the smooth cool wood when the mechanical orderly spoke to him in that soothing female voice. Darien hated the voice, always a stark contrast to the appearance of the mechanical's square and dark grey form. It moved to confront him on the hidden wheels that allowed the unit to glide silently along the corridors.

Darien pulled his fingers away from the wood, clenching his fingers into a fist and walked slowly back to his own room. When he returned he was holding the stainless-steel intravenous stand upside down. The first hit shook the mechanical orderly unit to the left.

"Excuse me, sir," it said in its soothing voice.

The second hit smashed the top right corner forcing a crack to run down the side. "Stop this act. You will be charged for my replacement." Darien pushed it over as it tried to flee on its hidden wheels and swung the stainless steel intravenous stand again and again until it stopped talking.

Sweating from the exertion, Darien looked down at the unit at his feet. The intravenous stand clattered to the floor as he let go of it, the sound echoing down the corridor. The cool white of the hallway light changed to a dark red as ear piercing alarms began to sound.

He walked to the elevator and pressed the button. It did not light up. He pressed another call button, this one on the second elevator. With a satisfying sound, "bing," the call button glowed with a yellow light.

The doors opened. Standing inside were four mechanicals. However, these were not mechanical orderlies. Man-like in appearance, these were the more expensive control units, black, sleek bodies with a single glowing blue spot crossing back and forth across the facial area. They stepped menacingly into the red lights of the corridor. Two of the units grabbed Darien by the shoulders and spun him around to face back toward his room. He pushed against them as they walked him past the destroyed nurse unit and the silver intravenous stand.

The mechanicals never left his room after that. As night fell and the lights dimmed, two mechanical control units would stand with their backs to the door and power down. Darien didn't know if they were actually off, but at least the blue dot would stop sliding left and right. One night, out of sheer boredom, Darien poked one of them only to have it power up instantly and take a step toward him.

The treatments and tests continued, but now Darien was more than happy to travel to the unpleasantness on the sixth floor if only to get a glimpse of another human. The people there never looked at him.

Are they already counting me among the deceased patients named on the racks of the refrigeration room?

Weeks later, the car salesman, greasy grinner, was back to inform Darien he was clear of the cancer.

"And good day to you Mr. Mamon," he said, opening the door. "I have a few forms for you to sign." He walked past the mechanical control units to the edge of the bed.

"Hello, Mr…" Darien trailed off, sounding more like a question than a greeting.

"Oh, don't worry. My name isn't important to you. In fact, this might be the last day you ever see my face."

"It's only the third day I've seen your face," Darien said.

"Too true. Too true," he said. A writpad appeared in his hand and he motioned for Darien to type his name in several locations on the digital forms, following each with a fingerprint scan.

"What is all this for?" Darien asked.

"You're being discharged."

"Why?"

"You're cured. No reason to keep you in here any longer. The results came back about a week ago."

The greasy grinner looked back at the mechanical control units. "Break a few rules, did you? How long have you been in solitary?"

"Three weeks."

"Shame," he said, shaking his head and looking over the marks on the writpad. "If we had seen this result when it was determined we could have saved you a lot of money."

"So, I can leave today?"

"Almost immediately." Greasy grinner pressed a button on his writpad and a mechanical orderly arrived.

"Where are the clothes Mr. Mamon was wearing when he collapsed at work a couple of months ago?"

"They were placed in the patient storage." The mechanical pointed to the locked and sealed cabinet on the wall.

"Hmm. We probably should have had those cleaned. Still, who knew you were going to get well?"

Two middle aged men in uniforms entered the room. "Hello? Is this the patient leaving today?" one of them asked.

Greasy grinner nodded, smiling. The two men took hold of Darien's arms, pulled him from the bed, and roughly removed the hospital gown, leaving him standing naked.

"Are his personal effects in the storage compartment?"

"I think you'll find they are."

The uniformed man on Darien's left twisted Darien's arm, incapacitating him, and said to the other, "I've got a hold on him, Ned. Can you open the storage compartment?"

Ned retrieved Darien's items from the compartment as Darien winced in pain at the wrenching his arm was getting.

Darien twisted his head to read his assailants name tag, *George Wells*. "Hey, George, I don't think you need to be so physical."

George applied a bit more pressure and Darien decided to shut up.

The pair marched him naked through the door into the hallway and over to the elevator bank.

"Have you seen the new SHD 67?" Ned asked George.

"The shuddergun? No, but I've heard we're going to be getting them. Have you used one before?"

"Just once. They leave a hell of a bruise. It's just the thing if you get an unruly patient." George twisted Darien's arm a bit more, emphasizing his point.

"Why don't we just use the stun guns?"

"Sure, I suppose you could," George answered. "But the shuddergun works like a bullet proof vest getting hit by a bullet. It spreads the impact across a wider area to reduce the lethality."

"Dumb as a bag of rocks," Ned said. "Just another way to reduce our effectiveness." The elevator doors opened and they ushered Darien inside.

"You work in a hospital, now. We're not supposed to kill them anymore," said George as he pressed the button for the lobby.

"Do you mind if I get dressed?" Darien asked and got another twist in response.

"Well, just be careful not to drop them," Ned said, "I heard an SHD 67 went nova and exploded over in Kentucky. Killed six people."

George laughed. "The thing was thrown from the roof of a building. If you play with fire, someone's going to get burnt."

When the elevator doors opened, George and Ned walked Darien all the way through the lobby and out the front door. Releasing their grip, they dropped him naked on the sidewalk with his pile of dirty clothes.

"Have a good day, sir," Ned said to Darien as he closed the door.

Chapter Seventeen

<pre>
Report Subject: Darien Mamon
Origin Location: Oneida, NY
Current Location: Tucson, AZ
Subject Age: 27
Subject Status: Viable
</pre>

"Who is Octavio Medina?" Darien asked Mrs. Mouse, who was a lot nicer when she wasn't reprimanding him.

"He's a board member for PEPM." Mrs. Mouse opened a drawer and, pulling out a small container of mints, offered one to Darien. "But, I haven't met him. He shows up about once a year and spends a lot of money keeping this place running to not release any significant product." Helen put the mints away after popping one in her mouth. Sucking on the mint, she was silent a few seconds while she logged off of Darien's writpad. "Ok," she said around the mint, "this is all set," and handed him back his writpad.

Helen, her name is Helen, not Mrs. Mouse, Darien reminded himself. He already had enough irons in the fire without causing trouble with the HR lady.

"What do you mean, we don't produce anything?" Darien took his writpad from her and sucked on his mint.

"The company actually makes a lot of things. They just don't make them here. You work for MemorSingular but it's really just an arm of Phoenix Electronics and Pharmaceutical MicroSystems. MemorSingular makes programs for education and," she lowered her voice to a whisper, "sometimes they do a little work for government intelligence services."

"What? Intelligence services like Larry and Agent Curtis?"

Helen rolled her eyes, laughing. "Those idiots? No, I'm talking about real government boys, not the corporate wannabes."

She actually has a nice laugh, Darien thought. He hadn't thought about Helen much since the last time she talked with him, yelled at him was closer to the point. She was nice.

After his return through the tunnels from Cindy's silo his writpad had buzzed with a new appointment from Human Resources. *So much for a day off,* he had thought grimly. He was so fried from his sessions with Dr. Hollister and his meetings with Larry in security, he couldn't remember if he was coming this way or that. Throw all of that in with his emotions over Cindy, sexual tensions notwithstanding, and his chance to reconcile his tumultuous relationship with Nancy, and he was stuck inside a pattern of cerebral vertigo.

"Your appointment with Mr. Medina begins tomorrow at 9:30AM." Helen raised her eyebrows and nodded her head toward the door in a silent gesture the meeting was over and he should see himself out.

Darien ran his hand over the panel in his room, sparking the music system to life. Out of the speakers the voice of a long forgotten indie rapper shouted his lines into a stage microphone.

Look out people. This is the next step in evolution.
    Solution of the fools who got to start reducing,
    The population, that might at least reduce pollution.
    Put the plan to work, it hurts and then face the retribution,
    Revolution of your ideas and fears introducing,
    Machinery and microchips, electrocution
    Contribution to my skills and still I feel I'm not producing.
    Infusing fantasies, Please, that's how we losing.

My mic is a magnetic prosthetic.
    Integrated circuits embedded, with no anesthetic
    So don't even sweat it. It only hurts if you let it.
    Was simple surgery, splurging, but not simply cosmetic.
    Swerving, nerve system shredded. Now my spine is synthetic.
    Electro-kinetic is it, if you can get it.

Genetically programmed for each man, you just set it.
Do you understand where I'm from? No? Forget it.

Digital anomaly encasing all my arteries,
   Power running through my vocal cords, ejected orally,
   Gorily ripping through my flesh, taking more of me,
   Made of steel, yeah it's real. I was human formerly.
   All meat, metal ripping up inside the core of me,
   Screaming because I'm steaming. There's a puddle on the floor of me.
   Melting as the heat goes up to forge a piece of me.
   And everybody sees but they won't open up the door for me.

Electrical inside my eyes, can't cry.
   Pain got me fetal on the floor screaming out why.
   Too tired to try, too wired to fly,
   String me down to machines with cables and wires and I,
   Can't survive, but I reach for the sky.
   Through the window. Hope I can make it so high.
   Become one with AI. Make my worlds collide.
   Fantasize inside my electric lullaby.

Look out people,
   Because I'm becoming technological,
   Why? I don't even know,
   and didn't even think it possible,
   Or Plausible,
   Don't understand How I became robotic,
   Record company keeping me working,
   To try and make a profit,

Where are we at? In between awareness and dreams.
   Machines keep us alive as electrical teams.
   Street soldiers with weapons busting out of the seams,
   Components get so hot, I'm vaporizing with steam.
   Burns like you can't believe, but it's keeping me clean.
   Scrub away the blood until I start to gleam.
   Beside the scene, I've been powerless to intervene.

And I've seen things you people wouldn't believe.

Put me to sleep because we're getting back to basics,
Use my body for power just like inside the matrix.
I hear a language in the back of my head. I can't place it.
I think it's binary, ones and zeroes, I try to trace it.
Can't escape it. Be careful or you'll wind up wasted.
Wait for the number trip the latch and straight up erase it.
Shoot for freedom, know it's a dream, I know I've got to chase it.
Fresh air, damn. It's the best thing I ever tasted.

Listening to the song, Darien thought back to the mechanicals in the hospital from so many years ago. Each mechanical control unit was basically an emotionless entity doing the job that should have been performed by a human. *Are we becoming obsolete?* he wondered. The song had been written by someone who had obviously felt they were losing their own identity by becoming part of the machine and longing to break free. *Is anyone free?*

Darien lay on his bed and checked the clock. Dinner with Nancy was in half an hour. A dweeb would head down to the cafeteria now. *Are you a dweeb?* he asked himself, and with that thought, Darien fell asleep and missed his chance to sort things out with Nancy.

When Darien awoke from his nap, dinner had long come and gone. He looked up at the white ceiling in his room and berated himself. "You're such an ass, Darien." Even in college she couldn't stand the sight of him. This wasn't going to help.

The walk down to the cafeteria was filled with regret. Just that morning Nancy had been happy to see him. Would she feel the same tomorrow? *No, idiot,* he answered.

Just as he expected, the cafeteria was empty. Even the kitchen staff of mechanicals had shut down. The tables were clean and washed. As he scanned around the cafe and thought about how this was yet another mistake in his long line of failed personal relationships, he put his hands over his eyes and sat down at

Nancy's table where, only a few days prior, he had met Cindy.

He rubbed his eyes, pushing away the sleep sand, and let his gaze travel along the grain pattern in the faux wood until he came across an irregularity. On the table, a couple of feet to his left, the surface held a blemish. He slid along the bench seat until the blemish was in front of him. The normal gloss of the table had been worn off, wiped away as if someone had run their hand along the same spot repeatedly over the span of several years, wearing it down like a wooden bannister in an amusement park line. Darien tilted his head to allow the cafeteria lighting to reflect off the surface, making the blemish easier to see.

It was a number. "704," Darien read. *What could that mean? A room number? A time?* It was a strange place for such behavior. Someone, or some persons, had sat here over and over again, and traced the number into the table. *Who would have been here long enough to wear a pattern like that and why hasn't it been fixed by the mechanicals? The company doesn't seem to have any issues with cash flow. Fixing something like this shouldn't cost much money at all.*

He ran his fingers over the numbers, feeling the difference between the normal gloss and wear pattern before standing up to leave the cafeteria.

Back in his room again, Darien scrolled through the music on the server system, his fingers tapping the acrylic display keyboard as he searched for songs that might break him out of his sour mood. Artists listed on the display in front of him: Spandesire, Sandy Parker, Mandy Annie, First Page Rennie Junkies, 700 Toxic Monkeys, Rhapsichord, Comicon Chronic, Greased Axle Cun—

Darien flipped back to 700 Toxic Monkeys. He didn't know the band that well but it made him think of the numbers on the table seen in the cafeteria. He typed, '704.'

Nothing.

Not seeing anything else worth listening to, Darien selected Rhapsichord from the list. He let the soprano singer tell her story, nodding his head to the mixture of stringed instruments, drums, and DJ.

The illuminated music display went blank and the vid-screen on the door came to life again, the second time in a little over a week. As before, images flashed on the screen in time to the music.

The first image was a picture of him at his home. His mother was holding him on her lap as she read a book. She didn't appear to be reading to him as he was not sitting still in the picture. Darien's little arms stretched away from his mother to reach the plastic drink cup on the table in front of the two. The next digital image was of the staff in his house. It flashed away on the next beat. Reaching out, Darien was able to back up to it. Holding his finger on the screen, Darien kept the image from flashing away again. Using his fingers, he stretched the image, allowing him to zoom in on their faces. One after another Darien recognized them, but not a single name came to mind.

He pulled his hand away, letting the image display continue. The next image was also a picture of people that appeared to be a household staff. Darien zoomed in on their faces and recognized each of them as staff members from his home. Darien scrolled back to the previous image, zooming in on the faces. These weren't the same people. The two images contained staff members of a household that he remembered as his own, but they were two completely different groups of people.

Blinking, Darien flipped between the images. *Her,* Darien remembered, *Mrs. Katz. She was my tutor when I was thirteen. I had a crush on her.* There was no way he could forget that year. He pushed to the second image. A bushy eye-browed man stood in the back of this image. His receding hairline and frown were unmistakable. *Him, Mr. Harris, he was my tutor when I was thirteen.* Darien remembered the unusual man and the way he spoke, leaving the letter 'R' out of every word that should have contained it.

He did not have a change in teachers that year. He remembered the entire year with Mrs. Katz. He remembered copying the equations from her expensive paper textbook into his calc pad so he could cheat on the exams. He also remembered how Mr. Harris had called his father a stupid pissah, leaving the 'R' off at the end.

Darien remembered both events, both experiences, though they conflicted with each other as being concurrent in the same timelines. There was no doubt in his mind it was the same year and, as he questioned his memory, he could not help feeling like he had lived it twice.

Darien sat on the bed and allowed the pictures to flip on their own, still pondering the memory confusion. He had to have had one of the years wrong, but the staff, he remembered the staff from each picture.

Image after image flipped past on the door vid-screen. Memory after memory rang in his brain. The last picture was a distance shot and it stayed on the screen. There was a bridge or a high platform over the ocean. Buildings in the background displayed the logo for Miami Tech. Two figures sat on the platform engaged in conversation.

Rising from the bed Darien walked to the screen and used his fingers to zoom in on the two figures, one man and one female. The man was sitting on the platform and he had something in his hands. It was a sneaker.

Chapter Eighteen

Report Subject: Darien Mamon
Origin Location: Oneida, NY
Current Location: Tucson, AZ
Subject Age: 27
Subject Status: Viable

"Good morning, Mr. Mamon." Octavio Medina's hand stretched out toward Darien. He was about sixty years old, the same height as Darien, and he wasn't wearing a business suit. Octavio wore jeans and a button down short sleeve shirt. His hair had the salt and pepper edge at his temples but was otherwise blond. *Probably dyed,* Darien thought. Smile wrinkles lined Octavio Medina's face and crow's feet adorned his eyes. "Hello, Darien, I'm Octavio Medina. Helen said you'd be ready."

"Uh, yeah," Darien said, taking the man's outstretched hand.

This guy? Darien asked himself. *He's a board member? He looks like a loser.* Darien was surprised at how ordinary Octavio Medina looked. He hoped it wasn't obvious.

Mr. Medina looked him up and down. "So, are you ready?"

"Ready for what?" Darien asked, genuinely curious.

"We're going hiking."

"Oh, I'm sorry," Darien said. "I thought we were just having a meeting."

"Well, you can go to the boardroom if you like but I'd rather be spending my time outside." He glanced around at the walls and acrylic furniture. "I never liked these upgrades they made to my beautiful silos."

Darien looked down at his uniform. "Do you mind if I change?"

"Into what?" Mr. Medina said. "I'd bet your drawers are only filled with uniforms and maybe the suit you arrived here in." He looked Darien up and down. "Was it a suit?"

"No," Darien said, smiling. "It was a shirt and tie, though."

"Well, you're dressed well enough for a hike."

"Is there time for coffee? I haven't had any yet," Darien asked.

"Coffee? Yuck! Bitter stuff. I prefer tea. And no, we don't have time. We should get out there before the sun is too high."

Mr. Medina led the way up the several flights of stairs to ground level. At the exit door he opened a small locked compartment by punching in a series of numbers and letters. Inside were a multitude of supplies to handle the heat and sun inherent to this part of the state. He handed Darien the sunscreen. "Gotta protect that skin. The sun here can be brutal. You don't want a bad burn and neither do I." Mr. Medina donned a hat and handed another to Darien. The last thing he pulled out of the compartment were a couple of backpacks. The backpacks were water pouches allowing one to bring water from the pack through a tube attached to one of the shoulder straps. A closer inspection of the pack revealed a knife, a rope, extra sunscreen, and a couple of protein bars.

"You can never be too careful when you're walking out into the desert. You might get lost. You might get bit by something. You might even run into some bad dudes." He lifted his shirt to show an old snub nosed revolver. "Always be prepared, I say."

Darien tightened the straps on his backpack. "I won't need a gun, will I?"

"I doubt it."

"It's just that I've been working with the security team and I thought maybe I'm coming along as some type of protection. Is that right?"

"No, I don't think we'll need any kind of protection. The gun is just a precaution." Mr. Medina reached back into the compartment. "Sunglasses. The sun is bright enough out there." He handed a pair to Darien. "When was the last time you were outside?"

"I went shooting with Larry not long ago. I think that was the last time."

Mr. Medina waved at the security camera in the corner by the door and the door buzzed as it unlocked. Waving again at the camera, Mr. Medina opened the steel facility exit door.

Glancing up at the camera, Darien followed.

An hour into their hike they reached a steel tower, a remnant of a time when towers were needed every few miles to allow seamless communication between personal devices. A ladder guard surrounded the ladder, its steel bands connecting every few feet to help protect a climber from falling.

Mr. Medina took off his hat and placed it behind a loop on his belt. He looked up at the ladder block set in place to keep anyone from climbing the derelict tower, and said, "You probably aren't aware of your importance to our business, are you?"

"Me?" Darien asked poking himself in the chest. "I'm just a programmer. I'm nobody."

Mr. Medina had taken off his backpack and was searching through the pockets. "Have you programmed anything since you've been here?"

Darien shrugged his shoulders. Should he tell this man the truth? "Not officially."

"Right, with all this technology around you how could you resist the temptation to make your life a little bit easier by hacking a bit of code?"

Darien was a little ashamed. Mr. Medina had hit the nail on the head. He hadn't been authorized to change any code but he had made a few modifications to the systems in his room. Was he in trouble?

"No," Mr. Medina said, reading his mind. The man dug around in his pack. "You're not in trouble. Ah!" he said, pulling out a large set of keys. "They don't have any camera systems or automatic locks out here. It's silly, really. I don't like keys and locks but they don't want anyone climbing the tower. "Mr. Medina fumbled through the keys in silence and finally selected one. He climbed a few rungs on the ladder to unlock the ladder block.

"Are you going to climb this old thing?"

"Yes, I am." Mr. Medina put the keys back into his bag. "And so are you."

"That's a 'no' from me, sir," Darien said. If the air had not been so dry the sweat on the back of his neck would have stained his shirt. He felt dizzy just thinking about the height.

"Don't worry. There's a landing on the top with a railing and everything."

Darien felt his breakfast coming back and, turning away, he threw up, hunched over at the waist, hands on his knees.

"Well, I'm glad you got that out of the way. Any more?"

Darien retched again.

"Tell you what, you go first and I'll climb behind you. Keep your eyes closed and when you reach the top of the ladder the rungs will run along the floor of the landing for two more rungs. Use those to pull yourself onto the landing. At the top, you just sit on the floor and breathe for a few minutes." Mr. Medina was gently pushing Darien toward the ladder but Darien resisted.

"Mr. Medina, you don't understand. This is about as hard as it gets." Darien inhaled deeply. "I feel my heart is going to jump out of my chest."

"In order for things to grow, other things need to die." Mr. Medina guided Darien over to the ladder. "We all need to grow sometimes. Parts of ourselves need to die to allow new and improved attributes to flourish. It'll be easy. Don't look down. Keep your eyes focused on the rungs of the ladder."

Darien took off his hat and placed it in his belt loop. He gripped the ladder and looked up. The vertigo grabbed him and his shoulders slumped.

"Looking up and looking down are pretty bad ideas, right now, Darien. We need to live in the moment, no future, no past."

Reaching up with his right hand Darien started climbing. Soon he was high enough above the ground to be inside the steel protection rings. He didn't look at them. Looking at them would cause him to look out away from the rungs and he was certain the fear of his predicament would cause him to freeze.

Darien focused his mind. There was no tower. There was no ground. There was no Mr. Medina. There was only the ladder.

You're in no danger, Darien, he said to himself.

Yes, you are, he replied and his arms wrapped themselves around the ladder rungs. His eyes clenched shut to push out reality.

In his mind he was falling, falling from the tree, hitting the branches, *meeting Kenny.* His bones broke. Scratches and cuts from the branches covered his shoulders and back. *Oh, he's handsome.* Landing on the ground knocked the wind out of him. *Yes, I'd love some coffee.*

Darien's arms unclenched from the ladder and he continued climbing. Had Mr. Medina noticed his failure? It had felt like an hour but it could have not been more than a few moments. The rungs in front of him passed by as he closed his eyes to shut out the height.

Darien fixed his mind on the memories of Sam Matheson, of the way he liked his coffee, of the way he walked and talked, what it felt like to use his voice, of the way his heart beat so fast when he had met his lover, Kenny. *I'm Sam,* he thought. *I'm Sam Matheson and I'm not afraid of heights.*

Then, Darien was at the top of the tower. He sat with his head pointed down at the steel floor under him, breathing deep, eyes not really open or closed, but in that state where you know you accomplished something profound, something life changing. His fingers pressed against the grit of the rusted floor, feeling the divots and grains of the decaying metal. It didn't give way as his hands pressed. There was no flex in the steel, even rusted as it was. It stayed solid and reassuring, like the staircase.

Mr. Medina came through the hole in the floor and laughed. "You," he said. "That was impressive. I gotta say I didn't expect you to make it all the way to the top." He stood up and put his hands on the railing, looking out at the desert. "Hell, yes, it's beautiful up here." He pulled the hat from the loop on his belt and put it back on his head. "I never had a fear of heights." He turned, putting his back to the railing and leaning on it he asked,

"You all right, son?"

"I think I'll be ok. I just want to sit a moment."

"Straighten your back. Sit upright and stretch your arms out wide." Mr. Medina was doing this while leaning on the railing.

Darien got to his hands and knees, positioning himself away from the hole in the floor. Reaching his left hand forward he grasped the bottom rail of the steel railing and climbed his way to the top rung with his hands until he was standing at the edge. The railing, like the staircase inside the silo facility, had the permanent feel he liked. He began to relax a bit and reflect on what he had managed to do. Darien looked down, and for the first time, he fought back the feeling of vertigo and loosened his grip on the railing.

"You need to step out of your safety zone, Darien. You won't know what you're capable of doing until you try."

Darien looked out at the horizon. Mr. Medina was correct. It was beautiful up here.

"Mr. Medina, thank you."

"Don't thank me yet," Mr. Medina laughed again. "You still gotta get back down."

Chapter Nineteen

Report Subject:	**Darien Mamon**
Origin Location:	**Oneida, New York**
Current Location:	**South Miami**
Subject Age:	**24-27**
Subject Status:	**Non-Viable**

The humidity of the Florida summer drained the life from Darien as he walked. Hair too thick and too long, his hands came away from his head slick with perspiration as he brushed the strands from his eyes.

When was the last time you got a haircut, scrub?

Haircuts were now a luxury. Synapse had a reputation for paying far below the standard wage.

His hands hurt. The coding schedule was always short. Deadlines were tight and increasingly filled with the pressure of losing potential customers. The tighter the schedule the more problems arose to make the task even harder. Sometimes there would be a password requirement Darien didn't meet, forcing him to reach out to another office just to wait for the authorization to do his own job. Too many tasks required learning a new tool, a new system. There was so much to learn and never anyone available to teach or guide entry-level employees.

Darien reached up to his neck and squeezed away some of the stress. There was so much to do. It was the weekend and here he was feeling guilty about not getting enough done, about leaving on time. He had been slipping up. Procedures went into one ear and out the other. There never seemed to be enough time.

The sign at the tram station held more bad news. The tram for the westbound neighborhoods was still out of service from the breakdown suffered the week prior. He walked past the station. He was going to have to walk the whole way home again.

Home, the EasyRest apartment, a hole in the wall, a tube.

He laughed at his misfortune, getting a small feeling of relief from his dark humor. What else was there to do about it?

How does it qualify as an apartment?

Darien checked his pockets, feeling out of old habit that there should be a key in there. *Empty.* The hole in the wall had a hand scanner. A little high tech for a hole in the wall but any corporation that could fit this many personal boxes into such a small footprint was raking in the dough. He longed for an apartment again. Even something small would have felt like a mansion.

Years ago, when he had found himself naked on the street after the medical expulsion, his apartment was already long gone, along with all of his possessions, taken as initial payment for his growing medical bill. His job was gone too. BioMedTricks had been kind enough to notify him in the cancer center during the first week of treatment.

After his stay in the hospital, Darien started over with Synapse. It was a different atmosphere, a new place to hang his hat, but it didn't make him feel like he was getting ahead anytime soon.

Two years at Synapse should have left him with a feeling of security. His seniority level was actually one of the higher ones in the coding group. People came and went so fast it was hard to learn names. There was always someone at his workbench asking how to do the most menial of things. He supposed that must be how he had looked when he had started. To the new employees he must appear to be so knowledgeable about the workings of the corporate maze, but he still felt just as lost as any of them.

Logging into the EasyRest message system Darien scrolled through his notifications.

A notification from Synapse. Not good.

"We regret to inform you that your services are no lon—"

He stopped reading aloud and punched the button, turning

off the system.

Seventeen hours, his shift had been seventeen hours. Darien looked at the clock ticking away slowly. It was one of those clocks, round and white with the number twelve larger than the rest. Three minutes dragged on like they would never finish, as if the anticipation of walking out the door slowed down time.

He shouldered his backpack and pushed open the door, almost groaning audibly at seeing who was waiting outside, Kevin Nesse. Kevin had been hired at Electo Motivations the same week as Darien, creating an unnatural friendship, one based on only one thing. They had something in common.

"How's it going, Darien?" Kevin asked.

"How's it going?" Darien responded, rubbing the fatigue from his neck. "I spent the whole day at the customer service desk. I could punch a puppy right now."

"Did you get the raise you were expecting?"

"No." Darien spat on the ground. "And I can't afford to pay rent this week. I'm out of my box, for sure."

"What do you mean box? The EasyRest apartment?"

Nobody else called them box apartments. They were luxury compact living spaces. Darien wasn't down with those terms. It was a box in a wall space, a tube, a hole in the wall.

"Dude, it's a body bag. You'll find another EasyRest next week. Suck it up."

Darien walked past the homeless on the street, men sitting in unwashed clothes, leaning forward in despair. They held out their hands as Darien walked by them. He walked on. His own clothes hadn't been washed in a week.

The pounding in his head echoed from ear to ear. *You're getting sick again.* He thought grimly.

No, You're fucking not, he argued back. *You can't afford a free clinic, sick boy!* He looked back at the men on the sidewalk and shuddered. How far away was that reality?

Stay on your path and dig your way out, sick boy.

He turned the corner and looked back again.

Those poor men.

A rumble in his stomach reminded him he had not eaten in more than twelve hours. He did a mental check of the funds in his account, added the money he would receive from his weekly blood donation, and stopped at a street fruit vendor, deciding to splurge just a little. He grimaced at the taste. The synthetic fruit was supposed to have the same nutritional advantage of a real apple.

This isn't real food, Darien said to himself. He longed for an apple, a real apple. Continuing on his walk to his hole in the wall home, Darien ate the synthetic apple, the rumbling in his abdomen subsiding from the influx of carbs and sugars.

The streets became dirtier as he trudged along, chewing. Buildings in disrepair showed evidence of jimmy-rigged solutions to obvious architectural problems. Plastic yellow tape spanned across one front porch, signifying a crime scene in block black letters. Three people had been killed in that small one room home six weeks ago. When the police had arrived, they removed the bodies, locked the door, and stretched the yellow tape across the porch. That was the last Darien had seen of the police. Solving crimes in the poorest sections of town did not seem to be a high priority.

One less person is one less drain on the system, he quoted his college paper.

Maybe I could break in and squat there until my finances are back in order. Darien glanced behind him to the tape across the front porch. *Who are you joking?* Darien asked. *You ain't gonna do it.*

Sitting on the sidewalk outside of his block was Mara, a little girl Darien had seen often, waiting alone as her parents worked. Arriving at the family's EasyRest apartment first, she could only wait until her father arrived. He was the only one with the correct print for the hand scanner. Her parents were in horrible financial trouble, as bad as, maybe even worse than, Darien's. The three of them shared a single occupancy EasyRest.

Darien frowned. Personal EasyRest boxes were meant for one. *If anyone finds out they're going to be evicted.*

Darien guessed her age at seven. She was so skinny. She sat staring at the pavement in front of her. Matted and dirty, her hair hung over her eyes in strands and her dress was too large, taken probably from a trash heap.

Darien stopped, looking down at the synthetic apple in his hand. This was more food than she had probably eaten in a week.

"Hey," Darien said to her, holding out the synthetic apple, "are you hungry?"

Her sudden intake of breath answered that question. She reached up with both hands, taking what Darien was offering. She ate the synthetic apple, oblivious to the chunks Darien had chewed away and thanked him in between bites.

The box apartment seemed smaller than usual. Darien climbed in and stripped off the shirt and tie. The tie, Darien looked at it in his hand. The symbol of his enslavement, it hung like a chain around his neck. At one time the world had been full of rampant slavery. For all he was aware it still had not come close to being eradicated.

He scolded himself for his self-pity. He knew he shouldn't have been complaining. He wasn't experiencing anything remotely close to the level of cruelty endured by actual slaves, not by a long shot. However, Darien didn't feel free either.

Working seven days a week, week in and week out, Darien felt he was making no progress. Eighty-five percent of his already meager check went to his debt. Each day Darien worked, some increment of his indentured servitude ebbed away unnoticeably.

And now you're going to be on the street again.

The coding job at BioMedTricks Darien held before the cancer hit him had refused to hire him back. Darien was a bad investment they said, too much of a risk to their bottom line. They had lost money on him, they said. Darien didn't know how. They hadn't been paying him that much.

It was still a lot more than Darien was making now.

A notification appeared on the personal box door screen, a red number, 753. Darien had 753 unread messages, junk mail, porn advertisements, prostitute thank you cards. Darien was a very busy man. He read the headline and opened the body of the message skeptically.

Dear Mr. Mamon, we have reviewed your resume and verified your records from the South Miami University. We feel your skills would improve our profitability in the near future. Please contact us in the soonest possible time manageable.

Henner Mills,
   Phoenix Electronics and Pharmaceutical Microsystems, LIRC

Darien read the message again. They were blunt, mentioning how he might improve their profitability. This was a job offer. *Where is the contact scan?* Darien flipped the displayed page to the Information Highway System, opened the Goo Diamond search engine, and typed Phoenix Electronics and Pharmaceutical Microsystems, LIRC.

The first result showed a towering grey building in Phoenix. There were stock prices listed. *Rising,* Darien noted. The PEPM logo was an image of the letters PEPM surrounded by two half circles of opposite colors, like a yin and yang symbol.

Darien scrolled down. PEPM had their fingers in a lot of systems and several subsidiaries were listed; Genetibotics, MemorSingular, Bytronics, SecondStream. One company caught his eye, BioMedTricks, PEPM. He used to work there.

What am I getting myself into?

"Show me contact information for PEPM."

"PEPM, No contact info found," a computer female voice answered.

"Search contact information for Phoenix Electronics and Pharmaceutical Microsystems, LIRC."

"Found, Phoenix Electronics and Pharmaceutical Microsystems, LIRC," the female voice answered.

Darien passed his scan card over the small screen and reviewed it carefully to make sure the information was identical. His card had been acting up lately. He held up the card to the communication lens and waited.

A young pretty face appeared on the screen. "PEPM," she

said.

"Hello," Darien said, realizing he had not put his shirt and tie back on. "I'm Darien Mamon."

"Yes?"

"I just got this mail that your company might be interested in speaking to me about a position?"

"Oh, that's good news for you," she said. A number of forms appeared on the screen beside her. "If you're interested in a position with us you will want to fill these out. Please, press the 'acknowledge' button on the screen and then press the 'submit' button in the bottom corner when you're finished." She pointed at the bottom right corner of Darien's screen.

"OK," Darien said. As he pressed the 'acknowledge' button the visual connection to the pretty woman slid away and the forms took center screen. He racked his brain, trying to remember the information needed for the forms and entered the data to the best of his ability. *Isn't this all available in a database somewhere?* He knew it was. This exercise seemed unnecessary. Reaching the end of the last form, Darien pressed the 'submit' button and the pretty woman slid back into view.

"Very well done," she said.

Darien asked the question, "Wasn't all of this information available from my public record?"

"Yes, it was." She scrolled through the forms Darien had filled out on her end of the video conversation. Darien could see his information displayed backwards and faded as if he were looking through the back of a piece of paper. "We like to have an understanding of how much you know about yourself."

Odd, Darien thought.

"Everything seems to be in order. We will send a pod for you straight away."

She waited until Darien nodded his head.

"Now, if you will just swipe your hand over the screen so we can get your hand print?"

Darien complied.

"I think that's it, Mr. Mamon. Your travel pod should be arriving shortly. Good day."

The screen blinked out and Darien reopened his email account.

Pages and pages of junk mail stared back at him. He could easily have missed this message.

The pod glided in, lowering gently down onto the sidewalk outside of Darien's EasyRest, the nicest one Darien had ever seen, nicer even than the several his parents had owned. The exterior's gloss white reflected the rays of the setting sun. The pod door opened and a cool, calm voice invited him inside.

"Good morning, Mr. Mamon," it said. "This pod will bring you directly to MemorSingular, a Tucson division of Phoenix Electronics and Pharmaceutical Microsystems. Miami to Tucson travel time: three hours and forty-three minutes."

Dropping his bag, Darien slid into the chair and activated the safety harness system. As the door closed he found himself deactivating the safety system and getting back up.

"Wait just a moment, please," he said as he pressed the exit panel and stepped outside.

Hair matted and tangled, her dress too large, synthetic apple gone, Mara waited. She sat looking at her feet, bare and dirty as they were. Darien walked to his box, scanned his hand and punched in a few passcodes. He opened the box door and looked for anything else of value he might need. *Nope.* Everything he might have wanted had been thrown hurriedly into the bag now resting on the floor of the pod.

"C'mere," Darien beckoned Mara over. She didn't move.

She doesn't know you. Can you blame her if she doesn't trust you?

She looked at him, seemingly ready to run if need be.

"Ok, don't come here," Darien said. "After I get back in the pod, then." Darien pointed to the scan unit. Red lights were blinking and increasing in frequency. If a new hand was swiped, the lights would stop and the system would beep confirmation of the change. Otherwise, the system would time out. Darien reset the light frequency to allow more time for confirmation. "Swipe your hand here and the EasyRest is yours for the rest of the week. I don't think I'll be back."

Stepping back into the pod, Darien sat down in the chair. As the door closed he heard the confirmation beep of the EasyRest scan unit.

A blast of heat embraced Darien as the door to the pod opened. Entirely different from Florida's oppressive humidity, the Arizona heat was like standing in front of an oven. When the wind and heat teamed up, it hit like a giant hair dryer, taking Darien's breath away.

Surrounding the pod was a sea of solar panels reflecting the pink of the evening sky. The sky surprised Darien instantly. It opened up wide before you, displaying the vibrant sunset. A rainstorm, miles away, stood as a single isolated red cloud. The skies in Florida had been hazy and sometimes gray, perhaps the result of pollution and smog. There, the distance you could see had been limited by the trees and buildings around you. In Arizona the sky stretched away, appearing to go on forever.

Mountains stood in the distance, rising above the earth as if they had been specifically placed there, like decorations on a cake. In a video on a social networking site, Darien had once heard someone call the mountains in Arizona 'dirty mountains.' He had laughed at the expression on the little girl's face when she had said it, her nose crinkled, looking up at her mother from her seat in the travel pod.

"What's up with the dirty mountains?"

Now that he was here, he agreed with her assessment. The mountains lacked the tree cover he was used to seeing over them. Florida did not have mountains of its own but there were many near his childhood home. After a few glances he decided he liked these, even if they did look a little 'dirty.'

The attendant meeting him at the pod wore a suit and tie, dressed impeccably for the level of heat in the air. He wasn't even sweating. His hair was black and cut short and his eyes were a dark brown.

Darien looked down at his own clothes, dress pants, wrinkled. His faux leather belt had splits in it near the buckle and around the holes. The stain in the short sleeve shirt, thankfully, was covered by an orange and grey tie. Looking at the man waiting for him, Darien felt foolish and underdressed.

"This way, Mr. Mamon," said the well-dressed man, extending his arm. The pod had landed on a top of a squat building and the suited man led him to a concrete staircase that brought them below ground level.

Darien followed, wondering if he should start a conversation. Sometimes a long awkward silence can lead to several encounters of long awkward silences. He finally relented and said, "The suit, really nice." Darien looked down at the stain on the edge of his tie. "Does everyone dress so formally here?"

The well-dressed man answered without turning, still walking down the stairs ahead of Darien. "No, sir. But I don't think one should dress so casually." He glanced back at Darien. "I see from your dress that you might disagree."

"Sorry, I couldn't afford a suit."

"No matter. I work for the international subsidiary of Phoenix Electronics and Pharmaceutical Microsystems. We are a bit less casual. I am Takoya."

"Nice to meet you, sir," Darien said, holding the green painted steel handrail for support as he walked down the stairs behind Takoya.

Takoya opened a door at the first landing off the stairwell and motioned for Darien to enter before him. At the end of the hall a thick vault door stood open, attended by a woman in a yellow dress.

"Good morning, Mr. Medina," the woman in yellow said, closing the vault door as if it weighed no more than a folded shirt.

"My name isn't Medina," Darien answered.

"Not yet," she said, receiving a reproachful glance from Takoya.

"Right this way, sir," Takoya prodded again. He led Darien to an office, one level down from the vault door. The sign on this door read, 'Henner Mills, Administrator.' She was waiting, slender and lovely, her skin as pale as pearls. Bright red hair fell on her shoulders in curls. Takoya led Darien into the room and stood to the side after he closed the door behind Darien.

"Good morning, Mr. Mamon," the woman said, rising from her chair and extending her hand. "I'm Henner Mills. Welcome to Tucson. You probably have questions for me." She was in her late thirties. Her eyeglasses did little to hide the beautiful eyes behind them.

"You can call me Darien," Darien said, taking her hand. Her fingers were slim and dry. *Soft*, Darien thought. Her hair curled around her face and she had the light scent of lilacs about her. She smiled and offered a chair, which Darien took.

"Ok, Darien, do you have any questions?" she asked again.

"Yes," Darien answered. "This facility—"

"An old missile silo," she answered. "With our level of required security, it is convenient." She smiled again. "You look like you're in good health, Darien. How are you feeling?"

"Fine."

She made a note on her writpad. "Well, then, let's start the first phase of your physical."

"Excuse me?"

"The physical is a condition of your employment here. If you'd rather not, we have a pod waiting to return you to Florida."

"Can you describe the job?" Darien asked.

"Of course," she said. "You will be working directly with our team of engineers in the field of human memory storage and retrieval. I see from your records at the Tech in Miami that you studied this field." She paused. "Your grades were quite impressive until your unfortunate," she coughed, "decision."

"Isn't there a number of candidates available who were not," Darien paused, half unintentionally mimicking her and half looking for a word that wouldn't injure his ego too badly, "disgraced?"

"None with your qualifications, Darien." She smiled again, not looking as genuine as before, and rose from her seat. "If you agree to the physical you can follow Takoya." She gestured to the suited man.

"I'm sorry," Darien said. "I do have a couple more

questions."

Henner Mills raised her eyebrows, leaned on her desk and tilted her head, waiting for Darien to begin.

Darien cleared his throat and asked, "How long after the physical will it be before I find out if I have the position?"

"Oh, we'll know almost immediately. You'll know in a matter of hours."

"Well, that's good." Darien searched for the next question. He had tried to memorize them during his travel time and before he stepped out of the pod he could snap them off one after another. The heat outside and the strange environment seemed to have erased them from his consciousness. "Where is the housing for most of your employees?"

"We house our employees on site. We find that it is more efficient for MemorSingular though difficult for some families."

"What is the compensation?" Darien asked.

Henner Mills punched a few numbers into her writpad and pushed it over to Darien. Looking at the figure Darien's heart raced. He hadn't expected so much. Keeping his face blank, Darien wrote a new number on the writpad and pushed it back.

She examined the new figure and knocked it down by five percent. None of his other employers had bothered to negotiate. They had a whole 'take it or leave it' attitude back in Miami.

Frowning on the outside and jumping for joy on the inside, Darien turned the writpad to him and signed his initials.

With Darien's agreement for the yearly salary signed, she motioned for Darien to follow Takoya again.

"I think you're going to like it here, Darien. I think if you even ask around after you start you'll find some people never leave."

Outside in the hallway, the woman in the yellow dress laughed.

Chapter Twenty

Report Subject:	**Darien Mamon**
Origin Location:	**Oneida, New York**
Current Location:	**Tucson, AZ**
Subject Age:	**27**
Subject Status:	**Selected**

The buzzer rang through Darien's ears, piercing a path down his spine. Under his fingers, the grate of the metal floor vibrated in time with the noise. A chill air, cascading around and in-between his fingers, flowed in through the gridiron. Darien waited for the noise to happen again, keeping his hands on the grate, feeling the cool steel.

Where am I?

Darien scanned away from the floor, searching around him for clues. On both sides of him sat rows of prison cells, their barred entryways closed, dark, empty, *lifeless*. The metal underneath his hands gave way to concrete paths.

It's a prison block. Where is everyone?

Light filtered into the room through square holes in the walls, illuminating the dust in the air like beams of pollution.

He looked up at the elevated gangways crisscrossing the hall. Stairs traveled up to each level, railings continuing on every floor as the gangways extended away toward their destinations.

The buzzer rang again. *Where is that sound coming from?*

It rang again. This time, Darien noticed a blue light flashing in time with the buzzer. It rang again, hitting Darien's spine. The light was five levels up.

He headed for the stairs, taking two at a time. He had to get to the light, to the buzzer ringing down his back. He swung around the railing at the first landing and ran across the gangway to the next set of stairs. The buzzer rang again.

He took the next set of stairs two at a time, running across the gangway to the next flight up.

He looked down and, feeling dizzy, took these stairs more slowly, one at a time in the center of the treads away from the railings. The buzzer sounded once more, lighting the hall with a cool blue light.

At the next set, Darien climbed one at a time with both hands reaching out to steady himself on the rails. Trying not to look down, Darien walked the gangway, still holding the rails to the next—

Darien woke. He pressed himself away from his pillow and sat up in the bed. The buzzer sounded again.

It's your door, idiot.

The walk to the door was shorter than he remembered and Darien bumped into the plastic and steel. Rubbing the sting away from his head, he found the call button and pressed it.

"Yeah, this is Darien." The vid-screen flashed, showing Cindy standing outside, Cindy Barnett. Her eyebrows were raised and she smirked into the screen. Darien pressed the 'unlock' command and the door slid up into the ceiling with a hiss.

Cindy's smile spread across her whole face. Her eyes held Darien and he was unable to look anywhere else. Her smile changed back to a smirk and she crossed her arms, berating him mockingly, "It's a good thing I know how to check body stats on this panel or I'd have left. I've been ringing forever. You're a sound sleeper. It was like waking the dead."

Darien stared back at her, smiling without knowing why.

"Are you going to invite me in?" she asked, cocking her head.

Embarrassed at his delay, Darien backed up, clearing the door. "Come in."

"I had a little extra time today and I saw on the schedule that you're free as well."

"There's a schedule?"

"Yeah, stupid. Geez, you're clueless." She pushed him until he was sitting on the bed and leaned in to kiss him.

"So this is what you've planned for today?"

Cindy shoved him, laughing. "Oh, you think so, huh?" She put her hands on her hips. "A couple of kisses and I'm all yours? Get dressed. You're coming with me."

"Where are we going?"

"We're going out. We're going into town."

"But I don't have any mo—"

"It's on me. Get dressed."

Darien got up from the bed and she pushed him toward his shower, taking his seat on the bed.

Smiling a crooked smile, Darien spun the handle on the water and turned to look at Cindy. "A little privacy?" he asked.

She closed her eyes as he got into the shower but a few moments later she watched him through the glass, only closing her eyes again when he emerged.

The taxi pod was void of air conditioning systems and they opened the window on the ride into town. The hot breeze was a better experience than the stifled interior.

Cindy held Darien's hand. Her fingers played against his palm as they looked out the window. The desert passed by, each mile nearly indistinguishable from the next, bushes and low trees sliding by, blending into each other. If it had not been for the approaching skyline and mountains with their unique rock faces changing their location on the horizon, Darien might have questioned if they were moving at all.

Tucson appeared around them a little at a time, first one house on the outskirts, then a small store. The buildings around them increased in number until they were uncountable, stacked on top of each other, so crowded that the sheer number of people living there must have been several million.

The taxi pod stopped at a skyscraper, glass windows reaching into the sky. Cindy stepped out of the pod and payed for the ride by sliding her card against the doorframe. She led the way, still holding Darien's hand.

"Are we going up?" Darien asked, remembering his experience on the derelict tower with Mr. Medina.

"Not yet," she said. "There's a restaurant here on the ground floor I like." Cindy opened the door, ushering him inside.

"How long for a table?" Cindy asked the man at the podium.

"At least an hour," was the reply.

Busy beyond belief, it seemed half the city was here. Packed into tables and booths people ate, drank, or waited for their own turn to eat or drink. As Darien searched for a place for them to wait for their table two people left their seats at the bar and headed for the door.

"Can we sit at the bar?" Cindy asked.

"Yes, of course, you can," the doorman said.

Pushing through the crowd they finally made it to the long mirrored bar and sat in the high stool chairs. Cindy grabbed menus from the stand in front of her and handed one to Darien.

"Pick something."

"Should I worry about the price?"

"I don't have the debt you do but I warn you, don't order the lobster. One, the price is ridiculous here, and two, it's a desert. The lobster isn't exactly going to be fresh."

Darien scanned the menu, turning the pages. "I'll have the chicken."

Behind the bar, a vid-screen with the sound turned off displayed a news story. The newscaster walked around a burned out warehouse and office building. The screen wiped to show the aftermath of an explosion and Darien dropped his menu.

"What's the problem?" Cindy asked.

"I've seen this."

"How?"

"It doesn't matter." Larry Enderby had shown Darien the video.

The newscaster came back on and his mouth moved without sound, explaining the scene and situation when an image of a man appeared on the screen next to him. The man in the image was apparently the one filming the destruction, the one that caused it. Darien recognized the man. It was Kenny, Sam's Kenny.

Darien spilled his water on the bar mid sip and choked,

coughing and wheezing to regain his breath. When he was able to inhale normally, the image was gone from the video screen.

Had it been Kenny or was his mind playing tricks on him again like it had earlier concerning his staff? There was no way there could have been two separate sets of staff employees in the same year. He still remembered both of them. *I must have my years confused,* he reasoned.

"Are you all right?" Cindy asked as she wiped up the water with a linen napkin.

"Yeah." Darien coughed again, one big cough to clear out anything still in his windpipe. His voice was hoarse and raspy. "I just thought I knew the guy on the screen a moment ago."

She turned around to look at the screen above the bar. "On the news? What? Did he win an award or something?"

"No," Darien wheezed. "It was a bit about a terrorist attack. They showed the assailant and I thought I knew him."

"Well, that's gonna throw you off. No wonder you inhaled your drink. How do you know him?" Cindy had her elbows on the bar and rested her chin on her knuckles.

"Know him? No, I don't know him. Sam does."

"Who is Sam?"

"Sam Matheson." Darien coughed again and his voice began to clear up. "I've been watching his memories, living his memories. He was, apparently, an employee in my silo."

"You've been taking part in the memory experiments?" Cindy picked up her drink. "I don't have them in my schedule for at least another three months."

"Really? Why would you take part in those? I thought they only did them in my silo?"

"Well, your silo is the programmer section. Have you been doing any programming?"

"Some, I suppose, but mainly I've been meeting with Dr. Hollister and Larry Enderby."

"Larry is the hothead security fella, right? Kind of stocky?"

"Yeah, that's him. Does he work security in your area, too?"

"No, that's not how I know him. I went to visit Human Resources about some surveillance issues from my childhood, that tracking wire I had removed, the one in my leg. He was there. I couldn't get over how he stared at me. He creeped me out."

"You know, I can totally picture that. He's a bit of a dick."

"Some people have said the same thing about you." Cindy raised her eyebrows, smiling.

"Well, they're not wrong but I'm working on it." Darien sipped from his half empty glass of water. "So, tell me about the tracking wire. Did you figure out where it came from?"

"I still don't know how it got installed without my knowing. Maybe when I was getting my wisdom teeth out?" Cindy rolled her eyes. "My parents were creepy. After I left my parent's house for college there was this company keeping track of me for them. I had to sue my family to get it to stop, nasty business. I still haven't talked to them."

Darien put his water down before he choked on it again. "What was the surveillance like?" He remembered college. The lawyers had wanted to keep track of him, too.

"Oh, it wasn't all that noticeable, I guess. I started seeing the same people everywhere and you think, it's a college, there's lots of people. But they showed up when I wasn't at college, when I was at the beach, when I went hiking, when I traveled across the country. It took a while to figure out what was going on. I eventually confronted one and ran his face through some software and figured out who he was and who he worked for."

"And who did he work for?"

"It was a hotshot private eye firm. Why?"

Darien pushed away his water and, waving down the server, ordered something stronger.

Cindy walked up the stairs. Their meal at the restaurant had been good but it was the conversation that left the impression on Darien. Their childhoods had been similar. Cindy had distant parents. She had a wealthy household, though not at the same level as Darien's. She was followed, spied upon after leaving her home. After college she had a job or two, though she hadn't experienced the same poverty as Darien. Eventually, she had been offered her employment at Genetibotics, PEPM. Her work in biomedicine had made her a perfect candidate for the nutritional studies she had been taking part in. Everything fit together like pieces of a puzzle, like it had been planned out for her in advance.

Walking up the stairs behind Cindy, watching her ass, Darien couldn't get the thought out of his mind. This was too perfect. His job seemed perfectly suited toward him, her job to her. Cindy, like Philip in the hospital, had the same strange upbringing.

She turned the corner at the landing, hand grabbing the railing firm and letting her body swing around the corner on its axis. Darien smiled. He liked to do that too.

At the next landing, windows stretched floor to ceiling with only a horizontal steel bar breaking up the illusion of the wide opening. As he approached the window Darien felt a woozy sensation in his head and he grabbed the railing to slow the spinning in his mind. Leaning forward, Cindy wasn't touching the railing. Her head was pressed against the glass, looking down to the street below.

"We're so high up. Do you feel it. The rush?"

He did not. Darien felt sick and leaned away from the glass, peering from a distance, over the ledge at the small figures below. It was like the looking through the glass floors at the silos. The city moved like the floor of an infested house. Figures barely recognizable as people moved about, intent on tasks needing to be done. Like ants in a nest they moved about, each individually, but each one making up only a small portion of the whole.

Darien sat on the landing, leaning on the railing where it met the two staircases together. Behind him, the gap centering around the staircase fell away like at the window. Realizing this, Darien moved to sit at the outside edge of the stairs on the lowest step leading to the next landing.

"Cindy."

Her head was still against the glass, turning left and right, leaving a grease spot on the window as she marveled at the people below. "Yeah?"

"People watching you in college, when was the last time you were aware of it happening?"

"I told you. It ended after I confronted my parents."

"Yeah, you did say that. But, are you sure?"

"Why do you ask?"

"Let's just say I know something about being under surveillance."

"Really? What happened to you?"

"I caught them while I was in college. I proved it to my girlfriend and everything. At least I think she believed me."

Cindy pushed away from the glass. "What are you suggesting?"

"I don't know. I just find it strange that our life stories are so similar. It's like we weren't just hired. It's like we were groomed to work in the silos."

"Except you can't look down when you're in the central hub." She laughed. "Are you always so full of conspiracy theories?"

With a grunt Darien got up from his step and started walking down the stairs. Cindy followed. "What?" she asked.

"Being up here isn't fun for me. I want to go back."

Sucking at her teeth, she turned and followed him down the steps, dragging her hand along the steel handrail. "So what other conspiracy ideas have you got rolling around in that skull? Moon landing stuff? Mars mission horror stories? Maybe you were killed and replaced with an exact replica? No, no, I've got it. You are from the future."

"Hey, I think it's all as crazy as you," Darien said without looking back. "But, this is the strangest I've ever felt."

"You're not from the future? Too bad. That could have come in handy."

"Oh, the secrets I would possess," Darien played along with her.

"You keep messing with your memories with that Dr. Hollister and I bet it gets a lot weirder. I hope I get a choice on who to work with when it comes to my memory experiments. Hollister's a weirdo."

Darien's legs ached. The climb had been longer than he expected and now walking down the stairs he could feel the jolt as each leg gave way under the weight and caught itself on the step below. At the next landing Darien opened the door to the building interior, thankful it wasn't locked. He was going to have to take the elevator, even if he hated them.

The door opened to a hallway of offices with glass walls. Every door had a complicated keypad panel near the handle, and every door was closed. There were lights on in every office. The glass interiors were draped, vertical blinds obscuring the view of the interiors.

Darien stopped to peer in-between the blinds on one of the offices. Inside was a desk, a vid-screen and writpad. A jacket was draped over the chair. Pushed away from the desk, the chair was visibly stained even in the low light of the office. Someone had a habit of eating at their desk.

"This guy stepped out," Darien said.

"Who cares?" Cindy pushed past him. "Where's the elevator?"

"Wait a minute. I want to check something." Darien pushed on a door to the glass walled office. It opened.

"It's not locked?" Cindy asked. "What's the keypad for, then?"

Darien stepped into the office and sat in the chair.

"What the hell are you doing?" Cindy held the door open. "Get out of there! You're gonna get us in trouble."

"Yeah, in a minute," Darien said, pulling the chair up to the screen. He pressed a short series of keys and the screen lit up, displaying the personal information of hundreds of people. "Just keep a look out."

"You're in? How did you get in?"

"I know a few back door commands, this one worked. Dumbasses."

Cindy leaned out into the hall, looking for any signs they had been discovered. She turned back to Darien. "What are you looking for?"

"Shhh! Not so loud," Darien said. "I've been cooped up for

so long at the silo that I was hoping to get a little information, maybe some public press about PEPM and their history." His fingers danced across the keys. "Might even Goo Diamond a few names and see what comes up."

He typed 'Nancy Williams.'

A public profile of Nancy appeared on the screen. "Wow, what a goody two-shoes," Darien said under his breath. "Not so much as a jaywalking fine."

He typed 'Lawrence Enderby.'

Subject not found.

He typed 'James Curtis.'

Agent James Curtis.

The public profile scrolling past showed records of kidnapping, theft, fraud, suspicion of murder, records fraud, sexual assault, and simple assault. Some of these were convictions. Some were investigations.

Darien scrolled back to the suspicion of murder investigation and rolled through the specifics until he came across, 'witness missing.'

"You gonna look me up, too?" Cindy asked from the door with a snarky attitude. "Maybe you want to look up another girlfriend?"

"Just do me a favor and keep an eye out. I won't be long."

She stepped out into the hall and let the door close.

Not taking the hint, Darien pressed a key and opened another file for the murder investigation.

Three years ago Agent Curtis had been a security specialist for another company, Wessar Inductor Energy. Darien scrolled on, reading. After several minutes he shut the system back down and pushed away from the screen, shuddering.

Illuminated at the end of the row was a sign for the elevators. Men and women lifted their heads from whatever tasks they were assigned to watch them walk past. As Darien and Cindy made their way to the lifts a small fat man in a grey uniform stepped out of an adjacent room and stopped them. His hair was long and pulled into a ponytail at the back of his head. The edge of a tattoo was visible under his collar.

"Pardon me," he said in a raspy voice. "Do you have your building identification?"

Cindy looked at Darien and answered the small fat man, "No, I'm sorry. We don't work here."

"And you're wandering this floor because…" The small fat man trailed off his question.

Cindy smiled and winked at him. "Well, we were using the stairs and we got tired on the way down and we figured we would take the elevator down."

"Down from where?"

"From here."

"What floor were you on originally?"

"I don't know. Sixteen or seventeen?"

The small fat man stood in front of the elevator button without turning his back to them and spoke into a shoulder microphone.

"This is 3327. Confirm trespassers on tenth floor. Please, advise."

"Take into custody, 3327. Assistance is on route," came the reply. The microphone was a speaker as well.

"We weren't trying to cause any trouble. I just wanted to look out of the windows."

"Not really my job to worry about what you were doing in the stairwell, but when you came onto this floor and started snooping into offices I had to call it in."

"We weren't snooping," Darien protested, but the small fat man wasn't listening.

Over the course of the next hour Darien and Cindy were collected by law enforcement. They were handcuffed, searched, brought to the local police station, separated, retina scanned, and run through the system.

As Darien sat in the white-walled holding cell he thought about the building, about the empty office, and wondered how he had managed to infiltrate their computer system so easily. The backdoor password had popped into his head so suddenly. On a whim, he tried it.

And look where that got you.

The database appeared to be official, a government run entity, or maybe he had come across an information repository for a personnel vetting firm. The standard encryption had been in place. Without his knowledge of a backdoor, it would have been unbreakable. Why was it so heavily protected?

The cell door opened. Takoya was waiting.

"Mr. Mamon, will you come with me, please?" He was dressed in a black suit, vest, and tie. Darien winced at the vision, thinking about the heat outside. *How does this man stand it?*

Darien walked out into the hallway to find Cindy standing behind Takoya. She was smiling and Darien smiled back.

"I don't think," Takoya said, "that smiles are in order. You have been accused of industrial espionage by Encapsulated Meta, Incorporated. It is only the weight of your employer and the company's influence that affords you this opportunity at dismissal." He wasn't looking at them and spoke as he walked away, expecting them to follow.

Cindy took Darien's hand and squeezed it playfully.

"I'm afraid you will both be reprimanded and your travel privileges will be curtailed for a period of no less than eight days. You will be confined to the facility."

"How did you find us?" Darien asked.

Takoya stopped at the guard station and signed the form on the writpad handed to him. The officer checked the signature and pressed a button opening a door leading out of the holding area.

"We have our ways Mr. Mamon. There is the receipt trail of the travel pod to the restaurant. There are the security cameras located in the staircase you ascended. There is the satellite tracking of your uniform's embedded signature. Each of those would have led us to you, but it was even simpler than all that." Takoya opened the travel pod door and motioned them inside. "We got a call from the police."

Chapter Twenty-One

Report Subject:	**Darien Mamon**
Origin Location:	**Oneida, New York**
Current Location:	**Tucson, AZ**
Subject Age:	**27**
Subject Status:	**Selected**

Darien was almost glad to be back on Dr Hollister's schedule. He'd been busy for the past week on tasks assigned by Larry, Agent Curtis, and Human Resources. His and Cindy's run-in with the law had been quashed by corporate muscle, but HR wasn't going to let them forget about it. At their direction Darien had spent some time working as part of the janitorial staff. The work had been tedious and terrifying, hours on his hands and knees cleaning the clear floors of the central hub. The janitors laughed at him, watching him clean under the influence of the powerful depth illusion until he passed out from fear. On one occasion he lost bladder control upon passing out, resulting in him having to clean the same spot again.

Dr. Hollister bustled about his office. Headphones in his ears, he bounced in time to music only he could hear. Five writpads sat strewn about the desk. Dr. Hollister typed furiously on one writpad and paced a few steps before grabbing another to fill a page with his thoughts and notes.

Darien walked in, put his writpad on the desk, and sat down in the visitor chair before Dr. Hollister acknowledged him.

"Oh, hello, Darien," Dr. Hollister said. He popped out one ear bud and left the music playing on the other one. "Been gone a while."

"Yes," Darien said, logging in to his writpad. "I've been handling some other duties assigned by HR." He didn't mention the police incident.

"I heard you might have a new girlfriend," Dr. Hollister said.

Funny, thought Darien. *Dr. Hollister doesn't seem the type to be in for gossip.*

"Yeah," Darien said. "I'm feeling pretty lucky about it. Nothing serious, though. It won't get in the way of our work."

"Not to worry. I'm sure it won't." Dr. Hollister turned off the music. "How have you been sleeping? Any changes since I've seen you last?"

"I've been having some strange dreams if that's what you mean."

"No, I meant the frequency of your sleep, duration, levels of fatigue."

"No, no problems there. Just the dreams."

"Stranger than usual? The 'usual' meaning before you and I started working together?"

"Yeah," Darien said. "Is this related?"

Dr. Hollister nodded his head in reply.

"Is this something that's gonna go away?"

Dr Hollister shrugged.

"It would be nice to be able to dream about something more pleasant, maybe a sandwich, or a ballgame, or—" Darien snapped his fingers, "sex. You can hook that one up right? Let's build the next session so that my subconscious opens the sex orgy door in my dreams, say, me and fifty women."

"If I had that level of control, you can bet I'd have that dream every night." Dr. Hollister smirked. "Though, I don't know that you really need more than one woman. Who needs a second boss? I have a hard enough time pleasing one." Dr. Hollister sat down across from Darien. "So, what brings you here today?"

"I thought we had an appointment to continue with our experiments."

"No, I'm sure I canceled that. I have to prepare a simulation for the next subject." Dr. Hollister cocked his head to one side and looked up at the ceiling before he looked at Darien and asked, "What time is it?"

"Around 10AM."

"You're kidding," Dr. Hollister said in exasperation.

One of the writpads on the desk buzzed and Dr. Hollister picked it up to read it. His face paled and he shut the pad.

"What's the matter?" Darien asked, and receiving no answer, he followed with, "Are you all right?"

"Huh?" Dr. Hollister's eyes darted around the room as if his train of thought had come to a shuddering halt. "I can't work with you today," he said. "Some work with a previous subject has gone horribly wrong. We're going to have to reorganize everything to try and meet our deadline."

"Well, I'm here. Maybe I can help."

Dr. Hollister looked dazed. He stared at the calculation board on the wall and turned to Darien. "Again, I'm sorry, Darien. I can't work with you today." Dr. Hollister picked up five writpads from the desk and stacked them under one of his arms. One of the writpads clattered to the floor and Darien picked it up, handing it to Dr. Hollister. Nodding a gruff 'thank you', and without saying another word, Dr. Hollister opened a door to a separate office and disappeared inside.

Darien watched him hustle away and wondered what was up with him. He had never seen Dr. Hollister so flummoxed. What kind of news had he received? Normally, he was such a solid, yet eccentric, personality.

Shaking his head, Darien picked up the only writpad left on the desk and headed for the door. As he passed the gaussian board he glanced to see a strange symbol in the calculations. Greek symbols were standard. Letters are so common in calculations as to be mundane to anyone past the most rudimentary knowledge in mathematics. This calculation had a bird, a burning bird, used in one of the parentheses.

"The hell?" Darien wondered. "Why the hell is he using a phoenix in his calculations?"

Back in his room, Darien powered on his writpad only to see the battery at its lowest point before shutdown. *That's strange*, Darien thought. He'd been charging the writpad all night and only took it to Hollister's office. The battery should have been good for the whole day. Mouthing a popular expletive, Darien hurried to place it on the charging pad. The charge symbol appeared in the top right corner and flashed green to indicate the battery was charging.

The battery was still too low to do any work but Darien thought it might be a good idea to check his schedule. Seeing as his appointment with Dr. Hollister had been canceled, he had a block of free time, a rare occurrence. Cindy might be available and there was ample opportunity to connect with her about getting lunch together.

He touched the screen and the password function popped up.

That's weird. The pad should have recognized his biometric signature. Darien typed in his password.

"Login Failed."

He entered his password again.

"Login Failed."

Darien didn't want to visit HR to get this fixed. Who knew what assignment they might push onto his schedule if he messed up again? He entered his password.

"Login Failed."

Darien hit his hand on the desk next to the writpad and his mind flared into anger. He had punched in the right numbers. The last time he had moved his fingers slowly so there could be no mistake.

"What?" Darien said and followed up with, "What?" Frustrated, he started punching in random numbers.

5150, nope.

5551212, nope.

6575309, nope.

123, nope.

704, the lock screen flashed away to reveal a list of books and papers about mind memory calculations. There were folders of videos, test subject theories, and numbered files.

Darien looked from the screen to the writpad itself. The scratch on the corner had not been there this morning. The mustard stain on the keys was missing.

This isn't my pad. This must have been one of the writpads Dr. Hollister had spread across his desk. Dr. Hollister must have my pad.

The number 704 had opened the writpad. Was this really Hollister's writpad or someone else's?

The number 704 is on the cafeteria table.

He flipped his fingers across the screen, looking through the numbered files. There it was, file 704. After a brief moment of hesitation, Darien double tapped the file and it opened to reveal a collection of seemingly random numbered documents.

Darien clicked on the first one to find a list of relocated PEPM employees. The second document was also a list of relocated employees. The third document was the same.

Pushing through the lists, Darien found the employee origin locations to be spread around the globe, but the employment relocation was always the same, Tucson, Arizona. Each listing contained records of birth, education, and previous employment. Some records contained the outcomes of memory experiments: failure, insanity, success, death.

Darien scrolled through the lists, scanning the names until he came across a name he recognized, Sam Matheson. The image in the file matched the face he recognized from the mem-sim mirror. He searched through the record to find Sam's listed memory outcome.

Pending.

Chapter Twenty-Two

Report Subject:	**Darien Mamon**
Origin Location:	**Oneida, New York**
Current Location:	**Tucson, AZ**
Subject Age:	**27**
Subject Status:	**Selected**

Darien paced Cindy's room. His walk through the tunnels was spent looking over his shoulder as every whisper of sound echoed behind him.

Hollister must have confused Darien's writpad with one of the five others strewn on the desk and collected Darien's when he scooped them up. When would Dr. Hollister realize he had the wrong writpad? Would Larry and Agent Curtis come looking for him? *Will they just send someone else?* With the knowledge Darien had just acquired he wouldn't be surprised if they tried to kill him.

"You're insane," Cindy said.

Darien flipped through the writpad and the room's vidscreen mirrored the display. "They've been building, with these experiments—" Darien stopped, a thought occurring to him. Explaining what he had found to Cindy, Darien began to realize his part in all this. "The experiments I've been running with Dr. Hollister, they're using them to deconstruct someone's mind. Sam Matheson, he's got to be the subject. They're trying to blur his memories enough so that they can wipe them." Darien clasped his fingers together and leaned his chin on them. "I'll bet he isn't the only one."

"But you're talking about removing memories. I've never heard of anyone who ever had anything like that happen to them. No one has ever been able to do that." Cindy sat on the edge of her bed, her hair still disheveled from sleep.

"Historically you're correct, but what if they didn't erase

them? What if they overwrote them?" Darien pushed his finger along the writpad screen, scrolling the data up. "This place, the silos, is only about thirty years in operation. They might have been working out of somewhere else before. And look at this, file after file, page after page. They're keeping track of so many people from birth."

Cindy was frowning, waving him off. "Overwriting memories? What do you think they're doing?"

"I don't know," Darien said, looking at the screen. "I haven't found proof of actual crimes, yet. But don't forget all the information I found about Agent Curtis. What are they thinking having a guy like that running security?"

"I'm gonna take a shower." Cindy grabbed a towel off the folded clothes pile on the bed. "You can keep talking but I need to get ready for work."

"We studied a little about this in school," Darien said, pacing again. "There was a series of companies in the end of the last century where they were just beginning to work with memory retention. One of the first uses of memory implants was spy work, before the corporations started claiming territory. Governments would implant a memory and use it as a way to smuggle information across international borders."

Darien watched Cindy's form and shape, blurred through the molded glass.

"So, what?" she said. "They would force someone to memorize something and then recall it later?"

"I guess it does sound funny, but that's how it was if you go back far enough. No, they would use a system like the headsets I used in college to implant the knowledge. The person would cross the border and after relaying the information they would be killed."

"So, murdered?" Cindy shut off the water and grabbed her towel.

"The government couldn't wipe memories."

"So, they just killed the spy?"

"I told you, this was an old system." Darien watched Cindy drying herself off through the glass.

"And you think we're involved in overwriting memories from people like this guy, Sam. Why?"

"Good question. Maybe they're getting involved in spying between corporations."

Cindy walked out from behind the glass naked, drying her hair. "How far have they gotten?"

Darien took in her image, choking on his answer, but seeing her act so nonchalant about being naked in front of him he forced himself to calm down.

"It seems from these calculations that the more memories are implanted, the more pliable the subject becomes, and eventually, according to Dr. Hollister," Darien displayed the calculation on the screen, "you can overwrite the whole thing." Darien scrolled the screen to the next formula. "If they overwrote with noise they could just clean the slate."

"That's a pretty stupid thing to do. Wouldn't that make a fully grown baby?" She smiled, winking. "I prefer the old fashioned way."

Blushing at the obvious flirtation, Darien continued. "You would expect that but some of the imprinting would remain. Things like language, common sense, general decency, those would stay instilled in the individual. But the things that make you who you are would be gone, gone with the troublesome memory."

"That's a pretty drastic way to keep a secret."

"Better than murder."

"Barely. Look, I gotta be honest here. I haven't seen anything sinister while working here, a few creeps, maybe. What can we do about it?" Cindy wrapped the towel around herself and drew an imaginary gun from her hip, brandishing it like a spy movie poster. "Do you want me to snoop around in my department a bit? Maybe I can—"

"You're not taking this seriously."

"No, I am. What do you want me to do?" She kept a straight face this time.

"I don't know. I need to think."

"So, if there's no pressing business…"

Cindy took the writpad from Darien's hands and put it on the desk.

"What—" Darien protested a moment before Cindy wrapped her arms around his shoulders and pulled him down, silencing him with a kiss.

Darien looked at the writpad in his hand as he walked down the stairs. As long as he had this, he was in danger. Should he throw it away? Should he leave it somewhere, the cafeteria?

No, he thought. *Dr. Hollister has yours. When he figures that out, he's going to come looking for this one.*

Darien repositioned the front of his pants. His time in Cindy's room had been unexpected. Sex, he hadn't had sex in months. Cindy's body had flexed against his and her lips held the flavor of her minty toothpaste. Even walking down the stairs from her room the memories of their romantic encounter produced physical arousal. He repositioned his pants again.

Had Cindy really understood what he had been trying to tell her? For some reason MemorSingular appeared to be willfully damaging someone's mind. Why? What did Sam have to do with the company?

Leaning against a wall in the staircase, Darien powered up the writpad. A glitch appeared on the screen, a visual display of white noise, before the system calibrated and offered a search bar prompt.

"Memory systems," Darien mouthed as he typed.

Hitting the enter function, Darien read the results. Dissatisfied, Darien typed different words into the search bar. *Records retention.*

Several menu items displayed on the screen. A map of the facility connections showed an entire silo numbered 704. He stretched the image to zoom in on the other silos. Each one of those had a function or subsidiary name attached to it; MemorSingular, Genetibotics, SecondStream. Snapping the image back to its original size, Darien scanned the map for directions to the strangely numbered silo, 704.

He had reached the door to the tunnels, but before he

opened it, he found the bathroom he had used on his first trip here. He always had to pee after sex and he didn't want to try and walk the whole way holding it in.

He leaned against the wall, relieving himself, the writpad on the counter next to the sink behind him.

Silo 704. That's where he was headed next. His mind made up, Darien washed, hurriedly dried his hands under the air blower, collected the writpad, and headed for the tunnels.

"Well, that took you long enough," a voice said out of the darkness.

Recognizing the voice, Darien said, "Larry?"

"Lawrence."

"What are you doing here?" Darien asked.

"I think you know why I'm here. That writpad isn't yours."

Darien's stomach dropped. What kind of consequences awaited him?

"Hollister asked me to find you. Said he accidentally grabbed your writpad instead of his own this morning."

"This one isn't mine?" Darien asked, bluffing.

"Bet you could barely play tic tac toe on it. We followed your signal, well, the writpad's signature. Been visiting that pretty little girl, Cindy?"

"Yeah, I—" Darien started.

"Did she put out?" Larry raised his eyebrows. "Wow, what an ass, and titties like little apples." Larry took the writpad from Darien's hands. The screen was dead. "I bet you had a hard time logging into this. It keeps a separate operating system for any user aside from the primary."

"It does? How does that work?"

"I don't really understand how the system works, but if you are a recognized system user then you will have some level of access on any writpad you pick up." Larry was searching through his backpack, eventually pulling another writpad out of it, Darien's. He handed it over. "Did it accept your password?"

"As a matter of fact, it did not. I thought I was going to have to take it to someone." Darien held up the writpad Larry had handed him. "So, this one's mine?"

"Yeah," Larry shook the writpad he had taken from Darien. "Did you manage to get any use out of this?"

"Some maps, a few games," Darien lied.

"Any porn? That guy Hollister's a real perv, I hear." Larry stuck out his bottom lip. "I might have to give it a once over before I hand it back."

"I did not see any porn," Darien said laughing, still nervous but being careful not to show it.

Larry put the writpad in his backpack and started walking back in the direction of Darien's silo, putting one arm over Darien's shoulder. "Hollister went a little nuts when he realized what he had done. I don't think he understands the level of protection within our system."

"It's that good?"

"The data protection? Agent Curtis hired this crack programmer years ago to build it. Her name is Nancy…" Larry screwed up his face visibly trying to remember something, but a moment later appeared to give up. "Well, I don't remember her last name, but she's a knockout, blonde hair, slender, bit of an ice queen, though. Jimmy got the recommendation from high up. She's supposed to be pretty smart or something. I don't care about all that." Larry rolled his eyes up. "Such a knockout! I've been trying to get her to talk to me for months." He lowered his voice and pulled Darien a little closer. "Did that Cindy broad send you any nudes?"

Darien sighed to himself before he answered, "No." He had known a lot of pigs like Larry. There's one in every room.

Darien knew if he called Larry on his behavior the response would be a brush off or some comment similar to, "We're all pigs inside. I'm just brave enough to be one on the outside too."

As he walked with Larry, Darien tried to get a little more information about Nancy. Was it the same Nancy he knew? Each silo had close to one hundred people working in it. That would not have been possible at their original size, but with the underground expansions, each one could have as many as several hundred people working without too much overcrowding. The chances it was the same Nancy were slim.

Larry started talking about the firing range again. *This guy likes guns.*

"I can't believe how good you did at the range, calm, collected, steady trigger squeeze. So, we're setting up a new scenario outside. Martin doesn't want to come and try it out but you're welcome to see how many bad guys you can drop. The new targets look so realistic. They're a mix of standard paper and hologram."

"They sprung for paper? What's the point of that? Is Octavio Medina coming to use it?"

Larry shrugged. "Maybe he will." He stopped walking and dropped his arm from around Darien. Both hands went to his temples and his face screwed up again. "Will. Will," he said. "Williams!" he shouted. "The blonde's last name is Williams."

Darien jumped a little inside. It was the same Nancy.

Chapter Twenty-Three

<table>
<tr><td>Report Subject:</td><td>Darien Mamon</td></tr>
<tr><td>Origin Location:</td><td>Oneida, New York</td></tr>
<tr><td>Current Location:</td><td>Tucson, AZ</td></tr>
<tr><td>Subject Age:</td><td>27</td></tr>
<tr><td>Subject Status:</td><td>Selected</td></tr>
</table>

Darien opened the door to find Nancy sitting cross-legged on the floor next to his bed. Wearing a buttoned up business suit and with her hair tied back in a ponytail like she used to wear in college, she typed away at her writpad for nearly fifteen seconds before she spoke.

"You stood me up."

Wincing, Darien walked to the end of the other side of the bed and sat, curling his knee up so he could see her while still having the barrier of the bed between them. "I did. I didn't mean to."

"I shouldn't have been surprised. You always were an asshole."

"No, I wanted to come." Darien felt like he was back in college.

She scoffed and got up off the floor. "Do you want to know why I wanted to meet with you?" She sat on the desk and pulled her knees up.

"I assumed you wanted to bury the hatchet between us."

Nancy shook her head. "You're pretty full of yourself." She lowered her voice and spoke slowly. "Let's get this straight. I don't like you. I never have. You're a dick."

Ow, Darien thought, *that stung.*

"You seemed pretty happy to see me the other day."

"That was an act, and no, it wasn't for your benefit. We're all being watched here. I had to fake a romantic interest in you because of the eyes on all of us." Her eyes traveled up to the corner of Darien's room and she pointed. "Hidden cameras, they're everywhere."

Darien's ego shrunk a size.

"You've been under surveillance all of your life," she continued. "I've only been under watch since I met you. I don't understand how you've never seen the extent of it. Those devices you found in college, did you think that was it? You're a walking time bomb."

"Huh?"

"Don't worry. You're not the only one."

"I'm sorry but I don't understand."

"Shara was a mark."

"Shara—"

"She didn't just happen upon you in college. She was supposed to meet you. I wasn't. As soon as she began a romantic relationship with you we were pulled into something bigger than us."

Darien's mind reeled. *Shara?* His breath caught in his throat, threatening tears of frustration and grief.

Shara was a mark? She was scamming me?

Darien swallowed his pain and said, "Look, Nancy, I don't know what you're talking about with this 'bigger than us' nonsense but if you know anything about the surveillance I was under then I want to know about it. I've seen it but I never got close enough to figure out who it really was. I always figured it was the lawyers looking for a way to keep me from receiving my college tuition."

"It wasn't the lawyers. It was this place, mostly."

"That figures. Why?"

Nancy pointed at him. "Why? That's a good question and one not easily answered. I don't even know if you're ready to accept it."

Darien's thoughts would not be silent.

"What did you mean about college? A mark? Shara? What does that mean?"

Nancy let out a deep breath. "You were snooping around inside Hollister's writpad today."

"How did you know about that?"

"Did your password work?" Nancy raised her eyebrows at him. "So, how did you open it?" Before he could answer she said, "704."

704, the number on the table. Nancy's table.

"What is 704?" Darien asked.

"There's a whole silo associated with it. You found it on the map." She pushed out her bottom lip. "Thinking about checking it out? Good luck getting there."

"What's there?" Darien asked, sweat starting to coat his temples.

"You are." She grinned at the puzzled look on his face. "You're there. Everybody is there. I bet Lawrence is there too. Agent Jimmy Curtis is there, for sure."

Yup, she's cracked.

"You were always meant to come here, Darien. That guy Martin you know, he was always meant to come here. That guy Sam you've been getting memories of—"

"Sam?" Darien found himself starting to hyperventilate. "How do you know about Sam?"

"He was always meant to come here. Cindy, that pretty little thing you were," she hesitated, "having sex with so recently, she was always meant to come here." Nancy checked her writpad and made a few passes over the code.

Darien just watched her. He didn't know what to say. "Shara?"

"Part of the system. She's pretty high up here. She has some pretty good connections but I think it's more than that."

"What do you mean?"

"She's so deep in the elite here. I don't know if she was ever being real."

"It wasn't real?" Darien's stomach turned knots. Even after so many years and knowing he could never reconcile his relationship with Shara this knowledge struck like an anvil falling from the sky. He had loved her so. "What's going on? Why is all of this happening?"

"Darien, you're a clone."

"I'm a what? You want to run that by me again?"

"You're not an employee. You are a subject."

"You didn't answer the last question. Here it is again with a new one. I'm a what? And what the hell is a subject?"

"You're a clone. You are also a subject. You're one of the reasons everyone is working in this silo."

"I'm the reason?"

"Not the only reason, but one of them." Nancy got off the desk and lay down on the bed covering her eyes with her hands. "I knew you would have a hard time with this. I was trying to use images and music as a counter effect to Hollister's manipulation of your memories."

Darien closed his mouth. He had not realized it was hanging open. A chill ran across his shoulders. "The pictures," he said. "That was you?" Darien looked over to the door vid-screen. It was currently blank, but the images that had flashed there previously had left him thoroughly confused. "Where did you get all of those pictures?"

"From your files, and from the files of everyone before you." She propped herself up on her elbows and in response to Darien's dumbfounded look she said, "There were others before you, other clones. You're right, the system has been in place for a long time. You, my friend, are a clone of a man named Octavio Medina."

The tower, we climbed the tower.

"I met him," Darien said shrugging his shoulders, feeling stupid.

"No. No, you didn't. You met a clone of Octavio Medina. But," she mused, "I guess that's correct. He is Octavio Medina, now."

"The pictures you had. Some were me. Some weren't. They all looked like me."

"Those were the other clones."

"From, what? From a previous generation?" Darien got up and paced about the room, keeping his composure as best he could. "So, who am I? Am I..." Darien stammered, the questions coming quicker than he could ask them. "Am I real?

My memories, are they just implants?"

"You're getting way ahead of yourself, Darien. You're reaching into science fiction territory." Nancy sat up on the bed and crossed her legs as she talked. Her fingers danced across her writpad. "You're as real as any person walking around. They didn't build you in a lab." She thought a second, cocking her head to the side. "OK, maybe they did do that, but you were born like any other baby. Your parents…" She hit a button on her writpad and the vid-screen sprang to life. A photo of Darien and his parents displayed in vivid colors. The image was soon replaced with another showing his parents looking older and, in the case of his mother, sadder.

Were they even my parents?

He thought of his mother, of the few times she had eaten with him. He thought of his father watching the soccer games from afar. He thought of his expulsion from the estate following their 'deaths' and of the lawyers he had blamed for the surveillance he now knew they were innocent of.

Mom.

"Why were they taken from me?" he asked.

"You were taken out of the program. Your fear of heights made you an unlikely candidate for future uses. So, they cut you loose."

"And why am I here now?"

"You survived the cancer."

Darien walked to his shower and turned on the water. He was feeling sick. The cancer he had survived, the one that had taken Philip's life, Leslie mentioned it the day he met her. She had mentioned it so nonchalantly while working on the solar array. Had she also survived that cancer?

Is that why Cindy and Leslie look so alike? Are they clones of each other?

Nancy sat up on the bed, raising her voice. Darien could just hear her over the sound of the water. "A strain of cancer started hitting all of the clones, the same one. Entire generations were lost." Nancy got up from the bed and walked to the shower. "You should have died. But you didn't, and when they found out that you had survived they began experimenting with the blood taken from you during your treatment. With your blood they were able to build a new treatment. I don't know if it works, yet."

Darien stuck his head under the cold water and snapped upright with a thought.

"Hey! Don't they have surveillance microphones and cameras in these rooms?"

Nancy held up her writpad. "What? Did you think I was playing Donkey Kong while we've been talking? I've spent almost a year on the security systems here. I shut your room down. Well, not down, but I created a loop of you masturbating from past footage."

Darien looked at her shocked.

"You dirty, dirty man," she said, shaking her head. "Nothing is private here. Wanna see the footage of you and Cindy?"

"Nothing is private," Darien said. "Damn, all that stuff I told Cindy about Hollister's writpad—"

"Has already been scrubbed. I knew when I saw it that it was time to include you in what I'm doing."

Darien stuck his head back under the water. The back of his shirt was drenched from the splash. "And what are you doing?"

"I want to put an end to all of this," Nancy raised her hands displaying the space around her. "How long have they been manipulating the global economy? How long have they been in control? So long," she answered, "that they have created clones of themselves in order to retain that same control over their board of directors."

Darien sat on the toilet, drenched, looking up at her. "I don't get it."

"Octavio Medina is a member of the board of directors. He had an army of clones to choose from, to take his place when he dies. Normally, one is chosen from the lot of you and the memories and personality of Octavio Medina are written over the subject's." She winked. "But, since you're the only one still alive due to the cancer, you will cease to be and Octavio Medina will have a new body."

"But…that's crazy," Darien said. "It's not like Octavio Medina will transfer consciousness from the old dying body to a new one," *mine*, Darien amended silently.

"That's correct. He won't." Nancy handed Darien a towel. "Octavio Medina will still die. But, his memory, his knowledge, will live on in a new body. That's what the corporation needs. They're not trying to extend his life. They're trying to retain his mind."

"And what happens to me?"

"You'll be overwritten." Nancy shut off the water. "You'll be gone. It's an all or nothing event. When it looks like Octavio Medina is about to die they will take his memories, all of them, and overwrite yours. That's why the fear of heights is such a big issue in your memory sessions with Hollister. Fear is a powerful thing."

"All or nothing?"

"If any piece of you survives the transfer, then all of your memories will restore over time and the implants of Octavio Medina will fade away. They've actually come a long way with this. It used to lead to insanity."

"What does it lead to now?"

Martin, thought Darien. *Is this why Martin tried to kill himself? He must be going through the same things.*

"If I'm correct, your fear of heights is increasing, not decreasing. Am I right?"

"How should I know? I've always been afraid of heights."

"No, you haven't. It wasn't until that fall from the tree. How old were you, eight?"

"So, what does it lead to? I'm not sure I'd like to live the rest of my days out of my mind."

"Is all of your mind yours, right now?"

Darien shrugged his shoulders, giving the matter some thought. "To be honest, I don't think so." Darien remembered knowing the back door to the computer system in Tucson.

The password came to you out of nowhere.

"I've had some knowledge of things that I don't think I should have had."

"I have to admit," she said, "I've been messing with you for a couple of weeks now, adding, altering, one or two deletes." She twisted the side of her mouth apologetically.

"What?"

Nancy turned her head. "Hold on." She walked back out into the room to check on her writpad. "Just making sure we're still not being recorded." She nodded her head at the screen and over her shoulder she said, "I've been manipulating Dr. Hollister's experiments with you, trying to see if there is anything to salvage." She typed a few commands on her writpad. "Well, the loop of you tugging your favorite toy is holding."

Darien came out of the bathroom and saw the screen, cringing at the visual. "Ugh! Can't you use another loop?"

"No, I don't want anyone studying the video. They should just be glancing occasionally to be sure you're still in here and alone. Besides," she cocked her head to one side and pursed her lips. "This one has an air of believability."

"Not really. I just had sex. Why would I be jacking off now?"

"Oh, they don't know that. I scrubbed yours and Cindy's passionate encounter." She smirked. "As far as they know, it never happened."

"So, you've been messing with my sims, putting information in my head, twisting my experiments with Dr. Hollister, to what end?"

"I don't like you."

"Damn it, Nancy! Stop it!"

She took a deep breath. "If we can keep them from getting too deep into you, we might be able to save your life."

"You just said you didn't like me."

"And if we save your life, we can save others."

"I don't care about others. I care about me."

"And that's why I don't like you."

Darien reached to shut off her writpad and she caught his hand. "Darien, you're either going to work for them or you're going to work for us, one or the other. I can make a few promises. If you work for them, they will eventually wipe your mind and you'll become a replacement for Octavio Medina. Your body will survive but your mind will cease to be."

"That doesn't sound pleasant," he said with a generous helping of sarcasm.

"If you decide not to work for us, I will wipe this memory from you before you get the chance to tell anyone. Then I'll find a way to kill you before they try to transfer Octavio's mind."

"Is there a way I get to live and keep my mind?"

"Yes, you can leave."

"Leave?"

"Escape, if you prefer that term." Nancy sat on the bed. "If you decide to work with us, you will make an escape attempt. We have people and the technology to hide you." She winced and rubbed her eyes. "There's one other option I want you to consider."

"And, what's that?"

"You have a chance to become the most powerful weapon we've ever had."

"I don't understand."

If you stay here and work with me, I can try to disrupt the overwrite procedure using your fear of heights."

"And then what?"

"Maybe, you come back. Maybe, you get to be you again. But now we have control of the board of directors."

"But it could, potentially, leave me insane? I think I'm choosing escape."

The room spun around Darien, his balance only saved by grabbing the side of the desk.

"Darien, don't you see?" Nancy implored, grabbing Darien by the hand. "It's your fears that hold you together. If we can keep a few, I think we can bring you back."

"Excuse me," Darien said before he passed out.

Chapter Twenty-Four

Report Subject:	**Darien Mamon**
Origin Location:	**Oneida, New York**
Current Location:	**Tucson, AZ**
Subject Age:	**27**
Subject Status:	**Selected**

Nancy had fiddled around with his writpad before she left. Darien's password opened a whole new file section. The screen held a distortion, as if the data coming in was encountering an encryption algorithm in real time, constantly shifting. He scrolled through the records, his records.

The first folder had reams of information about his parents, about their employment history, about their time in the company, about their duties concerning him. He was only addressed as subject number 2187.

Subject 2187 had a mother. Her real name was Evelyn Carter. An image of her appeared in the file.

At the sight of her Darien choked up, a tear rolling down his nose. She had been his mother, the only one he ever knew. In the image her hair was cut short and she wore a mountain climber's rig of ropes and clips along with an enormous smile. The image was taken from below while she rested against the ropes grinning down at the camera. Darien wiped the tear away and flipped to her exit profile. She had been instructed during her employment to take the prescribed emotion inhibitors. She had not. She was currently under evaluation in a psychiatric ward. According to the records she had attempted to take her own life several times.

His father's real name was Vincent Solder. His image showed him studying in a classroom, books piled up on the floor next to his desk. He scribbled on paper. Black hair hung over his unshaven face, obscuring one eye. His clothing did not scream wealth but what did Darien know? Darien had no idea of the fashions twenty, no, thirty years ago.

Where is he now?

Vincent Solder's current whereabouts were unknown.

Flipping through the records, Darien found the surveillance companies and their contact information. He found a timeline of his comings and goings, of his relationships, of his encounters. A sub folder beckoned him further and he found that some people he had known had disappeared over the years, victims of foul play, perhaps by the company.

How many people's lives are ruined for the sake of this one corporation? How many corporations are doing this? How many children are stolen from the ones who love them? Darien felt a chill across his neck and a dark thought entered his mind.

Are we loved?

Darien turned back to his mother's page. She had attempted suicide, many times. She loved him and she had been ordered to stay away. What had that done to her? Another tear rolled down his nose.

Where is she? Darien found the address of the psychiatric ward and memorized it. *If I survive this—* Darien looked around himself, at the prison his room had become after his discussion with Nancy. The paths before him all appeared to lead to his ruin, but only one left him with his mind potentially intact.

Darien thought of his mother.

I will find you again.

The writpad went blank. Maybe Nancy had decided he had seen enough for one day. She had told him to act natural as she worked out the security kinks to get him out of here.

The walk to the cafeteria seemed different. Darien walked past people he recognized and, though they seemed to speak to him as they always had, Darien could not help looking for any tell they might let slip to indicate they knew what he was. Perhaps many of them had known all along.

Dr. Hollister knew certainly, Darien thought as he made his way down the green painted metal staircase, hand on the railing all the way down. He didn't swing around at each landing on the rail this time. Too much had been told for his mood to allow any spot of happiness.

Yes, Dr. Hollister would have to have known, being the one preparing the subject for eventual wipe and transfer. *What a snake!* Darien seethed. He imagined Larry's gun in his hand as he confronted Hollister. *One right between the eyes,* he said to himself.

Does Larry know? Darien thought about his friend as he walked down the stairs. *Is he my friend? Larry's too open with his comments to be able to keep any kind of secret,* Darien reasoned. He seemed to be the wrong personality type to be involved in any kind of conspiracy.

He's security. You bet he's involved, he argued with himself. There was also no doubt in Darien's mind, Agent James Curtis was involved.

As he reached the bottom floor and opened the door to the cafeteria Darien was in a foul mood. The lines at the counters were long and he didn't speak to anyone around him. Watching them now, he wondered how many of them were manipulators and how many of them were subjects of the company, clones here to be used, to be prepared like the food on his tray for their eventual end.

What purpose could PEPM have with so many clones? *No, they could not all be clones. Some of the people here have to just be employees. Someone has to fix the networks and adjust the solar panels. Someone has to clean the floors. Someone has to run security. Someone has to fatten the pig.* Darien seethed again at the thought of his conversations with Hollister.

Walking through the cafeteria hall, Darien saw Martin in the last row of tables. Martin coughed and chewed hard on his burger when he saw Darien and waved him over.

"Martin," Darien said, not really wanting to sit with him.

"Go get your tray and get over here." Martin looked excited.

"Uh, yeah, sure."

Darien walked past the food available for this evening and selected four pieces of fried chicken and a salad. On his way back to Martin's table he grabbed a tall glass of lemonade and a cookie.

Don't mention the firing range, Darien said to himself. *No sense bringing up bad blood.* His lip had actually bled.

Martin's smile spread ear to ear as Darien sat down. "I haven't seen you around much."

"That's not surprising is it? You punched me in the face." Darien punched himself mentally.

"Yeah, I know. It's weird and not really like me. You wouldn't believe it but I'm a bit of a pacifist."

"You don't hit like one." Darien punched himself again.

"Yeah, I'm sorry about that." Martin really did look sorry. "I'm finding out all kinds of new things about myself and I can't say I'm happy with all of it. These memory sessions with Dr. Hollister are really getting to me."

Darien winced. His anger at being a subject of Dr. Hollister's experiments had wiped away the guilt he had felt when he thought he was an unwitting collaborator. It blinded him again to the reality that he was not the only one. Martin was surely a subject, like him.

"What kind of things are you doing in your sessions?" Darien took a bite of his cookie. *You should really eat the chicken first*, he said to himself. *But, I really want the cookie*, he argued back.

"Well, we're really working hard on changing some of the things I'm afraid of. Dr. Hollister says we need to wipe away the fear."

"That's a weird way to put it."

"He says that without the fear we can explore new sections of my subconscious. My memory is strong. I can pull things out of my subconscious so easily that it sometimes affects my speech patterns."

"What do you mean?"

"I'll be talking about one thing and get sidetracked with a little memory trail that leads me away from the current topic." Martin took a bite of his burger.

"I'm pretty sure that happens to all of us."

"Yeah," said Martin, chewing. "But mine will make me lose

my train of thought. It's new, just another thing I don't ever remember happening."

Should I tell him? Darien wrestled with his conscience. *If you tell him you might ruin Nancy's cover. Nancy will be caught. They'll find out she's helping you.*

Darien thought about his own experiences with Dr. Hollister. "Do you ever experience memories you don't think are yours, like memories of other people when you are alone or just relaxing?"

"No, that's odd." Martin finished the water in his glass. "What kind of memories are you talking about?"

"Sometimes," Darien began around bites of cookie, "I get an almost deja-vu thing happening about some puzzle I'm supposed to be solving, but I don't ever remember having a puzzle to solve."

"What kind of puzzle? Like a Hexxle Square or like a word search?"

"No, it's more like a code I'm trying to break, like programing."

They ate in silence for a few minutes, each making serious progress on clearing their plates. Darien finished his lemonade and he was preparing to leave the table, getting ready to say goodbye to Martin when Martin grabbed his sleeve.

"There's more," he said. "Please, don't go yet. I've had more serious memory sessions." Martin lowered his voice. "They feel realer than anything I've ever felt before. I've been waking up in my room standing in front of the mirror. My eyes aren't mine. My face isn't mine. Then I snap to myself again. It's like stepping outside, as if the person I've always been has been a sham, a blanket pulled over me for my whole life. I'm not me." Martin pulled tighter on Darien's sleeve. "I'm not me and I never should have been. I'm someone else, a strong powerful man who takes what he wants when he wants it."

Martin let go of Darien's sleeve and backed away from his plate. "I'm eating food I've never liked before. I'm having urges." He covered his face for a second as if to wipe away the feelings. "I'm having these urges where I want to put a knife to my wrist, again. I fantasize that the central hub glass didn't exist and I could throw myself to the bottom."

"You want to kill yourself?"

You have to tell him.

"No, that's just it. I don't want to die, but I want to kill the old me to move on as I am now." Martin pushed away his plate and silverware. "Every day I get this sensation. I am suddenly attracted to women I never felt were sexy before. Like that girl Cindy. She's totally not my type but I can't help but wonder if she is putting out for you yet."

"Martin, I don't think that's any of your business."

"You know what? It's not. But I can't help but think about it." Martin winked and Darien laughed, though he despised himself for it. "And that's a yes," Martin said, smiling.

"So what kind of girl are you usually attracted to?"

"I like a girl with a little meat on her bones. When I grab a woman I wanna feel her body give a little. Cindy's just skin and bones. She doesn't have any of the traits I'm usually looking for in a sex partner."

Darien was a little offended Martin had called Cindy skin and bones. He pushed aside his indignation and his urge to say, 'Hey man, that's my girlfriend!' and instead said, "That's a big change. I don't think that's a thing that can change on a dime."

"It did for me. My taste in food is different. My taste in women is different. I don't like beer anymore. When we were shooting, I could barely keep it down. Did you hear me? Beer! Who stops liking beer?"

"Well, for me there was a period during first year in college. I had way too much. Still can't drink the Untao brand anymore."

"I'm not talking about a hangover event here. I'm talk—"

"I get it. I was just trying to cheer you up a little."

A young woman passing by with a tray leaned in to speak quietly with Martin. Her light brown hair, pulled back into a ponytail, had let a few wisps fall loose to hang around her face. A strand fell across her eyes and she pushed it away with her free hand.

"Sir, I think you're going to be late for your appointment

with Dr. Hollister," she said.

"Yeah, that's right," Martin said as she walked away.

"A meeting with Hollister?" Darien asked. "This time of the day?" Darien tried to hide his concern.

"I got a message this morning." Martin pulled out his writpad and showed the screen to Darien. "Apparently, I passed some super important milestone in our studies. My status has changed from 'viable' to 'selected.' I'm moving up!"

Martin's words passed through Darien like water around a stone, enveloping but not penetrating. The bottom of Martin's writpad screen showed the change in Martin's subject status. Next to the status was the approval signature, 'Shara Musabayana.'

Martin said goodbye, put his tray away, and headed for the stairs.

And you didn't tell him.

Chapter Twenty-Five

Report Subject:	**Darien Mamon**
Origin Location:	**Oneida, New York**
Current Location:	**Tucson, AZ**
Subject Age:	**27**
Subject Status:	**Selected**

"Feel like hitting the shooting range again tomorrow morning? I could blow off some steam." Larry had interrupted Darien's music playlist, the buzzer ringing right in the middle of *It's Late*, by Rusty Knuckles.

Darien backed away from the doorway to allow Larry to step inside. "I'm not sure if squeezing off a few rounds is really what I need right now. I haven't been feeling very well. I was thinking about taking it easy tomorrow and watching a film."

"A film is a good idea. What the hell was that screeching when the door opened?"

"You can't be serious," Darien said. "It's a classic."

"Classic garbage. Why don't you play something from today? The new song from Tongue Cancer is amazing."

Darien laughed, "Tongue Cancer gives me ear and brain cancer. Now, that's some true garbage."

"Anyway, I want to press the trigger and I can't get anyone to go. I tried Martin already but he wasn't answering his door. We had such a good time last time." Larry sat on the desk.

"Until he punched me in the mouth."

"You're gonna let a thing like a few misplaced knuckles get in the way of your friendship?" Larry asked, smiling and shaking his head, following it up with, "Pansy."

"Martin didn't answer his door?"

"Not to worry, one less person means less waiting and more shooting. I might even let you try my antique Desert Eagle."

"That old thing? Maybe, if you could get your hands on

some rail guns, I might be interested."

"Rail guns, electric? Not too cheap. I think I could manage. What do you think, next week?" Larry asked as he walked out onto the landing.

"Yeah, sure," Darien said, and getting a nod from Larry, he closed the door.

He knows.

Darien argued with himself again about whether Larry was in on the whole cloning business at PEPM. Maybe he was just a victim manipulated by Agent Curtis. He was crass and uncouth but Larry didn't seem one to keep a secret so large. Darien shook his head with a smirk. It was hard not to like him.

Darien did, in fact, feel a little down and he thought of Martin. His mind rolled through the potential outcomes from his cafeteria meeting with Martin. *Why didn't he answer his door?* Darien checked the time, 10 PM. Sessions with Hollister rarely went longer than three hours. *It's been more than four.*

Shara had signed the selection contract. *Selection for what?* Nancy had said Shara was really high up in PEPM. *How high?* And Martin had an after-hours meeting with Dr. Hollister based on her signature.

Darien no longer trusted Dr. Hollister. He had admired the man during his college years and had been ecstatic to be able to work alongside him, but all the information provided by Nancy had opened his eyes.

He used you. You, Darien, have been his guinea pig.

When Nancy showed up at his door she appeared to be calm and collected, but after she entered the room and the door closed behind her, she all but collapsed in exhaustion, a layer of sweat around her hairline. Looking now like she hadn't slept all night, she slumped down at Darien's desk with her writpad and said, "Martin has been selected."

"Like for a job, right? He was pretty excited."

"No, selected for transfer." She turned on her pad and looked up at him. "Where did you hear this?"

"At dinner last night Martin showed me his writpad. It said

he had been selected and it was signed by Shara."

"Selected, condemned." Nancy turned her attention back to her pad. "It's all the same. He has been selected for the transfer procedure."

"He's a clone too? You would think we'd all look alike."

"You're not all clones of the same people. Some of you are board members. Some of you are managers. Some of you are engineers. It's the knowledge that's important. It's the continuity, the stability the corporation is aiming for with all this."

"And what are you aiming for? Why are you taking the risk?" Darien sat down on the bed.

"Are you worried I'm trying to screw you, that I'm not telling the truth?" Nancy shut her writpad. "OK, then. Ask your questions."

Taken by surprise at her directness Darien tried to ask his question again but only sputtered.

"Why am I going against the company?" she asked. "It's simpler than you would expect. My father was a great man. He was an executive for Alaskan Lumens. We didn't live in Alaska. That's just the name of the company. High enough in the hemisphere, Alaska goes without nights for months at a time. At least that's where he said they got the name for the company. But he was smart. He was loving. And he was my father. He was also a clone, like you. The cancer strain of his day passed him by. He survived, like you. And he had been pushed out of the program as an invalid copy, like you. Then, the board changed their minds."

"They took your father."

"Yes. According to several laws passed last century, a clone is the property of its corporation." Nancy brushed her fingers absently against her writpad. "He didn't know."

"But, I thought cloning was illegal altogether."

"For the poor. Every law is enforceable against the poor. The ultra-rich act with impunity. They are above the law. And a corporation doesn't go to jail. They pay a fine. The fine becomes part of the cost of doing business."

"And so, without any fear of repercussion, your father was

taken."

"He was."

For the first time Darien looked at Nancy as more than a rival for his girlfriend's time, as more than an adversary who didn't like him. Nancy was a little girl who lost her father. A single tear rimmed her right eye and she wiped it away.

"So, to stop all of this mess," she said, "I'm trying to disrupt the board. I want to put people on the board who are not memory clones of the original members. If I can get one, just one member on there, it will steamroll into two, three, four. Eventually the whole board will be new and the cloning operations might be rescinded."

"So what are your plans?"

"When they choose you, they are going to wipe your memories and you will replace the current Octavio Medina when he dies. If you escape they'll have to start over. I want to make it impossible to replace Octavio Medina."

"I don't understand why they can't just add memories. Why do they have to wipe?"

"They don't want *you*, even you with the knowledge of Octavio Medina. They want Octavio Medina. You will be gone. Like I said before, it's an all or nothing event. Every time in the past, where they went halfway, they terminated the subject as incomplete and started over with a new clone. I guess because they still have the memories on file, they can afford to take the time and get it right."

"They kill the subject of the failed attempt?"

"What else would they do? To them, you're not a person, you're a copy of a person. They have the original files stored in the system so they start over."

"But if they didn't have the memories any longer maybe they'd be forced to work with the combination memory of the validated subject and Octavio Medina. We could delete the original files after a transfer."

Her eyes rolled up to the ceiling. "It would take a special authorization. And unusual circumstances, like a potential breach of security scare." She scrunched up her face. "It's much easier to help you escape. The time they spend looking for you is time not spent on looking for and training the new replacement."

"So," Darien asked, "where am I going?"

"You know what? I don't know and I don't want to know. It's my job to get you out of PEPM and change your appearance in our files so the facial recognition software outside of the company can't track you." Nancy started typing on her writpad again.

"Who's picking me up?"

"I have a pod acquired. You're leaving in an hour."

"An hour?" Darien stood up quickly. "I can't leave in an hour. I need to take Cindy with me."

"No way. Are you insane?"

"After everything you told me I can't leave her behind."

"That's going to take twice as long to prepare and the pod is going to be here in an hour."

"I can't leave her here."

"Are you in love already? You barely know her."

"I didn't say I was in love."

"Men are all the same. One piece of ass and you fall like dominoes. Look at your dating history. Except for Shara, all the others have been—" She stopped herself. "You don't have the best taste in women."

Darien stared at Nancy. "Yes, I loved Shara. I still love her." Darien shrugged his shoulders. "If you're not careful, I might love you too."

"Now you're creeping me out." Nancy's fingers blurred across her writpad as she typed security interruptions into the code. "I'll reset the pod to four hours. Go get your girlfriend."

The corridors between the silos were a bustle of morning activity. More than once Darien had to squeeze to the side to allow a cart laden with white boxes, filled with food or clothing or blankets or who knows what, to zip by. The women driving the carts wore special eye goggles. Maybe the goggles helped the drivers see in the dark. They didn't slow down at all. Darien was sure that if he were to just stand in the middle of the hallway he would have been driven over without a foot to the brake.

At the first intersection Darien tried to remember if it were a left or a right to get to Cindy's silo. While he was trying to decide, a security personnel member approached in a narrow vehicle.

"Sir, where are you headed?" The security officer stepped out of his vehicle.

"I'm trying to get to silo three, Genetibotics."

"Can I have your ID card?"

In his mind he wondered if he could overpower the man in front of him, but he didn't try. "Oh, yeah, it's right here." Nervous, Darien pulled his ID card from his pocket and handed it over, hoping Nancy would have the forethought to account for his presence in the tunnel.

The edge of his collar began to sweat. He rolled his neck and heard the crack of his bones. *I bet that looks confident.* Darien thought. *Work on it.*

"I haven't been stopped in these corridors for three months. Have you guys been cracking down on the cross silo love affairs?"

"No, we've had more reports about unauthorized access and we're trying to find the perpetrators."

"What? Like intruders? Somebody broke in? Why would anyone want to do that? I'm working every day to get out of here for a few hours."

The security member laughed. "Aren't we all?"

"So, do you think I'm one of the intruders? Have you ever seen me in these corridors? Have you ever needed to stop me?"

"No. But you said just a second ago that you hadn't been stopped in three months. Why were you stopped then?"

"I'm afraid that information is classified," Darien said, bluffing. If Nancy hadn't been able to update his information, he'd be caught for sure.

Darien's ID badge passed across the scan and the security member listened to his headset as it relayed information about Darien. His demeanor changed. He stood straighter, almost snapping to attention.

"Do you have any more questions?" Darien asked.

"No, sir."

"What is your badge number?" Darien bluffed.

The security personnel scanned Darien's ID card a second time and he said, "I'm sorry, sir. You are cleared to continue."

"I should think so. You still haven't given me your badge number."

"I'm sorry, sir. It's 2181b. May I continue my duties?"

"Yes, you may," Darien said with an air of superiority.

"Thank you, sir," said the young man as he got back into his narrow vehicle. "Have a good day, sir." He drove away, accelerating quickly.

Inside, Darien felt ten feet tall. He pulled it off. He shook his head, smiling, appreciative of the level of personnel manipulation Nancy was capable of.

The screen flickered and an audible whine mirrored the patterns displayed on its surface. When it finally cleared, Shara Musabayana was sitting behind a large mahogany desk. A black curtain hung behind her, obscuring the windows of her executive office.

"Nancy," she said, "is everything ready?"

"Yes, he's just gone to get his girlfriend."

"That Cindy girl?" Shara frowned. "That's going to be a problem."

"It can't be helped."

Shara paused, tapping her finger on the table. "I want you to know I disagree with this plan."

"He won't leave without her."

"I'm not talking about her. I'm talking about you. Are you sure there isn't another way?" Shara leaned forward. Her dark brown eyes dropping to the desk in front of her. "This could be dangerous."

"It will be. I guarantee it." Nancy checked her writpad, watching Darien and Cindy make their way through the halls of the facility.

"The risk—" Shara started.

"Is worth everything. This is our best chance."

Shara put her hands to her face, rubbing her eyes. "You lied to him. You lied about me."

"Of course I lied to him. Do you really think it's safe to let him out there with that information rolling around inside his head? When they catch him, they're going to search his memory. The less he knows about you, the better."

"What he'll think of me."

Nancy closed her eyes, emphasizing her words with her hands. "Is better than what he'll reveal about you when the time comes."

"Nancy, I'll do my best to bring you back."

"You'd better."

Chapter Twenty-Six

Report Subject:	**Darien Mamon**
Origin Location:	**Oneida, New York**
Current Location:	**Tucson, AZ**
Subject Age:	**27**
Subject Status:	**Selected**

At Cindy's door, Darien hesitated. *What if Cindy doesn't want to go?* What would he be required to do? Would she sound an alarm? Would Nancy be forced to kill her? His hand rested over the call button. *How well do you know her?* He pressed the button.

The door slid up and Cindy jumped out of the room into his arms.

"Are you here for round two?" she asked, kissing his neck.

"I wish it were that simple. Let's go inside."

She pulled at him and the door closed. Her hands wrapped around his hips and grabbed his ass.

She smelled like fresh flowers and strawberries, *her shampoo,* Darien thought. Her lips pressed against his, softly, enticingly.

"Cindy, we don't have time." Darien pushed her back until she was sitting on the bed. "Listen to me. Your life is in danger."

"What? Because of the nutrition trials? I know I'm getting skinny but they've assured me that the trial is nearly done."

"No, that's not it," Darien said, sitting on the bed beside her. "It's more. It's so much more. The physical similarity between you and the girl topside working on the solar panels—"

"Leslie."

"Yes, her. It's not a coincidence. You and her are connected. That's why you look so alike."

Cindy started unbuttoning her shirt.

"Cindy, have you met Octavio Medina?"

"That old bastard? Yeah I've met him."

"Did he remind you of anyone?"

"Not really." Cindy's shirt was now completely open and Darien found himself looking at her breasts as she breathed in and out seductively.

The door vid-screen across from them sprang to life. *Nancy is watching.* An image of Octavio Medina displayed on the screen in bright colors.

"Did you do that?" Cindy asked.

"No," Darien said. "I didn't. I have some help in here, an old friend from college. She's manipulating your vid-screen function. And you might want to button that blouse. She has access to all video signals."

"Why should you need help? Is it about all that stuff you found on that pad?"

The image flashed to another of Octavio Medina, a few years younger than he was in the first image. Another image appeared and Octavio Medina looked younger by another decade. The pictures played in reverse chronological order and in them Octavio Medina looked more and more like Darien Mamon, until they were an exact match.

"What the—?" Cindy said.

Darien took Cindy's hand and said, "I'm a clone of Octavio Medina. I have been raised and educated and trained to take his place in the event of his death."

"Take his place?"

"Hollister is going to overwrite my mind and I will become —"

"What?"

"I'll be gone and Octavio Medina will have a new body, mine."

"And based off the first image, that could be any day." Cindy slid away from Darien. "Clones are illegal. I don't think it is a good idea for us to see each other any longer."

"But—" Darien started.

Another image flashed on the screen. This time an old and wizened woman stared back at them. In the next image she was a few years younger, and younger in the next, and even younger in the next. The images flashed in reverse chronological order until the wizened woman was the exact likeness in appearance to Cindy herself.

Tears began to fall from Cindy's eyes, rolling slowly down her cheeks and leaving wet spots on her still open collar. "You mean I'm a…"

"Clone," Darien finished.

"What? Why? Who was that woman?"

"I don't know. I've never seen her before." Darien reached for Cindy's hand. She recoiled, standing up and backing away.

"And you said my life was in danger. Are they grooming me to become her?"

"It would seem so. I don't know the timeframe, but you, like me, are in line to eventually have your mind wiped so that your body can be used to become the person you're a clone of. If we stay here, we are gone, effectively dead."

Cindy wrung her hands together pacing back and forth in front of the bed. "How long have you known? Did you know the last time you were with me?"

"You know I didn't."

"Where will we go?"

"I don't know that either. There is a pod coming to take us somewhere, but I don't know where that somewhere is."

Cindy shuddered and sat down on the bed next to Darien, buttoning her shirt. Looking into his eyes, she said, "Lead the way."

Darien's room had writpads strewn across the floor and Nancy crawled from one to the next typing corrections into her code.

"Your identity has been changed in the official records, as has Cindy's. I've given each of you new names. Cindy, your new name is Lisa Pallenter. Darien your new name is Lindsay Sue Brentwood."

"Lindsay Sue?" Darien asked, annoyed. "You couldn't just name me Meredith? Evelyn was too feminine? What about Sharon? I've always liked the name Sharon."

"Lindsay is both a boy's name and a girl's name. Whatever we can do to make it a little harder to find you, the better. Maybe, anyone looking into you two will think it's just a couple of girlfriends on vacation."

"You don't think it would stick out?" Darien raised one nostril, making a facial expression he didn't know he was capable of. "I'd remember meeting a man named Lindsay Sue. I couldn't tell you how many Michaels I've met, but a guy named Lindsay Sue, I'd remember that."

"Oh, all right. I'll change it, tone it down." She tapped a few strokes at the writpad. "You're Johnny Brentwood."

"So, what now?" Cindy asked.

"I've cleared the door locks on our path. We should be able to avoid getting into conversations with anyone. The less we make note of our passing— I don't want anyone to remember us. I still have to live here. I can't afford to blow my cover."

"Are there a lot of people like you working against this?" Cindy asked.

"You don't want to know. And more importantly, I don't want you to know. I'm not too pleased you know me." Nancy took a good look at Cindy. "Until we can get you to our memory systems in South America, you're a walking book. They only have to open you up and start reading."

"Are they going to alter my memory?" Cindy looked afraid. "Isn't that dangerous?"

"If they catch you, they're going to read everything you've seen. That includes me. I'm taking a huge risk including you in all of this." Nancy looked like she was ready to call it all off, ready to send Cindy back to her room.

"You've known." Cindy looked at Nancy accusingly. "You've known this all along and you didn't say anything. I have lunch with you almost every day."

Darien stepped in, "You're already helping me. You're already taking the risk." Darien reached out to touch Nancy's hand. "She isn't going to be any trouble."

Cindy gave Darien a look and called him out. "You don't think I'm gonna be any trouble?" She turned her gaze to Nancy. "This one has been holding out on me since the day we met."

Nancy lifted her hands at Darien and turned her attention to Cindy. "Listen here, we had some lunches and I like you. But, this here?" She spread her hands out wide. "This is more important than your life or mine. You can either get in line or —"

"Get in line?" Cindy asked, her tone of voice aggressive.

"Working with two instead of one is going to make everything twice as hard. Do you know how hard it was to get two complete sets of clothing even, one male, one female, in sizes that would fit you?" Nancy's face was turning red. "Piss off, then! Go back to your room."

"Nancy," Darien said, stepping in between the two.

"Darien, she's not helping."

"I'm not going without her."

Nancy pulled him close. "If they catch you—"

Darien shot her a defiant look and Nancy stopped talking.

The door locks in their path had been tampered with so as to allow them to pass through without delay. The cameras along their escape route were manipulated to show a loop of past footage and thus not give away their presence. Nancy even provided a digital bank number and funds to last for several years in one of the globe's poorest regions or for several months in one of the richest.

"The pod will arrive in an hour and twenty minutes. Don't take anything with you. Even the clothes on your back can be used to track you. I've provided a set of clothes for each of you," Nancy said. "Get changed."

"Here?" Cindy asked.

"Yes, here. You've already seen each other naked and I've been watching both of you for some time now."

Glaring at Nancy, Cindy unbuttoned her shirt. Both she and Darien stripped every article of clothing, donning the new ones.

"Do you think we should try and take Martin with us?" Darien asked as he buttoned his shirt.

"I know you're expecting me to say there isn't any time, but it's more than that. He's dead."

"Dead?" Darien and Cindy said simultaneously.

"Yes, dead. He was selected and taken to the memory overwrite procedure. The memory wiped as expected but the implanted memory did not take. Without standard cerebral functions the body died." Nancy was still working writpad to writpad.

"The memory was wiped. The body died," Darien said. "You're talking about a friend of mine."

"I thought he punched you in the mouth," Nancy shot back.

"Yeah, he did do that, but I didn't want him dead."

"I'm not sure there was anything you could have done to change his outcome. Now he's dead and a replacement clone will take his place. You've seen this happen already. Do you remember the purge of rooms that happened last month? We went from having dozens of empty rooms to being full up in a matter of days. This is a big operation."

Nancy walked the corridors with confidence as she led Darien and Cindy along their escape path. The doors opened easily and Darien marveled at the lack of security personnel. New ID cards were hanging from the lanyards around their necks. The new clothes were plain, with neutral colors that would not arouse suspicion if they were to be caught on any of the cameras outside of the silo complex.

After almost a quarter mile traveled within the underground corridors they arrived at a staircase that disappeared up into the darkness. Nancy led the way and beckoned Darien and Cindy to follow her to a small room at the top of the stairs, cramped and dusty.

"This is one of the access escape areas that exist in the event of a tunnel collapse." Nancy slid the latch to one side and opened the door to bright sunlight. Orange desert sand fell in through the newly opened door.

Waiting near the access hatch was a white pod.

"I don't know where this pod is taking you. I do know you will be met at your destination by one of my associates."

Shielding their eyes against the brightness of the sunlight,

Cindy and Darien opened the door to the pod.

"Nancy," Darien said as he turned. "I don't know how to thank you for what you're doing."

"You can thank me when this all works out. Get in the pod."

"You should come with us," Cindy said.

"I can't do that. There is way too much more for me to do here." Nancy started to pull the hatch closed.

Darien remembered all the times Nancy had shooed him away in college, how many times she had not invited him to important events, how many times she had encouraged Shara to break off their relationship. Now, Nancy was risking her life to save him. That he was in danger was unmistakable, but hundreds of others were in the same danger. Why had she chosen him, of all people, to save?

"Nancy, why me? Why are you helping me? You never liked me. How can I know this pod isn't going to drop us in the ocean or land us somewhere frigidly cold?"

Nancy let the hatch fall open again. "I know it doesn't sound right. My father told me I should help anyone that I can. I loved my father like you wouldn't believe. He was wise and strong and always knew the right thing to do. He's the reason I'm helping you."

"Your dad sounds like a good guy. I wish I could have met him," Darien said.

"You already have. You thought he was Octavio Medina."

Chapter Twenty-Seven

<table>
<tr><td>Report Subject:</td><td>Darien Mamon</td></tr>
<tr><td>Origin Location:</td><td>Oneida, New York</td></tr>
<tr><td>Current Location:</td><td>Unknown</td></tr>
<tr><td>Subject Age:</td><td>27</td></tr>
<tr><td>Subject Status:</td><td>Selected</td></tr>
</table>

According to the pod's programming, medicines and vaccines acclimated their immune systems to their destination via air circulation and inhalation.

"The inhaled vaccines do not offer the same level of protection as the standard shots," the pod's computerized voice explained, "but as far as the bio scanners are concerned, there will be no discernible difference." Like the automated vaccinations, the pod's endpoint had been programmed prior to its arrival. Blacked out, the pod windows gave no indication of their destination.

The chairs sat empty as Cindy and Darien huddled together on the floor, leaning against the pod wall, trying to guess what was in store for them.

They sat in silence. Each of them falling into stories of their pasts, looking for any detail that could have led them to this end. Darien already had a pretty good handle on what had transpired behind the curtains of his youth, but Cindy was running blind. What did she really know of her parents? Were her college years and grades a manipulation of the system to guide her to PEPM? Genetibotics had recruited her fresh out of college, making her a few years younger than Darien.

His arm around Cindy, Darien noted that she didn't lean in to him. Her arms wrapped lightly around her knees, head slightly tilted to one side, she stared at the far side of the pod where the floor and wall met, barely blinking. When Darien finally noticed, he thought she might be in shock. He pulled her close and she didn't resist. She didn't respond either. Sitting like that they shared warmth until the pod engine wound down.

The door opened with a hiss, causing Darien's ears to pop from the change in air pressure and he worked his jaw to allow them to adjust to the altitude.

Outside the pod, a cinder block wall surrounded a patio of broken and uneven bricks overgrown by weeds and tall grass. At the opening of the pod door, looking down at them, was Kenny, Sam Matheson's Kenny, the 'I blew up the facility in New York,' Kenny.

Darien felt a flush of emotion as Sam's memories came flooding back, love, anger, safety, and arousal all mixed together blinding and overpowering. Darien's breath stole away as a cloud came over him.

"Are you two all right?" Kenny asked. The question snapped Darien back to his senses. Cindy needed him.

"I'm ok, but I think she's in shock." The proper assistance to someone in shock as foreign to Darien as an ancient language, he asked the only question he thought might help. "Is there somewhere we can take her?" He felt useless. Dealing with the physical needs of others was so far removed from Darien's list of experiences.

Kenny reached into the pod, picking up Cindy with his muscular arms and as Darien followed, Kenny carried Cindy inside and laid her on a bed upstairs. Seeing an extra blanket, Darien threw it over Cindy and lay down next to her.

"There's a lot to talk about," Kenny said, "but it can wait until tonight." He walked to the door. "This door locks from the inside. I have my own key. Don't you open it for anyone else."

"Don't open the door. Got it," Darien answered.

After Kenny left, Darien touched the maroon paint chipping away from the wall next to the bed, feeling the cracks in the plaster. He squinted in the low light of the room, noting the bed, in which he and Cindy were sprawled out, a table, chairs, and an empty bookcase. Feeling the dampness under his clothes, he breathed in the air, humid and warm.

Like South Miami, he thought. *But where are we?*

He put his arm around Cindy and kissed her forehead.

Like you used to kiss Shara in South Miami.

The air carried a conversation in Spanish through the window.

"It figures," thought Darien. He had always told himself language courses were a waste of time. He studied as little as he had to and all he had ever cared about was to get out of the class so he could study something more interesting. Therefore, the only phrase he could remember how to say was 'where is the bathroom.' Unable to decipher any meaning in the conversation outside he turned his attention back to Cindy.

She was shivering, even in the heat of their current climate. Darien climbed under the blanket with her, breathing in the smell of her skin, until the two fell asleep.

Darkness pressed out the light of the day as Kenny arrived with a lit candle and carrying a small tray of bread, cheese, and fruit. Cindy seemed a little more like herself and chose a pear from the tray.

"So I said that we would talk tonight and here we are." Kenny pulled a chair toward the bed and sat. "My contact didn't tell me much about you, just that you were in need of some new identities, a memory purge, and a safe place to lay low. The pod came from a silo in Arizona. Can you tell me a little about what you did for PEPM?"

"Well," Cindy said, "I've been working in the area of nutrition and its effect on the human body for Genetibotics. They had me on all these crazy diets. In the last one I lost fifteen pounds."

"With your frame? That sounds pretty dangerous. Eat something. Eat a lot of somethings." Kenny smiled and held the tray out to her until she chose another piece of fruit. He turned his attention to Darien. "What about you?"

"I've had a couple of different jobs. Officially, I worked for MemorSingular. I was an errand boy collecting signatures from some of the other new employees. After that, I spent some time working with Dr. Hollister on memory experiments. I figured we were trying to increase the realism of the memory files. I worked a bit with security." Darien thought about his last sentence. "No, I didn't really work for security, but I made a friend there. He took me on a shooting exercise where I did pretty well."

"Tell me a little more about your memory work." Kenny put down the tray and pulled over a chair to sit in.

"I've been through several memory sessions recorded from someone named Sam Matheson."

Kenny blanched.

"You were in some of those," Darien said. "You're a good dancer."

"They're using his memories," Kenny said, obviously angry. He tried to hide it but his eyes welled. "Is he dead?"

"I don't know. Is that why you blew up that building in New York?"

"How did you know about that?"

"It was you, wasn't it?" Darien asked.

"Yes, it was me. But it wasn't about Sam. I was in love with Sam. He knew his role in our organization and I knew mine." Kenny selected a piece of cheese from the platter he had been holding and bit it in half.

"What is this organization?" Darien asked, uncertain he really wanted to know. "What is it for?"

"You only know your own history, don't you?" Kenny asked, chewing. "Here, let me guess." Kenny closed his eyes and raised one of his hands as if he were reading the vibes from Darien's aura. "I see a large expansive estate, servants, distant parents, nearly every need or fancy provided. I see college life, happiness, classes and goals easily achieved." He raised his other hand and built his voice to a crescendo. "I see a dream job coming after college with promise of an alleviation of any college or personal debt."

Darien and Cindy sat quiet and Kenny ate the other half of the piece of cheese, grinning at his joke.

"I guess it's easy to see the forest when the trees aren't so close," Cindy said. "Yes, that's my past." She poked Darien. "His, too. His is a bit sadder than that, but it's close enough. I assume you're going to fill us in on the real world. Let me guess," she said mocking Kenny. Cindy closed her eyes and raised her hands. "There's poverty everywhere. People are starving. The corporations control the laws and steal from everyone. A few brave and brilliant people are fighting back against the evil empire." Her volume increased to the last word, building suspense as Kenny had done.

Cindy's exhibition gave Darien courage. "You killed one of my favorite college professors in that blast," Darien said with a slight edge in his voice.

"Who?"

"Professor Becker."

"A friend?" Kenny's eyes softened. "I'm sorry. Really, I am. We've all lost people, too many. When the building exploded we did not expect a full staff to be there."

Disgusted, Darien said, "You're a terrorist and by association so is Nancy."

"I understand how you might feel. I also know you might have questions and I'm sorry but you're going to have to wait a little for the answers you want. I'll do my best to look out for you, even if I am a terrorist." Putting down the plate, Kenny sighed. "It's easy to ride your high horse when you don't have any skin in the game." He took in a deep breath. "But you have a lot of skin in the game, my friend."

Kenny got up and headed for the door. "I'll have some new clothes for you when I return. If you can, you should both get some sleep."

"Where are we, Kenny?" Darien asked.

"Mexico City."

Beside Darien, Cindy lay sleeping, deep in dreamland, her eyes sliding back and forth under her eyelids. Darien watched the door. Kenny hadn't locked it when he left. He had barely shut it. Curious, Darien crept out of bed. He checked to make sure he had not woken Cindy and headed for the door.

Cracked paint came off on his fingers as he opened the wooden door. He wiped the paint chips on his pants. Looking behind him, he could see that his room wasn't the last room in the hall. The boards complained under his feet as he walked to the stairs, touching each doorframe along the way. Even in a daze during his arrival he had made a mental map of where his room was in the house and he replayed the remembered directions in reverse now. *Down the hall past several doors, turn right, down the stairs, left through a kitchen, and out the door.*

He didn't know where he was going or why his curiosity embraced him at this moment. The kitchen hummed with the appliances and faded as he left them behind to walk outside, making sure the door wasn't going to leave him locked out of the house.

The pod was gone, returned to whatever storehouse it had been called from. The cracked bricks of the courtyard showed no sign of it ever having been there. Unable to see over the walls of the courtyard, Darien looked up at the stars. Washed out by the lights of the city, they were barely visible in the night sky.

The courtyard must have a door leading to the street, Darien thought. Maybe, he could get a better view of the city if he could get out.

A pair of steel grates covered by panels of fiberglass roofing material blocked his exit. The steel grates swung freely in the middle, there being no center pillar, but the chain was tight enough that he couldn't fit through.

The sound of a racking shotgun broke the silence of the night air.

"Can I help you?" The voice wasn't Kenny's.

"Uh, yeah, sorry," Darien said meekly. "I, uh…" he stammered, "I've never been to Mexico. I wanted to see what kind of skyline—" He stopped talking. It was a stupid reason to be out of bed, of his room, of the house.

"We keep the courtyard locked unless we're going out. I think you can wait until tomorrow to see the city. You're lucky to be alive. Maybe, you should take that into consideration."

A voice in the back of Darien's head pushed him to ask, "Why is it locked? Is it dangerous here?"

"No more than anywhere else, but don't worry, you won't be here for long."

"Because we'll be going somewhere to have a portion of our memories wiped?" Darien guessed.

"Yup. Don't worry. It's not a complete wipe. They're gonna dig a little and take out anything that could give us away. Your lady friend up north requested it."

Darien still couldn't see who was talking. The voice was high pitched like it belonged to a youth in the midst of puberty. Whoever it was they were above the courtyard, perhaps in one of the second floor windows.

Darien walked to the center of the courtyard away from the gates and saw a young man in the window of the room next to the one he and Cindy were staying in.

"You sound a bit young for guard duty," Darien said.

"I think you should head back to bed. Through the kitchen, up the stairs, and the fifth door on the right."

Not in the mood to talk, well, ok, Darien thought. He walked toward the kitchen door, and looking up, caught a glimpse of the young man giving him directions.

Philip.

Chapter Twenty-Eight

"You work with us long enough and you'll get used to seeing the same faces over and over again. Not everyone at Hiraeth is a clone of someone else but there are quite a few working here." Kenny flipped one of the pancakes. "Hell, it's in their own best interest."

Darien thought back to his first weeks in the silo at Tucson. Almost everyone he met stopped him to read his name tag. That name tag held more importance than his own face. He reached up to touch his cheek.

How many people out there have this face?

"Hiraeth," Darien said, "the people in Tucson called it a terrorist group."

"They would, wouldn't they? We stand for human rights." Kenny put a couple of pancakes on a plate and handed it to Cindy. "Eat," he told her. "Put on some pounds." Spatula in hand, Kenny put a few more pancakes on plates. "We stand for human rights, all humans. Just because you were copied from someone else's DNA shouldn't make you less."

"But those people in New York, Dr. Becker—"

"We're not perfect. Did I intend to kill anyone in that explosion? No. There wasn't supposed to be anyone working when we set it off. We had no way of knowing about the split shift." Kenny shrugged and handed Darien a plate. "But, I think if I knew, I may still have done it."

Darien took the plate, his stomach turning. He couldn't eat.

"That explosion, the news coverage, is that why you're down here instead of back in New York?" Cindy asked.

"How did you know I was from New York?" Kenny smiled.

"You haven't lost your accent yet." Cindy took a large forkful of pancake and chewed around her words as she asked, "Is that why you're here?"

"The message we sent to PEPM about why we did it was

hacked and they were able to create my face from several sources. It was supposed to be scrambled in the video. So, yes, that's why I'm here. My face is too recognizable to be out in the field."

Darien got up from the table, leaving his plate, and walked away from the kitchen to the base of the stairs. He sat down on the lowest step. Across from the stairs, a sitting room with couches and chairs placed cozily around a small fireplace of painted and broken bricks beckoned, promising comfort and quiet. He didn't feel like enjoying himself.

"So, what's here?" Darien could hear Cindy still asking questions in the kitchen. "This place, this building, what do you do here?"

"Here?" Kenny asked and took a bite of his pancakes. "We don't do anything here. This is a waypoint, a rest stop on the way to the real destination. You've got a couple of more stops yet to go. But me, I'm going to stay here for a month or two while my records are reset. I might even get a little plastic surgery to make me a little less recognizable." He put down his fork and framed his face with his hands turning both left and right. "What a tragedy, losing this face."

Cindy gushed mockingly. "Lovely. Absolutely beautiful." She looked down at Darien's plate and turned to the stairs to call him. "C'mon Darien, come back and eat. Your pancakes are getting cold."

Darien lay back on the steps, the rounded edges of the treads digging into his back.

That wasn't Philip I saw last night. He was too young to be Philip.

Darien's mind went back to his friend, to his voice, to his laughter, to his pain. The young man last night had not been him. He was a copy of Philip, or more accurately, he and Philip were a copy of the same person, whoever that might be.

My past, my pain.

It's nothing, nothing compared to the pain you've caused.

His own injuries were trivial when compared to others in the world. They had not always felt that way. Now, they felt like nothing, like mere inconveniences in comparison to the horrors that others around him experienced. *Philip's pain.* The pain of others burned inside of him, building like a bonfire of massive proportion. Their pain hurt deeper than anything he had ever imagined. The children being raised to fulfill a heartless corporation's need, the babies being born to either clones or economically disadvantaged women, women whose babies weren't even theirs, babies that they were not allowed to love, all of these images flooded through Darien's mind as he lay there on the stairs.

He had to do something about it. Sam had seen this, had felt this, and done something about it. Kenny was doing something about it.

Darien got up and went back to the kitchen.

"It's funny. You don't realize how lost you have been until you realize where you are and wonder how you got there. Everything I've done with my life, every need I thought I had, it's all just washed away. Those dreams, those desires, the craving for security, it's all pointless." Darien opened the window. He still could not see over the wall of the courtyard. "Kenny, I'm sorry. What you and Sam have been going through is devastating. How long have you been involved?"

Kenny sat at a writpad. He had been entering the information for Darien and Cindy's next leg of the journey and held up his hand as he finished. "I've been working with Hiraeth for three years, ever since they took Sam the second time."

"What do you mean, the second time?" Cindy asked.

"I met Sam in college and we dated off and on for a year. He disappeared with no explanation and about six months later he was back. He escaped. You see? I was living in Vermont at the time." Kenny leaned back in his chair and rubbed at the belly of his shirt, still wet from pressing against the counter while doing the breakfast dishes. "He filled me in on what he knew, which wasn't much. Man, he was scared. "Kenny shook his head, grimacing. "We moved to New York City, hoping to muddy the waters about where we were, but they were tracking him through me. They knew about us and when I went to work one day, PEPM took him back." Kenny shut off the writpad. "I get a message from him now and then. It's been a long time since the last one. Lucky for me, there are a few members of Hiraeth who managed to get hired at PEPM. I don't know who they are. The company is good at sniffing them out. They broadcast information, but they never last long."

"What do you mean? If you don't know who they are how do you know they've been caught?" Cindy asked.

"Codenames, we all have them. Sometimes they're letters. Sometimes a collection of numbers. Sometimes it's a brand name of an item, like Hiragana."

"What's that?" Darien asked quickly.

"Hiragana, it's a beer brand. All sorts of brand names. Some even use names of old authors or celebrities, Wilde, Hannah, Stefani, Brando—"

"So, are these some of the active names?"

Kenny made a face and shrugged. "I don't know, I'm just sharing examples."

"Do we get to pick our own? C'mon, Kenny," Cindy said, "What's yours?"

"You wouldn't believe me if I told you."

"So tell me and let's see if you're right."

"My codename is Slippery Nipple."

Cindy burst out laughing, breathing deep, "That's awesome!" She giggled a bit more and took another deep breath before she said, "I want to be called orgasm." She pantomimed a radio handset and said, "Orgasm calling Slippery Nipple. Orgasm calling Slippery Nipple. We have word that the Golden Lady is on her way. She's coming, and not quietly." She laughed some more.

Kenny joined her in laughter at her last comment before he composed himself and said, "Taken."

"Orgasm is taken? Figures. Black Widow."

"Taken."

Cindy looked up at the ceiling as she tried to think of something original. "How about Blush?"

"Oh, that's a good one." He nodded his head in approval.

"Good Band. I haven't heard anyone using it. You might be in luck."

"I really want to know who is using orgasm, though," Cindy said, frowning playfully.

"So, what's the next step?" Darien asked. "When is the pod coming?" Joking about codenames didn't seem funny to him. He had felt a jolt of recognition at the mention of the codename Hiragana. *That was Shara's beer.*

"I've called the pod. It should be here in an hour or so," Kenny said. "The next step, I think, is the memory purge. They might copy some memories before they do that, to see what you know. Might be something useful rolling around in that thing you call a head."

"Well, I'm ready," Darien said. After breakfast he had spent some time in the courtyard staring at the wide blue sky. His thoughts kept bringing him back to Philip, to the other children being born in the cloning operations, to the little girl in Miami. His doubts were gone.

"Kenny?" Darien asked. "How many cloning operations have you managed to shut down?"

"None."

"How many clones have you managed to help escape?"

"Since I've been here, around fifty."

"Fifty escapes. That means around fifty memory transfers have been stopped. Is that globally?"

"Yes." The front of Kenny's shirt was still wet and he pawed at it, pulling it away from his stomach.

"So, what do we know about the positions the corporations were trying to fill? Did they eventually succeed in filling those position from the ranks of clones that had been set aside?" Darien leaned against the windowsill.

"I think so. We monitor the outside postings of the companies with cloning procedures that we know of."

"Have you managed to get anyone, any clone," Darien corrected himself, "into a position of power with their memory intact?"

Kenny didn't answer. He was looking at Darien funny.

"You're asking a lot of questions. I think that kind of question might be better answered after your memory purge. Sometimes you don't want to know too much."

Darien waved it off. The answer didn't matter. He knew what it was he had to do. Nancy had told Darien he was in line to be the replacement clone for Octavio Medina, a position her own father had been forced into decades earlier. She also told him his fears might protect him, protect his mind from the memory transfer.

There was no question. He had to go back and take the risk. If he made it through the memory transfer with his mind intact, he would be a member of the board for one of the biggest companies in the world. He would have access to the apparatus that ruined so many lives. He could break it.

I have to get caught.

Chapter Twenty-Nine

How long are you going to wait, this time? Lawrence asked himself.

Every ten years or so, Larry put a gun in his mouth and pulled the trigger. There was always another Larry to take the place of the last. The company backed up his memory every day and it was no real effort to remove the last couple of days leading up to the suicide. They could just rewind to that point and continue with the next body.

Lawrence Enderby had been one of the subjects in the first round of clones for PEPM, a prototype before they started working on the sections of the highly educated workforce, even before the members of the board.

Raised in a household of brutal violence and abuse, Larry felt disgust at how the company recreated the atmosphere perfectly, creating generations of little Larrys to suffer through years of mistreatment until they experienced the death of their mothers at the hands of their fathers.

Larry packed some clothes in a bag.

Darien Mamon escaped. He even brought the broad he was banging with him.

Larry didn't want to chase Mamon and wondered if they could just let this one go. He actually liked the guy, even if he was a bit stuffy.

Martin. They killed Martin. He had liked Martin, too, maybe even a little more than Darien.

Martin lost his mind.

"No, he didn't," Larry argued with himself out loud. "He didn't lose his mind. Someone stole it."

How many years have you been in this job? He asked himself. *You've been here longer than anyone should have to.* A hollow chuckle escaped, aimed at his dissatisfaction with his position. What was he thinking? The company wasn't going to offer him a retirement package. Work until you die. Get born again in the next body.

Rest? Nope.

Retirement? Nope.

Career advancement? Nope.

Every day he endured a constant suicidal state, just a few nudges away from ending it all. But even when Lawrence pulled the trigger, the end never came.

There is no stepping outside of your area of expertise, silly boy, not as long as you're useful to the company.

Larry packed his gun, zipped the bag closed, and hung it over one shoulder.

"I don't want to do this anymore."

"Don't want to do what anymore? This is what you do." Agent Jimmy Curtis opened the pod door for Larry. "This isn't open for discussion."

Larry climbed into the pod and buckled his seat belt, stashing the bag with his clothes and gun under his seat.

The gun.

Larry thought about the gun in his bag, an old fashioned snub-nosed thirty-eight. What if he just pulled the gun out and shot Agent Curtis?

There would be a six to ten hour wait on this mission before the replacement Agent Curtis stepped in to take the place of the one you shot. As punishment, you would probably spend some time with Dr. Hollister playing in the fairytale land of recorded pain. Larry shuddered at the thought.

Dr. Hollister had recordings of pain, taken from people with unfathomable experiences. One woman had every bone in her hands broken by slowly descending hydraulics, bones splintering under the pressure, shattering to slivers. Another had been boiled in a large cauldron. A man had been skinned alive, his screams of despair and agony rang in Larry's memory as if he had lived them.

That was the thing about memory recordings, they were engineered to be almost as real as if they were original. All recorded moments of agony became new memories for the subject. Larry shuddered at his past sessions with Hollister, the resistance as he tried to pull away from the strong hands stripping the skin from his arms like a pair of long concert gloves. Larry put the thought of shooting Agent Curtis from his mind. It was pointless.

"Just wait until we're across the border. This will all fall into place," Agent Curtis said, powering up the pod. "You've been in a funk for a long time, Larry."

"Lawrence."

"Maybe, I can put in for a vacation for you."

"I'd like a vacation *from* me." Larry looked over at Agent Curtis for a second before facing front again to look out the windshield. "You don't get it. I don't want to be me anymore." Larry sat up straight in his seat as the pod lifted from the ground. "How can you be so content to just do the same thing, day in and day out?"

"Are you kidding me? I'm living the dream. I like the authority. I love the uniform." He flipped his black collar. "I get to use a little violence, just a little." He winked. "And then, a little more. If I remember correctly, you used to enjoy that part."

"That was fifty years ago, Jim."

"Even so," Agent Curtis said, "what choice have you got? We're here for the long run."

Larry took control of the pod. This was something he still enjoyed, actively driving a travel pod. He let his fingers feather against the controls, getting the feel of the pod's motion in response to his touch. It was like sex. *When was the last time you had sex?* he asked himself before telling his inner voice to shut up.

The travel pod soared left and right like an old airplane; a setting Larry enjoyed immensely. It even had the combustion engine noises piped in over the hum of the pod's standard electric engine.

"Do you have a signal?"

"Yes, I've got a signal," Larry said." What do you think I'm looking at, moron?"

Agent Curtis stared back at Larry. "There's no need to be a jerk."

"Well, what else have I got? Personally, I think it's my best feature."

Larry maneuvered the pod only inches above the desert scrub, barely out of reach of the shortest trees, moving wildly and abruptly to avoid the taller ones.

"You do know you can change the pod travel setting so it doesn't do that." Agent Curtis reached for the control panel but Larry blocked his hands away gently.

"I don't get to go out much, so I think I'm gonna try to have a little fun with it."

"What's the current destination?"

"Mexico City. They haven't moved for the last two hours. I expect they're settling there."

"If we're lucky, they've already made contact with Hiraeth. Those kids are so hard to pin down." Agent Curtis grimaced, checking his weapon. He was using an MX7 automatic with case-less ammunition. He popped the slide closed and pressed the safety. The grip was similar to the old Smith&Wesson forty-five caliber.

The Mexican border passed underneath them. They would need to be more careful in Mexico. It didn't have the toothless legal system so inherent to their home country when it came to corporate law and powers. At home they could pretty much do whatever was needed to meet the goals of the corporation. No lawmaker dared shake the boat. Corporations had their own armies, their own police forces, even their own states. Petrotex Oil officially annexed all of Alaska only a few years prior.

Larry watched Agent Curtis with the new firearm. Larry didn't like the new ones at all. They were too easy to trace. It was an unnecessary risk as far as he was concerned.

Give me an old fashioned wheel gun any day.

They were twenty minutes past Nogales when the signal they were zeroing in on disappeared.

"Where did it go?" Agent Curtis asked. "It was strong, up to now."

"Don't get your panties in an uproar. I know where I'm going, kind of. Mexico City is a big place but the signal was coming from the south-east side."

"You're talking about one of the highest population cities in the world, Larry."

"Lawrence."

"Yeah, I know. It's going to be like finding a needle in a haystack." Agent Curtis pushed his writpad screen to display across the windshield, blocking out Larry's view just as a large tree needed to be avoided. The autopilot kicked in, jerking them sharply to the right.

"Dammit, Jim!" Larry said, rubbing his neck after the abrupt autopilot correction. "You gotta warn me when you're about to do something like that." The autopilot increased altitude and adjusted for crosswinds, smoothing out the ride. Larry unbuckled his lap belt and stood up to get a closer look at the data from Agent Curtis's writpad displayed across the windshield.

"Where's the autopilot taking us?" Larry asked.

Agent Curtis checked the coordinates. "It's putting us down outside the city, about fifty miles. When we get there we should get something to eat, after checking to see if the signal has been reestablished, of course."

"And if we don't establish a signal?" Larry asked. "We've never lost a runaway signal before."

"Sure, we have," Agent Curtis said. "Yours, once."

"I never ran." Larry said, still looking at the map of Mexico City on the windshield. "I'm the 'eat a bullet guy.'"

"One time, about thirty years ago, you ran. You're a wily ass when you want to be. You got connected with a little whore out of system security and the two of you went on a walkabout. It took us a month to find you."

"I don't remember that," Larry looked away from the screen.

"You wouldn't, would you?" Agent Curtis rummaged in his bag for a moment and held up what he had been searching for triumphantly, a synthetic apple. "They wiped it." He took a bite of the apple. "Just rewound your memories to not include it, like they always do."

"Where did we go?"

"New Hampshire, weird place to go hide, if you ask me. They found you working in a hardware store in Goffstown." He took another bite. "What the hell is a Goff?"

Larry sat back in his chair. *New Hampshire.* He remembered the girl, her laugh, her hair, her smile, and the fact she didn't care that he was fat. *One more thing stolen.* Her accent, Boston-but-not-Boston had always made him smile. She was from New Hampshire.

"Anyway, the whole needle in the haystack thing," Agent Curtis continued. "Stupid expression. Have you ever seen a haystack? We need a new expression. Like finding a pubic hair in a fur ball. Don't like it? I figured that was right up your alley. There I go again, up your alley."

"Jimmy."

"Yeah?"

"Shut up."

The headset in the pod was almost the same as the one in the labs back at the silos. Larry put it on his head and let the system back up his mind. He used to fight this procedure but there was no winning against PEPM. They had him, lock, stock, and barrel. He was their gun.

Wearing the headset, he tried to close his eyes and sleep. Maybe he would dream about the girl.

You don't even know her name. Is she still alive? Thirty years is a long time.

Not for you, he argued. *Maybe she'd be in her sixties. Would she remember me?*

An audible beep from the headset signified the end of the backup procedure. The memories he experienced between this moment and the next backup were his and his alone. If he died now or any time before the next backup he would be taking those inner thoughts, those memories, to the grave. It was a sense of privacy he barely thought of anymore.

He stepped outside of the pod. With no sign of Agent Curtis, the trees of *Desierto de los Leones* called to him. He walked up the gentle slope, rustling his feet through the low undergrowth. He could keep on walking, just keep walking clear to the other side of the forest. The direction didn't matter. *Freedom.*

He knew it would never be his. The snub-nosed thirty-eight in his holster called to him, called him to freedom. How old would the next Larry replacement be? *Twenty? Thirty?* Larry pushed the thought of the gun from his mind. The other clones, his clones, every day he suffered as a slave to PEPM was a day they got to live their own existence, their own lives. If he put the barrel in his mouth, one of them would lose all of that to take his place.

Chapter Thirty

Orders had come from the board of directors. They needed Darien back. Stationed in Mexico City until they found Darien, Larry was not unhappy with the change of scenery.

With no direct way of knowing how long it would take to find Darien Mamon and Cindy Barnett, Agent Curtis and Larry found apartments in Mexico City, one above the other. They were small and didn't breathe well in the humid air but Larry looked forward to some time away from Jimmy Curtis.

Coming from the upstairs apartment, a loud thump woke Larry with a start. Someone was screaming in Spanish and it wasn't Jimmy Curtis.

"What the hell has he gotten into, now?" Larry asked himself out loud. Climbing out of bed he threw on a pair of shorts and made for the door. The screaming got louder, more shrill, more panicked. Larry stopped at his door to listen, looking up at his ceiling. The screaming stopped suddenly in the middle of a word as a gunshot rang out. The pitch of the voice had been so high.

Larry ran out the door and up the stairs two at a time. Outside of Agent Curtis's door he couldn't hear the voice any longer. He knocked.

"Just a minute…" Agent Curtis called from inside. Jimmy opened the door and peeked his head out. "Oh, it's you," he said and opened the door to pull Larry inside.

"What is wrong with you, Curtis?" Larry asked when he saw the man on the floor. Blood pooled on the sloping tiles against one of the painted white baseboards. Agent Curtis still held the MX7 automatic in his hand.

"Who is this?" Larry asked.

"He followed me. I was down at the corner cafe getting a cup of coffee and a breakfast sandwich. I noticed him looking at me as I waited, and when I headed back he trailed me."

"So you killed him?" Larry started looking for the man's identification. "Not too smart, Curtis."

"Watch your tone, Larry. I'm still your superior."

"It's Lawrence. And when you stop swinging your gun around like it's a dick, I'll treat you like a superior." Larry found a wallet in the man's chest pocket. His left eye was still open. His right eye was gone, along with that portion of his face.

Larry checked the identification in the wallet. "This says he's a cop." Larry looked closer at the plastic card. "I don't think he is."

"I didn't think so either." Agent Curtis put his gun away and came back with a writpad and a small medical bag. He handed Larry the writpad and opened the medical bag, taking out a flat sample collector. Agent Curtis touched the collector to the pooled blood and let it soak into the material. Sitting down next to the body, Agent Curtis took the writpad back from Larry and handed him the bag.

The collector sent the DNA data to the writpad screen.

"No way this guy is a cop," Agent Curtis said. "Look at this." He scrolled down. "Match, Leonard Benson. This guy's a clone from—" Agent Curtis zoomed in on the company name. "Whiteboard Syndicate."

"Hiraeth?"

"Has to be. We're on the right track, I think."

"We have to clean this up." Larry stood. "Get some rags or towels or sheets. Do you have any trash bags?"

"Just the takeout bags from last night."

"It's a start. Let's put him in the tub."

Larry and Jimmy spent the better part of a day removing any sign of Jimmy's murder victim from the front hall of Jimmy's apartment. By the end of the afternoon they had several garbage bags filled with bloody towels and sheets, and a number of others filled with the more incriminating evidence.

The bar on the opposite corner held a small moment of rest for the two. Blocks from their apartment building, partitioned into several black garbage bags, Leonard Benson rotted in the

Mexico heat.

"This means one of two things," Jimmy Curtis said. "One," Agent Curtis held up a finger, "either we're really close and Hiraeth is keeping an eye on us, or B," Agent Curtis held up the thumb of his opposite hand, "it was all a coincidence and that guy just thought I was really cute."

Larry laughed, stress and anxiety falling away as he attempted to breathe in between his outbursts, tears filling his eyes. He tried valiantly to place his beer on the table before he failed and spilled it. The puddle of cheap beer dripped off the table and into his lap, causing him to slide out of the booth and stand up.

"There he is," Jimmy Curtis said. "I've been dealing with your Mr. Melancholy personality for a few days now. Are you back?"

"Yeah, I suppose." Larry pushed the beer away from the edge of the table, gave the seat a cursory wipe and sat back down. "I don't dig cleaning up after you but I guess you didn't have a chance, did you?"

"Hey, the guy followed me. I wasn't stalking him."

"All things being what they are, we should switch apartments." Larry downed the last bits of beer from his glass. "Don't think you want to be around when someone finds your friend. How old was that kid? Eighteen?"

"They're getting younger and younger." Jimmy sipped his beer. "I wonder if we're slipping."

"Us? Naw, that kid was from Whiteboard Syndicate."

"Still, someone is slipping."

Larry, standing, pushed away his empty glass.

"I'm going to the pod. There has to be something we missed. We had a signal. Don't pick up any more tails, ok?"

He left Jimmy alone at the bar and headed for the parking garage where the pod was stored. The signal had been strong on the way down here. The tracking device had been secured magnetically on the pod as it landed near the silo escape hatch back in Tucson. Larry had to hand it to Jimmy, the magnetibots with their tracking signals had been a good idea, even with the hassle of having to place them near every silo exit. The signal was easy to follow.

The magnetibot battery must have died or, maybe, it was discovered and removed.

It was beginning to look like they were going to have to rely on Hollister's implanted memory and who knew when that was going to trigger? It could take a year.

The crowd on the streets didn't appear to be going anywhere. Throngs of tourists lined the sidewalks and even the road, watching street performers and shopping at the roadside carts that came out every Saturday.

Not a bad idea. Larry stopped, and digging out some cash, bought a turkey leg from one of the vendors. *Pretty skinny turkey,* he thought as he took a bite. It was still better, and more expensive, then the synthetic meat some of the other vendors were selling.

He had to admit he liked it here. The buildings didn't have that plastic feel like they did back home. Everything at home looked like it could be put up in a few days, something he had seen happen when he was a boy. Cookie cutter neighborhoods were laid down in a month, whole streets replaced in a week. This city had been here a good long time and he liked it.

Turning a corner, he headed for the pod garage at the end of the block. This was one building unlike the others.

Larry wondered how like his grandfather he was becoming. He was already several decades past his grandfather's dying age. The man had hated everything, even most of his own children, but he liked Larry. The boy would listen to him complain about how nothing was like it used to be. Nothing was made to last anymore.

"When I was a kid," his grandfather used to say while inhaling the cloud of a vape pen, "a refrigerator would last ten years. You're lucky now if it lasts five." Larry smiled at the memory of the old man's squeaky voice. "Hell, if we paid for the air in our lungs, more than the pittance we do now, mind you, they'd have found a way to make that obsolete too."

That was the world they lived in back home, a scattered collection of planned obsolescence. The trash heaps grew and the consumer kept spending, spending more than they could afford, and throwing away the things that could not be fixed as one after another they failed, as intentionally planned by the manufacturers. Everything failed, *except you.*

Even as Larry admired the old buildings the thoughts kept coming. *Everything fails, except the mind, except the knowledge.* Larry tried to push away the inner voice. His mind in turmoil, he marched as much as walked. The lazy stroll spent admiring the architecture was now a mission to get to the pod.

You've made PEPM a fair bit of cash. Nice investment they made in you there, Larry boy!

Up the stairs he went, two at a time, turning at each landing with his hand on the handrail, until he reached the level where his pod was stored. All the while, he berated himself.

You are worse than any of them, you know?

Larry opened the pod door and grabbed his bag. As Larry walked away, fishing inside his bag, the pod door behind him closed slowly to lock itself.

You keep the wheels rolling along, keep bringing back the others. You can't even get free yourself, coward!

The outside edge of the pod storage park was concrete, three foot high, smooth and devoid of any character, any originality. Larry set the bag on top of the concrete barrier and pulled out his gun.

You know what. Larry? I bet next time you don't last two weeks. Did you get your backup today, Larry?

"It's Lawrence," Larry said as he checked the chamber for a round. Then, he put the gun in his mouth and pulled the trigger.

Chapter Thirty-One

Agent Jimmy Curtis waited a week, impatiently looking out the window, watching the streets. PEPM was usually quicker than this. They knew Larry's history. They knew the volatility of his moods. There should have been six replacements waiting in the wings for such a predictable event.

During this week of waiting Jimmy moved out of the apartments, cleaning his own as well as he could, removing as much of the murder evidence as possible before he vacated to another building on the North side of town. Shortly after Larry's body had been found in the pod park, Jimmy quietly moved the travel pod to another garage closer to the new apartment.

Tired and angry at Larry for yet another stunt, Jimmy Curtis waited for the replacement Larry to arrive. He knew he shouldn't take it out on the replacement, but it was getting harder and harder not to do so.

The knock on the door was a welcome sound even as he knew the following conversation would not be. He opened the door to see Larry, looking fifteen years younger than before.

"Hey, old man," Larry said, "you wanna back up a few steps and let me in?" Jimmy acquiesced and waved a welcome gesture as he stepped aside. Larry wasn't smiling and he looked to be all business. He set his bag down on the floor.

"They sure took their time getting you back here."

"The body," Larry spread his hands out to display himself, "went for a run. They had to get it back and you and I were nowhere around to help. They actually had to hire outside to get the body back, this time." Larry checked himself out in a spotty mirror on the inside of the door. "Good hairline on this one."

"We've got a lot of work to do," Jimmy said, picking up Larry's bag and looking inside for a writpad. "Your writpad was with you when you died, and when the police looked into it the security system wiped it. I've been running almost blind here. Have we received a signal yet?"

"Yesterday," Larry said.

"Well, Larry, let's hope they haven't moved too far."

"Jimmy?"

"Yeah?"

"It's Lawrence."

Chapter Thirty-Two

A red topless combustion automobile passed by as they walked the streets of Mexico City. Combustion vehicles were still popular in Mexico with the youth spending a good chunk of their free time learning about the antique engines. The first time the car went by, Kenny paid it no attention. The second time it went by, he stopped to watch it take a corner two blocks away. The third time it went by, Kenny started looking Darien and Cindy up and down.

"We need to get off the street, " he said, motioning them into an alley.

"Why, what's going on?" Cindy asked

Kenny pushed Darien and Cindy back into the space between the buildings. "They've found you, I think." Kenny looked at Darien. He spun each of them around, looking them up and down. "What did we forget? All new clothes, new shoes." Kenny crossed his arms. "I've read your files. We've run scans on both of you. Neither one of you has a wire implanted, anymore." He backed away from them and peeked out of the alley.

"I never had a wire implanted," Darien said.

"I know. In college you found a wire in your shoelaces, but you never had anything, implants, like Cindy had." Kenny looked at her. "I heard you were a wild one, once."

"How did you know about that, the wire in my laces?"

Kenny snapped his fingers three times as he said, "Hey, Darien. Are you in there? I've read your file. I know more about your past than you probably do. But, how did they find us?" Kenny leaned against the wall, watching Darien. "There's something I don't know."

Darien felt guilty. He had wanted to be caught and the thought of going back, of taking the risk, of losing himself forever in an effort to burn down the system, to free hundreds, if not thousands, of people had blinded him to the danger into which he would be placing those around him. What if any of them were caught alongside him? He had weighed his own life against the lives of all of the others facing a life of servitude to the corporations, and in that comparison his own life had felt cheap indeed. The lives of those around him had value. It was something he didn't want to risk. He needed a plan.

A plan, one thing I do not have is a plan. He had no idea how to get caught without putting Hiraeth, Kenny, or Cindy in danger. He had hoped that after the targeted memory wipe, and before he learned too much about Hiraeth after the wipe, he could just pick up a phone and call.

Phone. Darien hadn't seen one since they visited Tucson, the day they got arrested. He hadn't been allowed one when he started working for PEPM, but then he had a writpad, and the writpad was the standard form of communication as well as the tool for the brunt of the work taking place within the company. He hadn't thought of it much because no one at the silo facility had a phone.

When he arrived in Mexico with Cindy he noticed that no one in Hiraeth used one either. Most of their communication was relayed in person with runners coming and going from the courtyard.

"It's in the company's best interest to keep you on a digital trail," Kenny explained. "That's why none of us are using phones. We learned that lesson a long time ago. A paper trail can be burned. We burn the trail, message gone, no trace, no record."

Now, he was in an alley and they were being tailed by a red convertible, or so Kenny thought. Darien pushed off the wall he was leaning on and walked toward the street.

He said to Kenny and Cindy, "Don't come with me."

"Where?" Cindy asked.

Kenny stepped in front of him.

"Move please," Darien said. In a fight he knew Kenny would win every time.

"Where are you going?" Kenny asked.

"It's me they're after. If I get caught you can get away."

"You want to get caught?"

"No," Darien lied. "But I don't want either of you to," and that was the truth.

"Stick with me for the moment," Kenny said. "It might not even be us they're looking for."

"It's just—" Darien lost his voice. He spun on his heel heading back into the alley, then spun on his heel again and rushed at Kenny, trying to knock him out of the way. The larger man caught Darien in his outstretched arms and lifted him from the ground, holding him there until he stopped struggling.

"I have to go," Darien said.

Kenny set Darien back on the ground but did not let him leave.

"We need to get you to the overwrite station, today."

"I don't need the wipe. I just need to go back."

"Are you nuts?" Cindy asked. "You're going back?" She threw her hands up. "You want to go back."

"It's not his fault, Cindy," Kenny said. "Dammit, we gotta get you to the station." Kenny looked Darien over. "You don't know, do you?" Kenny said to Darien before he looked at Cindy. "They never know."

"Know what?" she asked.

Shaking his head, Kenny pulled Darien by the hand and Darien followed the tall man. "Let's get you both off the street." He pulled them both into a shoe store.

"So, what are you trying to tell me? I don't really want to go back but I'm following some kind of preprograming?"

Kenny nodded in response.

"And these ideas aren't really mine?"

Kenny nodded again.

"And they're coming for us?"

"Yes."

"How much time have we got?" Darien held a pair of shoes, much too small for him as he sat on the worn bench in the shoe boutique. He didn't believe Kenny.

"You saw the car, didn't you?" Kenny asked.

"Yeah? So, what?"

"During your time at MemorSingular you had run-ins with security."

"Doesn't everyone?"

"I think you might be working for them, unwittingly."

"There's no way I'm working for company security," Darien said indignantly.

"That's the thing isn't it? You wouldn't know. Who can tell what might have been fed into your mind without you knowing? You know, your memory isn't even all yours. Your brain might be the booby trap they've been waiting to spring."

"So, what? Am I going to start sabotaging everything?"

"You might have already done so. There's no way to know," Kenny said, "until we can give your mind a full reading. We don't have the facilities here in Mexico City," Kenny looked out the window. "We've got to get you out of here. If you sent them some kind of signal then they will all be joining us soon."

"Can we get back to the house?" Cindy asked.

"I think the safe house is trashed."

Kenny grabbed Cindy's hand and, pulling her close to him, whispered in her ear. Stepping away again, he said, "Get off the street. Get inside somewhere and have lunch. Take your time. It should not look like you're in a panic. Act as nonchalantly as you can." Kenny looked at Darien. "I have to go and shut down the safe house and then I'll give the new address a once-over before you arrive." With that statement he was out the door.

Chapter Thirty-Three

Up on the second floor a cat lay on the windowsill, drinking up the early afternoon sun. There was little to no movement from inside. Kenny sat across the street from the courtyard entrance, the concrete tables and chairs of the park empty aside from him. Out of the corner of his eye, he watched. He waited, watching the streets, watching for runners, watching for messages from the other safe-houses.

There's one, he thought. *That's Eduardo.* The boy looked like his father, eyes squinting when he smiled, his voice strong and deep when he laughed. He traveled along the sidewalk, oblivious to the danger in his path.

A sharp whistle would have been quicker at gaining the boy's attention but the recognizable and predetermined tune would alert the youth to danger without awaking the suspicion of any other eyes, or ears. Kenny put his lips together and whistled the theme to *Treasure Island.*

Without turning his head towards Kenny, Eduardo walked, passing by the entrance to the courtyard without stopping. As he rounded the corner, the boy broke into a run. No doubt, Eduardo was headed for the small store on the next block where he would relay the danger signal by whistling the same tune. Word on the loss of the safe-house would spread from there. Kenny didn't know each of the message houses. He didn't want to. Knowing too much was risky.

How many got caught in the net this time? PEPM didn't usually fight so hard to get back one man. What was it about Darien Mamon they wanted so badly? Kenny watched the windows, mentally listing the names of the people that might have been inside, *too many.*

How many of PEPM's men are in there? he wondered. *Another safe-house gone, and with it at least four friends.*

Kenny got up from his seat and walked the path of Eduardo,

whistling the *Treasure Island* theme until he reached the store on the opposite corner. When he reached the small store at the end of the block he changed the tune, from the theme song for *Treasure Island* to the theme song for *Jaws*, walked in, and bought a drink.

As he sat on the store's front step, sipping his drink, Eduardo returned, handing over a small plastic shopping bag. Kenny felt through the plastic and, putting down his drink, pulled out a small recoilless pistol grip and detachable stock from the bag. Turning to rest his back on the doorframe of the store, he put one foot up on the step and began to assemble the gun.

Their walk back to the safe-house started lonely, but as they passed by doorways and alleys, they were joined by six other young men and women, all carrying recoilless guns, all lips pursed with grim determination, all eyes promising death.

The chain holding the courtyard gate rested on the ground, cut. Kenny pushed open the gate slowly, expecting gunfire at the slightest movement. Inside, sprawled on the cracked brick, *Danny,* the young man Darien said he had confused for Philip, was dead. His eyes closed, Danny's chest lay open exposing the bones of his ribcage and the mangled flesh around them. His hands gripped the shotgun he loved so much. No spent shells lay around him.

He didn't get a shot off.

They shot him, probably before even announcing themselves. *How many are there?* Bricks, even broken ones, don't show footprints.

Kenny and his soldiers moved across the courtyard two at a time to take their places near the two sets of doors. One of Kenny's soldiers, Maria, pushed open the door. It swung silently on its hinges.

Peeking inside, she stepped in to find the body of another of the building's inhabitants. Shirley, a young redhead from Argentina, lay on her stomach and stared at nothing out from under her crimson locks.

One by one, they all followed Maria. She made her way to the stairs where she crinkled her nose at the smell of rotted flesh flowing down the steps. Kenny covered his nose and mouth with his sleeve.

The bodies down here, why don't they smell this bad. Why does it smell so badly from upstairs? Kenny questioned.

"Hey, Kenny," Eduardo whispered and motioned him to one of the downstairs rooms, "look at this."

Three of the young men had searched the downstairs rooms, finding no sign of anyone, but coming across many unusual large and locked plastic chests, several in each room.

"I can pick these locks."

"Are you sure?"

"Yeah, give me five minutes."

Kenny winced. "How many are there?"

"Thirty?" Eduardo guessed.

"Maybe, just bring them outside."

On the staircase, Kenny crept up as silently as he could, avoiding the creaks he had memorized over the past month. Reaching the top of the stairs, Kenny found three more bodies. These were not his friends. These were the bodies of the invading PEPM force.

Kenny grimaced at the stench. The smell came from them. *They couldn't have been dead longer than Danny or Shirley, not here on the second floor. They would have had to pass by Shirley and Danny on their way here. Why do they smell so much worse?*

On inspection, Kenny found them wet with a chemical accelerant, speeding up the rate of decomposition.

They used the smell to draw us in. To draw us into what? A trap?

The door at the end of the hall sat open, allowing the sunlight to line the floorboards.

"I can hear you out there. There's no sense sneaking around." The voice was hard and gravelly, a voice of age.

Kenny continued down the hall, his gun out in front of him. The other three behind checked each room as they passed them.

In the room at the end of the hall, an old man sat in a chair, his suit jacket and jeans spattered in blood. On the table beside him rested a gun. He didn't reach for it.

"It's about time," he said. "I wasn't sure we'd have any

company at all but I'm glad you're here."

"Me? You know who I am?"

"No," the old man said, "and I don't really care."

"So, you're glad, why?" Kenny said, leveling his gun.

"I was afraid I'd have to die alone."

Kenny's associates entered, took hold of the man by his arms, and stood him up.

"Maria, we've got him. Get the others out."

"Check," she said, heading back to the hall.

"Oh, don't worry," Kenny said to the old man as he sat on the windowsill next to the cat. "You'll die."

"Yeah, I knew that, but it's such a shame to die alone." He smiled.

"Where are your other men?" Kenny asked.

"I'm the last one." With Kenny's friends holding him by the arms, he held his hands out to the side feebly.

"So what makes you think you're not going to die alone?"

"You found my boxes?"

Kenny thought of the four downstairs working on the plastic chests.

"Want to know what happens when you open one?"

The building exploded.

Chapter Thirty-Four

"So what happens to the old Octavio Medina?" Cindy asked Darien.

She had both hands wrapped around the tallest burger Darien had ever seen, buns, tomato, lettuce, onions, meat, cheese, another slab of meat, more cheese, guacamole, and a collection of onion rings.

How do they think anyone could open their mouths that wide?

Cindy cut the burger in half and tackled the meal by biting first the top section of the burger then the bottom half, the juices of the burger running down her hands to drip onto the plastic tray.

"From what I hear, the executive is always close to death when they run this procedure. Sometimes they live for hours more, sometimes a week."

"Does the executive have any say in the matter?" She took another bite.

"The executive belongs to the company."

"That's creepy," she said with her mouth full.

"They signed away the right to refuse."

"Why would anyone do that?"

"The original executives did it when they devised this plan. They set it all up. Since the beginning, any new body for an executive had all of their memories wiped— That's not the right term, overwritten," Darien corrected himself, "and were replaced with the memories and knowledge of the executive. Then, they pass a knowledge test and are confirmed to be the executive. Therefore, they are destined to follow the same rules as the original executive." Darien picked up a few of his fried onion rings and dipped them in ketchup, looking out the window as he took a bite.

"Yup, creepy as hell. And they're grooming you to be… What? The next Octavio Medina?"

"So it would seem."

"You still don't know who they were grooming me to be?"

"No, I don't. I've been with you since you found out and I didn't know then." Darien took a gulp of water and glanced out the window again. This time, a red topless automobile sat empty in the parking lot. "Hey, we paid when we ordered, right?"

"Yeah, why?"

"The car that freaked out Kenny is parked outside."

Cindy put down the second half of her burger and wiped her hands on the napkin before cleaning the juices from her lips. "We should go. Follow me," she said, dropping the napkin on the table.

Cindy walked into the kitchen like she owned the place. They passed by the cooks and waiters without giving them a glance and found the back door. In the alley behind the diner, Cindy leaned around the corner of the dumpster, before she waved for him to follow. As they reached the next block Cindy asked, "Did you see them? How many were there?"

"The car was empty." Darien looked around. "I have no idea where to go. I don't know if the police can help us. Maybe we should rent a car of our own instead of walking around aimlessly."

"Maybe we could, but I don't know how many credits I have on this card," Cindy said. "I left most of the other cards back in the room. Kenny will collect them while he's there. I suppose we should just walk."

"Where are we going?"

"Don't worry, Kenny gave me an address."

"But, if we're being followed," Darien said, shrugging, "we probably shouldn't go there. Maybe you give me an address to meet you at later, away from the new safe house. We split up. Maybe I can lose them alone."

"No, I don't think so. You're sticking with me. We'll make sure we aren't being followed, and then we're going to the new safe house."

Cindy took Darien by the hand and they walked in the heat of the noon sun, trying to stay in the shadows of the tall buildings as much as possible.

"I wish I had thought to get sunglasses or a hat," Darien said. "I feel like I'm frying my brain."

"Oh, we can't have that." Larry's voice carried from far behind them. "A mind is a terrible thing to waste."

Cindy and Darien turned to see Larry and Agent Curtis crossing the street. The pair of security agents had been gaining ground silently and now their presence was given away. Agent Curtis looked at Larry, an annoyed expression on his face.

Darien and Cindy turned and ran as fast as they could around the corner of the next building, entering and making for the staircase past a very confused receptionist. Moments behind, Agent Curtis and Larry crashed through the door. The receptionist nervously pointed toward the staircase.

Lungs bursting for air, Darien and Cindy opened the door on the fourth floor landing just as their pursuers entered the stairwell. Cindy pointed out the elevator. "I can't climb anymore." She looked pale as she walked, leaning on the wall. "Is it the altitude of this place?"

"Up or down?" Darien asked, chest heaving.

"Up, I guess," Cindy said. "Increase the distance between us." She hit the up button on the wall and when the elevator doors opened she pressed floor eight.

"That's not very far," Darien said. "There's twenty-five floors."

"And when they look at the elevator we'd still be going up. They could just watch what floor we were—" Cindy stopped short and hit three other floor numbers. The elevator would continue its journey with or without them. At the twelfth floor they entered the stairwell again and, as quietly as they could, they descended one floor.

The eleventh floor appeared to be a data center for a number of banks. Ten young men sat around playing a game, papers, books, and dice littering the table. They were obviously supposed to be working and they started at the appearance of the two fugitives.

Two made as if to be busy and the rest laughed at them.

"Welcome to the party!" one shouted. "Which archetype do you want to play?"

"Shut up, Reggie," said another of the young men. "You're going to get us fired."

"By who? This is the dumbest job I've ever had. It's only a matter of time before they don't need us anymore either."

Darien and Cindy ran past them down the hall toward another exit sign, the door to the opposite stairwell underneath it. Cautiously, they opened the door to see if the stairwell was occupied. It was.

Agent Curtis waited on the other side, out of breath but ready for them. His gun stared Darien in the face as his other hand pulled the door open far enough so he could follow Darien and Cindy back into the hall.

"Neat trick picking so many floors with the elevator," Agent Curtis said to Cindy. "Backtracking a level off one of the floors, that was another good one. Changing stairwells? I saw that coming." He turned to Darien. "I should have expected better of you though, Darien. You saw who it was following you and you didn't offer any real usable advice." He grinned, still pointing the gun and searching his chest pocket for zip restraints. "What department do I work in, Darien?"

"Security."

"That's right. And security is famous for cameras. Security cameras," he said tilting the gun left and right with each word. "It just has a ring to it." He was beginning to get a handle on his breathing. "Larry found the camera room and told me where to meet you. Don't worry. He'll be here soon." Agent Curtis handed zip ties to Darien. "Here, bind her hands behind her."

Darien followed the instructions, tying Cindy's hands behind her back. He didn't tighten the zips too forcefully, though.

"Now zip one around your left wrist and push another tie inside the first." Darien followed Agent Curtis's instructions again and held his hands up for the security agent to tie his right hand in with his left. "Oh, I think we'll wait for some back up before I lower this gun to finish binding you."

Moments later, the elevator beeped and Larry's arrival could be heard down the hall.

"Uh, hello?" one of the gaming employees asked.

"Pay me no mind," Larry replied.

"We're really not supposed to let anyone in—"

"Well, you failed at that one already. So, what's the point now? Hey," Larry called down the hall toward Agent Curtis and the two fugitives, "why don't you come this way? Let's take the elevator down. I can barely breathe."

As they got closer, Larry held his hands out to Darien and Darien allowed Larry to zip tie his right hand to his left. He wasn't gentle, zipping them painfully tight.

"Hey, you look great," Darien said to Larry, trying to defuse the situation. "Did you color your hair?" He really did look younger.

"No."

"Something's different."

"Shut up."

"Why did you come after us?" Darien asked Larry.

"Just doing my job, man."

"Larry, let Cindy go," Darien said as the elevator doors closed. "It's me you want. You can bring me back to Tucson."

Agent Curtis pulled Darien close. "We've been in a deep investigation of the Hiraeth terrorist organization for some time now. We can't let this slide, Darien." He pushed Darien away. "But, thanks. We knew you would lead us to them eventually."

Agent Curtis pushed Darien out into the lobby as the elevator reached the ground floor.

"If you thought I was one of the terrorists why did you ask me to keep my eyes open for suspicious activity?"

"We ask everyone. Did you think you were the only one we trusted? Now, that is cute." Agent Curtis opened the door to the street. "We've got a pod coming. Just stand still."

"It's nothing personal, Darien," Larry said. "I've been in this job a lot of years. I got to say that you're one of the ones I actually liked. You've got a decent trigger squeeze and you can take a joke. Most of the dopes that come through here couldn't hit the ground if they threw themselves at it."

The pod drove around the corner and came to a stop in front of them. It had three seats.

Agent Curtis grabbed Darien and pulled him toward the pod as he said to Larry, "It's time."

Time for what, Darien thought.

Larry pulled the gun out of his holster and pointed it at Cindy's head.

"I thought you needed us," Darien shouted at Agent Curtis. "I thought you came to bring us back."

"Us?" Larry said. "Not, really. We only need you."

Larry pulled the trigger.

Chapter Thirty-Five

Report Subject:	**Darien Mamon**
Origin Location:	**Oneida, New York**
Current Location:	**Mexico City**
Subject Age:	**27**
Subject Status:	**Pending Transfer**

"Don't worry, buttercup," Larry said to Darien. "There's always Leslie."

"Larry, what the—?" Darien's head spun. *Cindy is dead.* She lay on the sidewalk, blood pooling away from her crumpled form.

"It's Lawrence. And what are you worried about? You liked that little piece of ass. And guess what? There's going to be a lot of those coming through. At the very least you could ask Leslie out."

"Leslie isn't Cindy."

Larry closed and locked the pod door behind them.

"Put his seatbelt on," Agent Curtis instructed Larry.

"Not Cindy?" Larry said, buckling the belt. "Sure she is. She looks exactly the same. She's a clone."

"And, what," Darien asked, "being a clone doesn't make someone human? We're replaceable, expendable?" Darien twisted his wrists against the zip restraints. The pain of struggling against the ties didn't help. As Larry sat down and readied the controls, Darien said through his tears, "If I survive this, Larry, I'm going to kill you."

Larry spun in his chair, grabbing Darien by the shirt. "What do you know about anything? You're gonna have to get in line for that one." Giving the moment thought, Larry relaxed his posture, then he punched Darien in the eye, saying, "It's Lawrence."

* * *

Blind and naked in the darkness, Darien searched for the toilet. He needed to pee. Unsure of his balance he placed his hands on the toilet seat and set himself down. As the urine hit the edge of the bowl to slide down silently, Darien rested his elbows on his knees.

All of his clothing had been taken when Larry and Agent Curtis locked him in. He still had his blankets for warmth but he was to be held as a prisoner until his appointment with the memory wipe procedure.

Overwrite, Darien thought to himself before telling himself to 'piss off.'

Darien shivered. Underground, the heat of the day could not penetrate or overpower the cooling systems of the MemorSingular silo. He couldn't decide which extreme temperature was better at the moment. The searing heat of the day could easily kill a man who didn't have the sense to prepare. Dehydration works fast in the desert. But at that moment, as Darien shivered on the porcelain toilet, he wondered if it would be so bad to die of dehydration.

Cindy was dead. The bullet had sprayed her brain matter across the front of the building. She fell, hands bound behind her, to bounce off the wall and roll away, her blood pouring down the sidewalk into the street.

Is it my fault?

Taking her with him had been his idea. Nancy had tried to talk him out of it, not strongly, but she had tried. Had she understood what the company had done to his mind? Had she known Darien was inevitably going to sabotage his escape? Darien couldn't believe that.

Larry was to blame for Cindy's death. Larry had pulled the trigger, pressed the steel as if Cindy were no more than a channel to be changed or a book that could be replaced with another off the shelf.

"Just replace her with Leslie," Larry had said.

Asshole.

Darien flushed the toilet and let the bowl empty. The vid-screen illuminated, lighting the room as he washed his hands.

"Mr. Mamon?" Octavio Medina asked from the screen. "Mr. Mamon, are you awake?" He was dressed in a pair of red pajamas and he lay in a hospital bed far from the camera. "Mr. Mamon, this is Octavio Medina."

"I know who you are."

"Do you? That's a funny statement. Do any of us know who anyone is? Do we ever know who we are?"

Darien shook his head. "You're pretty philosophical for someone who's about to die."

"What makes you think I'm about to die?" Octavio Medina leaned forward in his bed. "What do you know about death? I started a system over a hundred years ago that ensured I would never die. Sure, the body dies, but I live on. I learn more every year, as does every member of the board."

"Knowledge doesn't make you immortal."

"Ah, but knowledge is immortal. If you know it, you won't forget it. The human mind is more flexible than any hardware ever invented. Granted, it is not made to last, and that is a problem we might solve. And, yes, this body will die, however, I will live on in you." Octavio Medina looked into his vid-screen which was still absent of Darien Mamon. "You can come out now. What, are you camera shy?"

"I'm naked."

"Yeah, sorry about that. I'll have some clothing brought in. Typical prisoner strategy." Octavio Medina nodded to someone offscreen. "Being naked makes you uncomfortable?"

"Of course, it does."

Darien's door buzzed and slid open to let in a slender woman in a light blue jumpsuit wheeling a cart. In the low light Darien couldn't make out her details but she looked like Nancy, her hair in a ponytail. The door slid shut as she exited, and with the closing of the door the lights came on.

On the cart, under an ancient blue book with frayed fabric at the corners, was a pair of blue jeans, underwear, socks, sneakers, and a white button down shirt. Pushing the book out of the way, Darien put the underwear on, out of the view of the camera. He could not help wondering if, in fact, that was Nancy, and if she knew that he had been captured.

"Fear is a funny thing. Isn't it?" Octavio Medina asked.

"I don't think I know what you mean." Darien stepped into the camera view still buttoning his shirt.

"You fear little things. Things that don't matter." Octavio Medina rested easily in his bed, nonchalant, sipping tea from a small cup while Darien put on his pants. "You, worried about being naked in front of someone you barely know. Why? You're exactly the same as I am. Your penis is the same. Your chest is the same, albeit a little thinner. But you were still afraid to have someone see you naked." Octavio Medina took a long slow slurp of his tea. "Yet, you didn't flinch when a woman entered the room. A little sexual bravado, was that?" He cocked an eyebrow. "Fear of me? Perhaps, you think I'm gay and appreciating a younger version of myself?"

"No, I don't think you're gay."

"Why? I might be. How would you know?"

"I don't know. And I don't really care." Darien laid down on the bed.

"Sure, you care. It's your body right now. Soon it will be mine. You care about what happens to it." Octavio Medina sipped some more tea and scratched his nose. He set the cup on the table beside his bed.

"Yours. You said that before," Darien answered, sitting up. "How could it be yours? You. You in that body." Darien pointed at the screen. "You will be dead. I will live on as someone else."

Octavio Medina clapped his hands together. "That's right! That's the spirit! You will live on as me. And thus I will survive." He laughed and pressed a button on the side-rail of his bed. With the laugh came wheezing, followed by a severe coughing fit, and ended with the older man wiping tears from his eyes.

"So," Darien said, "what's wrong with your body?"

"This body?" Mr. Medina said hoarsely.

"Yeah," Darien said. "You're not that old. I don't even think you're sixty, yet. Why are you trading bodies so young?"

"This one is sick." Octavio Medina hit the button again. His head lolled to the side and Darien could see the sweat reflecting off Octavio Medina's brow.

"Sick? Oh, you poor baby," Darien said sarcastically.

"I have a rare form of cancer that affects my glands. I'm fairly sure you've heard of it."

"Is it the same one I had?" *The one that killed Philip?*

"Yes, it is. We tried to make a cure from your blood but we've been having trouble. And, you know, we don't want to risk it any longer so we decided to continue with you. You survived the cancer. After the transfer we might even begin cloning a new strain directly from you. That way we can avoid the whole cancer issue."

"Didn't you always have the cancer issue?"

"No, it entered our DNA, somehow."

Darien didn't care much about how at the cancer strain had infected their cloning system. He didn't care about the corporation. He hoped Nancy would bring PEPM crashing down around their ankles soon. Darien decided he didn't want to talk to Mr. Medina any longer.

"Can you kindly get lost, now?" Darien asked. "Go drink your coffee and die?"

Octavio Medina nodded and pointed to the cup. "Tea. Coffee is nasty. So, you want to live in peace for a few more hours? Not in the cards, my friend. You have another session with Dr. Hollister before this is all over. Or did you think maybe someone was going to rescue you? That's not likely to happen." Octavio Medina picked up his cup and sipped at his tea. "You didn't recognize Nancy."

"What are you talking about?" Darien feigned ignorance.

"Nancy, the person who brought you your clothes. I thought the ponytail was a dead giveaway." Octavio Medina's voice was weak. Even barely above a whisper, Darien could hear an edge of contempt in it.

"I didn't recognize her," Darien lied.

"You didn't really look, did you?"

"I was a little preoccupied and surprised to see a woman bringing my clothes."

"Still uncomfortable?"

"I was. I'm fine now. Thanks, I guess, for the clothes." Then, Darien remembered the book that had come sitting on top of the clothes and walking to the table, picked it up. "What's with this? An expensive present?"

Mr. Medina paled at the appearance of the book. He had not seen it on the cart brought in by Nancy. He said in a soft voice, "I don't think you need to worry about the book. Just put it on the floor, would you?" Mr. Medina's voice dropped, falling away at the last word.

"Why?" Darien turned the book over in his hands, noting the age of the pages and the worn cover. When he looked back to the screen, Octavio Medina, overtaken by a sudden exhaustion, had spilled his tea on his chest. His head fell back to his pillow as he frantically pressed the red button on his bedside rail, calling for help that would never come.

Octavio Medina's life ebbed away while Darien watched, fingers pressing into the frayed corners of the book.

Chapter Thirty-Six

Report Subject:	**Darien Mamon**
Origin Location:	**Oneida, New York**
Current Location:	**Tucson, AZ**
Subject Age:	**27**
Subject Status:	**Pending Transfer**

"Well, hello, Darien. How are you today?" Dr. Hollister appeared on the screen.

Darien didn't respond. He sat looking at the floor and sighed.

"I guess that was a stupid question," Dr. Hollister said. "Hello, Darien. I'm here to run a few more tests on you. I'm not actually going to be in the room with you today. In your state I'm not sure you would be able to restrain yourself from tearing out my throat."

"That is an astute observation," Darien said still looking at the floor. "Why don't you join me and we can find out?"

"I don't think I will. I know you don't think I was trying to be a friend to you, but I was. You really are very bright. Had you been an actual colleague and not a subject, things might have been different."

"You're not going to come in to the room and hook me up? Maybe play a few more games with my memory?" Darien clenched his fists. He surely would like to get his hands on Hollister. For years he had admired the man and his work. Now, when Darien looked at him he just saw a money hungry freak. "How much are they paying you for all of this?"

"You'd be surprised, Darien. This is where most of the funding for memory storage and transfer comes from. It's not just me." Dr. Hollister hit some numbers on his pad and put it aside. "And we don't need to hook you up anymore. We have a solid understanding of your brainwave pattern and how to connect to it. We'll be doing this work remotely."

"And what will this work entail?"

"Ahh, Darien. You know I can't say anything about that. Suffice it to say, we need to understand where you are in the sequence. We had to accelerate your transfer schedule. Had they been able to get a cure for the cancer from your blood, you wouldn't even be on the list. But, since they failed to reach their timetable, here we are."

The screen went fuzzy, distorting Dr. Hollister's image and slurring his speech. Darien looked up at the screen finally to see the image reduced to a still pattern of Hollister, flickering as the sound slowed to silence.

His door panel illuminated. On the door lock image, a number pattern ran through a sequence. Several seconds later, the door slid up into the ceiling.

"Hello, is there anyone in there?" It was Sam's voice.

Sam Matheson is dead.

Unsure of himself, Darien answered, "Yeah, I'm here."

Wearing a black security uniform, Sam stepped into the doorway. He looked thinner than Darien remembered from the sims of his memories. "Do you want to let them go through with their plan or do you want to come with me?" he asked.

"I'm coming with you." Darien pulled on the shoes and followed Sam without tying them. "Is there a way out?"

"There is, but we're going to have to shoot our way through. Do you remember how to use this?" Sam handed Darien a semi-automatic pistol.

An alarm sounded, piercing and high.

"Dammit!" Sam said, touching his ears. He reached into a pocket and handed two small white pieces of plastic, noise canceling signal generators, to Darien. "Put these behind your ears. They'll cut the intensity," he shouted.

Darien placed the plastic behind his ears as he had done at the shooting range with Larry. The intensity of the alarm subsided considerably. Checking to ensure Darien was stable, Sam waved for him to follow and they ran across the glass span to enter the stairwell.

"We have a small group of people internally right now. We

entered through the southern silo and forged ID passes to get you out. The problem is, now that we've sprung you from your cell, our badges aren't going to work." Sam opened the door to level six and peeked out. The coast was clear. "We've got to save one more. C'mon."

They crossed the clear floor of the central hub to a door on the other side. The level six floor was a little easier on Darien's fear. This level had the spiderweb of steel girders under the glass, and that had always made Darien a bit more secure when crossing it.

Sam made a number of connections between his writpad and the door. "It'll just take me a few minutes to get this open. Elizabeth isn't as far along in the program as you are but we won't get this chance again."

Elizabeth, Darien's memory reached back. *She slapped you, stole your keycard, and kissed you.*

"Elizabeth is still here? I thought she got away."

"Well, you helped her get into the tunnels, but," Sam pushed some popups on the screen of his writpad, "she didn't make it out."

Darien looked to the stairwell door on the other side of the central hub, waiting for a team of security agents to bust through. The cameras had to be giving away their position, unless Nancy was already doing her thing.

Elizabeth's door slid into the ceiling. She wasn't there. Larry was.

"Hey, fellas," he said.

The big man grabbed Darien by the shirt and threw him into the room behind him before leaping forward and grabbing Sam by the neck. Larry drove Sam with such force the glass floor vibrated as they landed on it. In his surprise, Sam had dropped his writpad, but in his hand now was a shuddergun. Sam rolled on top of Larry and, pressing the shuddergun into the larger man's chest, he pulled the trigger. The floor under them splintered with a spiderweb of cracks as Larry bellowed in pain.

Clutching his chest with one hand, Larry continued to squeeze Sam's neck, pressing into Sam's windpipe. They rolled together, each fighting for purchase on the smooth floor. Sam pulled the trigger on the shuddergun again but, in his struggle with Larry, he missed and hit the floor directly. The spiderweb shattered sending the gun and Larry falling down to sub level seven. Sam managed to hang on to the steel support beam of sub level six and hung from it, arms wrapped around the beam.

Upon impact with the glass on the floor below, the shuddergun exploded, breaking the clear floors in the direction of the impact, three more. Underneath Sam the transparent floors were now missing for sub levels seven, eight, nine, and ten. At sub level eleven the falling glass and steel rested, obscuring the view any further down.

Sam struggled, pulling his slender body over the top of the steel girder, pushing away the remnants of the glass floor still on top of the steel. His voice raspy, Sam called out to Darien. "Hey, are you all right?"

Darien stepped out of the doorway to stand on the edge of the precipice. He reached for Sam. "Give me your hand. I'll pull you in."

"No point in going that way," Sam said. "The way out is the stairway. C'mon." He crawled across the girder in the direction of the stairwell.

Sweat rising around his collar, Darien looked at the girder, the narrow girder and the five story fall below it. There was nothing but open air all the way down to sub-level eleven. A dizziness came over Darien and he fell backwards against the wall next to the door.

Closing his eyes, steeling himself as he used to when stepping out onto the floor, Darien pushed off the wall and stepped forward, placing one foot on the steel floor support spanning the silo. The dizziness came back in a rush. Darien's hands went out to each side and he balanced, one foot on the beam and one foot on the steady floor. He leaned forward, settling his weight over the forward foot, and in a rush of panic, shoved himself backward where he rested against the wall once more.

Sam reached the other side. "Darien, we have to go, now!" He held the door open and looked into the stairwell. "C'mon

Darien! More security will come." Indeed, the sounds of people running down the stairs echoed out of the opening.

Darien felt the chills fanning down his spine. Sam was calling from the other side. He knew he had to cross this span to escape, but Darien couldn't move.

"Well, that didn't go as planned," Dr. Hollister said.

Still locked in his room, Darien looked up at the screen. The pain, he could still feel the pain, the lingering pain of the memory-creation, where Larry had struck him. Except it hadn't been Larry at all.

Darien's mind fought against itself, reorienting to his actual surroundings. "What?" Moments ago he had been on the landing, watching Sam leave him behind. In an instant, Darien was now standing back in the middle of his room looking at a perturbed Dr. Hollister on the screen.

Randy Hollister fiddled with the writpad in his hand, reading the output of the simulation.

Realizing what had happened, Darien shouted at the screen in rage. "You son of a bitch! A memory creation? A new memory? None of it happened, did it?" Darien demanded.

Dr. Hollister frowned. "No, when the screen glitched, that was the beginning of the input memory scenario. I was hoping in the blur of an escape attempt we could get you to overcome your fear of heights again, like you did climbing the tower with Mr. Medina."

"And Sam, you just brought him back from the dead to break me out?" Darien spat.

"What makes you think he's dead?"

Darien did not answer the question and Dr. Hollister followed with, "We thought that your multiple memories shared with him would force a bit of bravery out of you." Dr. Hollister frowned again and punched some more at his writpad screen. "Maybe we should have used Cindy. Then again, you saw her die, didn't you? Yeah, that would have been harder to pull off."

"Heartless. Is this who you've always been? I admired you." Darien shook his head, seeing the forest through the trees at last. "If I could get my hands on you—"

"Careful now, you're starting to sound like Martin."

Martin is dead.

"You did this to Martin, didn't you? You killed him."

"Killed Martin? No, I didn't kill Martin." Dr. Hollister didn't look up from his work. "He is dead. I can confirm that. Martin's mind could not take the strain of the transfer. Sad, we're going to have to prepare another for—" he checked his notes, "engineer Billy Mathias. It's funny. We've had issues with his line before." Dr. Hollister looked up and away thoughtfully as he talked. "No matter. We'll just pull the next into position. I figure engineering can live without Billy Mathias for another month."

Darien's breathing deepened and he lowered his voice. "If I ever get out of here—"

"That would be a neat trick. I'm not sure how you would manage it." Dr. Hollister tapped his finger on his writpad. "It's pretty clear. You are going to be Octavio Medina."

"I saw Octavio Medina die this morning." A thought occurred to Darien. "I could kill myself. How long can the board wait for the return of its board member?"

"Kill yourself? With what? You have a set of clothes and a stupid old book." Hollister took a sip from the coffee cup on the desk next to him. "It's true that the board can't go long without Mr. Medina. He's head of the board. We needed some more information. That's why we ran the last simulation," Dr. Hollister explained. "Generally, if any piece of your memory or personality remains after the wipe, all of your memories will eventually return. It will be like nothing ever happened. That's why we spend so much time working on your fears. Fear is a deep psychological tool. It keeps us alive in the darkest moments. It boosts our strength and increases our speed when we need it most. Fear is the first thing removed."

"And what? I have too much fear?"

"I thought so, I just got word that there's a plan in place. Octavio's assistant, Shara Musabayana has approved the transfer." Dr. Hollister got up from his chair and shaking his head, said, "No reason to listen to me. I mean, I only invented the whole transfer thing. Whatever. There's a plan in place and I've got the approval right here." Dr. Hollister showed Darien his writpad screen and the approval signature read, *Shara Musabayana.*

"Oh, yeah," Hollister said, "I almost forgot. The woman who came in here earlier," *Nancy.* "we know you were lying about knowing or recognizing her. It's a funny thing, memories, all kinds of secrets in there. Thanks for sharing."

Darien sunk to his knees on the floor as Dr. Hollister continued. Darien's grief blurred Hollister's words. His thoughts were not his own, not secret. He had betrayed Nancy by merely knowing her.

"Well, when we found out who it was who helped you escape we knew what to do." Hollister began packing up his materials. He emptied the coffee cup in one large gulp, spilling a drop of coffee down his cheek. "We made a copy of her mind for our files and wiped her memories. She's a blank slate right now, like a child. We will eventually have everything we need to fight Hiraeth after we analyze her knowledge base." Hollister put his writpad in a bag, zipped it shut, and slung it over his shoulder.

"That was Nancy who brought you your clothes, but Nancy can't help you anymore."

Dr. Hollister put his finger on the power function for the screen in his room and said, "Goodbye, Darien."

Chapter Thirty-Seven

Report Subject: **Darien Mamon**
Origin Location: **Oneida, New York**
Current Location: **Tucson, AZ**
Subject Age: 27
Subject Status: **Pending Transfer**

Nancy Williams was on Dr. Hollister's mind. She had orchestrated Darien Mamon's escape. She had procured a pod and programmed it.

How long had that taken?

She wasn't anything to worry about at the moment. Her mind had been copied and overwritten, replaced by that of a simple child.

The memories they had taken from her were incomplete, despite his boasts to Mr. Mamon. A series of scrambled data filled Dr. Hollister's screen, scrolling like hieroglyphics when he had tried to view several mem-sims of her recent days. It was blank, as if she had hacked into her own brain to keep anyone from learning her secrets. Someone with coding skills so advanced could damage a company's file system without anyone finding a trace of it for years to come. There may even be some malware at work, now. What kind of malicious programs were lying in wait for the right conditions or keystrokes to be pressed? He reassured himself, *She's nothing to be worried about.* But, he was still worried.

We should have killed her, Hollister thought. The chance of her regaining her memory was as dangerous as anything else he could think of.

He was letting his own fears get to him. There were literally thousands of people writing code for the company. Nancy Williams didn't run every system.

He mustn't fear.

In his office, Dr. Hollister held his writpad up and inspected the approval signature for today's procedure, *Shara Musabayana.* There couldn't be any mistake. She had signed her own writpad by hand. It didn't look like a digital signature representation or a copy.

He shook his head in disgust. It was unusual to receive approval so quickly. If there was a reported fear event leading up to a transfer, more care was warranted. Thankfully, he felt the free time scheduled between the last simulation attempt and the memory transfer to be sufficient enough to deaden the effect.

Shara must have some reason for pushing this today, Hollister thought.

The last program he had run on Darien had focused on Darien's fear of heights. In the program, Darien was supposed to follow Sam across the steel beam. Doing so would have cemented into his psyche as a personal victory over his most intense phobia.

Hollister laughed. Sending that moron Lawrence tumbling to the bottom of the silo had been a particularly fun section of the program to write. It did have the unintended effect of making Darien recoil that much more. Dr. Hollister laughed again. He would have to make sure that the vid section of Lawrence hitting the bottom got leaked to the general vid libraries.

The last simulation had been an important stage in determining Darien's readiness. Had Darien crossed the span in that simulation Hollister could affirm the transfer would be a guaranteed success. Darien failed. His fear had held him back.

Fear within the subjects had been the reason for so many mistakes in the past. The danger, today, was that subjects with deep strong fears would eventually recover their own memories, effectively nullifying the procedure. If the transfer went badly they could just start over and re-upload the data, as long as the data was not erased from the network.

Dr. Hollister preferred the old system when the subject would simply go insane under the onslaught of two different memory timelines. Reshaping a mind from that state had been both interesting and rewarding.

Of course, neither of those mishaps had happened in several years. The system of memory overwrite had reborn thousands of personnel for the last three generations.

Darien's fear of heights is too great.

It was still risky. No matter how he looked at it, he would never be completely comfortable with continuing the procedure while there was still a significant fear present in the subject at hand.

Dr. Hollister had, once again, expressed his concerns to Ms. Musabayana in his report, stating his reasons for wanting to extend the memory preparedness protocol. He didn't feel Darien Mamon was ready for this transfer and, once again, his concerns were pushed aside by the signature of Ms. Musabayana. She made one good recommendation, her recommendation being the addition of a window of time between the last simulation of the steel beam and the beginning of the overwrite.

Dr. Hollister checked on the status of the memory recovery from the old host of Octavio Medina. Every moment had been captured in perfect detail, every one except death.

There was no need to share the memory of death with a new host and the memory recording was always terminated prior to the expiration of the old host. In past experiments a memory such as that could lead to depression and even eventual suicide.

Hollister punched in his security codes and waited for the data to load fully. While waiting, he checked the signals within the transfer room where Darien was being held. Darien's brainwave pattern was noisy but the room frequency looked clear. He checked the frequencies again.

Clear, absolutely clear. He shook his head. *There should be some frequencies traveling through that room, even if we're not broadcasting an overwrite.* He refreshed his writpad screen and as he expected, the screen now displayed normal activity.

The transfer program worked on the same system as the memory creation algorithms. Like the previous test performed on Darien Mamon, the subject did not need to be connected to physical wires. The signal was sent directly to the subject by aligning to the brainwave patterns. This made the transfer less stressful and reduced chances of injury as there was no need to restrain the individual during transfer.

Having a confirmed sign off at each stage he ran through the checklist. When all items in the list had been satisfied he had been ordered by the board to proceed at the allotted time.

"Two more hours," he said out loud. "Two more hours with no additional stimulation."

If we get that, this might work.

"Yeah, I got really lucky. I don't usually get a chance to," Agent Curtis raised his fingers to show quotation marks, "interrogate someone right before a transfer. Oh, don't worry. You're not going to remember any of this."

"Then, what's the point?"

"You made me follow you. I hate that." He smiled. "Because of things like that, I need a little fun, now and then. So," he bobbed his head, "what is fun?" He rubbed his palms together and laced his fingers. "Murder is fun. But, murder? Sure, I can do it. But, it leaves evidence. It leaves a trace. It means there's a body to cut up and get rid of. It's a hassle. I don't like it."

Darien couldn't see a way out of this. The transmission of signals into brainwaves within this room had to be powerful enough to overwrite memories. Someone could surely manipulate the signals. It was inescapable. If Agent Curtis wanted to use the memory system to torture him, it was going to happen.

"What should we start with? Skinning alive? We could put you in a pot of oil and start it boiling, nice and slow. Maybe, we could tie you down and let the rats eat you. I really like that one. They like eyes. I don't know why."

Agent Curtis paced the room on the other side of the screen, waving his hands wildly, breathing deeply, smirking like a child who let his sibling take the blame.

His eyes went wide and a cruel smile appeared on his face, followed quickly by a frown.

"No, I don't think I have time for that one. I'm going to have to write it for next time."

"You write these yourself?" Darien was surprised. He hadn't thought of Agent Curtis as a programmer.

"Me? Write? Sorry, I misspoke. I can't write these, never learned how. I do have quite a few programmers with the same affinity for pain as myself." He rubbed his hands together.

"So, are you going to fill me in or are you going to keep being a psychopath."

"Oh, I am a psychopath, can't help it. I tried for a while to walk the straight and narrow. In fact, when you met me I bet that is exactly how you pictured me, by the book, stick up the ass, jackass."

"Spot on, there," Darien said.

"This idea is grand. It would take a while. Oh, not the actual pain part, that's instantaneous, like the snap of a finger. The memory would be years. Get this." He held his hands up as if displaying his idea in front of him. "I make you fall in love with something, a woman, a dog, maybe a child, then I kill that thing in front of you."

Things. He called his potential victim a thing. We are things. Darien knew he was in trouble. Agent Jimmy Curtis had no compassion, no empathy.

Neither did you, once.

Even in his current predicament, Darien winced at his own criticism. He had once been like Agent Curtis, perhaps not as deranged, but he had been as unfeeling for others, caring only for himself.

"Do it."

"Do what?"

"Whatever you're going to do, do it. Let's go."

Agent Curtis stopped pacing. "You're not afraid?"

"Of you? No, I'm not."

"Oh, you poor man, you poor, poor, man. Did you think I was going to lose interest?" He pointed his fingers back at himself. "Oh, no, not me, never me. I'm going to record this. I can look back at my old files whenever I want. It's the best part of this job, the only reason I stay really, that and tormenting Larry. I just want to let you know that I might get a good laugh about this part of the conversation. You appear brave, so very brave, and it's not going to matter one bit, not one bit."

Agent Curtis looked for a reaction and got a single finger salute.

"Don't like heights, huh? I think I'll drop you off a building." He put his hands on his hips. "No, too boring." He paced about slowly, savoring the moment. "Falling down stairs? Nah, too common." He raised his eyebrows and pursed his mouth in appreciation of his next thought. "Sliding off a cliff ledge." He nodded.

Agent Curtis raised his hands, and with an effort to make it appear over the top and deliberate, pressed the execute button on his writpad.

Chapter Thirty-Eight

Report Subject: **Darien Mamon**
Origin Location: **Oneida, New York**
Current Location: **Tucson, AZ**
Subject Age: **27**
Subject Status: **Transfer in Progress**

The white plastic walls closed around him, pressing into his psyche, his feelings of self. Darien sat on the floor, arms wrapped around his torso, waiting for the inevitable.

No way out, he thought. This moment could be his last living as Darien Mamon.

Nancy's no longer here to save me. I came back for nothing.

He tried to remember his parents, his mother, her face, her laugh, how she used to dress. What he did not remember was her embrace.

Did she ever love me?

Had his father ever cared as he had watched the soccer games from the balcony?

They were not his parents. They were employees of the system, the system that led him here to this end.

Nancy had been a friend. He had never expected her to be, and now she was doomed as well, trapped in the web, just like Darien. In possession of secrets one could only imagine, she was a prize in PEPM's fight against Hiraeth. Her mind would reveal all.

She would never kiss him. He was precisely 'not her type.'

Kiss.

Cindy, the thought of her broke Darien's heart. He loved her, the touch of her lips, the crinkle in the bridge of her nose when she laughed. The way she smiled at him even as they fled for their lives pierced him and scattered fragments of his heart to the wind. He remembered her brains scattered against the wall of the building in Mexico City. That was a memory he could lose.

Mexico City.

That's where Larry had shown his true colors. Trust wasn't a word one associated with an individual like Larry; camaraderie, boyish endeavors, stupid tricks, and braggadocio, maybe, but words like trust, dependability, and friend were far-fetched in any relationship Larry was part of.

Friend.

Even as one might believe that the brash front Larry put on was just that, a front, he was as it turned out every bit the misogynist pig, every bit the callous braggart he appeared to be on the exterior, as dark and unfeeling inside as a corrupt bureaucrat.

Friend.

Darien's mind fell to Philip, the boy who had taught him how to love another without reserve, without feeling jealous about the gifts others possessed. His friend had passed too early, a victim of the cancer strain affecting the clone population. How many others like Philip had there been?

A tear fell from his eye, rolling down through the stubble on Darien's cheek to his neck. He couldn't cry for himself anymore. Such a thing, now, seemed petty and small. Darien's tears were for the others so affected by merely being near him, being near one destined to be erased. He was powerless to help them, but he was aware of how many more there were in the world adversely affected by the increasing greed of industry. How many clones out there destroyed the lives of those around them, just as he had.

Relationships.

How many had he pushed away during his life? The boy who had been with him when he was climbing that tree for the last time, had been there when he fell, what was his name? Darien struggled to remember and instead fell into one of the memories from college. He was a little girl looking happily at his birthday cake and burning his fingers on the candle.

No, that wasn't him. That was a mem-sim at Smami Tech.

Darien once again searched his mind and came up with Smami Tech, no, South Miami Tech. Only Shara called it Smami Tech.

Shara. Her beautiful brown eyes grabbed his and he remembered kissing her soft lips, her beautiful brown skin, while running his fingers through her silky blond hair and watching her ass as they stepped aboard the roller coaster.

Darien shook his head in frustration.

Shara has dark brown hair, not blonde.

And her ass, it wasn't her ass he was watching on the mem-sim in Dr. Becker's class. That girl had been blonde and had held his hand. She smiled at him and winked.

His eyes held his gaze in the mirror. Cold water filled the sink to flush over the side, soaking his shoes, soaking his sweatshirt as he lay in a pool on the floor unable to move next to the broken sink.

"Mr. Likmand is going to lose his shit," Darien said, recalling the voice of someone else years ago.

The children, tray after tray of small orange children, like an assembly line of planned death, rolled underneath him, stretching into both his future and past where the hospital halls were increasingly covered in filth.

The dream.

Darien's memories were becoming more and more jumbled, bleeding into one another. Recognizing this incongruity, Darien tried to focus on the tower climb memory with Octavio Medina, on the fear he had felt even as he continued to climb. Cold sweat covered his palms in the heat of the desert. Quick evaporation of the climate should have prevented the slick under his hands as he grabbed the rusted metal of the ladder, but it was there, increasing his chance of falling, absorbing the orange color of the rusted metal.

Like the children.

He watched Octavio climb above him. The steel under Darien's fingers was slick with the sweat in his palms. *One rung at a time.* Darien kept pushing on steadily, one rung, one step, one more. The fear was subsiding. The wind rolled around him, echoing in his ears. Darien's courage surged over him.

I am going to be able to do this, he thought. *I am not me. I am Sam, and Sam is not afraid.*

He watched Darien climbing below as he pushed open the trap door to the tower landing. His fingers splayed across the metal floor, pulling himself up. Once on the landing, he walked over to the railing and leaned on it, sighing contentedly, waiting for the sweaty young man below to reach his goal.

He remembered leaning on the railing at the top of the tower, looking out at the wide expanse of colors in the sky, and saying to himself, *I am Octavio Medina.*

Confusions of his surroundings argued. Rippled experiences rolled away, sliding into the darkness, and screaming like a man lost, personality faded. Another personality emerged reborn from the digital code.

On the floor at Octavio Medina's feet, a book carried the dust of decades. The paper jacket had fallen apart long ago. Blue fabric frayed at the corners and the silver book label had almost completely rubbed off, showing only fragmented letters. Yellow pages crackled as he picked it up, opening the front cover to read the words penned in black marker.

My mind breaks like ripples on the shore, ebbing ever so slightly, wetting the same sand. Over time and sped to the frequency of my thoughts, the sound changes from the tranquility of water to the noise of a dead channel.
When time has no value, the little pleasures dissolve.
—Elizabeth Medina

The book Octavio Medina caressed in his hands had been a gift from his first wife, Elizabeth. She had been lovely, not just on the outside as many define beauty, but on the inside as well, her days spent in the support of others.
Others, except for you.
She had been against PEPM's knowledge extension plan. The year she died she had given this book to Octavio, writing the inscription inside to remind him in the years to come why she chose not to participate, why she chose to die.

Unnecessarily.

He looked at the cover, 'The Picture of Dorian Gray' by Oscar Wilde.

I'll read it this year, he thought. He knew he wouldn't, but that didn't stop him from making the same promise every time he saw the book. In Elizabeth's will she had requested the book be present at every transfer from the old clone to the next involving her husband.

Maybe I'll read it, but not today.

Mr. Medina pressed the door panel, bringing the screen to life. A series of passwords flowed from his fingers onto the lighted wall keyboard.

After his passwords were recognized by the mainframe, the door screen glowed a golden hue before dissolving to show the office of Shara Musabayana. She sat behind a large mahogany desk covered with stacks of data and legal folders filled with the forms required to perform a memory transfer. Behind her, through wall sized windows, the New York skyline stretched toward the harbor and the sea. PEPM executives rarely lived near the silos and Shara had always been partial to the change in seasons that came with her New York office.

Rising to approach her vid-screen, she smiled and picked up one of the folders on her way.

"Ah, Mr. Medina, good morning. Welcome back," she said. "I trust you are feeling well? No lagging confusion from the transfer?"

"Thank you, Shara. I am well. Has the old host expired?"

"Yes, last night. It was lucky the reports from Hollister's preparation came through clean. We gave the subject an open window of two hours after the last simulation. We had a bit of a hiccup but it all worked out in the end. All in all, I figure you only missed a half a day. And based on Hollister's assessment of the transfer we can purge the system of the transferred memory recovered from the expired host."

"You've always proven to be a person of good judgement. I am lucky to have you on my side, Shara."

She nodded her response.

"But, eliminating the backup so close to the transfer is against protocol. What's the reason for the accelerated deletion?"

Shara opened the folder she had carried over from her desk. "We've had reports of a break-in to our carrier database." Shara swiped a hand at the screen and Nancy's personnel profile lit half the area. "Nancy Williams, an employee to the Tucson silo data security team has been apprehended in connection with the escape attempt of Darien Mamon."

"She's been with the company for four years, starting right after you. What are your recommendations?"

"Currently, she is in a state of limbo. Dr. Hollister copied, then overwrote her memories until the matter could be ruled on by someone from the board. The question of erasing the backup is predicated on her abilities. Nancy Williams was able to hack a portion of her brain, so I don't believe keeping her memory within our system is wise. I would like her memory restored to her and then wiped from the system. I want to be able to talk with her. Maybe we can get to the bottom of this."

"Granted."

"Thank you, sir."

"So, the backup of my own memories, are they in danger of corruption?"

"Yes, sir. We believe Ms. Williams leaked access data back to the terrorist group Hiraeth." Nancy's personnel page disappeared from the screen.

"Well," Octavio Medina stretched and closed his eyes, saying with a yawn, "I've never felt better about a transfer than this one. I feel good. I feel right. In the future I think we should wait until the body and mind are a bit more mature when we select a clone for transfer."

"Yes, sir."

"And so saying, I don't think we'll be needing to retain the backup." Mr. Medina scrunched up his hand into the shape one would use to hold a pencil. He signed the screen and said, "Deletion, authorized. Let's avoid, if we can, any access to the carrier data."

"I agree, sir."

"Shara," Mr. Medina held up the blue frayed book. "Did I give the order again to leave this here?"

"You did, sir. It was an old order you implemented three generations ago, you requested this book at your feet whenever you wake from a transfer."

"I'm not that man anymore. Let's kill that order in the future."

"Yes, sir, Mr. Medina."

"I'm hungry. When was the last time this body was fed?"

Shara scanned her writpad. "It has been more than a day, sir. The subject, Mr. Mamon, had been in solitary since his return from Mexico City. Would you like to order something?"

"No, I think I'll eat in the cafeteria today. I would like you to check ahead to make sure the coffee is fresh. One thing I can't stand is stale coffee." He gave a quick assessment of his cleanliness and clothing and said, "Open the door."

Shara smiled. "Yes, sir. Enjoy your breakfast, sir." The screen went blank and the gloss black door slid up into the ceiling with a hiss.

Mr. Medina grinned, taking a deep breath and letting it out slowly. This new body felt vigorous and strong. He flexed his muscles, enjoying the stretch that followed as he walked through the door.

Octavio Medina stepped out onto the glass floor, feeling a bit dizzy at the depth below, and tried not to look down as he crossed the nearly invisible span. Arriving on the other side of the central hub with a sheen of sweat building up on his neck, he inhaled deeply, opened the door to the stairwell, and let out a sigh of relief.

As he walked down the stairs his fingers enjoyed the touch of the sturdy metal railing. Unlike the plastic world around him, it eased his tensions, giving him a feeling of permanence, of strength.

THE END

Thank you for sharing my adventure. This is a book where it isn't
always clear where the story is going, where it isn't all in front of you
like a map. Littered with clues, this story should have different
perceived endings based on how many of those clues you picked up.
The next time you read it, you might discover the ending isn't what
you thought it was. Maybe, it will be your memory that was reborn.

Reach out to your friends about what they thought the ending was.
You might be surprised as to how differently they saw it.

**If you enjoyed Memory Reborn and want to read more, you can
help by leaving a review. Reviews sell books. Reviews get movies
made.**
Ask your local bookstore to carry the book. Mention it to your book
club. Discuss it at your school. Show it to your neighbors. Give it as a
present. Nominate it for an award. Wallpaper your house with it. Read
it to your goat. Send a copy to your favorite star. Make fan movies out
of it. Get a tattoo….
OK, I got a little carried away there. Well, that's me.

Other published works by Steven M Nedeau

The Soulweb

In the Under Realm (short story)

Marla's Message (short story)

Simple Principle (short story)

The Unlikely Hero: A Fair Play Renaissance Fair Play (holy crap, this guy wrote a play!)

Upcoming works from Steven M Nedeau

Soulweb Sleeping.   ***Soulweb Shattered***

I love hearing from my readers. You can find me:
on Twitter **@StevenMNedeau**
or Instagram **@StevenMNedeau**.

www.StevenMNedeau.com